MW01131364

Other books by John Kovacich

The Lost Art of Magic

THE MOTHER OF ALL VIRUSES

by John Kovacich

The Mother of All Viruses

Copyright © 2012 by John Kovacich

Photography credits:
Digital Dreams by Flavio Takemoto
Digital Board by Ilker

In loving memory
of Phyllis Kovacich
1932 – 2005

CHAPTER 1

The morning sun was just peeking over the eastern skyline of the small Norwood University campus, as Professor Dierdre Jennings darted in between the buildings and through the hallways toward her office. There was still another hour before the start of the first period, and only a few students were milling about, leaving her a clear path to her office. This was the time of morning the faculty would spend preparing themselves for the coming day, and especially for their first period. For some instructors, standing before a collection of students was no different than standing on stage before an audience, so they develop a morning ritual which may include warming up the vocal cords, or simply rehearsing the lecture they were about to present.

Professor Jennings ritual usually involved consuming large quantities of coffee, and this morning would be no different. She entered the physical science office building, clutching her valise in one hand, with disheveled papers jutting out of the top, while her other hand held her dark glasses firmly on her face. The glasses remained on as she turned and slipped into her office. She dropped the valise on her chair and let her overcoat slip off her shoulders onto a guest chair. She turned in the direction of the ladies room, just across the hall, but was ambushed at the door by her secretary.

"Morning Sunshine," came the sweet sing song voice dripping with sarcasm and malice, "Girl, look at you, aren't you a sight for sore eyes? Or was that a sight with sore eyes?" Aimee Takahashi, one of Dierdre's few close friends on campus, and the only one from whom she would tolerate this kind of verbal abuse, stood in the doorway smirking and wagging her finger at the professor. "Didn't your mother ever tell you not to stay up late on a school night?" Aimee would often accompany Dierdre on her evening romps, and would frequently be in a similar condition on the following morning, so she took particular delight in teasing the professor on this occasion.

"You know," Dierdre said, "you really should have considered a career in the medical field. Your bed side manner would have taken you places. I'm sure we could find you some brochures in the administration offices." She hastily squeezed by her smirking friend and headed across the hall, a trip she was bound to repeat several times through the morning.

"You can run," Aimee added, "but you can't hide. I'll still be waiting here when you get back."

"As long you are waiting with a fresh cup of coffee, OK?" Dierdre disappeared through the opposite doorway.

Aimee cleared a space on Dierdre's desk, placed a coffee on the blotter in the center, and lined up a stack of unanswered messages in a semi-circle around the cup. Aimee was one of the departmental secretaries assigned to five different professors, but she only had a personal relationship with Dierdre. They hit it off right away. Aimee, the dark haired voluptuous Asian with the network news anchor looks, and Dierdre, the tall, thin blond, with extra-long legs. They made a perfect one-two punch and have exercised that punch on many occasions.

"What are those?" Dierdre asked as she slinked back into her office, "They don't look like Christmas cards."

"They aren't get-well cards either," Aimee shot back, "though you look like you could use one. This one is the dean asking if you have submitted your research paper to the review committee yet, and so is this one and this one and..."

"OK, OK, I get the picture."

Aimee pointed at her watch while she said, "Time's running short."

"It's not ready yet."

"Then maybe you should have been working on it last night."

Dierdre gingerly replaced her dark glasses with her regular pair and sat down behind her desk and said, "Maybe I was."

"Be serious."

"I am, sort of. My paper is about predicting random quantum events, last night I was researching a random encounter, of sorts."

Aimee placed both hands on Dierdre's desk and leaned in close. "You know as well as I do that they want something from you this century. Look on the calendar. It's 2005 already. I don't think they are going to wait for 2010 to roll around before you publish something. Heck, I doubt that they will wait for 2008. You're going to lose your grant and you'll never earn your tenure if you don't write something."

"I can't. I got researcher's block and writer's block all rolled up into one."

"Yeah, yeah, you're a regular block head." Aimee traced a finger in the air as if writing on an invisible blackboard. "She shoots, and scores! The crowd goes wild." She cupped her hands together and made hissing sounds.

Dierdre sipped her coffee. "Don't you ever get tired of kicking me when I'm down?"

Aimee's face turned serious. "You are my best friend. I don't want to lose you. I'd write the paper for you if I had your brains. There is no doubt in my mind, you are the most intelligent woman on this campus, but you insist on hiding your brains and acting like an idiot. I like to party. I'm usually right there beside you, but it's time to get down to business."

"You sound like my grandmother. Aren't pretty young Asian girls supposed to be quiet and demure?"

"Now you sound like my grandmother. I thought you were supposed to sound like the brilliant young researcher who was going to make a name for this university?"

"I know. But, I have this idea, only it's kind of like remembering a dream. I can't quite form this idea into words. Like a word on the tip of your tongue. I have an idea on the edge of consciousness, and I don't know how to make it pop into my mind. I feel like I just have to bide my time and wait for it come on its own."

Aimee fetched the pot and freshened Dierdre's coffee. "Getting some sleep wouldn't hurt that idea, I think."

"Yes, Grandma," Dierdre said as she settled her head onto her desk, "sleep sounds good to me right now, you take my class."

"Oh no you don't," Aimee said as she pushed the aromatic brew closer to Dierdre, "You get out there and improve those young minds."

"OK, but while I do, maybe you can find an org chart about our working relationship, cause sometimes I get confused about who's the boss here."

"Pulling the boss card will only get you yesterday's coffee instead of this fresh pot I made for you. You might want to retract that."

"Retract what?" Dierdre shrugged. "I'm just saying that I'm confused."

"I'm just as confused, honey. If I keep sounding more and more like my mother, I'm going to need to find a shrink."

"Speaking of shrinks," Dierdre said as she gathered her papers and headed out the door for her first period class, "you know Ross Bagley who teaches in the school of dentistry?" She held up her hand with her thumb and fore finger about two inches apart as she left the room.

* * *

Dierdre walked briskly down the cold hallway, stepping on her toes as much as she could stand to prevent the click of her heels from echoing down the corridor. She hoped that the less time she spent out in the open, the less chance she would have to endure another uncomfortable lecture reminding her that she was hired for her research. She was expected to put Norwood University on the map, which was a promise she has yet to fulfill, and was more burden than any fresh young academic should have to shoulder.

Dierdre was still a post-graduate student when she wrote a paper about the interaction of sub-atomic particulate and non-particulate matter. Real geeky stuff, far too technical for anyone to get overly excited about, but they did. Her professor gushed over the paper and showed it to some colleagues, copies were made, they told friends who then told more friends, and the next thing Dierdre knew, a publisher from one of the Science Journals wanted to print her paper. Dierdre was filled with new found ambition, and having a published paper led to dreams beyond a simple PhD. She visualized Nobel Prizes and new foundations in her name.

The problem, she soon found, was that it was much easier to dream things than it was to make them real. She remembered writing the paper that made her famous, but even that seems like a dream to her now. Expressing her ideas in that paper was certainly a lot easier than it is now, with everybody having such grand expectations that every word she puts on paper should unlock doors to some profound new world of understanding. But she wasn't profound, more and more, she felt like she was just a girl that got lucky once. She had a brief flash of inspiration and managed to record it all on paper. Now the world wanted her to do it again, but she couldn't.

She rationalized that with a new position as a researcher, she would have more resources at her disposal. She convinced herself that with more resources, surely there would be more inspiration, but when it did not come, she found herself relying more and more on the one brilliant moment of her life, and milked that paper for every drop she could get out of it. And when that started to dry up, she left the confines of the university in search of mental and physical distraction. And now, as the weight of the universities expectations came crushing down upon her, even her extra-curricular activities were becoming more work than fun. Just about all she had left, was the teaching, and she was just starting to like that. But, if she didn't find something to put in a report soon, she may end up losing that too.

* * *

A chill rippled up Dierdre's spine and the hairs on her neck and head bristled. She re-focused her eyes, which had glassed over in her thoughts, and realized someone was holding her arm. She sucked in her breath and turned her head to the side. "Dr. Whitfield," she gasped, "you startled me."

"Please forgive me," he said with a warm southern drawl as he motioned into the doorway of his office, "that was not my intention. I have something very urgent to tell you, but let's not discuss this in the hallway."

Dierdre had no idea what was on his mind, but followed him and stood in the doorway to his office, sizing up the diminutive man. Stillman Whitfield was a quiet man. Standing just five foot six, he was a bit shorter than Dierdre, but it wasn't just his size, it was his persona that made him appear small. He was nice to the core, and was probably a boy scout, and still lived by all the virtues of the scouts, but he was square through and though. Even the geeks found him odd. He was the kind of man that would wear tweed and a bow tie. But most of all, he was likable and trustable, and from all reports, a very good teacher.

Dierdre stepped into his office and asked, "What can I do for you Dr. Whitfield?"

"Please call me Stillman. I just wanted to warn you. Dean Smithers came by the labs looking for you last night. I overheard one of my lab assistants tell him they had not seen you all evening. That's when I stepped in and told him that I had just left you in your lab, and you were at a very critical part of your research and did not want to be disturbed."

"Really Dr. Whitfield, I mean Stillman, you needn't lie for me. I would hate to see you get caught covering for me like that."

"Don't worry about me, but I've seen them like this before. You need to worry about yourself. They want something, and they want it soon. Perhaps there is something I can do to help you? I've already submitted my research, and I've got a pretty clear calendar for a while now."

"How incredibly sweet of you!" She poured on the charm. How unfair, she thought it was that such fine gallantry should be confined in such a mousy exterior. "You are such a doll, but I'm just wrapping up the finishing touches on my paper," she lied, "I plan to turn it in at the very last moment. I'm keeping it all a big hush hush surprise." She added one of those girlish giggles that left Dr. Whitfield wondering how anyone so incredibly attractive ever developed brains like hers.

"Well, if you change your mind, or if you just want someone to proofread it first, you be sure to call me, anytime at all."

"I will then!" She wriggled her nose, which as far as Whitfield was concerned, was as good as a kiss on the cheek.

* * *

Aimee clicked the button on her headset to answer the ringing phone, "Norwood University, Physical Sciences Department, how may I help you?"

"Aimee Takahashi, please."

"Ramiro? It's me. I was just thinking of you."

Ramiro Vasquez and Aimee had been good friends for a long time. Intimate on occasion, but had never really been serious until recently. He was a lawyer, an assistant district attorney with an eye towards politics. Neither of them had consciously made the bold decision to commit to the other, they just found that they enjoyed each other's company more than anyone else. Each of them had noticed this, but neither wanted to risk spoiling what they had discovered in each other by putting the subject out on the table. But it was only a matter of time.

"Aimee, you interested in an early lunch?"

"How early?"

"Now?" Ramiro Vasquez, six feet tall with dark hair, perfect olive colored skin and a giant smile, stepped into Aimee's reception area, with his cell phone pressed to his head. He wore a crisply tailored Italian suit, eye candy to the hungry secretary who drooled on the inside.

She rose from her chair, licked her lips and meowing like a cat, took hold of his arm.

"I still haven't received anything from your friend," he told her, "You know I won't play favorites. I will only guarantee that it is expedited to the committee, and that it is examined."

"Believe me," she said, "I would never ask you to do anything wrong, she just needs a little push."

"As long as you get it to me at least two or three days before the final meeting, which is less than two weeks away, I will get it to the members of the review board. That's what friends are for."

She smiled warmly at the handsome man.

* * *

"Dimitri, have you heard yet?" Arion Panopulous dropped his backpack in an empty chair and seated himself at the table alongside his professor, Dimitri Pietre.

"Arion, my friend, I'm so glad you could join me." Dimitri's Russian accent was not overpowering, but his syntax was unmistakable. He was raised by parents and grandparents who spoke little English. Russian was the native language in their home. His grade school years were in a private Russian school, and they occasionally attended the Russian church. His conversion to English began in middle school or he might never have survived high school. His accent added a pleasant lilt to his English. In college, as he discovered his aptitude for sciences, he also discovered that his Russian accent fit the stereotype of a scientist, so he made no efforts to lose it.

"What's that you're reading?" Arion asked while he unwrapped his sandwich.

"Nothing special, just car brochures." Dimitri tossed the document aside and smiled broadly at his protégé. "It is looking like our hard work is paying off for us."

"What about the other candidates? Who are we competing against?"

Dimitri shifted in his seat, and leaned forward so he could speak in a lower voice. "Our chief competition, dear Dr. Rupert Karlyn, has withdrawn his name from the consideration. It would seem he has the problems at home. I heared that his wife learned something about him and one of the coed students."

"Ow, guess that's a lucky break for us."

"Yes, is lucky." Dimitri shifted in his seat again, not sharing what he knew about how Mrs. Karlyn learned of her husbands supposed infidelity. "The only other person remaining in contention is Professor Jennings, and she has yet to complete her submission. From what I am hearing, she has not submitted the progress report in very long time. I am thinking she is not even spending much time at her lab lately. "

"So you think we are at the top of the list?"

"Da, and once we have top grant for whole university, we will automatically qualify for grant money from government."

"Then we can build the prototype you wanted."

"Money makes world go around, I think." Dimitri glanced at the Porsche brochure on the table and imagined how some money could make his world go around in better style.

* * *

Aimee found Dierdre in her office when she returned from lunch. "Ramiro says hi."

Dierdre looked up from her notes and nodded.

"OK, that's a lie. He wants to know where your grant application is."

Dierdre nodded again and said, "I'm working on it."

"Is that it there?"

"Yeah. I'm still stuck on my idea, but I'll force something onto paper and give it my best shot."

Aimee walked around Dierdre, peered over her shoulder and asked, "Anything I can help with? Form filling that is, can't help with the geek stuff."

"No, thanks though, but I got it. I'll leave it on your desk tonight. You can give it to Ramiro tomorrow."

Dierdre worked on it through the afternoon and early evening. She still could only glimpse the idea that floated around in her head, like a hazy fog that she could not get her fingers to grasp, so she reasoned that she only needed more computer power to bring it to life. At least, that would be her excuse. If she had to wait for the idea to germinate, then she would have to find some way to keep her position until then.

So she wrote up a proposal to build a giant supercomputer. She thought that not only would a new supercomputer buy her some time to work on her project, but it would bring a bit of prestige to the university, which was all they ever wanted anyway.

For all she knew, this really was what her idea was waiting for.

As the evening progressed, she noticed a change in her reasoning. She had gone from trying to convince the grant board, to trying to convince herself. That was when she decided to wrap it up and put it in the hands of fate. She had class in the morning and still needed to catch up on some of the sleep she had lost the night before.

She printed the final copy, and slid it, unfolded, into a large manila envelope with a string closure on the flap to hold it shut. She left it on the center of Aimee's desk, collected her things, and left the office. She was a mix of emotions over what she had just done. She felt good to have finished it, yet she knew she didn't really finish anything, but only turned in a paper that she hoped would buy her another year.

She tried putting it behind her and not thinking about it anymore. It was now officially out of her hands. Even if worst came to worst and she lost her grants and her position, her idea was still stuck in her head, and would go with her. She only hoped that when it decided to surface, she would be in a position to explore it.

She entered her apartment, still trying to leave her work at the university, but that was easier said than done. Perhaps soaking in a bath would help. If that doesn't work, maybe reading a book might get her mind off it. She just hoped she could stop focusing on it before she went to sleep. She didn't want nightmares about it.

* * *

Ramiro walked briskly into the conference room. He proceeded to the head of the long conference table, pulled a gavel out of his briefcase, rapped it on the table and said, "Quiet please, the senate subcommittee for the distribution of government research grants to further scientific study is now under way." He rapped the gavel on the table again and then sat down.

"Very funny Ramiro," said the lone attending female, "Senate sub-committee, hah."

A stern looking gentleman to her left smiled broadly and said, "I think you are missing the point, Brenda, look at the gavel." Everyone shifted their attention to the gavel, a new finely polished gavel awarded to ambitious lawyers on their first bench assignment as Judges.

Ramiro beamed as his colleagues gathered around to shake his hand and congratulate him. Brenda was less enthusiastic, but still went through the motions and shook his hand, weakly and briefly. As the commotion subsided, Ramiro stood up and addressed the room, "If I may be serious for a moment, this will be my last time presiding over this meeting, but we may still run into each other, as I am bound to be placed on the panel to review this committee's findings." After a few more exclamations and brief applause, he continued, "so I think perhaps, we or rather you, should, elect a new chairman before we close tonight's meeting."

Ramiro Vasquez had always veered his career towards politics, so it seemed only natural that he would become a district attorney and learn the ropes of public service, and in that capacity, he volunteered for various causes, which brought him to this committee. This is the first stop for grant applications from the regional universities. Each university is allotted at least one application to be passed up to the review board, and all others must earn their way on their own merit.

"OK," Ramiro said, bringing the meeting to order, "The first order of business. Professor Jennings has requested additional funding to build a super-computer she needs to model her theories. I assume everyone has reviewed her reports. I further assume that someone here speaks Martian and can explain it to me?"

"I am fluent in Martian," said an elder voice from the other end of the table.

"Dr. Gruber," Ramiro said, "you have the floor."

Dr. Gruber, with several PhD's to his credit, stood and said, "Professor Jennings is a very intelligent young lady. I have met her before and I must say I am quite impressed by her. Her specialty is in quantum mechanics. She has some rather unique notions about the ability to predict the outcomes of essentially random events. For the laymen present, quantum mechanics is a field of physics that deals with some very small sub-atomic particles that don't behave in the same manners we are accustomed to, but seem to bounce around randomly. While most researchers are dealing with ways to control these quantum events, she has this notion that learning to predict them could lead to ways of harnessing them while consuming far less power than controlling them would require. In other words, if you had a hot air balloon, and wanted to go from point A to point B, you would wait until the wind was blowing in that direction before you launched your balloon, rather than trying to control nature and force the wind to blow where you want." Dr. Gruber scanned the room. "Does that analogy help?"

"So," the gentleman to Brenda's left chimed in, "She suggests that we wait around until the wind is going our direction and then use it when it is convenient to the wind? That does not sound very efficient."

Brenda felt an overwhelming need to come to her fellow woman's defense, "On the contrary, it may not be very convenient, but it must be far more efficient than trying to control the weather. Plus, if you had lots of people going in different directions, then every time the wind changed direction, someone would get a ride. You only need to schedule them in the same order the wind was going. I think that is the Professor's theory."

"Quite right," Dr. Gruber confirmed, "but the problem is that quantum events are random and can't be predicted".

"That's exactly the point of her research, she believes they can be predicted, and wants a chance to prove it." Brenda, always the feminist's advocate, never backed down from an argument.

"Dr. Gruber," Ramiro said, "is it your opinion that her theories are groundless and will never work?"

"No, not at all. I think her theories are both novel and intriguing. I just don't think they are very practical. Ms. Jennings has a spark for fanciful theory, but I don't think she has thought it through to how her theories could be applied in the real world to produce real world products."

"Do we have anyone else working in this field?"

"Yes. There is Professor Pietre and his assistant Mr. Panopulous..." Professor Gruber was interrupted by some chuckling from the man to

Brenda's left. "Reverend Johnson, did I say their names wrong?"

"No, you pronounced them correctly, I just find them funny, as a team, you put them together and you get 'Peter Pan'." This brought smiles and chortles from all around the table.

Dr. Gruber found it difficult to finish without smirking while he spoke. "Well, Dr. Peter and Mr. Pan have been working with lasers and linear accelerators, and another team I read about is using lasers and rotating mirrors to do something or other."

"Thank you Dr. Gruber, I would like everyone to submit a vote on whether we should approve this project for further review, and if so, how much do you think the project should be granted. I will count the vote and if affirmative, deliver the papers to the panel for review."

"Next order of business..." The meeting continued on into the night, project after project, finally ending in the election of a new chairman, and a round of drinks at a nearby pub for the departing Judge.

* * *

With the weight of the grant application lifted from her shoulders, Dierdre could concentrate on her teaching for a bit. She stood center stage before the large class, shuffling her notes and preparing to speak. Her voice was clear and unwavering. She glanced briefly at her notes, and watched her students intently as she delivered her lecture. She paused occasionally, swiping a stray hair from her face, but mostly, she paused for effect, to allow the students' time to comprehend what she had just said.

"An accumulation of seemingly random events may not be random at all," she said, "when viewed as a group. Consider a rainstorm. Meteorologists can see and predict the coming rain. We can observe the storm come in and go out. Yet each drop of rain is, by itself, random. All the many microscopic events that led up to the precipitation were equally random, yet we can predict the coming of the rain. And while we can't predict exact rain storms for the next ten years, we can pretty safely predict that we will have rain each and every year for the next ten years."

Dierdre had been teaching quantum physics for almost three years now, though these lectures to the underclassmen sometimes felt more like statistical theory than physics. She considered it her job to not only teach the facts and formulas, which can easily be retrieved from the text books, but to try and help her students visualize matter and energy in motion. A difficult task, when your field of interest defies exact precise mathematical definition, yet can only be described by mathematical formulas.

"So," she continued, "if we can predict the coming and going of rain storms, what does that say about the randomness of raindrops?" The professor's clear voice reverberated over the classroom. She stared out at the faces of her students. She saw one third of them listening raptly while another third sunk down in their seats content to let other students respond to her questions. Dierdre continued, "If we can predict the course of millions, perhaps billions of raindrops, what does that say about their randomness?"

A few students scratched their heads and faces, providing visual clues that they were listening but were stumped. One student tentatively raised, lowered, and then finally raised his hand.

Dierdre pointed to him, "Mr. Lewis, what does that say about the randomness of raindrops?"

Albert Lewis straightened up in his seat, and in a voice void of any kind of conviction, said, "Well, the raindrops aren't really random, are they? They never fall up. Their motion is influenced by gravity, and air currents."

"Exactly!" Dierdre Jennings paced around the podium. "Gravity is pulling the raindrops, but it is not in control of them. Many forces have come together to lead to the formation of each raindrop, starting with evaporation, humidity, rising air currents carrying the water vapor aloft, cooling air temperatures causing the vapor to condense, gravity pulling it down, side to side motion of air currents knocking them about, electrostatic attraction between different forming droplets, rising air currents from warm land masses, an endless variety of energy has caused these drops to form and fall, but not one of those, not even gravity, controls the drops. While they are not fully random, the endless bombardment of causes creates an endless, virtually random series of events. And this very observation is true at the planetary scale, solar system scale, microscopic scale, and subatomic scale. A constant bombardment of external events can create a random like outcome, but, fortunately for us, the outcomes represent a subset of possible outcomes, which means we can predict the overall effect."

Dierdre returned to the podium and closed her notebook. "That's all the time we have today. Read chapters four and five, and prepare a small paper describing a real world example of a predictable random environment that does not involve weather. Try to get your papers to my office by Wednesday." Like clockwork, as she completed her sentence, the bell rang and the students poured out of class.

* * *

Dierdre filed her notes and books back into here valise as the students exited the lecture hall. She saw Aimee approaching with an envelope in her hand. The envelope was a portent of either good or bad news, and the professor's heart skipped a beat. Aimee waved the envelope in front of her as she approached the podium. "It's here! It's here!"

"What did they say? Did I get it?"

"I don't know," she replied while trying to shove the letter into Dierdre's hands, "You read it."

"I don't want to open, you open it!"

Aimee was astonished by Dierdre's reaction. "Oh come on, you know they've got to give it to you this time!"

"Oh, all right, give it here." Dierdre snatched the envelope from her friend and held it to her bosom with her eyes closed, offering up a brief prayer for good news.

Aimee held up a letter opener, which Dierdre accepted and slid into the crease of the envelope flap. She slid the knife along the fold of the flap to reveal the fate which her research would be taking.

> *Dear Professor Jennings,*
>
> *We are pleased to inform you that your budget for computer time has been significantly increased. We regretfully decline to fund a new super computer designed solely for your project. We are aware of some other projects which are building new computers, and if you wish, we can inquire as to whether they have any plans for their old equipment. Perhaps you might be able to purchase one of those.*
>
> *As always, good luck with all your endeavors.*

That's how they did things. They turned down her request for a new super computer, but wrapped it up in a pretty bow by increasing her computer budget. This wasn't going to please the dean. She had little choice but to accept their offer and pursue one of the used computers.

Dierdre could feel the hope slip from here chest, as clearly as she could feel the blood drain from her face. Being prepared for bad news did not make it any less disappointing. Neither did being through this before. There were only two things that could help at a moment like this. One would be revenge, completing the project in spite of all the setbacks and thumbing her nose at the naysayers, reminding them how they could have been in on the ground floor, but were not. But that was a long term goal and of no practical use at the moment.

Aimee saw her friends face, and immediately recognized what was required. "Well," she said, "you have far too many papers to grade for us to go out tonight, so that leaves us with only a couple choices: chocolate or vanilla?"

It's always good to have a friend who knows how to pull at least a half smile out of a bad situation. They dropped the class materials off in the professor's office, and headed out to the local gourmet ice cream parlor, where they could carve scoops of ice cream into little voodoo dolls, and dispense migraine headaches and life altering cosmetic modifications to the doll's bodies.

CHAPTER 2

The following morning found Dierdre empty and listless. The sword that had been hanging over her head was gone, and with it the promise of something better over the horizon. She found, quite to her surprise, that she missed the pressure which had forced her to produce her grant application. All she had now was her work. As her disappointment waned, she found herself staring at a pad of paper, tapping a #2 pencil. Even though it was Saturday morning, Dierdre fell into her research. She would jot down ideas from time to time, but then cross them out as being the same ideas she had already dismissed previously. Occasionally she would actually work an idea into a mathematical equation.

So she wrote equations, long calculus equations. A lay person could not distinguish any of the equations from scribbling. They all looked, at the same time, like nonsense and genius. But a physicist or a mathematician would see where they were going, and would probably see that they all hit a dead end where she would scribble them out and start a new one. Her theory that she would just have to wait for her idea to pop out of her head on its own seemed to be the only theory that was proving true for her. She continued off and on throughout the weekend with nothing to show for her effort. Monday brought classes and the first smattering of class assignments, which provided some relief from her mounting frustration, but did not prevent her from starting a new pile of paper wads.

Aimee stepped in and saw the pile of crumpled papers and the many doodled equations. "Oh my God," she gasped, "I've seen this movie. You let me know if you start seeing or hearing people, OK? It's just the two of us here now, right?"

"Ha ha. Can't I do a little work without getting the third degree from you?"

"Sure, don't mind me. Here's some more homework assignments. Your morning classes have been canceled. They said something about maintenance changing the lights in the classrooms."

Dierdre crumpled up another failed formula and tossed it onto the mounting pile in her trash can. "Why can't they do that work on the weekends?"

"They're union."

"Well, still, what a pain."

"Why are you complaining?" Aimee motioned to the growing stack of assignments and said, "Looks to me like you got plenty of assignments to grade. If you need a break later, I was thinking of going out for pizza at lunchtime."

"That sounds fine to me, you mind if I bring some of this homework with me?"

"As long as you can talk and grade at the same time, I don't mind."

"That won't be a problem, I've decided to experiment with multiple personalities, and then maybe together, we can get my ideas on paper."

Aimee placed the back of her hand across Dierdre's forehead and said, "You are hearing voices, aren't you?"

Dierdre looked at her with the straightest face she could muster. She tried holding that face for as long as she could until a smile cracked through.

Aimee got right in her face, and looked her dead in the eyes. "You are scary. I think I should warn you that I have been trained in all manner of martial art, and should you ever go postal on me, I will defend myself with lethal force."

"Yeah, right. The only martial art you were ever trained in was how to be drop dead gorgeous."

"Damn, no wonder I can never win at poker."

"You never win at poker," Dierdre said, "because you like to play strip poker with the boys, and you don't make much of an effort to win."

"If that's the way you're going to talk to me, then maybe you should have some imaginary friends to keep you company."

Aimee grabbed a rolling cart with a stack of papers on it and headed toward the door. "I'm going to the media center to make some copies for Dr. Shapiro, I'll be back to meet you here for lunch. Have fun, all of you."

* * *

With Aimee gone, things slowed down again. Dierdre read the class papers, made notes on them, and pulled grades out of thin air, mostly good grades, for each of them. From time to time her mind would wander, and she wished she could have imaginary friends to do the work for her.

But, back in the real world, the only company Dierdre had at the moment was the papers she was grading. Most of her students seemed to understand the concept, but there were a few that had no idea what her lecture was about and turned in papers filled with double talk and fancy clichés, obviously stalling for time, a tactic for which she could not, under the circumstances, fault them.

Mary Salzen apparently could not free herself from the weather example Dierdre had given them in class. Well at least she was paying attention, even if she didn't quite get it. She used water drops traversing down a glass shower door, but she complained that the requirement for them to not use weather in their examples was unfair, because the water droplets are clearly much more interesting on a car's windshield, where gravity pulls them down, and the angle of the glass increases the incidence of any drop veering off its course, and if the car is in motion, air friction on the glass would push the drops up or aside even, but since that was too close to weather, she chose a shower door, which was pretty boring. Mary gets a point for listening in class, a point for understanding that she was not supposed to use weather, and no points for effort, no points for originality, and no points for elaborating on the weather theme that she did not actually use. Dierdre tossed in a free point for turning it in early, just to bring it up to a dismal C minus.

She dropped the disappointing paper onto a pile of completed homework and shuffled through her in-box looking for one with a little more promise. Marcia White, no, she kept looking, Steven Hsiu, no, Patrick Cage, hmm, she pulled out the paper for Patrick. Dierdre never understood why he would take Physics classes anyway. He always seemed to be on an environmental soapbox. Best she could figure out, was that he saw science as the enemy, and either just wanted to know his enemy, or wanted to infiltrate them. In either case, his paper should provide a change of pace.

> *Chlorofluorocarbons (CFC's) are used throughout the world in randomly spaced intervals, often for randomly measured quantities, and certainly for a variety of reasons (such variety represents a kind of random application). Certainly there is no way to accurately predict how much CFC is released when a man or woman sprays*

deodorant under their arm, just like we can't predict when a sealed fluorocarbon refrigerant system is going to spring a leak, and how much would be released into the atmosphere, but we can predict the outcome and measure the effects of the declining ozone layer, and in time as we inch nearer to catastrophic consequences, we will be able to more accurately predict the warming of the Earth due to the greenhouse effect and the melting of the polar ice caps. Random events, predictable results.

Patrick's paper was short and sweet, well maybe not so sweet. Dierdre chuckled as she placed a B on the paper, thinking that the paper itself was predictable too, then added a post script, "They don't put CFC's in deodorant anymore".

* * *

The morning progressed with little fanfare. Each paper was read in turn, marked, and placed on the pile of graded papers. Some would elicit a chuckle, others sympathy, and some were just plain sad.

"Are you making faces at the papers you're grading?" Aimee asked while she transferred large stacks of copied documents from the cart to a table just inside Professor Shapiro's office.

"Was I making a face? Didn't mean to, but some of these papers are just so sad, I can't read them without some kind of reaction."

Aimee finished transferring the documents and picked up her oversize bag. She turned to face Dierdre and anxiously asked, "Ready to go?"

"Sure, sure, I think I'll only take a few of these with me. I can finish the rest this afternoon and have my grades in early."

"OK, who are you and what have you done with my friend Dierdre? Never mind, let's just get some lunch, or some Prozac maybe."

Dierdre made a shocked face and pushed her friend toward the door saying, "Let's just hit the cafeteria and bring it back to the lounge today, OK?"

"I know you want to get through those papers, so I'll do the cafeteria with you, but it's too nice a day for us to be cooped up in the faculty lounge. What if we go find a cozy spot on the small bleachers by the practice track? You can use the bleachers as a desk, and we can talk in relative privacy."

Dierdre cocked an eyebrow and asked, "Aimee, sweetie, is there something you want to talk about?"

"Things dear, just things."

They headed down the hill leading from the physical sciences building to the center of the campus where the cafeteria, student services, administration and a small amphitheater could be found. A large looping drive provided easy access to buses and carpools, and the student parking was not far. Most faculty members were granted privileged parking spaces outside their primary buildings.

The cafeteria was quieter than usual, probably due to the unseasonably warm weather outside, where most of the girls gathered around impromptu picnic lunches, and the boys congregated on the basketball courts and the grass fields where they played football or soccer. Norwood University was on the cusp between being an Eastern and a Southern college, and as such, you were more likely to see footballs than Frisbees, but there were exceptions. Everyone accepted the practice of allowing token hippies and other California natives on campus to provide cultural diversity.

Aimee and Dierdre walked past the rows of vending machines and headed straight to the steamer tables where the staff served up the hot meals. The girls worked their way down the buffet and filled up their Styrofoam boxes for their take out lunch. It was a short walk out the opposite side of the hall towards the practice track.

"Have you heard about Dr. Pietre?" Aimee asked as they neared the bleachers.

Dierdre climbed to the third row of bleachers, sat down and put her lunch to one side, and the papers she was grading to the other. "Dr. Pietre? No, but I've heard Dr. Karlyn's name mentioned in low tones." She started reading the papers.

"Dr. Karlyn, now there's a story." Aimee kept her hands too busy punctuating her story for her to eat her lunch, "Poor man had the misfortune of getting caught with one of his students in a very compromising position."

Dierdre turned a page and added, "Wendy Brenner was the name I heard. I had her in one of my classes for a while, but she dropped out after a couple weeks. She had excellent grades on her transcript, but it sure didn't show in the work she turned in to me."

"Her name has come up before, in fact, she is in Dr. Pietre's class and is getting straight A's there."

Dierdre looked up from her papers. She shook her head and said, "A's? Wendy? Imagine that."

"Yeah, imagine." Aimee took a sip of her drink before continuing, "She only recently signed up for Dr. Karlyn's class, but she was already getting A's in Pietre's class. She left Pietre, transferred to Karlyn's class, and two weeks later, his wife gets wind of her, he drops all his research projects to concentrate on patching up his marriage, and she transfers back to Pietre's class."

"Are you suggesting…"

"Damn right I am, and I'd bet money that if you swung the other way, she would have tried a little harder in your class too!"

Dierdre took a bite of her lunch and resumed grading her papers. "But why? Does Pietre hate Karlyn for some reason?"

Aimee rolled her eyes and said, "I swear. How can you be so naïve with all the brains you have tucked away in your head? Pietre, Karlyn and you were the front three professors vying for the university research money. Whoever turns in the best pitch is in line for the big federal money. Now with Karlyn out, it is just you and Pietre."

"And I guess it was no secret that I was not producing much data lately."

"Right, so as a result, Pietre got the grant money he asked for, basically, he got the computer you wanted."

"That son of a bitch," Dierdre hissed, "Well, I should probably put together a nice congratulatory letter for him and Panopulous."

"Ooh!! Ooh!! That reminds me! Ramiro heard a funny one at his last committee meeting. Reverend Johnson called Dr. Pietre and his assistant Panopulous, Peter Pan!!"

"I can see Panopulous as Peter Pan, he always did seem a bit fruity to me."

"Do I have to spell it out for you?" Aimee reached out and put her hand on the class assignments until Dierdre looked up at her, "Pietre and Panopulous, Peter and Pan, Peter Pan. And it was Reverend Johnson that cracked the joke!" Aimee waited for a more spontaneous reaction from her friend, but got none. "I want the old Dierdre back, the one with the emotion chip. She had a sense of humor."

"I'm sorry, go on."

Aimee paused at that point. It was clear that she had more to say, but was unsure how to word it. Dierdre had seen this look before. It usually preceded a difficult life altering decision, like dumping a boyfriend. But she said nothing, and instead went to her lunch, as if courage were one of the ingredients.

Sensing where this might be leading, Dierdre decided to help by asking, "So, how's Ramiro these days? "

"Oh, he's great. He got promoted you know."

"Promoted? So he's a full blown DA now? Tell him I said congratulations!"

"DA?" Aimee shook her head, "No, better than that, they made him a judge."

"A judge? That's terrific! You sure have been seeing a lot of him. Getting serious? Or seriously tired of him?"

Aimee glanced at Dierdre, then her eyes darted up and to the left as if the answer were written in the sky somewhere. She clutched her milkshake and sucked mightily on the straw which was reluctant to share any of the chocolate within.

"Aimee?" No response. "Aimee?" Still no response.

Suddenly, Dierdre's face changed. She shifted her posture and cocked her head to one side. "Aimee? Did you know that killer bees were no more toxic than regular honey bees?" She picked up one of her papers and read, "A single killer bee is no more deadly than a common ordinary honey bee, and in fact, is far less venomous than some other bees and wasps. It gets its reputation from two facts. First, it is very aggressive and will attack with little or no provocation, and second, it will attack when it senses another bee attacking, so they attack in large swarms."

Aimee's jaw went slack, as she looked, bewildered, at her friend. "I am trying to share a deeply personal moment with you and you are talking about bees?"

"No," Dierdre said, "you weren't actually sharing anything. You went quiet and unresponsive. Do you know anyone who can confirm this behavior in bees? Never mind, it doesn't matter, the concept is all I need to know."

"Dierdre? What are you talking about?"

"I am talking about power. A drop of water has very little power, but a river is mighty. The research I want to do requires vast amounts of computer power. The traditional way to get that power is to build bigger and more powerful computers, and to feed them bigger and more powerful programs. But killer bees harness all this power without making a bigger bee, and without all of them following the same program. Each one of them is operating independently, going about his daily tasks, random tasks. The only difference, is, that when provoked, he attacks. And when one of them attacks, others nearby attack. They are each independent, and if they all attacked someone different, there would be no harm done, but if they all attack the same person, they become killers, stinging him hundreds, maybe thousands of times."

Aimee just stared blankly at her friend.

"I'm sorry." Dierdre put away the papers. "I'll work this out later. You were going to tell me something. Something about you and Ramiro I am guessing. You aren't going to break his heart and dump him, are you? Not now, right after his promotion?"

Aimee stared straight into Dierdre's dark blue eyes and blurted it out, "He asked me to marry him."

Dierdre hemmed and hawed, searching for something coherent to say, "So soon? I mean, you've known each other for a long time, but you haven't really been dating seriously, have you?" Then, as a new thought dawned into Dierdre's mind, she glanced at Aimee's abdomen and started to ask, "You're not..."

"No, no, he is just the sweetest man, I love him dearly, but I'm not sure if I'm ready for marriage. I'm not sure I'm ready to give up having fun, like with you. I don't know what to do. What should I do?"

"I can't tell you what to do. Besides, when I stop to think about it, it's been a while since we really let loose together. What do you want to do? What would it change? If you become a judge's wife, will you keep your job? He's not the kind of guy who would make you stay home is he?"

"No, he would never do that."

"Well I think you'd make a beautiful bride, and a wonderful wife. When is he expecting an answer?" That was when she noticed a thin glint of metal on Aimee's finger. "Wait a minute, is that a ring? If that's a ring, where's the stone? If he's going to be a judge, I think he can pop for a stone." Dierdre's mind was buzzing with thoughts. Her mouth fell open and she asked, "If you are already wearing a ring, does that mean you've said yes already?"

Aimee slid the ring around so the stone was no longer hidden in the palm side of her hand.

"Jesus, would you look at that monster?" Dierdre grabbed Aimee's hand by the finger tips and pulled it closer to her face for a proper inspection. "It's beautiful. Must be almost two karats! Damn, girl, congratulations. So, what's the big problem? You obviously love him, and he must love you."

Then it all came gushing out of here like a geyser, "I haven't met his parents yet, but he warned me. His dad is prejudiced and doesn't like Asians, especially Japanese. It goes back to his service in World War II. How can we do this if his parents feel that way? What am I going to do?"

"You'll be fine. You and Ramiro are both American born, and neither of you share much more with your folks than just family genes."

"But Ramiro's family will want a big wedding, and my family can't throw a big wedding like that."

"If he was a rich white boy, from a family with old money, you might be in trouble, but I have a feeling that for his family, a big wedding means lots and lots of guests, even if you throw it in their own back yard."

"I hope so."

"One thing," Dierdre said, "Why didn't you tell me you were engaged right away? Why were you so worked up about telling me?"

"You know, I didn't want to mess stuff up."

"Stuff?"

Aimee swallowed hard and said, "How many girls do you know that got married in the last five years?"

"I don't know, a couple, I guess."

"And how often do you see them now?"

Dierdre could see where she was going with this now. "I don't think it's a fair comparison. Alice married that boy from Portland, and he got a job back in his home town, so they moved west."

"Yeah, well Mary Sue didn't move out of town, and we never see her anymore."

"Mary Sue has been kind of busy popping out babies! "

"Well she should have come by and shown off her babies!"

"She did Aimee! You are getting all worked up over nothing."

"Don't tell me it's nothing!" She was almost sobbing now. "I don't want to become one of those newlyweds that disappear off the face of the planet."

"Then don't."

"Ooooh!" she growled. "You make it sound so simple, but what if it's not simple? I don't want to lose you. I want to stay friends."

Dierdre realized that no amount of talking was going to soothe her friend, and it was time for a simple old remedy. She leaned across the bleacher and put her arms around her friend, patting her on the back, and at the risk of sounding like a twelve year old, she said, "Best friends, forever."

This brought more tears to Aimee's eyes, but they were softer tears. "Were you planning anything special this week?"

Dierdre threw her head back flipping her hair out of her face. "Possibly. I feel this idea coming out and I may spend most my nights in the lab designing a new simulation, but if you want to do anything, then I'm your girl. I will probably need some moments to clear my head anyway. This idea feels like it might be a good one."

The two of them picked up their stuff and headed down to the steps from the bleachers to the ground level. When they reached the bottom and started on the path, Aimee said, "I'll call you later then, if I need you."

* * *

Dierdre sat down at her computer and looked at some of her earlier simulations. She was trying to define a way to predict the flux of quantum motion and how it affected the varying levels of energy required by the unification of matter, energy and gravity. The proof of her theory was locked away in a long mathematical equation, the very equation she had published years earlier. But harnessing the theory into something practical would require a computer of the future. The speed and power required was still years away from today's state of the art computers. Her only recourse was to create a simulation. The simulation would run at a pace today's computers could achieve. It would have to model various quantum events while another program would try to predict upcoming events.

The largest supercomputer being built at the time housed around sixteen-thousand to sixty-four-thousand processors. Dierdre estimated that modeling quantum events in real time would require millions of processors, and the prediction process would require even more. So it was unlikely that she was going to see a machine fast enough, even in her lifetime, to harness quantum events through predictions. But, if she could find a way to prove the concept in practical terms, she might be able to enlist enough support to at least build a machine that might come close.

But it's not all about hardware. The only way these giant machines can work was by putting all those thousands of processors to work at the same time. That takes very sophisticated programming. She would need to take both of the simulations, the one that simulated the event, and the other one that simulated the prediction, and break each of them up into tiny pieces that could all run on the individual processors. This is where she ran into her limitations as a programmer. In order for this to work, the simulations had to be broken up into tiny pieces and scheduled for all the processors, and the scheduling step had to be fast or the time savings of all those processors would be lost.

The killer bee paper she read started her thinking about this whole process. There was no master bee in charge ordering all those bees to attack. They each attacked on their own. They each chose their own method of attack. And most importantly, they each attacked more or less instantly. If she could program this kind of independence into her simulation, then instead of loading all the processors with tasks when something needed to be done, they would load themselves and find something to do on their own. The more she thought about it, the more this seemed to fit in with her notion of predictions.

Dierdre stared at her old workstation. She already saw it as her old model, even though there was no new one to replace it yet. She was good with computers, better than some of her colleagues. She had a simulation that worked, but it would take days to compute a fraction of a second. Her first attempts brought the computer to a halt and never completed. She needed more power, lots more power.

The phone rang. "Hello?" she asked, her voice sounded slightly groggy.

"I'm sorry," Aimee said through the handset, "Am I disturbing you? You sound like you were sleeping."

"It's OK. I was working. What's up?"

"Will you be working tomorrow night? I was hoping you could come to dinner with me."

"Sure," Dierdre said, "I can always make time for you sweetie. You probably have your hands full making plans and stuff. Have you set a date yet?"

"Well that's kind of why I wanted you to come to dinner with me."

"No problem. I don't know what help I can offer, I've never been married, or even part of a wedding, but I'm there for you anytime you need me."

"You're the best." Aimee took a deep breath, and then spit the rest out as fast as she could talk, "Ramiro and I will pick you up around seven, and we'll all meet his parents at Giuseppe's at half past. Bye now, gotta go." And before Dierdre could either object or express her astonishment, Aimee was gone. Dierdre had never known Aimee to be so intimidated by anyone before, and she wasn't sure if her presence would be as an advocate, there to defend her friend, or as a soft shoulder to cry on. She knew Ramiro was a strong man, and an excellent lawyer, but she had no idea whether he would stand up to his parents. Some very strong people in this world melted before their parents.

Dierdre looked at her program again, and wondered if it was time to enlist the aid of a programming specialist. She couldn't shake the fear that she ultimately might have to, and wondered if she knew anyone who could help, or if she would have to advertise and interview for an assistant.

CHAPTER 3

Aimee knew that Dierdre thought she was overreacting, but as nervous as she was, Ramiro was worse. He stood in front of his closet matching ties with shirts, shirts with socks, socks with trousers. Then he would shake his head and start over again. He coached Aimee on things not to say, especially to his father. He might have been preparing for trial, the way he rehearsed everything he could say, while in the shower, while driving. Everywhere he went, he was preparing responses to every conceivable outburst he imagined from his father.

Aimee stood in the doorway to the bedroom and timidly said, "I asked Dierdre to come with us and stand by me."

Ramiro dropped what he was holding and backed out of the closet. He looked at his fiancée and asked, "You what?"

Ramiro's world was upside down with everything backwards. In the real world, it would be Aimee's parents who thought he was not good enough for their daughter. He reminded himself that he has not crossed that bridge yet. And, if this evening went badly, he had no reason to expect better treatment from her father.

"You're mad at me," she said, "I know, it's stupid. I'll call her and cancel."

"No, wait. It's brilliant. It will probably take both my mother and me to get my father to see reason. You should have someone with you."

Silence passed for a moment and Ramiro returned to pulling ties from his closet.

Aimee tiptoed behind him and reached around his girth pressing her cheek to his back. She looked around him at the tie he held and said, "No, not that one. Try the blue tie with the single gold stripe across it."

Ramiro knew just the tie she meant, and collected it to lay over the coat and shirt on the bed. She was correct, it was a good match. It was a fleeting moment, shared between them, but he learned much about himself, and about them. He stared into her eyes and pulled her close. It was a passionate embrace, not one filled with abandon, but a warm embrace that leads to unspoken bonds between them. Both of them realized that the evening was not about their future together, but about his future with his father. Aimee also knew that in some ways, it might be their future together, because she could never be the same if she caused a split between them. She still needed to find some kind of acceptance with his father.

* * *

Aimee ended yesterday's phone call before Dierdre could even ask her what to wear. Dierdre searched through her closet. Giuseppe's was an upscale Italian place, and this was a very special, although awkward, occasion. She had to find something that presented her as a strong supportive friend, but also a successful, intelligent, and accomplished woman, but most importantly, it had to be something she was sure Aimee did not have in her closet.

She pulled out a mid-length black dress, more of a utility dress and less slinky. She felt safe betting that Aimee would not wear black to announce their engagement. She laid the dress against her body and leaned back to see how it draped on her in the mirror. She shifted her weight to her other foot, and nodded her head. With her gown and shoes selected, Dierdre was free to go about her day.

She had nothing special planned for any of her classes. Over the few years she had been teaching, she had developed some lesson plans that served as a foundation she could use, year after year, and today, she simply followed one of those lessons without variation. All through the day, her mind would occasionally touch on the evening ahead. She wanted to be prepared if she had to speak on her friends behalf, and she wanted her statements to be rehearsed in her mind beforehand. Her mind would inevitably drift off to her simulation too. She tried to picture how she could get so many program threads to run without bogging the computer down. She was nearly resigned to the fact that she would have to call in an expert.

She scanned the faces of the computer science instructors in her mind. Michael Green taught computer sciences geared for math and science majors. Dierdre doubted he could handle the task, besides, they had dated once, and she wouldn't give him the time of day, even if he was the last man on earth.

She ultimately decided it would be too difficult to maintain control of the project if she partnered with another professor. She needed someone who had bright ideas, but didn't feel he always had the only solution. When the time came, she would have to look for a graduate student. She needed someone who was willing to do grunt jobs, and willing to accept a minor mention in the credits. She would have to take a closer look at some of her students to see if any of them had an aptitude for computer work. Throughout the day, she eyed her students, as they sat in their places waiting for her to launch into her lecture. She made mental notes of those that carried notebooks, or PDA's, and tried to spot those that could pass for nerds. She realized that she was profiling them, and that profiling wasn't a satisfactory way to find an assistant.

The day passed, and she had not identified anyone. Next chance she gets, she'll have Aimee cross reference her students for computer science classes.

* * *

Ernesto Vasquez was still a strong man for his age. He was eighty-one, and still stood straight. He was never a tall man, but as the years went by and his friends gradually began to shrink and hunch over, he had become tall, or so it seemed. He was an angry man, perpetually in a bad mood. There was little anyone could do to change that, and this night certainly was not going to be an exception. "I just don't see why we have to meet him at such a fancy hi brow place for dinner. He's our son. We should have him here for dinner."

His wife scowled at him. "You mean I should slave in the kitchen for him when he is trying to make a special good impression on us?"

"What special impression? What do you know that you aren't telling me?"

Esmeralda was in on the secret. She knew everything. She was sworn to secrecy, but she would not have spoiled her son's announcement anyway. She spent the whole week subtly preparing Ernesto for this night. One morning, she shared a dream that she had made up about them bouncing grandchildren on their knees. Another morning, she was examining her face in the mirror counting wrinkles and exclaiming that by the time they have grand babies, she would be an old prune and would scare them away. She was every bit a woman with a ticking clock, except her clock was for her son to have children, which of course meant to get married and start a family. So a seed had been planted in Ernesto's mind that the two of them were not getting any younger.

She turned to him and slyly hid the truth. "Your big shot lawyer son wants to take us to dinner in a fancy-schmanzy place. I can add two plus two. He must have an announcement to make."

Ernesto's face brightened slightly. "Maybe he finally accepted the job with that big law firm that wanted him when he graduated. I never understood why he would turn down so much money to be a public servant."

"He's just like you, only instead of running off and joining the army, he became a prosecutor."

"Well something is up. He knows I don't like these fancy expensive places. That fancy pretentious food always gives me gas."

Esmeralda tapped her foot and shook her head. "I just don't believe what is coming from out of your mouth. You act like you grew up poor, like your family never had money."

"My father taught me the value of a dollar. He came to this country poor. His father struggled just to keep them here."

"But your father turned all that around"

"Yes," Ernesto replied, "My father made his fortune, but he did not do that by wasting his money on fru-fru food. He worked hard for his money, and taught me to guard it by investing it wisely."

"Nonsense. Your father may have worked hard, but he made his money by being in the right place at the right time."

Ernesto was getting frustrated. He felt his wife couldn't even hear him. "I like what I like. I like my beer cold with a lime in it. I like my food simple and traditional. When I have an announcement to make, we gather on Sunday with a big pot of menudo. It was good enough for my father, and it's good enough for me."

"Well thank goodness your son has set higher standards for himself. It's his announcement he wants to make, and he should be able to make it in whatever way he sees fit without you ruining his day. Now I expect you to stop acting like a child and show some love and support for your son."

Ernesto started muttering Spanish expletives under his breath, and threw up his hands in despair. He turned and headed for his lazy chair, where he planned on brooding and muttering a while longer.

"Ernesto Hidalgo Vasquez," Esmeralda wagged her finger as she scolded him, "I don't want to hear one more complaint from you, not a single peep! Your only child wants to buy us dinner at a very nice place, and you are going to enjoy it whether you like it or not!"

"Just who do you think you are talking to?"

Her voice softened as she said, "I think I'm talking to the man who was gentle once, and had manors enough when he came home with me to meet my parents."

"That was a hundred years ago." He waved off the thought with his hands as if it was too insignificant to consider.

"Then I am talking to the man who has shared my bed for fifty years, but is going to share my rolling pin on the side of his head if he does not behave himself. I mean it. Don't you dare embarrass either your son or your could-be-separated wife."

Ernesto looked at his wife and the normally foul mood melted off his face. He loved how his wife let him know which things were important to her. It was that spark of independence that first attracted him to her a lifetime ago. "OK. OK. My best behavior."

"And when your son wants to pick up the check," she leaned over his chair and thumped her index finger against the center of his chest, "you let him. I don't want to see any of your macho pride ruining my finely balanced budget. Do you hear me mister?"

Ernesto pulled himself up to attention and saluted. "Sir, yes sir! Ma'am!"

* * *

Aimee's left eyebrow arched high on her forehead when she heard Dierdre's plan. "You want a WHAT?!?"

"I wouldn't say I WANT a partner, exactly. I am just admitting the possibility that I may need some expert help with my computer model."

"And you want one of the students?"

"Yes. Hopefully we can find a computer major who has also taken my course."

"OK. Just a sec." Aimee brought up the student registry and the screen filled with pictures. "He's kind of cute," she said. She entered some parameters to narrow down the list. The screen blinked and provided an empty list.   "Apparently, none of your students are computer majors."

"Oh well, thanks for looking."   Dierdre hung her head a bit and headed back to her office.

"Wait just a sec, I'm not done here."   Aimee changed a few parameters and added, "Just because none of them are computer majors doesn't mean that none of them have the right stuff. Let's see if any of them enrolled in any advanced computer classes."   Again, the screen took her requirements, and a moment later blinked, and displayed only a single student.

Dierdre leaned in to read the name. "I know him. He's very bright, but kind of weird. What class did he take?"

Aimee pushed a function key to display the courses he took, but it displayed a blank list. "It looks like he enrolled in some computer courses, but didn't actually finish any of them. Let's see if there are any notes about him from that department." She punched another function key and up came another screen with some notes. "Hoo hoo hoo," Aimee exclaimed, followed by a melodic whistle.

"What did you find?"

"Looks like your boy here was refused admission to the computer sciences departments, because, in his youth, he had gotten himself in some trouble with the law by hacking some government computer systems."

"I don't need any trouble makers, I'll just have to take care of this myself, I guess."

"Dierdre, my friend, I think we have all made mistakes at one time or another in our lives, and if he can hack into a government computer, he probably knows a thing or two that you don't, plus, he seems to be doing well in your classes too."

"He is. Well, I'll keep him in mind. Thanks."

Dierdre was just closing up her appointment book and about to lock her drawers when the phone rang. "Hello?"

"Professor Jennings? This is Rupert Karlyn. I understand that you had requested funding for some advanced computers, but that your budget was only marginally increased."

Dierdre knew project funding was not secret, yet it was still unnerving to have the facts quoted to her by someone she barely knew.

"You may have heard," he continued, "that I had withdrawn my name from this year's grant program."

"Yes, I heard something to that effect."

"Well," he said, "I never doubted that my affairs would be public."

"Perhaps 'affair' is a poor choice of words, especially under such dubious circumstances."

"You have your suspicions?" he asked, "Good. While there were photographs involved, the photographs did not tell the truth, and the entire situation was completely fabricated. I am very fortunate that I have a wife who sees all this as well."

"I'm glad to hear that, but I'm not sure why you are sharing all this with me?"

"Of course," he said, "sorry. What you may not have heard, is that I am leaving the university. My wife sees the truth. Even Dean Smithers believes in me, but sadly, this plot against me has made its stain upon me, so we are packing up and starting over elsewhere."

"I'm sorry to see you go, but I hope all goes well for you both."

"Thank you," he said, "you are kind. I've decided to correct one injustice before I leave, so I'm transferring my computer to you. I will have the paperwork ready and waiting on your desk in the morning. My student assistant can dismantle and deliver it to your lab over the weekend, but you may need to find someone to help you install it I think."

"Dr. Karlyn, I'm speechless, thank you." She knew his computer would not have thousands of processors like the giants that IBM announced every other year, but she knew that it would be much larger than what she had now.

* * *

"I'm curious," Dr. Karlyn's wife posed her question as he hung up the phone, "why did you choose her? I'm sure there are plenty of others who could benefit from your computer. What put her at the top of the list?"

"Well, my dear, first of all, the university put Dr. Jennings on a very high pedestal when she arrived here, and they put a great deal of pressure upon her to produce something new. Then when it was time to fund projects, they treated her like a silly girl who could only dream pretty dreams and would never have a useful invention, so they never gave her serious money. Second, her research looks very promising. She really has some very unique ideas. Lastly, her field of study is the same as Dr. Pietre's, and while his work is strikingly similar to my own, her theories are directly opposite, so much so, that if she can prove hers to be correct, his, and mine, could not possibly be correct, and right now, I would very much prefer hers to be correct, even if it proves me wrong too."

His wife smiled a sly sinister smile. "Good. I was hoping that was the reason, the last one anyway."

The doorbell rang at the Karlyn residence and the professor handed some documents to a courier at the door. "Please rush these to Professor Jennings' office and leave them on her desk." Dr. Karlyn knew this courier was familiar with the campus and could be relied upon.

Outside the door, standing behind the courier, was Dr. Karlyn's senior assistant. After the courier left, they embraced warmly. "Dr. Karlyn, it has been a pleasure and an honor. I am so sad to see you go, especially like this."

The professor put one hand on the boy's shoulder and said, "Bobby, I hate to leave you like this. Now you won't have a project on your transcripts." He reached into his jacket pocket and pulled out a letter size envelope. "Here. This is a letter of recommendation. Give it to any instructor, or save it for any employer you want. I hope this will help, I wish I could do more."

"Thank you," he said as he accepted the letter. They turned and stepped down the walk to the car where Mrs. Karlyn stood by the open passenger door. Bobby stopped at the end of the walk and asked, "Have you spoken with Professor Jennings?"

"Yes, just a few moments ago. Those were the papers the courier just took. I told her you would deliver the equipment to her lab this weekend. I think we are doing a good thing."

"Are you sure you don't want me to send a special gift to Dr. Pietre?"

"I'm sure. You don't need that kind of trouble. Maybe, I think, I will just imagine that you did such a thing. Perhaps that could bring me sweet dreams for a while."

"Yeah," Bobby nodded his head, "I think I'll dream it too."

* * *

Dierdre was touching up her lipstick in the hall mirror when the doorbell rang. "Coming," she yelled at the door. She quickly blotted her lips, and pursed them once more for a visual check and twisted shut the lipstick canister as she walked to the door. She swung the door open, and as she expected, Aimee stood in the door way looking like a million bucks, a very anxious million bucks. She noted a complete shift in Aimee's posture since their last meeting, instead of being frightened, even petrified, she was excited, and anxious to step up to the plate and do her best. This was comforting for Dierdre to see, it would be a lot easier for her to support and defend a confident woman, than a cowering, probably sobbing, shell of a woman. The outlook for the night had already improved.

Aimee looked at Dierdre, and smiled. "You look great, thanks for coming with me."

"So what happened? You seem more relaxed now."

"Nothing really, I just realized that Ramiro and I have already made our decision, and Ramiro is not going to choose his father over me, so I'm not the one that should be scared."

Dierdre joined Aimee on the porch and hugged her warmly. "That's great. I knew he wasn't going to be a wimp."

Ramiro waited for them at the curb, holding the rear door open for the both of them. He stood straight backed and ushered both of them into the back seat. He was in good humor, and had no problems with Dierdre's presence. He was relieved she was there. He anticipated engaging his father in rather lengthy oral arguments, and was glad Aimee would not be alone, and hopefully, might not have to hear everything that was said.

"Thank you James," Aimee said as she slid in first.

"Very well mum," he replied.

"Thank you, sir," Dierdre added as she entered the car, "He certainly is a handsome chap, but what will your father say when he learns you plan to marry the chauffeur?"

"My father," Aimee said, "is a very practical man. He will say that I will be going places."

Ramiro closed the rear door and walked around to the driver's seat and added, "Personally, I'm thinking it might make a better impression than telling him she is marrying a lawyer."

"Ahem," Aimee interrupted, "I will be Mrs. Your Honor, the judge's wife."

Ramiro bowed his head and replied, "I stand corrected."

The restaurant was not far. The university was located at the hub of many of the city's cultural activities, including museums, theaters and some of the trendier restaurants. There were also plenty of smaller food vendors that catered to the students, who were fonder of hot dogs and pizza by the slice, than veal or pasta. The drive took them in a circle around the campus. The campus was not fenced in, except for the sport courts, but there were numerous walls of trees and hedges that marked the borders, and the streets that followed the exact contour of the campus border were often lined with trees on one side, and homes on the other. The homes were mostly older, and while many showed signs of age in the fences and sheds, the homes themselves were all relatively well cared for, as were most of the yards. This town was every bit the look and feel of an upscale Ivy League town, even if it was south of the Dixon.

Ramiro swung the car around the final turn, a left onto University Avenue, then around to the right and pulled up in front of the restaurant. The restaurant itself was upstairs over a bookstore. The three of them walked past the latest literary masterpiece, stacked up in pyramids in the window, and up the stairs on the right side of the building. The stairs were sturdy, and made of elegant woods of a variety of types and colors. The hand rails were covered with grapevines, though at this time of the year, the foliage had already been clipped off. There was an elevator at the base of the stairs, but on nice nights like this, most patrons opted for the stairs, which ended in a deck that extended to what would be the back of the restaurant, as it was away from the street, but actually served as the entrance. The deck at the entrance was a beautiful piece of work with trees growing up through it, and benches circling the trees. Twinkling white lights were strung around the trees so there was always a wonderful starry night on the deck. The restaurant had three seating sections, the first section, in the center of the room, was for your more casual diners and appeared similar to any other restaurant, with tables and booths to handle as many diners in as comfortable a space as could be arranged. Around the outside along the walls of the room, were a few larger booths, capable of holding as many as nine patrons, with more space between the booths that provided a more private experience. These booths were by reservation only, and generally needed a good deal of lead time to get. Finally, there was the banquet room. Hardly large enough to handle more than a medium sized meeting, it was, however, available for private parties, by special arrangement only. This was where Ramiro had reserved a table, one of the perks of public service, and it didn't hurt to have made friends with the owner along the way.

The maître d' greeted Ramiro as he entered the front door, "Good Evening, sir, all is ready as you requested," but before he could lead them to the back, the owner stepped in and said, "I'll take care of this party." Ramiro had helped the owner maintain the deck and patio when the bookshop had moved in down below. Previously, downstairs was a coffee house that benefited greatly from the business brought in by the restaurant, and served as the waiting area for new arrivals. But when the bookstore moved in, they complained about the deck completely taking away their back yard area and the light. They pursued legal remedies to have it torn down. Ramiro, even though he was a prosecutor, helped the owner classify his restaurant and the deck as landmarks, which would be a step below a historical site. Landmark status prevented any further actions from the bookstore and earned Ramiro the royal treatment any day of the week. On this day, the owner had laid out a magnificent table in the center of the banquet room, lit not only with candles on the table, but he had small candelabras hanging from floor stands which provided a flickering ambiance to the room.

The three guests seated themselves, Ramiro at the head of the table, Aimee to his right, and Dierdre to her right. The opposite end from Ramiro was for his father, and his mother would sit opposite both Dierdre and Aimee.

Giuseppe's real name was Joseph, but as the owner of one of the better Italian establishments, he felt he should have a more fitting name, so he chose Giuseppe for the restaurant. His employees joked that Guido was more appropriate, but only in jest. Giuseppe motioned for the waiter, who rushed to Giuseppe's side.

Giuseppe bowed formally towards Ramiro and asked, "Shall I serve the wine?"

"Just decant it for now, my father is very punctual and will be here momentarily."

"Your father is here," Ramiro's mother announced as she came through the banquet room door.

"Ah, Mrs. Vasquez, please allow me." Giuseppe pulled the chair and seated Esmeralda. He motioned for Ernesto to take the remaining seat at the head of the table. After tucking her chair in, he hand signaled the waiter, and a sample of wine was poured for Ramiro.

Ramiro never considered himself a wine connoisseur, but he was a firm believer in ceremony, and went through all the motions of tasting the wine before serving it. His father did not care for this side of his son. He was a man to show what he felt and not put on airs, but he kept his tongue to himself as he promised he would and graciously accepted a glass of wine, even though he would much rather have had a pitcher of cervezas.

Ernesto scanned the room, his eyes paused briefly on Dierdre, too bad, he thought, that she was not sitting next to his son, or his wife's dreams of their son marrying might have been true. But with Aimee sitting next to Ramiro, he concluded it must be some business thing. Maybe he finally accepted a job at some hotshot lawyer outfit, and she was his new secretary. "So, son, what's this all about?"

"Later, dad, first let's eat."

The waiter handed menus to all at the table and listed the specials, pork medallions, stuffed peppers, and lamb meatballs with spaghetti. Aimee and Dierdre each chose lighter fare, not because they were watching their weight, but because they were not feeling their full appetites, and Aimee, at least, did not want to give the appearance of having an overly hearty appetite.

"Everything looks so good!" Esmeralda looked up and down the menu trying to select the one meal that looked the best, and tried her best to attract attention away from her husband who looked up and down the menu trying to select the item that would be the least fancy, as if nothing on the menu was regular food. "I think," she announced, "I'll have the chicken Parmesan with the fettuccine Alfredo."

"That does look good," Ernesto said. He knew what she was trying to do, and decided it would be best to one-up her, "except I'll have the VEAL Parmesan with rigatoni and marinara sauce. Can I get some red peppers with that please?"

* * *

Bobby Blain went to Karlyn's lab to run a couple jobs before he dismantled the computer on Saturday. Even though Dr. Karlyn did not request it, he thought he would back up all his research onto CD's and send them to the professor's new school. Bobby had every right to be there, but he left the lights off and locked the door, feeling it was easier if he did not attract anyone's attention rather than to explain what he was doing. While the data was backing up, he would have one last chance to play Rogue, a very old computer game that only the true geeks knew how to play.

Bobby had nothing against modern video games, in fact, he liked quite a few, but he had a romantic streak in him that gravitated to the old games that came from a time before graphical images moved around on screens, when everything was done in basic two color text. Dr. Karlyn knew of his fondness for the old games and allowed him to indulge himself, as long as they did not interfere with his research.

Bobby logged onto a second terminal which allowed him to see the progress of the backups while he played. The backups were mostly automated, but required someone to change the CD when it was full. The CD burner was a dinosaur. It burned at a steadily slow pace, which was fine with Bobby, since it gave him adequate time to mess around with his games. He merely needed to glance over at the master console to see when it was time to change discs.

With the backups underway, Bobby settled down at his station. He had some cold pizza, chips and plenty of soda to keep him going through the night.

* * *

The meal was winding down. The waiters were clearing the plates, and Ernesto took one last swipe at the sauce on his plate with one of Giuseppe's famous soft bread sticks. Ramiro and his mother both caught this, it was a good sign. It meant that he really had liked his meal and was no longer play acting, except, that he might continue play acting that he was really grumpy and only pretending to be good. Being grouchy was something he had raised to a fine art, and as much as he liked to believe that he did not put on airs around people, the truth was that he did not put on airs to please people, he only did so to displease people. For some sad reason locked in his past, he learned that not making others happy around you was far less disappointing than trying to please them. He made few exceptions, and even to his family, he guarded his expectations of happiness. So now, well fed, Ernesto sat back in his chair, unable to completely suppress the smile that lurked behind his face.

Seeing that now was a good moment, Ramiro gestured to Giuseppe that he would like the wine glasses filled again, and Giuseppe relayed hand signals to the waiters. It was not unlike a play being signaled into a football team huddled on the field. A finely orchestrated ballet followed, which ended with glasses filled just short of the brim.

Ramiro stood and cleared his throat. He raised his glass at arm's length and stared at the candles refracted through the burgundy liquid before he spoke. "I want to thank you for coming here tonight. I have a couple of announcements I would like to share with everyone. First, I wanted everyone here tonight to help me celebrate a new position which I will be embarking upon. I have resigned my post with the DA's office effective immediately."

Ernesto wanted to jump up and do those victory dances you see after touchdowns. He wanted to scream out, "I knew it. I knew it," but he resisted and held his breath waiting to see which firm his son had decided to join.

"Next week, and everyone here is invited to join me at noon on Monday, I will be sworn in to my new appointment as a District Judge."

Ernesto's victory dance stumbled over in his mind. He replayed what he heard over and over, as if he hadn't heard it right. It wasn't what he expected to hear. A Judge? He had never considered that before, and to his surprise, he did not feel disappointed in his son's decision at all. He felt a new different surge of pride come over him. In his mind, a judge was like royalty, like being voted into congress.

Ernesto lifted his glass and said, "Congratulations son, you make me proud. Very proud." It was a short toast, direct from the heart.

"Thank you Father. And now, for my second, and most important announcement." He reached over and took Aimee's hand and pulled her up so she stood beside him. "Father, Mother, I know this may be a bit of a shock for you..."

Ernesto did not like where this was going, the pride he had been feeling suddenly balled up in his throat.

"I want you to meet Aimee Takahashi." He turned to Aimee and said, "Aimee, I want you to meet my father and mother, Ernesto and Esmeralda Vasquez. Ramiro spoke in the most formal tones as if he were delivering a speech. "Father, Mother, Aimee has consented to be my wife."

Around the table, everyone sucked in their breath and turned towards Ernesto, to see how well he had taken the news.

* * *

Bobby had finished the last CD, but decided to stay a bit longer. He was never a master game player like many of his friends, but he was on level fifteen and wanted to see how far he could go down the dungeon. His game was interrupted when he heard voices out in the hallway.

He recognized one of the voices as Dr. Pietre, a man whom he had grown to hate as much as Karlyn was a man he had grown to love. Hearing the professor in the hall was not entirely uncommon, but he did not usually work this late at night. Then Bobby heard a sound that made his heart stop. The voices had stopped, just outside the doorway in the hall, and someone tried the door.

"I told you it would be locked," Dr. Pietre scolded his associate.

Outside the door, Dr. Pietre stood with one of his former students. He was an unpleasant young man who had once had aspirations to be a pharmacist, but had since found himself expelled from med school after being found in the possession of some questionable substances used in the manufacture of fancy designer drugs.

"Hang on, this should be easy," the young man said as he whipped out an old plastic school ID and tried to jimmy open the latch with it.

"Not so easy as it is looking?"

"Just a sec, I'll get it."

"And if you scratch the door jamb? We want to slip in, make the backups and slip out without leaving the trace we were here. We don't want to leave the evidence that there was a breaking-in."

"But," the young man said, "if it does not look like a break-in, and they do discover what you've done, they will know it's an inside job. Maybe we should make it look like a robbery."

"NO! I am meaning it! I have duplicate key in my office. The machine is scheduled for the dismantling on Saturday. Nobody will be knowing we were here."

The two men walked off down the hall.

Bobby's head was swirling. He knew he had to act, and he had to act fast. He also knew deleting the files from the computer would not be adequate. He had to run a program called deep-wipe that would remove every spec from the machines. He jumped to the console, and started scanning some security folders to find the deep-wipe program. He was lucky. It was already installed and ready to go. He fired it up and directed it at some of the most key sections of the system. While it was running, he grabbed the CD's he had burned, and put them in his backpack. He knew they would be returning soon, Dr. Pietre's office was just up the hill.

Bobby started a new session on the system console. He logged in under the system engineer's user ID. This was a secret user ID that the manufacturer used to configure the system. With this menu you could turn processors on and off and vastly rearrange the way they worked. Bobby used this menu to re-channel the disk drives into different partitions. A large computer like this had banks and banks of hard drives all working together as if they were one giant disk. Bobby tricked the system into seeing them as separate drives again, and started up another disk wipe program. He repeated this until he had four copies of the disk wipe running, each on a different drive, and each on its own processor. Each new process he started up meant it would finish that much faster. He thought he might have time to start another, when he heard a key inserted into the door.

* * *

As if a cloud had pulled overhead, Ernesto's face darkened, not a blush, but a deep dark red had replaced his usual ruddy brown complexion. His neck seemed to swell, and his fists clenched tighter and tighter.

"Ernesto..." His wife's voice was both pleading and warning. She held on to the last syllable for a moment as if singing his name. "Be calm Ernesto."

He looked at his wife, his eyes pleading to be released from his promise of good behavior. It was no use. He could not hold it in. Now his eyes looked deep into his wife's eyes, and while his face swelled with anger, his eyes apologized for what he was about to do.

"No," he said, quiet at first as if his voice could not get the sound out, "NO," he said again, this time with force. He slammed his fist to the table. "You can't do this." He was totally losing control and stammering out incomplete fragments of sentences. "You can't...not her...you...I...her...after everything...after everything...her?" It was clear that he had something to say but couldn't get it out.

Esmeralda mustered all of her strength into a great shout, "ERNESTO!!! BE QUIET!!!"

Ramiro had never heard his mother so loud before, but felt better having her support in such a vocal way.

Aimee had spent days preparing for this moment. She rehearsed in her mind what she would hear and how she would react, yet all the preparation in the world could not prevent the emotions which welled up in her bosom. Her eyes were wet, but tears had not yet stained her cheeks. Dierdre believed she had never seen fury like she witnessed in his face. She stood calmly, and stepped over to Aimee's side, which, if nothing else, would at least accent the fact that Ramiro's father was absolutely alone in this room.

Ernesto caught his breath. "How can you do this Rami? Can't you see what she is? Don't you remember what I told you? She killed them all, every last one of them. This is not right, you cannot do this."

"She never killed anyone," Ramiro said, "You are talking like a crazy man who can't tell the difference between today and something that happened over fifty years ago!" Ramiro's voice was steady and reassuring. Aimee released her grip on him, and moved over to Dierdre.

Ernesto stood, but stayed in his place. "Maybe she didn't, but her people did. They killed all my friends. They killed a whole village of people who had lived there for generations. They even shot me and left me for dead."

"Here we go again," Ramiro said, "the whole story of how you were shot and won your purple heart on Mt. Jinka. We've heard it before, it's old news."

Ramiro didn't notice, but Dierdre did. Something changed in Aimee's posture, she leaned a little heavier on Dierdre's arm and her legs started to buckle. To Aimee, the room seemed to be spinning around her. The room and everyone in it seemed to be slipping away, as if it were down a tunnel. Dierdre looked at her friend and thought she was about to pass out. Her eyes were glassy and jittered for a moment, before finally clearing. Aimee finally focused on Dierdre, then looked around the room. The yelling continued to rage on, and only Dierdre was even aware that anything was wrong at all.

* * *

Dr. Pietre opened the door and quietly slipped into the lab. He saw Bobby standing by the console and froze, so much for being in and out undetected. "You!" he shouted, "What is it you are doing here?"

"I am Dr. Karlyn's senior lab assistant in this lab, I belong here. What are YOU doing here?"

"Karlyn is gone. You are not belonging here."

"I am completing my final instructions from Dr. Karlyn. I am supposed to be here."

Pietre sneered, "I am not liking your tone. What is it you are doing?"

Bobby pointed at the computer and said, "I am preparing this computer for dismantling."

"You are wiping disks! All of dear Dr. Karlyn's research is gone now!"

"Of course, I can't deliver this to its new owners without wiping it first."

Bobby noticed that Pietre's burly assistant was trying feverishly to stop the wipe programs, but each time he managed to cancel one, another would pop up in its place, a favorite trick of Bobby's.

Pietre lunged at Bobby, and grabbed him by the collar, slamming him to a wall. "You fool! What have you done??? The faculty should backup systems first! Where do you take this when you are done?"

"I don't feel at liberty to say, and since this is not YOUR lab and I have work to do, I must ask you to leave now." Bobby was stubborn and stood his ground.

"I know you," Pietre spat, "You have past. You are finished at university! I will see to it."

Bobby shot back, "That's OK, I know who you are and I know what you've done!"

Pietre released him, wondering what the boy knew, and turned his attention to his assistant. "Why is it not stopped yet?"

"I can't, it keeps restarting itself."

Pietre went to the console and spent about half a minute trying to cancel the wipe before he turned away in disgust. "Bah, is useless." He pointed a finger at Bobby and yelled, "You will pay for this! You may mark my words. You will pay!" He ran out mumbling incoherent Russian curses under his breath.

Bobby was glad Pietre never noticed the Cd's in his backpack. He scooped up his stuff and left the lab. The wipe would eventually run out of disk and stop. As he left the lab, he reflected on the confrontation, and thought he detected something unusual in Pietre's face when he told him he knew who he was.

* * *

"They're just stories," Aimee said softly, "I never even knew him."

"Huh? What?" Dierdre barely heard Aimee speak through the din.

"Puju, Mt. Jinka, the harbor at Barrata Bay. I know those places." Her voice grew stronger and Ramiro heard her. He stopped yelling at his father and turned his head to see what she was saying.

"My grandfather was there. He died at the battle of Barrata Bay."

"You hear that?" Ernesto said, "I told you her people were there. She is one of them. You can't trust any of them."

Aimee continued, "My father said it was a terrible massacre. My grandfather died there. I never met him."

"And I'm not apologizing for any of the dirty Japs that I killed there."

It was like a twilight zone episode for Aimee. So much hatred exuded from Ramiro's father, and the coincidence of her grandfather being killed at the very spot where his hatred was spawned. As a child growing up, they had a shrine in their home honoring her grandfather and all those who died on the island of Puju.

"Even if I killed your grandfather," Ernesto said, "every Jap I killed deserved it, and more."

"You didn't kill my grandfather."

Ernesto puffed his chest out and said, "I might have."

"I don't think so. He was an officer in the four hundred and forty something battalion. He wasn't even supposed to be there, they were stationed in Africa and Europe. The army had a couple men from his battalion transferred to Puju, to help them intercept and translate radio broadcasts."

Ernesto had stopped yelling. The dark red and purple color was draining from his face.

"My great-great-grandfather was from an island off of Okinawa, where they spoke a dialect which was hard for the army's regular translators to understand. My grandfather was training them."

Ernesto slumped into his chair. His eyes glassed over, and his mind was back in 1943.

Aimee continued, "He only wrote home to my grandmother a few times. Most of what he wanted to share with us was classified, and even what he did share was redacted by the army. He said it was a funny place. Radio's everywhere listening to all different channels. And there were some other guys, some kind of Indians all speaking in some strange language that was even harder to understand than grandfathers."

"Navajos," Ernesto said. His voice was soft now, and without hatred, "They were code talkers. Their voices were like the wind through the trees."

"My grandfather wasn't supposed to be there."

"I remember," Ernesto said, "The Japs came in from the other side of the island and climbed over Mt. Jinka. They ambushed us from behind and killed everyone. I was supposed to protect them."

"In his letters, he spoke of a village at the base of the mountain where they would gather to eat."

Ernesto nodded his head and said, "Excellent food there. Wonderful people. All dead. They slaughtered all of them in their sleep. Then they moved on to our camp. It was all my fault. I was guarding them."

Ernesto stood up and reached for his wife's hand. "I am sorry, I think I better go. We can talk later."

Dierdre and Ramiro looked at each other blankly. Neither of them was sure what had just happened. A war had erupted and sputtered out. Ramiro looked at Giuseppe who shrugged his shoulders and said, "I'll have them bring the car around to the front for you."

Ramiro just nodded, and they started gathering their coats.

CHAPTER 4

True to his word, a bill of sale transferring ownership of Dr. Karlyn's computer sat on Dierdre's desk when she arrived in the morning.

Aimee was surprised to see Dierdre reading mail that hadn't passed through her desk first.

She hung her coat on a hook and stepped into Dierdre's office. "What's that?"

"Dr. Karlyn has left the university. He left his computer to me."

"Wow, that's a lucky break."

Bobby entered the lobby and knocked on Dierdre's door jamb.

Aimee stepped between him and Dierdre and asked, "Can I help you?"

"I need to speak with Dr. Jennings, in private. It's important. It's about a gift she'll be getting."

"Come in," Dierdre said, "and close the door. You can speak in front of Aimee."

Bobby closed the door and sat down. "I went to the lab last night, I wanted to make a backup of Dr. Karlyn's work and send it to him in case he ever wanted to continue it. Dr. Pietre showed up. He was there to steal Dr. Karlyn's research, I heard him through the door. I don't know if you know about him, but there is something very wrong about Dr. Pietre. It's his fault Dr. Karlyn had to leave. I think he is up to no good. Anyway, he seemed really pissed that someone was getting the computer, and he threatened to have me expelled because I erased the disks."

As Bobby spoke, his words came faster and faster until finally, Dierdre had to stop him. "Wait a minute, slow down. Pietre was there to steal Karlyn's research?"

Bobby nodded his head.

"Are you sure?"

"Positive. He said so before he knew I was there."

"You erased all the material?"

"Yeah," Bobby nodded again, "That really pissed him off."

"You know, you can't just erase files, the data is still there. He'll probably try to get it again."

"No, I wiped the drives. That's why he was so angry. Some big guy was with him and tried to stop the wipes, but I used a multi-channel process on several processors and each time he got one to cancel another would take its place." The thought brought a wicked little smile to Bobby's face.

"You really know this computer stuff then."

"Yeah, I always have, since I was a kid." Bobby hesitated a moment, then continued, "I got myself into some trouble on computers, when I was a younger."

"I know," Dierdre added.

"But Dr. Karlyn gave me a chance and let me prove myself to him. That's the real reason I'm here. He wanted me to deliver the computer to your lab on Saturday. But I think I should do it right away, like right now."

"Why? You wiped the disks, what else would Pietre want?"

"He doesn't need the computer, he's getting a bigger one, but he wouldn't want you to have it either. Once he finds out who is getting it, he'll be gunning to intercept it. I figured if it was already setup in your lab and you had all the papers to show it's yours, there wouldn't be anything he could do about it."

Dierdre and Aimee nodded.

"I can open the lab whenever you are ready," Aimee volunteered, "so Professor Jennings can teach her classes."

"I won't need to crate it just for a lab transfer, so I can have it there by noon, maybe even ten, assuming you will excuse me from first period class?"

"You are excused." Dierdre thought it was cute for him to ask.

* * *

"Dean Smithers," Pietre said, "how are you feeling this fine morning?" Pietre spoke into the phone using calm soothing tones, hiding any hint of the alarm that was racing though his nervous system.

"Fine, thank you, who is this?"

"This is Professor Pietre, I just heared about Dr. Karlyn's abrupt departure. A terrible scandal, I think. I was hearing the rumors but never dreamed they were true, until now. I think innocent man does not run like this."

"Forgive me Pietre, but I have no comment on this matter. Is there something I can do for you? If not, I have a rather heavy schedule this morning."

"Do for me? No, actually, I am offering my assistance for you. As you may know, I have extraordinarily skilled group of students with a vast range of talents, including some very qualified computer engineers. I am thinking to volunteer my services to help remove Dr. Karlyn's lab computer. I have contact with several colleagues around country searching for such equipment. I am thinking I might find one to buy from us. I'm also thinking maybe we donate equipment for the taxes."

"That's very generous of you," Smithers said, "but Dr. Karlyn has already procured a new home and filed all the necessary forms, so you needn't worry."

"That is wonderful news. Who is lucky person, if I may ask? Is maybe someone at university? I must send a card. Oh, silly me, what I am thinking? I am still offering my students to assist the moving of it."

"I will be sure to pass on your offer, but I believe Dr. Karlyn has already arranged for someone to take care of that for her."

"Very well then," Pietre said, "if you are so certain. Perhaps you could just tell me where I can send the congratulatory card?"

"An announcement will appear in the Gazette, and I promised them an exclusive on it. Now if you will please excuse me, I really have a lot of work to do."

"Good day to you then." Pietre hung up the phone. He didn't learn much, the dean seemed to be purposefully holding back something, but he did let it slip that the recipient was a woman. That should narrow down the field considerably.

Pietre pulled out his school phone directory and looked up the number for the school paper. He wrote down the main number listed, picked up his cell phone and headed out onto the campus.

* * *

Bobby knew the steps by heart, which was a good thing. The manuals which detailed how to shut down and dismantle this model may just as well have been written in some ancient forgotten language. He performed a full shutdown that parked the drives so they could be safely moved, even minor jostling can damage the fine surface of a high performance disk drive. After parking the drives and powering down the system, he disconnected the power, disconnected the battery backups, then shunted the emergency capacitors to totally drain any dangerous electricity from the power supply. With the power drained, it was a simple matter of pulling cables, sometimes marking where they came from, though he knew most of them intimately. Some parts had to be safe packed in anti-static bags, while others could be safely stacked and stored.

Tearing down was the easy part, stacking the parts on dollies and wheeling them over to Dr. Jennings lab was going to need some recruits. He hoped to get enough hand trucks and flat beds to move it all in a single procession. He had already called some friends who worked in the schools audio video center, and recruited their help. While he was tearing down, they were searching out more hand trucks and would meet him around ten o'clock.

* * *

Pietre crossed the campus until he was outside the offices of the Gazette student staff. He picked an isolated spot under a tree just outside the Gazette building, between the Gazette and the science labs which were up the hill. He pulled out his phone and dialed the number he had written down earlier.

"Hello? Norwood Gazette, this is Kim."

"Hello Kim, my name is Bruce Smith," Pietre said using a reasonably convincing Texas accent, "Dean Smithers said he gave you an exclusive on Professor Karlyn's computer. I thought you might want to take some pictures of it before we reassemble it."

"Thanks, but we weren't planning to write an article about it, just the announcement."

"Suit yourself," Pietre drawled, "but it seems a shame to waste such an opportunity for, what do you call them, a photo op?"

"Thank you for the opportunity, but all our photographers are in class right now, there's nobody I can send."

Pietre was getting frustrated, when was he going to get a break here? "That's too bad. It could have been front page stuff."

"Wait a sec, I thought you weren't moving it till Saturday? I could arrange for a photographer to be there."

"Someone needed the space and we are moving it now. Say, how hard could it be to snap a few pictures? You sound like a smart girl, why don't you grab a camera and meet me outside her lab. You can take a few pics and be back at your desk in no time."

"I don't know."

"Sure," he reassured her, "you'll be a hero."

"Well OK," she relented, "but I have to be quick. Are you there right now?"

"I'm here and waiting for you with bells on."

Pietre clicked the phone shut and waited for Kim to exit the Gazette office. Concentrating on his grammar was more exhausting than he would have imagined. It was only moments when a young girl popped out the door with a camera in her hands. He fell in behind her and followed her up the steps to the science buildings at the top of the hill. She turned into the second building on her left and went halfway down the hall where she stopped outside Professor Jennings' lab, looking very lost and bewildered.

Pietre walked down the hall nonchalantly and stopped where the girl was spinning around looking for the computer. "You are looking lost," he said, "Can I help you?"

The girl shrugged and said, "I was sent here to take some pictures of some computer equipment for the gazette, but nobody is here."

"I am Dr. Pietre. I am professor in this building." He reached out his hand and shook hers lightly. "Are you sure this is right place?"

"He said to meet him outside Dr. Jennings' lab where he was delivering the computer."

"Well, this is right place. I hate that you should go away with the empty hand, you can come to my lab. I have largest computer in school. You take all the pictures you want."

"I don't know. That doesn't seem to match the story the pictures are for."

"Who will know?" he asked, "I am having sandwiches sent up from cafeteria. Are you hungry? I think we eat and talk computers and you get very good pictures."

"I probably should be getting back."

"Without the pictures? You don't want to do that. Tell them you take lunch break. Eat with me and is not a lie, see?"

"Well, OK. I guess that would be all right."

* * *

Like clockwork, Bobby's friends started arriving at the lab shortly before ten and continued in a steady stream of geeks and nerds pushing or pulling all manner of hand trucks, wagons and those wheeled tables they use to for projectors. They came from either side of the building and lined up in single file outside the door. They entered the room, one at a time, had their carts stacked with various odd looking pieces from the computer and filed out where they lined up across the hall.

Bobby had no trouble getting them to help. No one questioned his rank as top computer dog. On many occasions, he had helped them get connected for LAN parties where they all brought computers and played games against each other. Not all of them knew about Bobby's past, but those that did respected his abilities, and most of them respected how he turned his life around.

The loading went quickly. Mostly because a lot of the carts brought could only hold a limited amount, and those with real hand carts could only really hold stack-able components, so nobody took a very large load. During the process, a steady stream of exclamations could be heard, "Far Out!" and "That's Bogus man," "You're trippin' dude!" Clearly this group watched too many old TV sitcoms. Any one passing within earshot could easily identify this group as the weirdos you find hanging out in the cafeteria playing magic games with collectible cards. After the last load was placed on the last cart, the lights were switched off and the door to the lab was locked.

The make shift convoy started off. They would have to exit this building, cross the main stairway leading to the very top row of buildings on the hill, and enter the building on the other side.

"Dude!" one voice shouted out for all to hear, "we're Centipede! Check it out!"

A few chuckles followed by another voice upping the ante, "Centipede? No way, we're Millipede!!"

The column slithered across and through the building on the far side, where they exited the other end into a small parking area with a roadway that led up to the last row of buildings on top of the hill. As the crew wound its way around the small parking area and made the sharp U-turn to get on the road leading up, they did indeed look like a snake winding through the complex.

Bobby dialed Aimee on his cell phone. "Hello? It's Bobby. We're on the access road now. We'll be there in just a few minutes."

"OK," she said, "I'll be right there."

* * *

"You get good pictures?" Pietre was trying to work an angle with the young girl.

"Uh huh, I think so."

"I am thinking you need to show how big computer is. Here, you give me camera, and I take pictures with you in them, so people see it is so big."

She handed him the camera, stepped in front of the computer and a little to the side, and flashed an instant smile. "Like this?"

"Da. Very good." He started snapping pictures. "Now you tilt head to one side...good, good...put hand on hip...da, like that, camera loves you, you must be model. Now tilt head back a little, yeah, like that, make the pouty lips, no wet them first, that's it, very nice. Maybe you undo top button or two and really spice up picture."

The girl was completely caught up in the moment, and without hesitation unbuttoned the top two buttons, and spread the top of her blouse to expose her cleavage. She bubbled over with excitement and smiled broadly for the professor, then she walked around to the opposite side of the desk with the computer console on it and leaned forward for the professor. "How's this?"

The professor had struck pay dirt.

* * *

Aimee opened the door to the lab, and the snake plowed right in like it was entering the hole to its den below ground. Bobby waited by a row of tables, and took the items from each cart and placed them on one of the tables. He would assemble it after they left.

Aimee waived at him from the door. "I'm going back to my desk, lock up if you leave. Call me if you need back in."

"OK. Don't worry, everything is going fine."

After the last item was placed on the tables, everyone slapped hands and did a number of hand gyrations as they said good job and good bye to Bobby. "Next week," he told them, "I think I should have a new router for you guys next week."

With the last of them out the door, he closed and locked the lab and started the assembly. In their haste to get it to her lab, he had never asked Dr. Jennings where she wanted it. Her lab was not especially large, but it was large enough. He was glad that there was no current computer in the way. He saw that her only computer was a single workstation on her desk. Workstation computers are generally pretty powerful, compared to PC's, but when he finishes this one, her old workstation will hardly be more than a nice terminal that connects to the computer.

He opened up a briefcase, and laid an assortment of tools out on a tray. He located the base of the main rack, and placed it on the floor in a spot he thought would be best. Next he located the large batteries that powered the backup system, and installed them in the base. He was glad he had done this before with Dr. Karlyn, it was all familiar to him now.

* * *

Pietre looked out the window and watched the girl walk off. He remembered her name was Kim from when she had first answered the phone, but had never bothered to ask her last name. He was always amazed out how easy and stupid these young girls could be. Stupid, but soft, he thought, and she smelled good. He wasn't really concerned whether she went away happy or full of regrets. He watched her bound off the steps below. Her short swingy skirt swished from side to side as she walked. She disappeared out of view as she turned the corner around the lower building at the bottom of the hill.

Then he saw something odd, as she disappeared from view, the walkway was suddenly covered with an army of strange boys pushing an odd assortment of carts and various other wheeled contraptions. They looked like ants as they filed through the walk way and all followed the same trail. His first thought was that it was one of those strange moments, when you wished you had a camera handy to take a picture to submit somewhere for no reason other than laughs. Something clicked in his head. He darted to his desk, put his shoes back on, grabbed a coat and headed out the building and down the hill to Karlyn's lab. He covered the ground swiftly, aided by the fact that it was mostly downhill. He jumped down the last few steps and sprinted into the building to Karlyn's lab. It was vacant. He was too late. The computer was gone. He smacked his palm against his forehead, he should have checked Jennings' lab first.

Now, he was the one with regrets. If he had not taken the time to nail the little girl from the newspaper, then he might have noticed something was up and found some way to stop it.

He climbed back up the stairs, already winded and quietly found his way to Dierdre's lab. The door was closed, and it was quiet inside, he tried the door, it was locked. The glass to the lab was frosted, so he couldn't see inside. He did not have a duplicate key to her lab, and unable to see what was inside, he would have to think up a new strategy.

He turned to return to his office when he heard a noise coming from the lab. Not a machine noise like a printer or tape machine might make, but a metallic ting sound, like two metal objects hitting each other, or a tool landing on the floor.

* * *

Aimee waited for Dierdre to return from her lecture and told her, "He's up there now working on it. You should have seen how many friends he had to help him. There must have been twenty or thirty of them."

Dierdre frowned. "So much for this being a big secret."

"It's not a secret, it will be in next week's paper, remember? The secret part was getting it into your office before anyone could try and object to your getting it. That's done. He had enough friends to move the whole thing all at once."

Dierdre settled into her chair behind the desk and asked, "What do you think about him? Have you talked to him? Gotten to know him any?"

"Not really, he's kind of young for me."

Dierdre rolled her eyes and said, "That's not what I meant."

"I can tell you that those boys that helped him genuinely respected and admired him. They treated him like he was the Dalai Lama."

"Maybe I'll go check on his progress, and get a feel for him myself."

Aimee smirked and said, "He's definitely too young for you."

"That's not what I meant! Stop it! Hey! Did you just call me old?"

Aimee scooted out the door and suggested, "Why don't you take some cokes with you. I think nerds like that while they work."

Dierdre shot up from her desk and chased Aimee out of her office, "You're avoiding the question!"

"It's almost lunch time, you should probably arrange for a pizza delivery too."

"Stop changing the subject!"

Aimee turned and took a stance on the opposite side of her own desk and said, "What are you standing around for? Go check on your new computer!"

"I will, but first I have to file these papers, check my emails, check the want ads for available attitude free secretaries..."

"Oh yeah? You'd be lost without me!"

* * *

Pietre arrived at his office to find his burly friend from the night before sitting in his chair.

"Where have you been?" The big man was always direct.

"Busy."

"Don't get cute with me. My employers have extended you just about every courtesy you are going to get. Your options have always been to either pay them, or give them what they want. But seeing that you can't seem to decide which to provide them, they have simplified your options to just give them what they want."

"I cannot." Pietre sat down in his guest chair and said, "You were there, computer was wiped."

"Do you really believe that kid wiped them without making a backup?"

Pietre had not really considered that. He was too focused on his more immediate problems. "Even so," he said, "I would be needing more time finding them."

"Then what are you doing here?"

Pietre took a moment to compose himself and wipe the sweat from his brow. "He's there now, in her lab. I think he puts it back together for her. The door was locked, with lights all off."

The large man smiled, placing his two hands together forming a diamond with his thumbs and forefingers. He stared at his hands for a brief moment, as if they were a meditation instrument, then he nodded his head and leaped up from the professor's chair. "Let's go pay him a friendly visit."

Pietre nodded, and followed dutifully behind.

* * *

Dierdre finished putting away her lecture notes, and stood by Aimee's desk watching her work. Aimee was busy entering grades for the quarterly updates.

"So, how's Ramiro?"

Aimee was in no mood to chat about last evenings proceedings. There was no doubt how Ramiro's father felt. She had thought she would have a chance to win him over, to show him she was really an all American girl, but that opportunity never came. She didn't want to talk about it now and merely answered, "Fine."

"His mother seemed nice."

"Uh-huh."

"Giuseppe was quite a character."

"Yup."

Dierdre could see this was going nowhere. "I'll just go check on Bobby."

* * *

Pietre tried the door to her lab again. It was still locked.

"Let me try." The big man stepped in and took a massive vice like grip of the door handle. He tested the lock, and it was really locked. He pulled a thin strip of metal from his pocket. It was very thin and pliable. He held it up for Pietre to see. "It's a slim Jim." He flexed the slim Jim like a pretzel and it straightened back to its original ruler like shape. "Beryllium, holds its shape for ever, yet is light and flexible." He slid the device between the door and the jam and slipped it down into the latch. The door popped right open.

Bobby heard that. His head popped straight up, but he could not see the door which was hidden behind the rack he was working on. "Hello?" he asked as he stood up to see who came in.

"Hello Bobby." The large man stuck out his beefy mitt to shake hands.

"You again? What are you doing here?"

"Bobby, Bobby, Bobby." He shook his head as if scolding a child. "We are just trying to be friendly. Nice computer you got there. See? That was me being friendly."

Bobby took a step backwards and said, "You shouldn't be here, I think you should leave."

"Now that was not very friendly," the large man said, "I have been following your career. You are a bright kid, with a tremendous future ahead of you. Too bad the school doesn't see it that way."

"The school's OK. We have an arrangement."

"I see," the large man swung his arms around in exaggerated motions as he said, "You work on computers for them, but they pay you peanuts, and they don't teach you the things you really should know."

"I'm doing just fine."

The large man walked to the windows and looked out over the campus. "I have a proposition for you. My employers would like to offer you a nice job. My employers are very generous, and are shopping for new projects to back. For example, Dr. Karlyn's project was one that my employer had invested in. But Karlyn left, and we just want to get the data that we have already paid so dearly for."

"That's not true," Bobby said, "The only money we got for this project was from the government grants."

"Maybe Karlyn did not share all the proceeds with the student help. Maybe he even pocketed it for himself. That project belonged to us. I can see that you are a smart kid. I bet you backed it up before you cleared the drives."

"Backed it up?" Bobby asked, feigning his best look of astonishment, "Never occurred to me."

"Too bad, if you had, I'm sure you could be well compensated for it, say ten thousand dollars?"

"Dang it," Bobby whistled, "I wish I had made a backup now. Oh well, anything else I can do for you?"

"Don't screw with me kid. My employers are quite serious about getting their money's worth. "

"Can't help you."

The big man was about to get a little more direct, physically, with Bobby, when Dierdre came in. "Hello Dr. Pietre," she said, "is there something I can do for you?"

"Professor Jennings," Pietre said, "Hello, how are you? We were just congratulating your assistant here on the fine job he is doing."

"Oh, he's not my assistant, but he is doing a job for me, and I would appreciate it if you didn't distract him while he is working."

"Of course, my apologies."

Pietre and the big man left, but before leaving the doorway, the big man yelled back, "We'll talk later Bobby. "

Bobby noticed the quick response that he was not her assistant, and suddenly felt uncomfortable about asking her for a job, "Professor Jennings, about that assistant remark…"

Dierdre turned her attention back to Bobby. "I'm sorry, what?"

"Well, I don't know if you want any assistants, and it kind of sounded like you don't, but I was hoping we could talk about it."

"I think I need to get to know you better."

"I know. It's my past. Maybe this would help." He went to his backpack and pulled out the letter Karlyn had given him, and handed it to her.

"Hmmm," she said, "Well, he certainly thinks very highly of you. How would you feel about a trial period?"

"That would be fine. Something else, keep your eye on Pietre, and be careful what you say around him. I already told you how he tried sneaking into Karlyn's lab to steal his work off this machine. That big guy was with him, and they just now were offering me money for a copy of Karlyn's work. I think we should put some extra security on this system, and you should change your locks. They will probably try to steal your work too."

"Dr. Pietre is part of the university faculty. I don't think you should be making such unsubstantiated accusations about him."

"Can you honestly say that he fills you with a feeling of trust?"

Dierdre couldn't say he did.   "Are you sure you didn't misunderstand them?"

"Positive. They are up to no good, and I got the feeling that the big guy was forcing Pietre to go along with it."

"I will get a copy of your classes, so I can schedule your time here. What classes do you have today?"

Bobby shrugged his shoulders and said, "Nothing important till after lunch."

"I don't want you missing any class work to do this. Before you set up any elaborate security measures, I think I'd like to have you write up a proposal outlining what you would like to do. I don't want Pietre to have any reason to bring suspicion on you directly, so all changes to the computer must be channeled through me. How soon do you think you can you prepare a proposal?"

"I should be done setting up by lunch. I could work on the proposal during lunch and my next class."

"Don't miss your class, if you are going to be my assistant, you will have to keep your grades up in all your classes."

"Don't worry," he said, "it's Karlyn's class, and until they find a replacement, they are going to set us up on self-study courses in the video labs."

"Karlyn just left, and it's not even public knowledge, how do you know all this?" Dierdre's voice was dripping with suspicion.

"Friends. I have friends in the audio/video department. They are the ones that delivered the computer."

Dierdre was relieved to hear that he was not hacking the school computer for his information. "Well I better let you get back to your work here."

"Dr. Jennings?"

"Yes?"

"Thanks. Thanks for giving me a chance."

"I think you are the one giving yourself a chance," she said, "and I am the one who is grateful. At least, I think I am grateful. I will be grateful won't I?"

"Aye aye, Mon Capitan!"

* * *

Dierdre left her lab with a new spring in her step. She already had a new model in her head, and now she had a computer capable of modeling part of her ideas. Somewhere inside her, veiled in a shroud of distrust, she was exhilarated to have Bobby's help. If he worked out, she might actually be able to achieve some of the goals she set for herself.

As she left the building and reached the long stairway, she saw Dr. Pietre and the burly man having an animated discussion at the bottom of the hill, or rather, the large associate was talking and Pietre was nodding his head in ascent.

"Good day Professor Jennings," Dr. Whitfield said, "you are looking quite chipper this morning, good news I hope?"

"Good day to you Dr. Whitfield, and yes, good news. It will be in the papers next week, so I guess there's no harm in sharing with you. Dr. Karlyn gave me his computer."

"Dr. Karlyn no longer requires his computer?" Dr. Whitfield's southern drawl was more pronounced in the mornings, especially when the topic turned to matters of Gossip.

"Well, I'm afraid I'll let you read about Dr. Karlyn's doings in the paper, suffice to say, that I have a new computer to model my theories now."

"My, my, that is certainly auspicious news Professor Jennings. I congratulate you with all my heart." He tipped his hat as he delivered that last overly dramatic line.

"Say, Dr. Whitfield," Dierdre asked, "do you know the gentleman talking to Dr. Pietre at the bottom of the hill?"

Dr. Whitfield walked to the edge of the stairs and leaned over the rail, as if an extra four inches would make the difference. He squinted his eyes and held his hand up for shade, "Hmm. He looks familiar, I think. Yes, he used to be a student here. A chemist I think, possibly a med school student too. Would you like me to ask Dr. Pietre for you?"

"Oh, no, please don't bother. I just thought he looked familiar."

"Professor Jennings, please allow me to more properly congratulate you on your fine acquisition, by accompanying me to lunch in our very own faculty lounge. I must confess, though this occasion certainly merits better, I haven't the time for anything more elegant at the moment."

"Dr. Whitfield, how sweet of you. I would love to."

"Please, I beg of you, call me Stillman."

"Very well," Dierdre relented, "Stillman. You may call me Dierdre. Deer like Bambi and dra like…dra." As she looked at him in the light, he was not as old as he acted or dressed. Somewhere in there was a regular guy trying like hell not to be noticed.

They descended the stairs and headed to the lounge where they would order up some food from the cafeteria. She made sure they delivered a couple slices of pizza to her lab for Bobby.

* * *

When Dierdre returned from lunch, Aimee was waiting for her. "So how's the kid working out?"

"Good, so far. I've offered him a trial assignment on my project. Can you see to the paper work for that?"

"Right away."

An uneasy silence filled the office as Aimee neither left nor spoke.

"Was there something else?" Dierdre's voice had a slight chill to it.

"About before, I'm sorry. I just can't figure out what happened. I thought I was prepared for every kind of confrontation going into that dinner, but I was never prepared for his dad running out of the room."

"Especially," Dierdre said, "when he seemed to soften, for a split second before bailing out."

"You saw that? I thought I imagined it."

"I'm sure everything will become clear in time. So how are you guys proceeding with your plans? Set a date yet?"

"Not yet," Aimee said, "we both wanted to give it some time and see how the dust settles, just in case there is any kind of acceptance from his dad."

"Don't set yourself up for a disappointment, just kinda hope for a long shot."

"I'll go get Bobby officially enrolled in your project."

* * *

At half past three, Bobby entered the main office and presented Aimee with an envelope for Professor Jennings. "Wait here," she said, "if you can, Professor Jennings may want to see you for a minute." She took the envelope straight in and gave it to Dierdre. "He's at my desk, if you want to see him."

Dierdre opened the envelope and immediately recognized that it was the proposal she requested. "Bring him in."

Bobby entered Dierdre's personal office. Aimee retrieved an envelope from her desk, and followed Bobby in, closing the door behind her.

Dierdre scanned the proposal and said, "Welcome aboard. We will pay you the same wages as Dr. Karlyn. In the event that our research develops a marketable product or concept, and you remain on board for the duration, I will offer you five percent of the net, assuming I have a buyer. Of course, you understand, that the research we are doing is unlikely to deliver a product any time soon, but if it does, you are part of the team. You are on probation. In twelve weeks, if you have not been excused from the project, you will become a full time non-probationary member."

Bobby was relieved.

"The team consists of you, me and Aimee. I will make ALL decisions, and the responsibility of everything on this project falls to me. Aimee will assist either of us as much as possible, but she does still have duties to the other professors, so you will likely share some of the burden for her. That means I might ask you to make copies or take my laundry to the cleaners." She tried making a joke, but the occasion was too serious to warrant humor. "OK, forget the laundry. Your duties are chiefly to operate the computer and assist me in some advanced coding concepts. I have some programs I am modeling, and I have done most of the hard work for the science part, but I need to get more results from the programs."

Bobby nodded his ascent.

"One last thing," she said, "We will be working closely together. When it is just us, I want you to call me Dierdre, but when we are in mixed company, especially with other faculty, call me Professor Jennings. This is more for your own protection than anything else. Let's meet here at five, and start going over the program. We need to transfer it from my workstation to..." she stopped mid-sentence. "Suddenly I feel it should have a name, like HAL had."

Bobby laughed. "But HAL had artificial intelligence. I don't think we are creating a personality here."

CHAPTER 5

Bobby had no more classes, but it was too early for dinner, so after leaving Professor Jennings office, he decided to hang around on campus and visit some of his friends in the A/V labs. They were preparing for a computer tournament they were hosting with a rival school. The tournament would be held on their campus, so Bobby suggested making sure that they had sufficient hardware to handle the larger crowd. He also wanted to impress the visitors with some really superior network hardware, hoping it would give them a psychological advantage, so the visitors will arrive and think they are in over their head. That was his plan, at least.

* * *

Dierdre finished her last lecture and had enough time left to go over some of her students' performances. She planned to pay particular attention to how well her new assistant has done in her class. He was always quiet and had never stood out, but that doesn't mean he wasn't following her lectures.

She regretted not having more time to get to know him better, but she had to make a snap decision. The letter from Dr. Karlyn was very reassuring, but she still worried about all the ways she could be wrong.

She would have to indulge her thoughts some other time, someone was knocking on her door. "It's open," she sang out. The door opened a crack and Dr. Whitfield poked his head in. "Dr. Whit-," she stopped herself and started over, "Stillman, I don't believe you've ever called on me in my office before, won't you please come in?"

He stepped into her office and closed the door behind him. "I fear that something is afoot with Professor Pietre. This can't be good."

Dierdre arched her eyebrows and asked, "What makes you say that?"

Dr. Whitfield spoke in a subdued voice, "His associate. I couldn't shake the thought that I had seen that young man before, so I looked back through some yearbooks, and there he was. I had him as a student in my own classes. As I had guessed before, he was a chem student, and he was in the Pharmacy school. He was expelled for combining his interests in chemistry with pharmacy. He made and sold what they call 'designer drugs'."

"Why would an expelled student be spending so much time on campus? Do you think he is selling drugs here?"

Dr. Whitfield shook his head and said, "I am more interested in learning what his association is with Dr. Pietre."

"Yes," Dierdre admitted, "And he sounds very much like the same young man who tried, in the company of Dr. Pietre, to get his hands on Dr. Karlyn's research."

"Of course!" Dr. Whitfield was more animated than Dierdre could ever have imagined. "Rupert was following up on some experiments in Cold Fusion, to either prove or debunk them. In the process, he had discovered some methods to balance thermal reactions with, a new kind of anti-thermal reaction. One could use these anti-thermal reactions to balance dangerous chemical reactions from exploding. I'm sure a drug manufacturer would find that highly advantageous."

"That explains the big guy, but what's Pietre's involvement?"

"Probably money. Those Russians will do anything for money you know."

This statement caught Dierdre by surprise. He did not seem the sort of man to hold a racial bias.

He shifted in his chair and said, "I know, that sounded terrible. Maybe he is innocent, maybe they have his family locked up in Russia and are threatening to kill them all. I still think it's just about money."

"Well, whatever the motive, something is very odd about that man. I think we should keep our eyes..." she stopped when she heard someone knocking at the door.

Dr. Whitfield stood up and opened the door. "Oh, hello Bobby."

"Dr. Whitfield, nice seeing you," he said, "Professor Jennings, I stopped at the lab, but it was locked, so I came here thinking I may have misunderstood you earlier."

Dierdre looked at her watch. "Oh my, look at the time! Forgive me Dr. Whitfield, but I was supposed to be in my lab at five. Do you know Bobby? He will be assisting me with my research now."

"Ah, yes, we are acquainted. Don't blame Professor Jennings, Bobby, it is entirely my fault she is late. Well Professor, I wish you a good evening. We'll talk again later."

"Thanks for stopping by," she said, "my door is always open to you."

Bobby waited for Dr. Whitfield to leave the room, then turned to Dierdre and said, "Professor Jennings, not many people know it, but Dr. Whitfield is way cooler than he lets on. He may dress like a square, but he's OK."

"Perhaps we should get up to the lab, and I'll show you what I have done so far."

* * *

In the summer time, the evenings hold their temperature long into the night. The buildings and the very ground itself act as radiators releasing all the warmth they suck in during the day. But approaching winter time, as it was now, the days may still warm up to a very nice comfortable shorts and short sleeve temperature, but as soon as the sun sets, the temperature starts to drop. Lows in the wee hours can drop to the low thirties. Earlier in the afternoon, a mild breeze was a comforting lick of coolness wiping away some of the afternoon heat. Now, in early evening, it was a brisk chill sucking away a bit of comfort. Later in the night, it will be a bitter sting whipping through their clothing.

"It's going to be cool tonight," Dierdre said, "Perhaps, since we will probably be spending more time in the lab, I should order some heaters from engineering." Dierdre was glad she threw her sweater around her shoulders, and she pulled it a little tighter around her neck.

"You won't need any heaters," Bobby assured her, "one of the side effects of having this much computer power, is it tends to generate a bit of heat. In fact, I am a little concerned it might generate more heat than your lab was designed to accommodate."

"Was it a problem in Dr. Karlyn's lab?"

"Dr. Karlyn's lab was larger, and handled it better. No offense, but your lab is more like a walk-in closet, and I am afraid that it might act like an oven and hold a lot of heat in, until we get the AC adjusted just right."

They reached the lab, and Dierdre opened the door. "It doesn't feel too warm yet, did you leave it on?"

"It's on, but it's sitting idle, it won't get really warm till you start to make it work, and from what I remember in your lectures, you will probably keep it pegged most of the time."

"Pegged?"

"Running at full capacity."

Bobby followed Dierdre into the lab. She closed the door behind them, but left it unlocked. Her lab had three rooms. The main lab was a twenty by thirty room with tables, sinks, power, and gas. It was a general purpose room that could be assigned to a chemist, biologist, physicist or any other natural science researcher with ease. Directly across from the door were tall windows facing out, the lab had an eighteen foot ceiling, and on the far left hand end of the lab were two adjoining rooms, one was just a closet with storage shelves, and the other was an auxiliary office. Dierdre's workstation was setup in the office. Bobby had set the new computer in the corner outside the office, by the windows, and opposite the corner with the door to the hallway. It was the only clear floor space free of lab tables, and since the lab tables were outfitted with gas and water plumbing, they were impossible to move without a general contractor.

Dierdre led him into the office and powered up the workstation. "Have a seat there, and I'll show you what I have, and how I want to make it work on the new machine. But first, some background."

"Einstein's theory of general relativity drew a thread connecting mass and energy with his famous $e=mc^2$ equation. His theories led us to control of the atom, and to the discoveries of sub-atomic particles and their properties. His Grand unifying theory that extends general relativity to include gravity, suggests that if we had enough energy, we could either crack or harness the bond that connects gravity to both mass and energy. Quantum mechanics, and other studies of the behavior of electrons and photons show one common behavior, and that is an apparent randomness in location. I believe this randomness probably is the result of our inability to properly measure these properties. I also think that the prevailing wisdom that states we would need massive amounts of energy to harness these quantum events are fighting against the nature of these objects rather than flowing with them."

"Imagine a Master martial artist," she continued, "When fighting an invincible foe, he does not try to overpower his enemy with strength and force, but he tries to use his adversary's power to his own advantage. This is what I want to do. By identifying the pattern of these motions that we perceive as random, we only try to harness them during the brief period in which they surge in the direction we want."

She paused a moment to see that he understood. "The problem is that they happen faster than our computers can possibly calculate, and we would need millions of programs running simultaneously to predict the correct sequence. We can't even hope to try these predictions for real, so we have to build models to simulate the flux events, and models to predict their behavior. Hopefully these simulations will teach us how we can harness enough power to attempt a real life prototype in the future."

Bobby was fascinated. She probably had calculus equations that were a mile long to define the whole problem, yet she was able to break it down into real life terms that he could understand. "So," he asked, "if we can't measure these changes, and they look random to us, how can we predict them?"

"Imagine a coin. Predict heads or tails and flip the coin. You have fifty percent chance of getting it right. That means, that if you flip one thousand prediction coins, and then flipped one outcome coin, five-hundred of the prediction coins should have correctly predicted the outcome. If you did it again, flipping only the five-hundred coins that were correct, two-hundred-fifty of them would have the right prediction, and those coins would have two predictions in a row. One more flip and one-hundred-twenty-five coins will have correctly predicted three in a row, it goes on and on, there is a chance that out of one thousand coins, one of them could correctly predict ten flips in a row. But you would need an astronomical one million coins to get nineteen flips in a row. In my theory, it wouldn't matter how many predictions were wrong, you only need one to correctly predict a long enough string of quantum motions to make a full connection to the grand unifying theory. And since we are letting the motions provide the energy, we only have to piggy back and follow to create our own connection for little or no energy output."

"But," Bobby said, "I imagine that it would take billions or trillions of predictions to make a string long enough to make a real connection."

"That is true. So we want to create a model that proves it can be done. Then we will worry about creating a computer that can do it. By that point, we may have molecular computers capable of fitting millions or billions of processors in a single rack."

"Hmm. Even the model may be a tall order for today's hardware. Even if we had millions of processors, we don't have an operating system able to control that many processors yet."

Dierdre smiled. He was already aware of the problem. "That's why I want to redesign the process so each of the threads runs independently. Instead of us creating a million threads, they create themselves, and then each thread operates on its own, without needing direction from a central source."

"You would need some creative way for each thread to choose a path that was different from all the others. And you will still have a lot of duplication."

"Yes," she said, "you are correct, but it gets worse. The number of threads and the amount of duplication is very dependent on the number of possible options available. A coin has only two outcomes, but unfortunately, the choices are more complicated than flipping a coin, and so it takes a great deal more attempts to get even a small string of correct predictions. If you had a coin with three sides, your string of predictions from a million coins would drop from nineteen to twelve. A four sided coin would drop to nine or ten, but a five sided coin would also drop to nine or ten, so you see, the odds drop slower and slower, but a million coins, is not enough. A sixteen sided coin, or dice cube would net about five straight predictions. If our quantum events have an infinite number of possible events, we are screwed, but if each event is limited to only four thousand possible outcomes, ten million threads would barely predict two straight outcomes. So, clearly, we are targeting this process for the future when we can harness enough computer power to make this happen in real time. Today, however, we need only make a model, so we can have our computer repeat the process millions of times instead of doing them all at the same time."

"But professor, you said that you did not believe it was truly random."

"True. I think there is a pattern we can't see."

"But your process is attacking it as if it were completely random. If it's not random, and if we devise a thread that figures out the pattern we wouldn't need as many threads."

"You are talking about a thread that can learn. That's fiction."

"Not really. You already said you wanted each thread to work independently. Suppose every thread spawned two copies of itself, but each copy had a slight variation in its program. Then after each thread completes its program, you take the best one, and kill off the other. If you have enough of them running, eventually you should see some real improvement."

Dierdre focused on that thought. She would just have to leave the programs running, until they got better and better at predicting the next path.

"OK. How would you go about programming that?" This was the moment where Dierdre fully realized she had a partner in her research.

"I'll need to modify the way the numbers are calculated so we can introduce variations. Then we just let them run and see what we get. Show me what you have so far. I want to see what kind of output you are generating, especially the range of data."

Dierdre pulled up some programs on her workstation and showed Bobby the sections that generated the predictions.

He looked at her algorithms and said, "I won't pretend to understand how you expect to take these numbers and apply them to the real world, even in the future, but I think I can come up with a way to generate them for you."

"OK," she said, "But I need to understand it, so whatever you come up with, I want you to be able to demonstrate how it works."

"No problem."

"One other thing, I've never had a machine with so many processors, I want you to show me how to make the threads harness them all."

Bobby smiled. While much of this project was in her area of expertise, there was also a lot in his area that she didn't understand. "Absolutely," he said, "I'll show you mine and you show me yours..." he immediately realized that it didn't come out like he meant it. "I mean..."

"It's OK," she said, "I think I know what you meant. At least, I hope I know what you meant."

"Let me work on this for a few days. By this weekend, I should be able to demonstrate how we can spawn different threads based on some made up gene sequence that will generate numeric sequences and match them up to the master program."

Dierdre reached into a drawer in her desk and pulled out a key. "Here," she said, "You might as well let yourself in and out."

"I'll leave progress notes in your email box."

* * *

"She is lying bitch. He is too her assistant," Dr. Pietre spat his words into the phone while he read the latest new hires on the faculty website, "she should know this can't be secret. Is public knowledge."

"Calm down professor," the burly man said with a steady and reassuring voice, "She does know that. She probably didn't hire him till after we spoke with her. I honestly don't know why you are getting so worked up over this."

"I think maybe I hire him for my project. Then we convince him to share Karlyn's research with us."

"Think that through a bit," the large man said, "If you hired him on your project, don't you think he might recognize how much of your research was stolen from Dr. Karlyn? Besides, he blames you for Karlyn's departure, how are you going to hire him now?"

"He is hacker. He has already criminal record. How hard could it be, appealing to his dark side?"

"He was a boy, and boys will be boys. Besides, he was never actually convicted. I have another plan in mind. I want you to leave him alone and let me worry about him."

Dr. Pietre did not want to let it go, but he took a deep calming breath and asked, "What is it on your mind?"

"I was thinking of helping him in his research, or rather helping her. We already told him that my employer has invested capital in Dr. Karlyn's project. Why not offer her some investment money? If I can find out a little more about her research, and her plans for her new computer, then maybe I can find some nice gift that she can add to her computer."

"What would you have me to do?"

"I think you've done enough," the large man said, "for now at least."

"But my research, I am still in running for final round of grants, I need to show the progress."

"Then maybe you should actually do some research on your project. I have to go now. Good day Professor."

Pietre had no answer. It's not like he didn't do any research, in fact, his senior assistant, Panopulous, was oblivious to the origins of some of Pietre's ideas, and he was actually researching them. Pietre reflected on his situation and decided that perhaps he could find some way to help Panopulous move forward.

* * *

Dierdre kept replaying Bobby's question in her head. How would she ever convert a string of numbers into real world science? The common theory was to introduce some kind of particle, either from a linear accelerator, or from a powerful laser. When one of these particles coincided with the quantum event, it was like a tumbler on a combination lock, but nobody really knew how many tumblers had to be turned in order to start the event. And nobody knew when they would reset and start over.

While Dierdre was trying to predict when and how to match the quantum events, others were using a more brute force method, by supplying a steady stream of particles, then you could match a quantum event almost by accident. The problem was that it required an enormous number of particles which required an even more enormous amount of power to produce. That is what made her theory different. Rather than spending an enormous amount of energy putting particles everywhere, her theory just put the particles where she needed them.

There is no existing method that can trigger the release of particles fast enough to satisfy this need. But nano-electronics was in its infancy. Perhaps she should enlist the aid of someone more familiar with the field of nano structures.

She glanced at her directory, and dialed the phone. "Hello? Stillman? It's Dierdre."

"Good morning Dierdre, how are you?"

"I'm fine, thank you. I was hoping I could pick your brain. Do you know anything about the field of nano-electronics?"

A warm smile crossed his face. "Yes, I know a thing or two."

"Could we discuss that over lunch today?"

"Certainly, I'd be delighted. I can swing by your office at noon to get you?"

"Thanks," she said, "You're a peach."

They hung up the phones and Dr. Whitfield added, "No dear, you're the peach."

* * *

The next few hours flew by for Dierdre. She busied herself preparing classes, giving lectures, and grading papers. She promised herself that she would not pester Bobby by spending all her spare time looking over his shoulder. She did, however, continue to check her email, frequently.

"Aimee?"

"Yes D?"

"Is the email down? I don't think I'm getting all my emails. Can you send me something so I can see if it's working?"

"Sure, but you're going to give yourself gray hair if you keep checking so often." Aimee opened up her email and sent Dierdre a simple note that said "RELAX".

Moments later, an icon popped up on Dierdre's monitor that she had received an email. "I wish I could relax," she said, "Maybe he has the wrong email address."

"No, he's got the correct address. You want me to…" Aimee was interrupted by the ringing of her cell phone and said, "Just a sec D, I better get this."

"Hello?" Aimee asked into the small flip phone. The expression on Aimee's face suddenly changed, at first it changed to a grave frightened look, then it morphed into bewilderment, and her voice became small and squeaky, "yes…OK…bye."

"Aimee?" The glaze had not left her eyes yet. Dierdre called her again, "Aimee?"

Aimee's eyes turned to Dierdre and slowly focused. Her mouth opened slowly, but nothing came out.

Dierdre rose from her desk and stepped to the doorway to ask, "Aimee! Who was it? What's wrong?"

"Nothing. Nothing. It was Ramiro's father. He invited us to lunch, both of us. He wants you and me to meet him for lunch. That's all he said."

Dierdre stepped back and leaned against her desk. "When?"

"Today."

"When today?"

Before Aimee could answer, her cell phone rang again, and again. Dierdre took the phone from Aimee and said, "Hello?"

"Hello? Who's this? Dierdre?"

"Hi Ramiro, yeah it's Dierdre. Aimee's busy."

"I wanted to warn you, my father called me a few minutes ago and asked for Aimee's personal number. He's going to be calling her sometime soon."

"Too late," Dierdre said, "He already called. Aimee is still recovering from the shock I think."

"Is she OK? What did he say to her?"

"He invited the two of us to lunch."

Life had returned to Aimee's eyes, and she took the phone. "Hi honey, your dad is seeing us for lunch. Are you coming?"

"I can't. I have to meet with some delegates from the State Supreme Court today."

"Oh, OK. We'll be all right. He just caught me by surprise."

"Me too," Ramiro said, "If I knew what he had up his sleeve, I'd tell you. I asked mom, but she wouldn't say anything. Call me if you need me, anytime. Don't worry about interrupting me."

* * *

Bobby was in the lab working on Dierdre's program when someone knocked on the door. He finished up the line of code he was working on, and hit the save button. At the door, he met a short thin man in a suit. He measured up the man, from his perfectly sculpted hair to his manicured nails, and decided he looked like a lawyer.

"Can I help you?" Bobby asked.

"I'm with the federal grant board. I've been sent here to verify research project number 638995. Are you Professor Jennings?" He was reading through some file notes and said, "Oh, I'm sorry, of course you aren't her. You must be one of her students." He flipped through more pages and continued, "Funny, it doesn't list any assistants."

"I'm new here. Professor Jennings is not here now, and I'm kind of busy, you should check the offices in the building at the bottom of the hill. If she's not there, her secretary Aimee can help you."

"I understand," he said, but took a step forward anyway. "These surprise inspections often go like this. I'm really here to observe the project. It's merely a formality, but we have to inspect all research projects to make sure they aren't just paper proposals."

"There's not much to see right now. I am in the process of porting the professor's work over to a new computer, but I have nothing working yet. We just started, you see. I'm sorry, but you'll need Professor Jennings to show you her previous work, like I said, I'm new here and don't know it that well."

"Very well," the wiry man said, "Is that her computer over there?" He pointed a long slender finger. He kept his elbow bent and his wrist supple. Something about his mannerisms just bugged Bobby.

"Yes that's the computer, but there's nothing to see. I really must ask you to leave. I'm sure you'll understand, but you need Professor Jennings to show you her work. I'm not authorized to admit visitors, and you wouldn't want me to lose my job, would you?"

"No. Of course not." He retracted and said, "I'll just go down and see her then." And off he went, out the door and down the stairs, but he did not go to Dierdre's office.

* * *

"Aimee?"

"D?"

"I have a problem. I already have lunch plans with Dr. Whitfield."

"Oh, I see." Aimee was crushed. Ramiro couldn't make it, now Dierdre was busy too. She didn't know if she had the nerve to see him alone. "That's OK, I understand."

"No," Dierdre said, "no, you don't understand. Be a dear, and get him on the phone for me. I'll fix it."

Aimee had all the professors on speed dial. "It's ringing."

Dierdre picked up her receiver. It was still ringing.

"Hello? "

"Stillman? This is Dierdre again. Something important has come up. Can we switch our lunch to dinner?"

"Dinner? I'd be delighted. Shall I pick you up then?"

"Yes. I'll have Aimee email my address to you. Thank you for being so understanding."

"Not at all," he said, "I'm quite looking forward to it."

Dinner and he was picking her up. Somehow, a simple question and answer session to pick his brain suddenly looked suspiciously like a date. Well, Bobby seemed to think he was pretty cool, but a notorious hacker was not the best reference in the world.

"Aimee, can you send…"

"It's already on its way. So, you and Dr. Whitfield? Only, it's Stillman now?"

"Aimee, it's business. I had some questions about nano-electronics."

"Uh huh." Aimee did not tell Dierdre that she added a personal note to Dierdre's address, *"She doesn't like red roses, pink and white are much better."*

* * *

The large man met his thin cohort in the parking lot. "What did you see?"

"Nothing," the slender man said, "He wouldn't let me in and suggested I see the professor. He said it wasn't working yet anyway."

"And?"

"The locks are the same as all the other labs and present no special challenge to us."

"OK," the large man said, "You're free to go. I'll meet you here at 1 a.m. Get some sleep, I want you sharp."

"Yes sir."

* * *

Aimee pranced around Dierdre's office singing, "If it looks like a date, and smells like a date…"

"It's not a date. We are just two colleagues going out for dinner to discuss science."

"First is denial, then comes acceptance."

"Oh, knock it off Aimee. I swear, sometimes you are just like a teenager the way you… what? What are you pointing at?"

"Don't look now," Aimee said, "but, you've got mail!"

Dierdre spun around and saw the little envelope icon on her screen. She lunged for her mouse and opened up her in-box.

> *Professor Jennings,*
>
> *I think you should know. I just got a visit from some guy representing the federal grant committee. He said he was here for a surprise inspection. I told him he would have to see you, that I had nothing to show him. He should be there any second now.*
>
> *I am close to running a full system test. I should have it started this afternoon. I'll leave it running overnight so we can examine the results in the morning.*
>
> *Thanks,*
> *Bobby*

Aimee was reading over her shoulder and said, "This guy better hurry, because we are leaving for lunch real soon."

"Why Aimee, you sound like you are looking forward to lunch all of a sudden. Does teasing me about my non-date dinner plans make your own sad little life feel that much brighter?"

Aimee sat against the edge of Dierdre's desk and started counting on her fingers while she said, "Face the facts sweetie. First, the two of you make a cute couple."

"No way!" Dierdre blanched, "Maybe an odd couple."

"Second," Aimee continued, "your best friend is getting married, which puts you in an awkward position. And third, if he brings flowers, then it's definitely a date."

"Flowers? No way. I know he has been like a puppy dog who wanted to follow me home, but he just isn't the type to bring flowers. And as far as me being in an awkward position because my best friend is getting married? You're nuts, I did fine before you came along, and I'll do fine after you run off with Ramiro. Face it. You're already off the market."

Aimee left Dierdre's office and exaggerated the swing of her butt while she said, "Well who are you gonna get to attract all the cute guys when I'm gone?"

"What?!?" Dierdre wadded up the nearest piece of paper and threw it in Aimee's direction. It was a decent throw, but Aimee had already ducked through the doorway.

Dierdre returned to her desk and replied to Bobby's email, *I'll meet you in the morning at seven to go over the results.*

"You ready to go?" Aimee asked.

"You really are anxious, aren't you?"

"No, I think I'm just curious now. I know there is nothing this man can do to ruin anything between Ramiro and me, only we can do that."

Dierdre snickered, "Yeah. That's what marriage is for."

"Thanks loads, but I was planning on having a good lasting marriage, and I'd thank you not to jinx it."

"I'm sorry, I meant that for me, not for you."

"So," Aimee asked, "you are thinking of marriage already? Maybe you should just get past the first date tonight and see how things go."

Aimee zipped out the door keeping as many paces ahead of Dierdre as she could.

"It's not a date! It's not a date!" She was swinging her purse at Aimee's fleeing form as they darted out of the building and towards the parking lot.

* * *

Bobby had finished a few last minute changes on the program just in time for lunch. He knew this would not be the finished program, but he expected to learn from its behavior and be able to fix it. That's how programming worked. You write a program, run it and see what things it did right and what things it did wrong, and you fix the wrong ones. You repeat the process until, eventually, it only has right things left. At least, that's the theory.

Finally the moment came to launch it. He started the initiator and watched the monitors as one processor after another began calculating. It was like a snowball, each processor would run for a bit, then spawn two copies of itself and they would run and spawn two copies.

Whether it was actually working or not, he would find out after lunch, and after his one o'clock class. That should give it sufficient time to either work, which seemed highly unlikely, or it would cause one of a number of problems which he foresaw.

In either case, it was on its own, and his most pressing problem at the moment was going to be selecting something from the cafeteria's vast selection of wholesome products. He shook his head at his reflection in the door glass and wondered when his private thoughts had become so sarcastic.

* * *

Dierdre and Aimee drove across town to the small taqueria where Ramiro's father said he would meet them. It was a dingy looking place full of mostly older men in dirty t-shirts and stained trousers, but also some younger boys with hip hop styled pants, oversize shirts and bandannas on their heads.

Aimee looked worried again and asked, "Do you think he brought us here to kill us?"

"No, I think he wanted us to be ravished by all those men so Ramiro wouldn't be interested anymore."

"Thanks, you are so comforting." Aimee scanned the building from the car. "I don't see him, do you?"

"Not a sign of him. Should we just go wait inside?"

Aimee breathed deeply. "Let's go. Ramiro knows where we are, and he will make sure that our murderers are dealt with."

The two left the car.

After they taken only two paces, Aimee asked, "Dierdre? Do you think we should lock the car so it's safe, or leave it open so we can escape?"

Dierdre paused and looked at Aimee, then she pressed the button on her key fob and unlocked the doors.

Inside, there were only a dozen or so tables, half of which were already in use. Several patrons looked the girls up and down, but when one of them started to speak, another at his table slapped him in the back of the head. Seeing the head whacking did not make the place any more agreeable to Dierdre. As the girls selected a table and sat down, a very nice looking young boy offered them menus and asked if they wanted something to drink. This boy definitely was out of place here, he wasn't wearing rags, tattoos, or a layer of dirt and oil.

Dierdre spoke first. "I'll have an iced tea."

"I'll have a beer," Aimee said.

Dierdre shot her a look.

"What? You're driving."

Dierdre looked around the establishment. There was still no sign of Ramiro's father. They looked over the menu. The scent wafting from the kitchen was very promising and the menu actually looked pretty good. When the boy returned with their drinks, they each ordered something to eat. Even if Ramiro's father was a no-show, the trip wouldn't be a complete waste.

Dierdre played with her tea, adding sugar, stirring, sipping, then adding more sugar. Aimee pushed the glass away, hoisted the bottle and took a big swallow.

Time ticked away. The meals came and Aimee was into her second beer, but there was still no sign of Ernesto. When the young boy brought them their check, another boy with a large brown bag darted in from the front, and asked, "You Aimee?"

Aimee raised her hand and said, "I'm Aimee".

Dierdre, suddenly fearing the boy meant harm slapped Aimee's hand and said, "Aimee, shhhh", but it was too late. The boy handed the package to Aimee and disappeared as fast as he had arrived.

Dierdre looked at the package, then at Aimee and asked, "Is it ticking?"

"Dierdre, be serious." All the same, she held it up to her ear and listened. "No ticking."

Dierdre picked up the bill and reached for her purse, but down at the bottom where the total was, it said "PAID".

"How do you like that? He's here somewhere, and he paid for lunch."

Aimee looked around, but there was no sign of him.

"So, what's in the package?"

Aimee shrugged and said, "I don't know."

"Aren't you going to open it?"

"I guess," Aimee said, "but not here. Let's go."

The two of them picked up their things, including the mysterious brown package and left. The car was where they left it, with all its tires intact. All in all, it was an interesting trip, weird, but interesting.

* * *

Bobby got back from lunch and his first afternoon class, and found what he expected. The programs partially worked, but something had gone wrong, and there were too many threads for the system to handle. This was a pretty big computer, and he was a little surprised it had choked so quickly. He sat down and started to analyze what went wrong.

Some things were more obvious than others. After each thread created two copies of itself, they each had to run a bit, then choose who was the best, and the other two had to die off. None of his had died. They just kept making more and more. An obvious mistake, fixing it would probably be a challenge, but he loved challenges.

* * *

"So," Dierdre asked again as she pulled the car out into the street, "are you going to open it or what?"

"I don't know. I don't like feeling manipulated."

"Yeah," Dierdre admitted, "I know what you mean. The more I look back, the more I feel everyone in that place was expecting us. Like they were all his spies. Pretty paranoid, huh?"

"Maybe," Aimee admitted, "but I had the same feeling."

"I wish I knew what he was up to."

"Well, this package," Aimee said, "may have the answers for us."

"Probably so, but all the same, maybe we should wait for Ramiro before we open it."

"What if it's something terrible that I don't really want him to know?"

Dierdre shrugged as she pulled the car into her stall in the faculty lot. Aimee became very quiet as they left the car and she carried the package to their office. Once inside, she hesitated before entering Dierdre's inner office, "D? Would you open it and just make sure it's not something really mean and awful?"

"You mean, would I open it and make sure it's not some kind of bomb or nerve gas?"

"No, I mean, I don't know. I'll just save it till morning and look at it then."

"Why morning?"

"That will give me some time to prepare emotionally and Ramiro will be able to come see me if I need him, and most importantly, you need to concentrate on getting ready for your date tonight."

Again a wad of paper was quickly hurled in Aimee's general vicinity, but she had already retreated to her desk where she laid the package in an unused bottom drawer.

The rest of the afternoon was consumed with Dierdre's late classes. Both of these were theory classes and consisted entirely of textbook study and lectures. These were the easiest classes to teach, the calculus requirements were minimal, and there was little need for physical equipment or experiments. Dierdre liked to add occasional videos, usually something from PBS, but she mostly taught straight from her syllabus.

When she returned to her desk, after the last class, she found another email in her in-box from Bobby:

Professor Jennings,

The first test run went as expected. I fixed some minor flaws and have now launched another run. This is the one we can check in the morning. Seven, as you suggested, is fine. See you then.

CHAPTER 6

It wasn't a date, Dierdre kept reminding herself. It was a professional meeting, but she still needed to be dressed appropriately. They had not discussed where they might go, but judging from what little she knew about Stillman, it would probably be more formal than trendy.

She could not take the chance that it wasn't formal so she had to find something that was versatile enough for any restaurant. It had to be something that said that she was a woman who could have dinner with a man without being on the prowl, hunting for him. She was a professional, and they were peers, equals.

By the time she had tried on everything in her closet, there was no time left to buy something new. She had to find something she already owned, but most of her wardrobe was date oriented, and therefore inappropriate. She must have something suitable. Why was this so difficult? It's not a date, she reminded herself again. It's Aimee's fault. Aimee kept teasing her all afternoon, and now her brain was so focused on not being a date, that she was spending just as much time preparing as she would if it were a date.

Time! It was getting late, and she still had her hair and face to do. Beige! Beige looks more businesslike. She narrowed her scope down to her beige dresses, and one after another, held them up to her body in the mirror. Too short, too low cut, too feminine, too much like grandma's dress. She banged her head into the mirror and screamed, "What is wrong with my closet?" She had to select between too short, and too low cut, and the too short sweater dress won.

It wasn't really that short, not these days. And her legs will be obscured by the table during dinner. Better that than too much cleavage staring him in the face, especially since she wanted answers from him. What made her think he would even notice? He might not even like girls. No, she reminded herself, that's not true. He practically drools over her in the hallway. Definitely don't want the too low cut. Too short was absolutely her final answer.

One crisis down, one to go. Dierdre looked in the mirror and with both hands grabbed her hair on either side of her head and started to panic. If she made her hair too nice, she might give Stillman the wrong signal, but she also didn't want to look bad if she ran across someone she really liked. How she wore her hear would probably have no effect on Stillman anyway. Having come to that conclusion, she no longer worried about over doing anything in her preparation, and she dolled herself up as if she planned to bump into a real prospect while she was out.

* * *

Dr. Pietre knocked on the lab door, "Helloooo? Anybody is there? Can you hear me?" He was carrying a bag of doughnuts and some coffee. He knocked again, then checking the hallway was clear, pulled out a new key and slid it into the lock and let himself in, "Hello? It is I, Professor Pietre. Anybody is here? Your door is open, and I am bringing you the refreshments."

He walked to the back of the lab, but found it deserted. He went back to the door, closed and locked it, then returned to the computer terminal where he sat down and stared at the screens.

Colorful graphs starting at the bottom of the screen stretched up, some to the top of the screen and some only part way. The graphs were alive and pulsated up and down. There was a set of numbers in the corner. They would increase and decrease occasionally, but only slightly.

He hit a key on the console to bring up a master control screen, but it asked for a password. He had hoped he would be luckier than that. He rummaged through the various drawers of Dierdre's lab desk, but found nothing indicating a password, or even any strange word combination that might be a password. He tried a few lame passwords, *"NORWOOD"*, *"PHYSICS"*, *"PASSWORD"*, but none of them let him in.

He went to the rack, and opened a panel in the upper processor box. Behind the panel door he found a set of switches and dials. He turned the dials till they read 9898465, the same number he read off a small strip of paper he pulled from his pocket. He located a switch labeled control processor interrupt and flipped it, then he located another switch labeled execute and flipped it. The display console which had been filled with the colorful chart just a moment ago, cleared to black, and in the lower left corner was a small prompt, *"CSRID>"*. He went to the console and copied the word *"OPOVERRIDE27"* from the same slip of paper. A moment later, he was presented with a blank control screen.

Dr. Pietre pulled a doughnut from the bag, took a large bite and a swig of coffee. He rubbed his hands together and typed *"DISPLAY PROCID ALL."* The screen started scrolling from the bottom with all the processes running. It was a never ending list that ran and ran and ran out of control.

"Oh my!" he whispered to the room. He hit the interrupt key on the keyboard, he tried the escape key, but nothing would stop the list. Then, while he pondered what he might try next, the screen blanked out and the colorful screen of graphs returned.

"I not do that," he said blankly.

He swept his stuff off the desk and swiftly and quietly left the room. If he did not cancel the list and return the other program, then who did? It was a question he probably would never answer. It was certainly a question he would not ask.

* * *

Dierdre was ready to go and was listing the questions she wanted to ask Stillman when she heard him rapping on the door. She slid the notes into her purse and opened the door.

He took one look at her and exclaimed, "Oh my, but don't you look absolutely stunning! I fear I may have misunderstood the nights festivities, for I find myself completely under dressed." Stillman motioned to his clothes, which were far more casual than Dierdre's.

"This old thing?" she said, "Don't be silly, you look very distinguished." She had to say something lest he think she had other things on her mind.

"Never-the-less, my pappy always taught me to never arrive at a ladies house empty handed." He pulled his right hand out from behind his back, and in it were three perfectly formed pink roses.

"Oh my God," she thought, "He has flowers!"

Stillman held the flowers up for Dierdre and said, "I chose three roses, only three, fearing any more might give the wrong idea, and pink because white also may send the wrong message and red is the color for Jezebels, and colleagues such as ourselves should lie somewhere in between where it is possible to have perfectly platonic relationships."

Dierdre forced the look of horror from her face and said, "They are beautiful, thank you so much Stillman, won't you come in for a moment while I find some water for these."

"Thank you, but just for a moment. I thought we would go to Uncle Billy's. It's a Jazz Bistro just off campus. I hope you like Jazz, they usually showcase Dixie, but tonight will be more contemporary, Miles Davis, Charlie Parker, I am partial to contemporary jazz myself."

"Stillman, you surprise me, and yes, I do like Jazz." She put the roses in a tall fluted glass filled with water and a sip of seven-up to keep them fresh. "All set here, lead the way."

* * *

"You didn't even open it?" Ramiro was shocked that anyone would accept a gift and ungraciously set it aside. He took one step away from her towards the door of her apartment.

"You don't understand. It's like he was playing some kind of game, like he was conning us and we were just his stupid marks doing everything he planned out."

"My father? Manipulating you to do what? Open a gift?"

"If it was just a gift, where was he? Why didn't he just give it to us?"

Ramiro couldn't answer that.

"And," Aimee continued, "how did two attractive young girls walk into that place filled with all those dirty sweaty Mexicans and not have a single one of them say something?"

"Dirty sweaty Mexicans? I don't think I have seen this side of you before." If there was one thing that made Ramiro's blood boil, it was bigotry.

"What? No!" she exclaimed, "They were DIRTY. They were SWEATY. They were MEXICAN."

"Perhaps it's just as well that I learned this now. I thought you were different."

Aimee was struck in the heart. Tears began swelling in her eyes as she began to realize what was happening. "What are you saying?"

"I'm saying you sound just like him, and I could never marry someone who was like my father. I backed you up at dinner. I was behind you one hundred percent and ready to defend your honor no matter what he said. I never expected to be caught between two bigots having to choose one over the other."

"But you're not hearing me." The tears flowed freely down Aimee's cheeks. "You're supposed to be a judge now. You have to listen to me."

"I heard your testimony. I heard it from your own lips." His voice was filled with anger, near hatred for what he was hearing.

"You see? This is just what he wanted," she cried, "He did this."

"My father is a plain old man. He never manipulated anybody in his life."

"He…did…this." She could barely talk now.

"You give him too much credit. He is not smart enough to do this. He is just an old man who gave you something, but you were too filled with hatred to open it. I have to go." Ramiro stormed out of Aimee's apartment.

She ran into her bedroom and fell onto her bed sobbing uncontrollably. It was a nightmare. Bad things just happened, and she did not understand where they came from. She cried herself to sleep, curled up on top of her bed.

* * *

The drive to Uncle Billy's was uncomfortably quiet. There was occasional idle chatter, but everything said was carefully crafted to sound like anything but date talk, leaving the conversation dry and uninteresting.

Dierdre considered asking her questions in the car, but really wanted to wait until they were comfortably seated so they could each relax and concentrate on the conversation. She may have feared their conversation might sound like a date, but the silence was far worse and sounded exactly like a date, so she had to say something.

"This is a very nice car." Oh God, that sounded like a date.

"Thank you. It gets me where I need to go."

More awkward silence followed, then he said, "So how's your friend Aimee doing? The rumor on campus is that she is getting married." Oops, he said the "M" word.

"She's fine. Her fiancé just became a judge, he's a lawyer."

"Well congratulations for her, that's a fine catch." OK. Good save.

Stillman pulled the car up in front of the Bistro into the valet line. While he was handing the attendant the keys, another attendant opened Dierdre's door, saving him from another awkward moment. Opening a door was something he had to do, unless someone else, other than his date, or in this case, he corrected himself mid thought, his female associate, opened it for him. Sometimes the proprieties of being born southern made him wish his daddy was a Yankee instead.

As the first attendant pulled the car away and Stillman joined Dierdre at the door, the second attendant gave him a giant thumbs up behind her back. She was, as his daddy would have said, a "prize filly." And, he had to admit, she was a stone cold knockout. He would be crazy not to want to date her. But she wasn't interested in him, and he knew he was not the great catch that anyone like her would go for.

They entered the club and Stillman held up two fingers for the Hostess who seated them in a small booth just off the dance floor.

Dierdre decided to wait until after they had ordered drinks and placed their meal orders before she began her questions. Stillman ordered a bottle of wine. Soft music played overhead, but the stage was empty. The entertainment would start later.

"Stillman, thank you for seeing me. I just have a few questions I want to ask you."

"Ah, yes, about nano-electronics as I recall?"

"Yes. My project involves manipulating the connection between matter, energy and gravity."

"Oh?" he asked, "Einstein's grand unifying theory? I had no idea that anyone was able to even prove it was more than a theory, let alone attempt to manipulate it."

"That's true, I can't manipulate it. I am only building simulation programs to demonstrate how it might be done. In order for it to become reality, however, I need to have processors that are thousands of times denser than anything we have today. They need to be smaller and faster. I know that the science of micro-electronics is starting to move from silicon based electronic gates to various kinds of experimental nano technologies. I was hoping you could fill in some details for me, so I could see if they would ever meet my needs."

Stillman scratched the small goatee on his chin. "Well, I will certainly try. Silicon gates have steadily gotten smaller and smaller.

The benefits of smaller size include increased speed and reduced heat loss. But there is a limit to how small they can get. Now to be fair, there were limits before which we found ways to exceed, but now they are getting down to limits that are being imposed upon them by the size of the molecules. As they shrink below ninety nanometers, the reactive properties of the electrons begin to change, so they need to find newer, better ways to build circuits. There are also problems with constructing circuits so small. At one time, they thought forty-five or maybe thirty-two nanometers would be the absolute limit because we couldn't focus photons well enough to go smaller. Some researchers still believe sixteen or possibly eight might be realized in the future, but eventually there will be a wall that cannot be breached. At some point a new process that is not etching electron pathways on silicon will need to be devised."

Stillman took a sip of his wine and continued, "One of the current trends is something called nanotubes. But, I think that what you really need to know, is how small can they get, and when will they get there."

"Yes," Dierdre replied, "My process is going to require millions of processors, something far bigger than anything we have today."

"Millions? That would be a lot of processors. Moore's law states that computing density will double every eighteen months, but in 1997 he already admitted that they were approaching the physical limits when they were at twenty-five microns. Some doubted they could go smaller than nine microns because of wayward atomic particles bombarding the circuitry causing errant results. Obviously, this was not the case, or at least has not been yet. At that time, it was predicted that progress using current technologies would come to an end around 2017. "

"That's fine. I am trying to build a prototype based on the future availability of improved parts."

"You must also consider that there are three ways to combine multiple processors. IBM pioneered the technique of putting multiple processors on the same chip. It was something they did for their own mainframe and midrange computers, but never reached the mainstream public until the chip manufacturers started to follow suit when they reached the limit of their ability to dissipate heat."

"But wouldn't two processors create twice the heat as one?"

"Yes, but over twice the area which makes it somewhat easier to extract. The second way to combine CPU's is using a parallel organization where they are all essentially part of the same computer. That is the type of system you currently have, the one you got from Dr. Karlyn. The last technique is called clustering. This is where you take a group of computers and make them work together as if they were a larger consolidated computer. One of the nice things about clusters is that they do not need to have matching specs. You can keep running some of your older equipment in a cluster with your newer equipment. Unfortunately, the new stuff is usually so much faster that the old equipment can hardly help at all. But in your case, needing millions of processors, you would definitely end up clustering, probably clustering a bunch of parallel systems. Assuming, of course, that quantum computers don't come on-line before that."

"Quantum computers?"

"The theory is that a quantum processor would actually execute so many instructions at the same time, it would be like executing your whole program in one instruction. Some even suggest that it would have an answer ready for you before you pose the question."

"That's exactly what I need!"

"Unfortunately, it's kind of like cold fusion. Some say they have done it, while others are skeptical that it can even be done. For now, it's still too far in the future to base any plans upon."

"How many processors are used in the fastest computers today?"

"Most of the fastest super computers range from two thousand to five thousand processors. But we are seeing ambitious plans to build new supercomputers with over ten thousand processors. Supposing that our ability to combine processors followed Moore's law. As the processors got smaller, we could fit more of them together, then every eighteen months you could double the amount of processors you used. If all that holds true, then we will be able to build your processor in twelve years. It's not that far away."

Dierdre's eyes lit up and opened wide. Her jaw fell slack for a moment, then spread into a broad smile. She had never really considered the possibility that this could be something that would happen within her lifetime, let alone during her research career!

"Wow," Stillman said, "that really must have been good news. You should do that more often."

Dierdre blinked, "Huh? Do what?"

"Smile."

Their meals arrived just in time to save another awkward moment. They stared intently at the waiter, their food, their drinks, the stage, anything but at each other. Dierdre reminded herself it's not a date, yet she found that her skin and her pulse reacted to all those small clues, as if it were a date. She wished she were a swami, able to stifle those pesky emotional reactions. She wasn't mad with herself, after all she had gotten what she came for, and it was an entirely enjoyable time so far. She just had no need for the heightened sensitivity one gets when the blood engorges and swells the erogenous zones, or when the skin on your arms, or neck grows taught. This was not one of those evenings where she was going to need the enhanced sense of touch that comes with such reactions.

And the meal was not helping. It was quite elegant for what appeared to be a small dime a dozen bistro. She wasn't quite sure if the food was as divine as it seemed, or if her taste buds were betraying her due to some crossed signals and hormonal overload. She didn't blame Stillman, he merely answered her questions, but never in her wildest dreams did she believe she could be so close to making her vision a reality. How lucky was she, to have someone available who knew all those answers so thoroughly? What a remarkable and intelligent man he was. Maybe you couldn't tell by looking at him, but he had quite a lot going for him. He wasn't that bad looking, either, under all his old styling, or maybe that was the wine that made him look better. Wine, mmmm she thought, time for another sip.

Good food, good wine, and the possibility of seeing her one dream to full prototype in another decade and a half. The house lights dimmed, and the overhead music was muted. Four men stepped on stage and seated themselves at the instruments while a deep baritone voice from the speakers said, "Ladies and Gentlemen, the Terry James quartet." Music filled the room. There is something about real music that recordings just couldn't capture.

Goose bumps ran from her wrists and wriggled up her arm across her shoulders, tickled the back of her neck, then ran down her spine. She crossed her legs, high, above the knee, and bounced her foot with the beat of the music. Her head nodded in a hypnotic rhythm. She glanced over at Stillman. His eyes were a bit glassy as he stared from musician to musician. She imagined, from his look, that he was analyzing the intricate rhythms and patterns as each man fell in and out of the central rhythm, yet never strayed from the main beat.

They remained entranced with the music, first one song, then two, and a third, until Stillman leaned over table and said, "Dierdre, do you like to dance? Please feel free, if you see someone you want to dance with. I don't want to hold you back. I might even do the same, if I see someone."

Once again, her body was way ahead of her mind, reacting to what she had heard, excitement, anticipation, confusion, hurt. Her mind was screaming what a relief, but her body was rejecting that notion feeling rather like she had been slapped in the face. She set her jaw a bit and coolly replied, "Thank you Stillman, I'll certainly keep that in mind." The nerve of him. If he sees someone he wants to dance with, of course he can dance with her, this is not a date, but that's no reason to pose the question like that. And him acting like he was always the southerly gentlemen, God's gift to ladies. The little twit probably can't even dance. He probably would do Mr. Robotic, he's such a know it all little geek. Dierdre filled another glass with wine, this time to the brim, and downed it in a hurry. No reason, she decided, for him to ruin her evening. She scanned the room looking for potential dance partners. Not the same crowd that circulates the more hip clubs. She saw mostly old dudes and misunderstood weenies. Her mind started to panic, what if he finds a dance partner and she doesn't? She glanced at him, he didn't seem intent on finding anyone at the moment, maybe he was just politely giving her permission should someone ask her to dance. Yeah, that's probably what it was.

"So, Dierdre, I'm curious. How do a million computer processors have anything to do with nuclear physics? You said you were researching the Grand Unifying Theory."

Dierdre's mind was abruptly pulled back to the dinner table where she composed herself the best she could. "Well," she said a little squeaky, she coughed to clear her throat, "excuse me, I was saying that the processors are required to model a quantum path. I believe that our inability to see and understand the path of quantum particles is what prevents us from seeing the unifying link. Einstein sensed it was there, and he put forth mathematical models to quantify it, but it remained a theory. Most theorists agree that any attempt to harness the link to gravity would require vast sums of energy. I believe that these quantum motions cross that link, and they do so without vast sums of energy. Any effort on our part to use energy to cross the link would only demonstrate our lack of knowledge regarding it."

"And you think that by knowing the paths of quantum particles, you can duplicate their motion? Is their motion a key? Do they follow a maze of some kind?"

"I don't know exactly what they do. But, I think that one day we will be able to move particles at our discretion, and if I can move them around in the same path as a quantum particle and at the same time, I think I can unlock the link. It would be like riding the quantum particle piggy back."

Stillman was interested. She could see him really absorbing her dream, and his eyes were dancing around in it. "And you think that if we could manipulate particles of matter fast enough, you could predict where to put them to catch the event?"

"No Stillman, I think that if I can predict where the event will occur, it won't matter how fast I can manipulate matter as long as I get it there ahead of the event."

Stillman sucked in his breath. "I think you should know that we are getting much closer to manipulating your particles even today. We have always had cyclotrons and linear accelerators. Years ago IBM pushed molecules around to form their logo."

He stopped speaking for a moment as if to size her up before he could continue. As he paused, the band stopped playing and stepped off the stage for a break. They both clapped for the group and nodded their heads to show their approval of the entertainers' performance.

"It occurs to me, Dierdre, that you might not actually know my area of expertise. An area I would have liked to research, if I'd had your background and clout with the administration. My interests are in nano-robotics. The field of creating very small molecular size machines. There is no reason, that someday, we wouldn't have small machines the size of bacteria, maybe even as small as a virus. These machines could be used in medical practice to roam the body and fight infection directly, possibly even alter damaged DNA. Before we can create machines, we need to learn how to manipulate the particles, and essentially build our own molecules the way we want them."

Dierdre saw the connection and poured another glass of wine. No wonder he got so stimulated, it wasn't her project, it was his. No, that's not right, the wine was giving her head a bit too much of a buzz to rationalize clearly. He was excited because her project somehow blended with his.

"Listen," she said, "I'm starting a brand new phase of my research, and I don't have anything to show just yet, but I should soon. When I do, would you like to look at my results? And if you like them, I mean if you believe in them, would you like to work on the prototype with me, and see if we can break a new barrier for mankind?"

"That's a might lofty, but, let's just say, I'm interested. Yes, I'm definitely intrigued by your proposal." Stillman stroked his goatee as he contemplated the opportunity. He stared into the bottom of his empty glass for a moment then reached for the wine bottle, but it was empty. He weighed the bottle in his hand for a moment. "Can I offer you something a bit stronger, Dierdre?"

"Are you trying to get me drunk Stillman?"

She meant it as a joke, and was surprised by the panic she thought she detected in his eyes. He stammered, "I...uh...that is...uh...no..." She thought he sounded like an actor who had forgotten his lines.

The band returned from their break and started to play. He stopped playing with the wine bottle and placed it back on the table. "Would you excuse me please? I think I see someone I know."

"Sure. Go ahead." Dierdre's mind was still caught up in the glow of going full throttle through the modeling phase directly into actual prototypes. The thought of providing a possible new energy source was more dizzying than the wine, which was dizzying enough already. If it worked, it would place her with the likes of Einstein and Edison. But she would have to really prove the process and create a prototype that could produce repeatable results. And no big publicity or it could be another cold fusion. That made her laugh. It very well might be a lot like cold fusion.

The vision faded out and her eyes focused back on the club. She couldn't believe what she saw. Across the dance floor, Stillman was dancing. Dierdre felt her face flush, not sure why. In fact, she was not sure why he was dancing with that girl. She wasn't very pretty and clearly did not know how to dance. Worse yet, she was much too young for him, and was probably a student, something she frowned upon. Dierdre had to look away for a moment, as the girl blatantly brushed her nearly falling out breasts clearly against Stillman's chest. Finally, mercifully, the music ended, and he escorted her back to her table, only to have her girlfriend jump up and drag him to the dance floor. Dierdre's jaw dropped open, for the second time this evening. She rummaged around various items on the table, as if she could find something to occupy herself that was equally interesting as dancing.

As she played with the salt and pepper shakers, a familiar voice said, "Professor Jennings, I've never seen you here before."

"Bobby, what are you doing here?"

"Me? I work here." He looked around to make sure he wouldn't attract too much attention, then leaned closer to her and cupped his hands around his mouth, and said in a deep voice, "Ladies and Gentlemen, the Terry James Quartet."

Recognition brought a light laugh to her face. "That was you?"

"I work the sound for them here on occasion. Listen, you mind if I sit down a minute?"

"Aren't you working?"

"Yeah, but once I get it set up, it pretty much runs itself." He slid into the booth next to her. "I saw you and Dr. Whitfield come in. He's usually pretty cool and stuff, I don't know why he's wasting his time with those stuck up sorority brats."

Dierdre glanced over in Stillman's direction. He caught her glance, as he danced lamely with the two girls, then, clearly a surprise to the girls, put his arm around one of the girls and pulled her around into a modest dip. The girls were clearly delighted. Dierdre was puzzled by their apparent interest in Professor Whitfield.

"It's his prerogative," Dierdre said a bit too stiffly, "we are just colleagues here. In fact, I was picking his brain for our project, learning a thing or two about nano technology. Besides, they are much younger than I am, why wouldn't he want to dance with them?"

"Baloney, you are clearly much hotter than both of them put together, not to mention smarter. Let's face it, if IQ's were batteries, those bimbos combined couldn't light up an LED. The only reason they got into the sororities, or the university for that matter, was their daddies' contributions to the college."

"They must be good at something. They look like they know how to have fun."

"Sure," Bobby said, "with each other. Guys are just toys for them to frustrate. They like to wind them up, then cut them loose."

"That would serve him right," Dierdre thought to herself.

"You want me to go tell Whitfield what a jerk he's being?"

"No, but thanks for offering. He means nothing to me, but all the same, you've done an excellent job of ego repair for me."

"No problem." Bobby popped up to leave, then stopped and asked, "Dierdre, would you like to dance?"

"I couldn't, you're my student."

"I'm also your employee and you might even consider me a colleague. It just doesn't feel right that he left you and is dancing, even if you were only here as co-workers."

"Oh," she said, "I see. A mercy dance."

"Are you kidding? Any time a hot chick like you dances with me, it's a mercy dance. But I prefer to think of it as a revenge dance, because, you might think of me only as an ex-hacker nerd type, but I can actually dance. Six years of training. I even thought I would be on stage at one point in my life."

Dierdre smiled broadly, and took his hand, rose from the table and followed him to the dance floor. She too, had several years of dance instruction, and even though they had never danced together before, all the training came back, for both of them. Too bad it wasn't ballroom music, she thought. Put on some big band and they could really turn this place upside down. But it was good enough, they made Stillman and the so-so sorority girls look like idiots.

After one of the sets ended, one of the musicians came up to them, and stared directly into Dierdre's eyes and asked, "Bobby, my man, who is this drop dead angel that dances on air and is so fine she even makes you look good?"

"Theodore, this is my boss, Professor Jennings, Professor, this is Theodore, a true life beatnik."

Dierdre reached her hand out to shake his. "I can't take all the credit here, Bobby is a marvelous dancer."

"He's a good kid too. You should give him a raise."

"Theo!" Bobby interjected, "She just hired me for crying out loud."

"Hey, just looking out for you, my brother. I gotta scoot. You two should stick around for the last set. You make us look good."

Bobby followed Dierdre back to her table. Stillman was there already, downing something amber colored. Dierdre caught something in his eye, something maniacal and calculating. He seemed to be exhibiting a devious side that she had never seen before, or perhaps, it was the alcohol making her paranoid.

"Ah, there you are," he said as she slid into the booth.

Bobby remained standing. "Good evening Dr. Whitfield, good to see you again." He turned to Dierdre and said, "I have to go set up some mikes, we usually get a few horns that show up for the last set. Make sure to come get me if you get stranded again, I'll be in that little booth right over there." He swung around and stylishly pointed to a raised booth across the dance floor where they kept the mixer equipment. He pointed with his fingers from his waist as if shooting a pistol in a fast draw, followed by him blowing out the smoke from the barrel of his finger. Then he dashed off to the stage.

"Dierdre, I had no idea you could dance. That is, I had no idea you could dance so well."

"You didn't ask." Either her paranoia was peaking, or she was sensing clear and disturbing vibes that Dr. Whitfield was carefully choosing his words. She felt that from here on, a simple conversation with him was some kind of chess game, and she didn't care for it one bit.

A waitress came to the table and Dierdre ordered a Piña Colada.

"Well I'm glad I didn't," he said, "You are far too good for me."

"Stillman, don't be so childish. Dancing with a stronger partner can only make you look better."

He went back to his drink. "Perhaps you are correct."

When the last set started, Stillman stood and formally, in the grandest southern tradition, requested a dance with her, which she accepted, and just as she had said, she helped him dance much better.

"Your perfume is quite intoxicating."

"Is it too much? Do you need to sit down?"

"No, my dear," he said, "I am quite fine."

"I'm sure I can find a designated dancer for you, if you need."

"Humor. A rare find in a woman so beautiful as yourself. Forgive me if I don't laugh with you, but I was being quite serious."

"Serious about being intoxicated by my perfume Stillman?"

"Indeed. Your perfume, the cut of your dress, your hair. You are a very handsome woman Dierdre, very very handsome."

When the last set had finished, Bobby crossed the dance floor, and met Dierdre and Stillman as they returned to their booth to collect her purse and coat. "Well professors, I'm glad to see the two of you had a good time." He eyed Dr. Whitfield closely and asked, "How are you feeling Dr. Whitfield? You OK to drive?"

"I'm fine, thank you," he drawled, "not that it's any concern of yours."

"But it is," Bobby quipped, "I would hate for you to have an accident leaving me unemployed again so soon."

Dierdre still eyed Stillman suspiciously. Although dancing seemed to have curbed his suspicious behavior, she still could not shake the gut feeling that she was some kind of prize in some twisted southern battle of the sexes. And if it was a battle of the sexes, especially if it was a battle of wits, she was not going to be one of those quiet southern bells that puts up a fake fight and falls prey to the southern gentlemen, crowning him the victor of the struggle.

* * *

The large man arrived on the college campus at half past midnight. As he approached the bottom of the steps that led to the labs, his small wiry associate stepped out of the shadows. The large man had to stifle a laugh. "You have got to be kidding." While he wore a dark suit himself, his smaller associate was dressed from head to toe in black, like a cat burglar in a movie.

"What?" the thinner man asked, "I'm in character."

"We didn't hire you to act. You have a real job to do. I sure hope you can follow through with it."

They climbed the stairs and entered the lab building. The small man pulled a handful of small odd shaped wire tools and a small magnesium flashlight from a small pack on his belt. He stuck the flashlight in his mouth and aimed it at the lock.

"What are you doing?"

"M hihn uh ahh," was all he could mumble with the flashlight in his mouth.

"Get rid of the stupid flashlight, the hallway is brightly lit."

The small man pulled the flashlight from his mouth and asked, "Was it hurting you? I'm a perfectionist, and when I do a job I want to do it by the book."

The large man rolled his eyes and wondered what the hell he had gotten himself into.

The smaller man picked the lock and quietly pushed the door open. The large man followed him in and to the back of the lab, where the console continued to display the colorful graphs.

The large man pointed at the console and asked, "What do you make of that?"

"I don't know yet."

"What about those numbers in the corner?"

"They look static," the smaller man said, "They may represent some input parameters when the program was started. Give me a moment. Let's see if we can get in." The small man tried a few keystrokes on the console, but was asked for passwords. "OK, we expected as much."

He got up from the console and headed to the rack. "What's this?"

"What?" the large man asked.

"Looks like this kid doesn't have control of his own process."

"Why do you say that?"

"He's been using interrupt vectors to force a new control console."

"Interrupt vectors? What interrupt vector?"

"9898465"

"Damn it." The large man shouted and paced now. That's not the kid, that's Pietre. I told him to back off, but he obviously didn't listen."

"Why do you think it was Pietre? It's not a completely secret interrupt."

"But it is the one and only interrupt that we gave him when Dr. Karlyn had the computer. Wait a minute, rewind. Pietre used the vector, and left it there? That idiot."

"Apparently he left the panel open, too," the small man said, "I wonder what would have made him leave in such a hurry?"

"I don't know."

"I could execute his vector and see if the machine tells us."

"Sure. Might as well."

The small man hit the execute switch, and the two of them lumbered back to the console.

At the "CSRID>" prompt, the small man typed, "SYSOEM647" and found himself at a control screen. He typed, "SYS USAGE." The screen returned:

ACTIVE THREADS:263,642
FORCED SWAPS: 1,023,455,679
MEMORY:567,445,293 STORAGE:365,349,888

The small man exclaimed, "That's a lot of threads."

"What's he doing with all those threads?"

"Not sure yet."

The small man repeated the command, "SYS USAGE." The screen returned:

ACTIVE THREADS:263,947
FORCED SWAPS: 1,023,735,260
MEMORY:567,463,037 STORAGE:365,351,524

"Whatever he is doing, it keeps using more and more of the system resources. My personal opinion is that it's not working. We may have come too...Hello! What's this?"

The screen flipped back to the color chart they saw when they first entered.

The large man asked, "You didn't do that?"

"No, I definitely did not."

"That's probably what frightened Pietre into leaving so quickly."

"I don't think we can figure out what he's doing just yet," the small man said, "but we can dump the password file, which should let us log in remotely."

The small man went back to the rack, slid a small optical disk into one of the drives mounted on the front of it, dialed a different vector and hit the execute switch. The optical disk started to whir, a few lights blinked away, and then it stopped and ejected the disk.

The small man turned the vectors back to all zeroes, flipped the control processor interrupt switch back to normal, closed the panel and removed the disk. "All done," he said, and the two of them left as quietly as they had arrived.

* * *

Stillman pulled the car in front of Dierdre's home and walked her to her door. "Perhaps a nightcap?" he asked, "To end the evening?"

She opened the door, but before entering turned to Stillman. She had no intention of inviting him in, and did not want any misunderstandings. She'd been stewing the whole drive home about him playing some kind of mind game on her, and was determined to close the evening with a win.

"No thank you, Stillman I..."

"Are you quite sure?" Stillman asked, "I'm feeling quite stimulated at the moment."

"Thank you, Stillman, but not tonight."

"Well, if you are quite sure."

She sucked in her breath and prepared the coolest most factual voice she could muster. "Yes, I am quite sure. You answered all my questions and have given me a renewed sense of hope in my research, and I am very grateful."

"Are you certain I have answered all your questions? I feel like we have only touched upon a new journey for your research. There is so much more we could discuss, perhaps over a cup of coffee, while it is still fresh in our minds?"

"That sounds wonderful, but I am so tired, I just can't wait to rip these clothes off and jump into bed." She was toying with him now.

"I see, yes, jumping into bed does sound much better than coffee..."

"What was that Stillman?"

"I mean to say... that is..."

"Perhaps a rain check on that coffee? Thanks again, I'll call you if I have any more questions."

"You are quite welcome. Call on me anytime." With that, he surrendered and gave up any hope of extending the evening, and leaned in to give her a very polite peck on the cheek, but she swung her head around and caught him full on the lips, and as he retreated, she leaned forward and followed him, matching his movements, maintaining a sensuous lock between her lips and his. He finally stopped retreating, and started returning the passion emanating from her lips, at which time she broke off the kiss. "I just wanted you to know, Stillman, that I had a really good time tonight. Really good. Too bad we are just colleagues isn't it?" And she slinked in through the door and closed and locked it, leaving him standing on the porch blinking with a silly expression on his face.

She stood inside of the doorway. Part of her wanted to do a silly victory dance, but instead she just stood there breathing heavily. She could feel the blood rushing to her cheeks. She shocked even herself that she could execute such a bold and forward maneuver. Now, with the blood rushing to her face and extremities and alcohol still coursing through her veins, she made her way to the bedroom.

CHAPTER 7

Dierdre left a little earlier than she needed to for her morning meeting with Bobby. She wanted some extra time to drink her coffee and rinse any remaining wine from her system. She was deeply grateful that she mostly just drank wine, and wasn't burdened with a hangover, but she was still a bit groggy, or maybe just tired.

She lost any sense of victory she had felt last night after executing her coup de gras. She remembered thinking at the time that it was a thoroughly well-conceived plan to gain control over a man she thought was toying with her, but all she felt now was regret, and she vowed to push it from her mind and concentrate on the tasks of the day.

She drove through Espresso Express and bought a double espresso for herself and a mocha for Aimee. She arrived at her office, but Aimee wasn't in yet, which was unusual. She left the mocha on Aimee's desk and dropped her valise on her own desk, then trudged on up the hill.

She barely had time to turn on the lights and take her coat off when Bobby arrived. Dierdre heard the door close and looked up in time to see him hold one hand up in the air, spin around and dance across the main lab to the smaller office.

"Good morning Dierdre, how are you this morning?"

She couldn't help laughing. "I'm just fine, and you?"

"Better than fine, I'm fantastic. I haven't had so much fun in a very long time."

Bobby danced his way to the seat in front of the main console. "Hmm, that's not good."

"What?"

He pointed to the numbers in the corner. "They aren't improving any more, or these numbers would be changing. We need to predict the locations a quantum particle might hop around, right?"

"That's my theory."

"How many?"

She took a long sip of her espresso and asked, "How many what?"

"How many hops do we need to correctly predict before you can tap the link that connects to gravity?"

"We don't know that yet. But it would probably take a lot of hops. I still need to find out how many possible locations there are, and how many locations we can manipulate."

"Manipulate? You think you can actually build a machine to tap this link?"

"Maybe," she said, "Stillman, that is, Dr. Whitfield claims they can move molecules around now, it's only a matter of time."

"Well then, I better get this process to provide a better range of numbers."

Bobby entered some codes to shut down the process. "What's this?" As the processes shut down, he came to a screen that was listing off all the processes running. That was not his doing. He hit the attention key and canceled the list, then typed the command, *"whoami"* which responded with *"OPOVERRIDE27."*

"Someone has been here," he said. He then typed, *"history alluser - 12:00:00"* to dump all activity for the last twelve hours.

A cryptic listing rushed up on the screen where he saw OPOVERRIDE27 login and start the process list. The terminal was reacquired by the master program before the listing completed, and no more entries existed for this person. Bobby's eyebrows arched up even further at the next entry.

Another login, many hours after the first, for SYSOEM647 was also terminated when the master program reacquired the console, but then there was a listing for UNKNOWN user. Someone executed a vectored interrupt to dump the user passwords onto CD. Bobby's lips curled into a mischievous smile, hoping that whoever their intruder was enjoyed what they got from that exercise.

"Bobby?" Dierdre asked, "What's going on? First you look surprised, then angry and now you are smiling."

"Nothing I can't handle. We had a couple intruders try to hack into our computer. Both went home empty handed, mostly."

"Mostly?"

Bobby hesitated before deciding to share all. "One of them tried using a special system command to dump all the user IDs and passwords to a Cd. It's there so the vendor can come in and rescue a system if a disgruntled operator changes all the passwords and quits. Anyway, he wanted our passwords, but I had already modified the system so it gave him some different passwords. And if he ever uses them, he will have a law enforcement convention breaking down his doors."

Dierdre tried not to laugh. She did not like how close this was to the kind of mischief that had gotten him into trouble years ago, but she could not ignore the irony. "Speaking of passwords, it seems that you have the keys to them all, and I think I should have those."

He pulled out a tablet, and wrote down a couple user IDs and passwords. "These are yours. You are the Master of this computer. You can go in and disable my password at any time. I promise you, I have no back doors to let me in if you do that. It's all yours."

She took the paper, and for the time being, stuck it in her purse. "Is there anything else that you did for our intruders?"

"Just one," he admitted, "I copied everything off the disk he was using. It included a program to get the user ID and redirect them to the CD, it might have had some old stuff on it. I might be able to identify the intruder if he is known. Right now, though, I want to see what went wrong with the program."

"I barely got here before you," she said, "and it looked like it was still running OK when I got here, I mean, it wasn't locked up or crashed."

"That part worked fine. It kept spawning new copies of itself, but eventually, they were not different enough to show any improvement. I think it's the way I'm generating the numbers. I need to break it up into more small parts, and have a different routine generate each part. Then I need to define a bunch of different ways for each routine to define those parts."

"So, each time it spawns a copy, it changes one of those routines to use a different method for its section of the whole number, that way each program is slightly different from the others. That's how it works like a genetic sequence. I like it."

"OK," Bobby said, "I can work on the programming part, but you still need to do the scientist stuff and see if you can determine how many hits we need to get. As I see it, we are trying to unlock a combination lock, only we don't know how many tumblers there are. I still don't know how you are going to tap it. You said something about moving a particle around to duplicate a quantum path, but I don't see how you will ever do it fast enough."

"That's one of the nice things about quantum events. They might lie outside of time."

"How's that going to help you? Last I check, nobody has invented time travel."

"We don't need to travel in time," she said, "We only need to predict the movement ahead of time, then we move them all at the same time."

"You are going to move one particle to several places at the same time?" Bobby asked incredulously, "If that doesn't unlock the mysteries of Einstein's theory, I don't know what would."

Dierdre wondered how deep his mind went. His I.Q. must be extremely high to grasp this as well as he has. "I'll catch up with you later," she said, "I have some classes to teach."

* * *

Dr. Pietre arrived in his office to find a note from Panopulous to come to the lab right away. When he arrived, he saw all of his assistants huddled around the main computer terminal. Panopulous was at the terminal furiously typing commands and tapping on this key or that key unhappy with the level of response he was getting.

"What is going on here?" Pietre asked the crowd as he entered.

"The system is looping and Arion has been trying all morning to get it under control."

Pietre rolled his eyes at the manpower being wasted. "Shut it down from main control on rack."

"Yes, we tried that," the young assistant said, "but it didn't respond to the shutdown command or the shutdown vector. We even shut down the power, but when we booted it up again, it repeated."

"What is it doing?"

"Whenever anybody logs in, it keeps repeating 'You aren't him' on the terminal. We can't get anything done, because it keeps interrupting any command we try to type, except logoff."

"It is sounding like we have hacker, or maybe a virus." Pietre believed that somehow he was the only one smart enough to make that conclusion.

"Professor, what does the message mean?"

"I don't know. Let me log in and see if it does to me as well."

Pietre waited for his assistant to logoff, and sat down in front of the terminal and typed his user id and password. Immediately after pressing enter the screen went black and displayed in the center. "You are him. Stay out of my business. Stay out of my systems. Stay out of my way." While the message glowed on the terminal, all the disks drives started to shut down in sequence until finally the whole machine shut down, and the screen went completely blank.

"Well. It would appear I have upset someone. Probably gave him poor grade on test."

A few chuckled behind him. Except for his dalliances with coeds, nobody knew of his escapades outside of the class. He took no one into his confidence except for the big man who had funded his project and who now seemed content to turn his back on him. He didn't even have a name for the big man, who never used it and never offered it to anyone. Pietre was sure he was an ex-student, but he could never find any records for him. But that was not surprising, he has learned that the man was quite capable and had ways of making things happen. There was no reason to believe that he could not make things disappear too, like his records.

* * *

Dierdre returned to her office and found Aimee's mocha still sitting on her desk, untouched and stone cold. Clearly Aimee was a no show this morning. She went to her desk to check for a message, but there were no calls on her phone, so she logged into her computer to see if there was an email. Nothing. This was not like her.

Dierdre pulled out her cell phone and recalled Aimee's number. She let it ring ten times before giving up. She thought Aimee might have spent the night at Ramiro's. She searched Aimee's phone for a speed dial with his name. She found one button with a conspicuous heart drawn on it and pressed it. Same results, it rang and rang with no answer.

A sudden irrational panic gripped her as she remembered them picking up the mysterious package and joking about it ticking. Dierdre reached down and pulled open the bottom drawer, the package was still there, undisturbed. She felt like a ninny for suspecting the package like that, and was relieved to see it was still there and Aimee wasn't blown to pieces. Of course there were still plenty of other equally devastating explanations that she did not need to dwell upon.

Dierdre decided to give Aimee another hour. If she doesn't hear from her by then, she will go to her apartment and break down the door if she has to.

* * *

The small man worked all morning long in his small little room on his overly powerful private computer. The phone rang precisely at eight. "Hello?"

The large man said, "It's me. Did you get them?"

"Oh I got them all right," he said, "Listen, maybe it's time you tell me who this kid is."

"Why? What's that got to do with anything?"

"It's got everything to do with everything. He's good, and you don't get this good without getting known somewhere."

"Why?" the large man asked, "What did you get that makes you say that? Weren't you able to crack the encryption on the passwords?"

"Oh I cracked the passwords easy enough. I have a nice long list of user IDs, their passwords, and the remote addresses where you can use them."

"Great! Email them to me."

The small man chuckled and said, "I don't think you want this list."

"Are you saying he made up a list of phony passwords in case someone like yourself tried to get them? He is good."

"No, I'm saying he produced a list of very real passwords in case someone like me tried to get them. In fact, they are not only real, but they are very secretive addresses and passwords. Anyone of them would instantly start a very serious trace and identify the person using it to the CIA, NSA, FBI and probably even Interpol! Now why don't you tell me who he is?"

The large man did not understand the problem and simply stated, "His name is Bobby. Bobby Blain. When he was in High School, he cracked the Federal Reserve Bank, the Treasury, and Wall Street, and transferred a ton of money into the President's bank accounts, but made the transfers look like they were several years old."

"WHAT?!?" the small man screamed, "YOU HAVE ME HACKING INTO BOBBY THE MIDAS'S SYSTEM AND YOU DIDN'T TELL ME???"

"Bobby the Midas? Is that what they call him?"

"Oh God, oh God," the small man panicked, "he probably dumped my disk all the while I thought I was dumping his passwords. He probably knows who I am already. I'm out. You can find someone else to do your dirty work."

"What are you worried about? He's harmless. And if he's so famous, why didn't you recognize him when you met him?"

"You don't get it. He pulled the greatest hack in history. He nearly got a President of the United States impeached, not to mention how many Wall Street tycoons were canned from their cushy jobs. He won't hurt me, he's a good guy. The problem is that he is royalty to the hacker community. He has fans, lots of them, including me."

"So what's the big deal?" the large man asked, "if he comes to you, you apologize."

"I'm not worried about him coming to me, it's the others. The Black Knight, The Trojan Croatian, those guys can really ruin me."

"I thought you were one of the best. Aren't you better than them?"

"Well, yeah."

"But you are saying that you aren't better than this Bobby kid?"

"No one is."

"Are you sure? Has he ever been tested?"

"I don't know," the small man said, "maybe nobody knows. He is very meticulous. Everything he did was elaborate and subtle at the same time. He hacked dozens of computers that went unnoticed, until going about their normal business, the information on them cascaded down to other computers and eventually was noticed by the SEC. It was three years before he was even suspected."

"Maybe we should be recruiting him, instead of trying to tap his work?"

"Why would we need him?"

"You said he's the best."

The small man shrunk in his chair and asked, "But what would I do?"

"You have a problem working with him instead of against him?"

"No."

"And if you end up working for him, is that a problem?"

"No."

"OK," the large man said, "I want you to think up some tests so we can lure him to us. Let's try to prepare a trap for him, so if he doesn't volunteer to work for us, we can entrap him and force him to work for us."

"I don't think you can trap him like that."

"I think you overestimate him. I've met him now, he is crafty, but I don't think he's as calculating as you think he is. Remember, they caught him. Perhaps he is not as good as his reputation."

"They only caught him because he became so famous. All direct attempts to learn his identity failed. It wasn't until they found some clumsy wanna be hackers who gave him up, just because he was so famous and they were so stupid."

* * *

Dierdre was about to leave for her first lecture when a figure appeared in her doorway, quietly standing there. She looked up and saw Ernesto Vasquez with his hat in his hands and his head hung low, as if he were studying his shoes. He glanced up now and then to see if Dierdre had noticed him yet. "Professor, excuse me. Is she here?"

"Aimee? No, I haven't seen her."

"Gracias," he said as he turned and left.

Dierdre cocked her head a moment then jumped out of her seat and bolted to the door yelling, "Ernesto!"

The old man stopped shuffling his feet and stood there a moment before turning around.

"Ernesto, what's going on? Why the cloak and dagger treatment yesterday? Why weren't you there to meet us?"

"It's all my fault. My shame. All mine. I'm sorry you were dragged into my mess." He turned to leave again.

"Do you know where she is? Is she in some kind of trouble?"

"I don't know where she is." He left.

Dierdre returned to her desk and tried calling Aimee again. Still no answer. Then, from her doorway she heard Ernesto say, "My son had a fight with her. He left her. I don't know where she is, but she probably needs you. He was wrong to blame her."

* * *

Bobby finished making his program changes and started another run. The graph screen came up again and showed all the programs running. He left it running, and expected he would have enough data to work with by lunch time. He sent a note to Dierdre that they should meet again around one o'clock to see the new results.

He grabbed his backpack and jacket and left the lab, locking it securely behind him.

* * *

Dierdre wasn't sure what to do. She had a class to get to, but needed to see if Aimee was OK. Her plan to wait an hour did not seem to make as much sense as it had before. She could give the class an assignment to work on, but that would only be busy work for them, she taught by giving them lectures and they were expected to read and research between lectures.

She checked her email one more time, there was a note from Bobby, but nothing from Aimee. Ultimately, she just could not abandon her class. She loved teaching as much as she loved learning. She was fortunate enough to teach a class that students signed up for when they really wanted to learn, not like English 101 which was a required course that some hated.

She quickly drafted a note to Aimee, "If you get this note, come see me or send someone."

* * *

Ernesto had not left the campus yet. He moved along slowly, looking at the faces of all the young people he passed outside. It had been a long time since he had spent any time looking at young people. Their faces weren't just young, but they were eager and filled with the anticipation of what was to come. Their roads stretched out as far in front of them as Ernesto's stretched behind him.

He made his way through the campus, zig zag fashion, shuffling his feet as he went. His chin was overrun with stubble, and his overcoat was overly stained with everything. He looked like an old retired gardener come to see how the tree he planted decades ago was doing. He turned the corner around the cafeteria, almost to the bus stop, when someone stopped him.

"Dad, what are you doing here?"

He didn't even lift his gaze from the ground for his son. "I came to fix things."

"Haven't you done enough?"

"No son, I haven't. You were wrong, but it was still my fault. It is my shame that has ruined everything. I must fix things."

"What are you mumbling about? Are you going senile on me?"

"Senile? No. Maybe I should. Maybe I wish I had Alzenhammers, so I could forget."

"Alzheimer's?" Ramiro asked, "I don't think you want that."

"Maybe not, I just want to forget. I thought I had forgotten. But it's all fresh in my memory now. It's all my fault."

"You still haven't told me what you are doing here. Did you see Aimee?"

"No," Ernesto said, "No Aimee, I didn't see Aimee."

"I have to see her, go sit and wait at that bench. I'll drive you home after I see her." Ramiro pointed at a bench by the bus stop, and took off towards her office.

Ernesto yelled after his son, "She's not there. No Aimee."

Ramiro stopped before he had even reached full speed. "What? You went to her office and she's not there?"

"Not there. The professor has not seen her."

Ramiro thought it over a moment and said, "Come on dad. I'll drive you home, then I'll find her."

* * *

Pietre sent everyone from the lab as the computer came back on. He had no idea what he was going to find, but if anything there implicated him in anyway, he did not want any witnesses. But, as things turned out, his precautions were completely unnecessary. The computer booted up clean and good as new. All his work, even the work he stole from Dr. Karlyn, appeared to be intact. He checked the logs, but could not identify anyone having made an unauthorized entry to the machine. He didn't know how, but he was pretty sure he knew who, and he was just as sure that his large friend, his previous benefactor, would have the resources to help him find out more.

He had no intention of letting some young punk intimidate him like this. He also had no intention of letting Dierdre's project steal away his benefactor. Whatever Bobby had done to his computer was a direct attack. This was war now. And he knew a trick or two, but mostly he knew some people with some very convincing ways about them.

Tonight he will place some calls and gather some support.

* * *

Dierdre finished her lecture, and spent a moment answering questions for some of the stragglers, then she briskly made her way back to her office. The message light on her phone was blinking.

"D, I'm OK, I just need some time off. I'll call you." Aimee's voice was tired, and it sounded like she had practiced what she would say over and over until she could repeat it without crying, but it was enough to relieve Dierdre's panic.

With one tragedy averted, Dierdre decided to have a peek at the project and see how it was coming along. If Bobby was there, maybe they could work on it a bit, and if not, she could try some of the commands he showed her to follow its progress.

* * *

Bobby stopped in at Dierdre's office, after lunch, but neither she nor Aimee was there. He turned to head up to the lab when Dr. Whitfield came in.

"Oh, hello Bobby."

"Dr. Whitfield."

"That was some show you put on last night."

"The music?" Bobby asked, "I didn't do anything, I just set up the mikes and the mixer."

"No, not the music, the dancing. You are quite some dancer, though I'm not sure it's entirely appropriate for a student to be dancing with his teacher."

"I agree entirely Dr. Whitfield, so I chose to dance with my project colleague instead. Dancing with a student would be a terrible social feaux pax, don't you think?"

"Clever as you are, I'm not sure that calling your teacher a colleague is sufficient to overcome the basic fact that the two of you were quite a spectacle."

"You may be correct Dr. Whitfield. Of course, it could have been worse. She could have been dancing with TWO students at the same time."

"I'm afraid you've lost me, my boy."

"You're a smart man, I'm sure if you put your mind to it, you'll recall the spectacle last night of a faculty member dancing with two students."

A light came on behind Stillman's eyes, but it was more like a giant slap in the face. He started to speak, he wanted to warn Bobby about being so insolent with a faculty member, but he stopped himself. He had pretty much forgotten about the sorority sisters, and in fact, fleeting pictures of Bobby and Dierdre dancing were all he had remembered prior to Dierdre's kiss which was etched into his memory.

Bobby started to push past him, when Stillman reached an arm out to stop him, not forcefully, merely a gesture requesting that he not run off yet. "Bobby, have you seen Professor Jennings? Is she up in her lab?"

"I haven't seen her since this morning. I'm pretty sure her morning lecture is over by now, maybe she's at lunch with Aimee."

"Aimee hasn't shown up or called in all morning. Her whereabouts are a bit of a mystery."

"I'm heading up to the lab now, if she is there, would you like me to tell her you were asking for her?"

"If it's not too much trouble, you may tell her I came to call on her."

Bobby went one way, and Stillman went the other.

* * *

Dierdre found the lab empty. She went to her small office and logged into the terminal. She pulled out her notebook and entered a command Bobby setup to show her a graph of how many sequences were being correctly predicted, and how much the threads were or were not improving.

According to the graph, there was considerable improvement when he started the process but, it quickly leveled off. According to her calculations, the results they were getting were very mediocre, and should be much better.

She pulled up a listing of the program he was running when she heard the door open and someone entered the lab. "Professor

Jennings? It's me, Bobby."

"We aren't getting the kind of numbers I was expecting," she said, "Is there some way to compare the algorithms that are being used by each of the threads?"

"Yes. This newest version creates a record of each spawned thread that shows which algorithms were utilized." He scribbled a name on a sticky note, "Here, use this command to view them. There are a lot of entries, I'm still working on a better way to filter out the ones we want to look at, but for now you can sort them by the time they were spawned, or by how many sequences they got correct."

Dierdre entered the command, and chose the option to sort them by the most sequences. She tabbed her cursor to the first one, and selected it to view. When she had seen enough, she tabbed down and looked at the second one.

She pointed at the screen and said, "These two are completely unrelated. They are using entirely different algorithms and getting the same results, and neither is very spectacular."

"Maybe we need to let it run longer?"

"No, I don't think that's it." She got up and paced around the room a bit. "How many different possible algorithms are there?"

"The algorithm sequence is composed of two-hundred-fifty-six unique sequential parts, and each of those can be one of sixteen different routines. That gives us almost three-hundred-trillion unique variations."

"OK," she said, "Ultimately, three-hundred-trillion may not be enough, but that's not the problem I think. Out of those two-hundred-fifty-six sequential routines, some are aiming at the right target and some are not. As long as we keep spawning the new threads with random differences, we will continue to get a mediocre result. But if we take two threads that work, and only take the good algorithms from each, and combine them to spawn a new thread, then the new thread should be better than each of the parent threads."

"True, if we could identify which algorithms made it work."

"We don't need to. Take two parent threads. Make up a child thread from parts of each parent. It might be better or worse. Make ten children, or a hundred. Now out of that group, select the best of them. Repeat that process and they should improve beyond where they are now, which is pretty average."

Bobby saw what she was describing in his mind. He was nodding his head. "I like it. I like it. Best of all, it fits nicely with what we already have, and won't be too hard to program."

Dierdre liked being able to describe the process she had in her mind, and then have someone else turn it into computer code. She was much better at reading what he programmed than she ever was at writing it herself. "I'll get out of your hair. I have some papers to grade."

"Dr. Whitfield asked me to let you know he stopped by to see you."

Dierdre's cheeks blushed as she remembered what she had done to him last night.

"Guess you made an impression on him last night. He also seemed to feel you shouldn't be fraternizing with your students. If I didn't know better, I would have thought he sounded jealous. Ridiculous, huh?"

"Yeah," she said, "nonsense."

"I set him straight though, I told him that we were technically colleagues, and that it's not even a felony when there is only one student involved."

"Oh no, you didn't!"

"Well not those exact words," he said, "but my implication was clear enough. I don't think he will be throwing any more stones in our direction."

"He really is a nice man," she said, "but last night he didn't seem himself."

"Maybe we should be checking for pods around the campus."

"Pods?"

"Invasion of the Body Snatchers, 1952. Alien plants land on earth and grow human clones in pods that replace the real people?"

Dierdre shook her head and said, "Don't know it."

"You need to get out more. I'm going to have to educate you."

* * *

Bobby continued to refine the program. Each program was made of two-hundred-fifty six segments. Each segment of the program had sixteen possible ways that it could influence the number it was going to generate. One method could add, another subtracted, and a couple methods used a computer mechanism called rotate left and rotate right, while still others multiplied. What it all boiled down to was building a number. What each segment did to build that number was critical, and so was the order they did them in.

The first version of the spawning routine took a single thread, and randomly changed between one and eight of the two-hundred-fifty-six segments. That made the new thread slightly different from the old thread, and if it was better, then it replaced the old thread.

Problems cropped up when a segment did something that had an enormous effect, like if after two-hundred-twelve segments worked hard to compute a number and the next segment then multiplied it by zero, negating all of previous segments. But the biggest problem was getting rid of that bad segment. Once one thread like that had a slightly better number than the parent, it was hard to get rid of.

The new solution, inspired by Dierdre, was to mimic chromosomes. Two parents would provide their sequences, then the program would break their sequences into eight strands, and swap every other strand. Now, if one parent owed its good results to segments fifteen through forty-five, and the other parent owed its good results to segments one-hundred-eighty-five through two-hundred-fifteen, then there was a chance that one of the offspring might benefit from having both sections of segments. But it was only a chance, so the process had to be repeated.

As Bobby went through the mental exercise of planning out the reproduction routines, he began to understand why mammals have so many children. He had previously thought it was only a numbers game, survival of the fittest. Sea turtles hatch hundreds of babies so a few might survive. But now, he saw that there was much more to it. The survival of any species also depended on its adaptability. More offspring meant more adaptability.

As he converted the thoughts in his mind's eye, he thought of one other thing, spontaneous mutation. There might be a need for some random modifications to the sequences, so he kept a copy of the old process that randomly changed a few segments, and he coded it to occur very rarely, perhaps every three to ten thousand spawns.

As he completed his changes, and ran a few preliminary tests, he stepped back and looked at his creation. The hairs on the back of his neck stood at attention. There have been many times that he has created programs that were grand achievements, but never before, had he come away with the feeling that he had truly created something.

Satisfied with the preliminary testing, he cleared the system, and started up the full tests. He went to his backpack, and pulled out a piece of cardboard he had his friends in the media center make for him. He placed it on top of the computer rack. Written on the front of it, with bright red ink, in OCR MICR letters, like the numbers on a bank check, was written, P.A.P.A. He had only intended it to stand for Parallel Algorithms for Pattern Acquisition, but now, as he watched the fledgling programs spawn brood after brood, it seemed to have much deeper significance.

CHAPTER 8

Dr. Pietre had been watching from his lab. He had already sent his team home for the night and told them that since it was Thursday night, they could take off Friday for a three day weekend. He installed a webcam and pointed it through one of the open vents over the door to his lab so he could see anyone enter or exit Dierdre's lab. Now he sat alone in his lab watching his monitors and waiting.

When Bobby left the lab and locked the door behind him, Pietre sat up and leaned forward in his chair. He directed his mouse over a button on the screen and changed the view to another camera which was directed down the hall so he could observe Bobby leaving the building. After Bobby was completely out, he crept out of his office and walked past Dierdre's lab. He had previously noted that Bobby only turns the small office lights out when he leaves for the final time, and he could see through the frosted glass in the door, that the office lights were out now.

He went back to his office, picked up the phone and dialed a number he had memorized long ago. When the other party answered, he spoke Russian into the phone, "He just left...Da...Da...One hour. See you."

His call had been expected. He had already contacted his friends earlier that day and formulated a plan of attack. He went back to his lab to wait the hour for his friends to arrive. He fidgeted in his seat the whole time. He browsed the Internet, played solitaire on the computer, but each passing minute just made him more anxious.

Finally he could stand it no more. He left his lab and crossed down the hall to Dierdre's lab, and used the special key he had made to let himself in. The lab was pretty much as he had seen before. The same program was running with the graphs going up and down on the screen.

This time, though, instead of trying to interrupt the main console, he went to Dierdre's old computer in the small office. He pressed a key to wake it up, but it asked for a password. He pulled a small mini-cd from his pocket and put it in the machine, then pressed the reset button on the computer tower. The screen blacked out, and went through the various boot phases, checking memory, checking add-on hardware, mounting drives, then the CD light started to flicker, and it started to load a new boot from the CD-ROM he had inserted. The screen continued to list various systems being initialized until finally it ended with a prompt for a user ID.

He pulled himself up to the keyboard and typed *"root"*, then when it asked for password, he typed *"noyb"* which stood for none of your business. The screen presented him with a *HOME>* prompt. He started browsing through the data on the hard drive. There wasn't much there, but he found a folder filled with documents including the paper that earned Dierdre so much notoriety. Also in the folder were some programs having names similar to that document.

Her programs were all about simulating the motion of quantum mechanics. He pulled another CD from his pocket and swapped it with the one he booted from earlier. He mounted the new CD and copied the folder onto it. Then he erased the folder, and wiped all the documents and programs within it from the hard drive.

"I thought I told you to wait for me?" It was his hacker friend.

"I save you some time. I'm done now anyway. Do your stuff."

The Russian, a short balding man with bad teeth went to the tower and ejected the CD.

Pietre swooped down and grabbed the CD. "That's mine."

The balding man then stuck his own CD in and pressed the reset button.

"The rest is automatic. What have we got here?" The short man went to the big computer and started inspecting it inside and out. "You should have told me, I could have prepared something for this machine too."

"No need," Pietre said, "Once she logs in from smaller computer, virus will spread to it."

"You idiot. The virus cannot spread from that machine to this one, they are totally incompatible."

"No matter. We can always come back and do this one later."

"Just how many favors do you think I owe you Dimitri? I think we are now even. Let us close this account forever."

"Just one more then," Pietre said, "Send me virus that would work on this computer. I will install it myself."

"Da. I can do that, if you promise that I will never hear from you again."

"Agreed."

The smaller computer finished booting, and the balding Russian ejected his CD and left. The virus was now installed in the boot sector of the hard drive. In the morning, someone will find their handiwork.

* * *

Early the next morning, around three, the large man's smaller friend entered Dierdre's lab. He too proceeded to the smaller computer and placed a CD in the tower and pressed the reset. After the CD completed booting the machine, he copied some spy programs onto the computer that scanned for terminal emulation programs and modified them to send passwords across the Internet to a small server hidden somewhere across the country in an empty office. As soon as anyone logged into the big machine, he would have a copy of their password waiting for him. He only had to log into that server from time to time and pick up whatever was captured.

After he copied the scanning programs, he ran a small job that inserted a call into the boot sector to make sure that his scanning program was loaded with the system, but that job crashed and gave him an error number. He ran it again to be sure, same error.

That was not supposed to happen. He called up a boot viewer that let him examine the boot sector directly. What he found was an already modified boot sector, a virus. And the date on the file showed it was only a few hours earlier. He checked the logs for that time period, but there were no entries, nobody logged in and no jobs were running. That's not impossible, what he was doing now wouldn't show up in the logs either, because he didn't boot off the hard drive, he wasn't running that operating system.

Quickly, before he did anything more, he ran a program that dumped all the memory, and all the disk caches into a file. He knew that whatever he found would be tainted because he had already accessed the CD, but there was a chance that there could be some buffer space that he didn't overwrite yet. He might find a clue as to what was going on, and he did.

One of the files on that CD had a Russian file name, which was no surprise since he had already caught Pietre interfering with this project before. He found evidence of an entire folder being copied to CD. The folder appeared to be deleted from the hard drive. He ran another tool that scanned the hard drive for remnants of that folder, it was cleverly deleted, but his program found enough check bits in the error correction code that he could reconstruct the folder and all the contents.

He was about to undo the deleted folder and remove the virus, when it occurred to him, that it might be beneficial for him, if he leaves it all there in its deleted state, and makes sure that Bobby can tell who did it. If he can distract Bobby by implicating Pietre, then maybe he can monitor things without being detected. And if the big guy really did want Bobby recruited, they wouldn't be adversaries if he ever approached him.

He modified his program to insert the password scanning code before Pietre's virus, and instead of sending the passwords to a remote server as he planned, he sent them to Pietre's private computer, he can still pick them up from there.

The last thing he did, before leaving, was run a cleanup program to clear the buffers he was just looking at, but to only clear the amount with his stuff in it.

Before leaving the campus entirely, he made a brief stop at Pietre's lab.

* * *

Friday morning showed no signs of the usual joy associated with the last day of the work week. Aimee, who was usually the first one in, was still a no-show, and there was no new email or phone message from her. Aimee was a big girl, and could take care of herself, but Dierdre kept picturing her spending the entire weekend moping in her apartment, and as her best friend, it was her responsibility to shake some sense into her. Her students can fend for themselves for one morning. She grabbed her coat and purse, and was about to head out when the phone rang.

"Aimee?"

"No, it's Bobby. I think you should come to the lab. You should see this for yourself."

There was something ominous in his voice. Dierdre bit her lip a moment, "OK, I'll be right there."

Now Aimee will have to wait, and from the looks of things, she is not going anywhere. Dierdre wondered if anything about this day would be normal.

Bobby had his laptop attached to the big computer and was watching the programs run when Dierdre arrived.

"What's wrong?"

"Wrong? Nothing, except maybe we need more speed, but look at them run. After running all night, we've spawned thousands of generations, and they still are managing to improve the formula every couple minutes."

"Every couple minutes?" she asked, "Yikes. I was hoping the simulation would be measured in seconds not minutes. Ultimately, we need a machine that can find a solution in less than thousandths of a second, not in minutes."

"Well that's where you're million processors will help."

"But we don't have millions of processors, this is all we got."

"Maybe," he said, "maybe not. I know some guys in these huge clubs. They throw computer parties once a month. Once a year, they throw a really big party with thousands of people all hooking up computers."

"OK, but where's this going?"

"I'm getting there. They usually ask me to help with set up, and sometimes I help them find some equipment. It just so happens, that you have some equipment they are looking for. If you loan them the equipment, I'll bet that most of them would let you borrow their computers while they aren't using them. That would add another thousand processors to your system."

"You mean you can load these threads across different platforms?"

"Yeah," he said, "Maybe not all platforms, just some, so far."

"Show me. Add this one." She pointed to the computer in her office. She reached down and hit a key to wake up the monitor.

"OK. Let me do some set up over here, just a moment..."

"Bobby?"

"Just a sec, I'm working on it."

"Bobby? What's this mean?"

"What's what?"

"I think you need to come look at this screen."

Dierdre stepped back so Bobby could see it clearly. Bobby left what he was doing, stepped around the desk and looked into the monitor. "What the…"

On the screen, where there should have been a boot up screen, was a sign with big letters reading, *"You have been caught hacking the wrong system. Now all your systems are mine."*

"Bobby, what does this mean? What have you been doing?"

"Nothing. I've only been working on your system. Remember before, I told you we had intruders? Well, they're back."

Dierdre's trust in Bobby wavered and she said, "What have you done to make these kind of people want to attack us like this?"

"What makes you so sure it's something I did? Maybe they are after you, or maybe they just want your project, or even simpler, just want you and your project out of the way."

"I'm sorry Bobby. I want to believe you, but none of this ever happened until you came along."

"It's not my fault. Remember also, that none of this happened until you got this computer. Someone out there, and I think I know who, has some hidden agenda, and for some reason, your project is in the way. First it was Karlyn, now he is out of the way and you are next."

"You are suggesting it was…"

"Shhhh." Bobby stopped her from finishing her sentence, "I'm not suggesting anything yet. I'm only saying something is going on."

Dierdre thought it was odd that Bobby would not mention any names, even though she thought she knew who he suspected. But it wasn't the strangest or worst thing to fall upon them. "I'm going to go check on Aimee, how long before you can get this guy fixed up?"

"It will probably take most of the morning. When I do get it up and running, I'll setup that demo for you."

"After lunch then?"

"Yeah," he said, "after lunch is fine."

Bobby sat down at the small computer and scowled at it. It really put a damper on what had been a pretty successful test of their system.

* * *

Pietre arrived at the his office pleased with himself for what he had done, but as he set his briefcase down on his desk, before he had even taken off his coat, the dean's secretary stuck her head in the door and said, "Before you get comfortable, you should head up to your lab and see what you can do to fix things."

"Fix things?"

"I don't know what needs fixing," she said, "but none of our computers are working and they say it's coming from your lab."

"What is it coming from my lab?" Pietre asked incredulously.

The woman was clearly tired of being asked stupid questions she had no way of answering and brusquely said, "I guess you had better move your buns up to your lab and see for yourself!"

Pietre hustled up to his lab and once again found all his assistants congregated around his computer.

"What is going on here? I gave all you day off."

"Some day off," said one.

"Where've you been?" asked another.

"Doesn't your phone work?" All their voices were sounding off together now. "Why does the dean wake us up instead of you?"

Pietre put his hands up to calm them down. "Slow down, one per time please. What goes on?"

"We can't get into the system to see exactly what it is doing, but we can tell you that it is using up network traffic and passing huge quantities of data all over the place."

"All over university?" Pietre asked.

"All over the world."

"Did you pull plug and disconnect from Internet?"

"We tried that, and the whole school went from being super slow to a dead stop. Somehow, every server in the school is being routed through this computer. But there is more going on than just routing the school through it, the disk drives are running constantly, and the traffic to the outside is enormous, I think it's downloading stuff, maybe setting up mirrors for someone. None of us can login to verify this, but maybe you can, like last time."

"Like last time," Pietre repeated. He dreaded being the one, if it were true, who could still log in.

He sat down at the terminal and typed his user ID and password. His screen immediately displayed big large block letters. *"I WARNED YOU ONCE. THIS IS YOUR FINAL WARNING. STAY OUT OF MY*

BUSINESS."

He hit the enter key and the warning faded away. He ordered a directory listing, and it was enormous.

His students gathered around him staring at the screen. "Look at the size of those files, and look at the file extensions, you know what those are?"

"Da," Dimitri confided, "I know what those are."

The disks whirred away as the system filled with more and more of the world's pornography, illegally copied music and movies. Pietre's computer had just become the world's largest illegal peer to peer swap site. And if that weren't bad enough, it was spamming the world that it was there and ready for business.

"Get me Dean on phone." Pietre tried shutting down the system, but he was relatively sure it would not be that easy.

Panopulous brought him the cordless phone they used in the lab. "Here, it's ringing now."

"Hello?"

"Dean Smithers? This is Dr. Pietre. Someone hacked my main computer and the school's entire LAN network. Before I start fixing this computer, we need network experts to fix LAN so regular servers work again. Yes. I think I know who did it. No, I have no proof. Yes, we will take measures to safeguard system in future."

The line went dead. He pulled out the slip of paper he had used yesterday. The short Russian never wanted to hear from him again, well maybe one more time wouldn't hurt. He dialed the number and listened to it ring, then it picked up and he heard, "The number you have reached is not in service and there is no new number. Please check your number and dial again."

* * *

Dierdre's mind buzzed with information overload. Intellectually, she believed Bobby, but she was having trouble taking the step from belief to trust. Doubts and uncertainty nagged at her. One thing she could not deny was his ability to convert her ideas into code far faster than she ever could. The advances she saw this morning were enormous, and the possibility of adding other networked computers was staggering. If adding her smaller computer proved a success, she could add her computer in her office, and Aimee's, which both sat idle during the night. And, Bobby said he had friends who could share their machines in return for her help. She wondered how productive that might be.

The distance to Aimee's apartment was not great, but it provided Dierdre with ample time to daydream about a nationwide club with millions of computers letting her share them. She pulled up in front of Aimee's apartment and climbed the steps to her door.

"Aimee?" Dierdre banged on the front door. Aimee had the upper unit of a split level flat. The front door was recessed in a small alcove at the top of a wooden flight of stairs. "Aimee, it's me! Open the door!"

Dierdre pressed her ear to the door but could hear nothing from inside. She crossed the porch and leaned over the railing. Aimee's car was still in her parking space. "Aimee! I know you're in there! Let me in."

"I don't think she's there," Ramiro said from the bottom of the stairway.

"She has to be here, her car's still in its stall."

"She wouldn't leave you out here like this."

Dierdre spun around and looked Ramiro in the eye. "Then that's even worse," she didn't mean to yell, but her voice was uncontrollably loud, "if she's not answering to let me in, something is seriously wrong. And what are you doing here anyway?"

Ramiro held up a finger indicating she should pause her tirade while he spoke on the phone. "Hello? Patricia? This is Ramiro. How quickly can you file an emergency entry order? Missing person, possible life endangerment, not a search or seizure. No visible signs of foul play. Next of kin? No, will a fiancé do? OK thanks, type it up and file it." Ramiro gave Aimee's address to the secretary then hung up the phone.

Dierdre shifted her weight to one side, placed her hands on her hips and waited. "What now?"

Ramiro pulled a key from his pocket, held it up in the light so Dierdre could see. "Now we go in."

"If you have a key, why did you file all that legal stuff to get in?"

"That was in case she is in there and doesn't want to see me, and I wouldn't blame her for that."

"A lawyer to the end I see."

Ramiro grunted and moved forward, inserted the key into the lock, and opened the door. It swung open quietly and revealed a dim but spotless apartment. They went straight to the bedroom, then the bathrooms and finally the kitchen and living room. Not only was Aimee not there, but there was no sign that she had been there. The bed was made, which considering the spotless condition of the apartment, did not mean anything one way or another.

Dierdre looked in her closet. "Look at this. Do you know how many luggage bags she has? Because this looks like a full set, there doesn't appear to be any missing."

Ramiro was rummaging through her medicine cabinet in the bathroom. "How are we supposed to know if anything is missing when she keeps everything so perfectly tidy?" Frustration was clearly evident in his voice. "I guess that didn't make much sense."

"No, in a strange way, I think I understood. Her purse is not on the hall table where she leaves it when she is here. Except for her car being here, it doesn't even look like she was ever here. This is a waste of time. If I were her, I might be out getting drunk."

"She's not in any of the nearby bars, I checked."

"How about the parks?"

"The parks?" Ramiro asked, "Why would she be there?"

"Maybe she was crying, or went for a walk and just decided to sit down and watch the sunrise."

Ramiro pulled out his phone again. "Patricia, ask Chief Henderson to send some patrol cars to all the parks in this area for a quick search. Yes, tell him it's for me." He left the apartment, locking the door behind him.

"She's probably OK," Dierdre said, "at least she sounded OK yesterday."

"You talked to her yesterday?" Ramiro sounded anxious, this was the first news he had of any contact with her at all.

"She left a message that she was OK and she'd probably be back in today. I haven't heard anything today."

"Maybe you should go back to the school in case she contacts you again."

After Dierdre left, Ramiro's phone rang in his pocket. He pulled it out and answered, "Hello? Ramiro Vasquez speaking."

"Good morning Your Honor, sir, Chief Henderson here."

"Mitch, you don't always have to be so formal."

"OK Ramiro, I don't want to alarm you, but do you want me to do a full missing persons check on her?"

"What would that include that we aren't already doing?"

"An APB would be sent to patrol cars, we'd check incoming patients in hospitals, and the morgue, plus a check of outbound airline, train and bus passengers."

Ramiro was stunned a bit when his friend listed the morgue among places to check. "Thanks Mitch, I'd appreciate it if you can check those for me. One more thing Mitch..."

Ramiro paused a moment to think how he would phrase his next sentence.

"Ramiro? You still there?"

"I'm here. Mitch, she's important to me. We're engaged to be married, at least, I think we still are."

"I'm sure she's fine, and we'll all laugh about this at your wedding."

"Whatever you find out," Ramiro continued, "good or bad, I want to know, but could you do me a favor?"

"Anything."

"Could you give me the news in person? I don't want bad news over the phone, and I don't want to think it's bad news just because I see you, so good or bad, can you come see me to tell me?"

"Sure Squeeze," Captain Henderson said, "I can do that for you. Don't you worry, we'll find her."

"Squeeze, nobody's called me that in a long time. Matter of fact, there aren't so many I would let call me that today, but from you, I like it. It reminds me how far back we go."

* * *

Bobby had his hands full with the old computer system. His first inclination was to restore it from a backup, but all of the backups were unreadable. Bad backups happen, but for all of them to be bad smelled like sabotage. Without the backups he was forced to rebuild the operating system from the install CD's.

He was busy entering configuration parameters by hand when the dean came in and interrupted him.

"Where is Professor Jennings?"

The dean's voice startled Bobby. "Professor Jennings? I think she said she was going to check on Aimee. I guess she's been sick the last couple of days." Bobby continued to work while he spoke.

"Can you please stop what you are doing, and explain to me what you are doing here?"

Bobby stopped entering the config data, and looked at the dean. He now saw the expression on the dean's face and knew that something was wrong. "You know she hired me as her project assistant, right?"

"Yes, I know all about that. I also have a sterling recommendation from Dr. Karlyn, which is why I came here alone. Are you aware of the problems we have had this morning with our computer systems?"

"No, sir, sorry, but I've been pretty busy with our own problems here."

"Problems?" the dean asked, "What kind of problems are you having?"

"Well sir, I can't really point fingers yet, but someone hacked our system last night, and it wasn't the first time, and more than one person has been in here hacking us. Last night, they loaded a virus on this computer and I think they destroyed all the backups, that is, the backups are ruined, I am only guessing it was done maliciously."

"Hmmm. Pietre's machine was hacked last night too, though I would suggest his is far worse than yours."

"Dr. Pietre? That can't be a coincidence."

"What do you mean?"

Bobby cleared his throat and explained, "Well, I can't prove anything, but there were bits and pieces of evidence suggesting that he may have been the one who hacked us last night."

The dean's posture stiffened as he asked, "Are you accusing a faculty member?"

"No sir, that's why I said I didn't have enough evidence."

"Bobby," the dean asked point blank, "did you hack his machine?"

"No sir."

"Not even in retaliation?"

"Absolutely not. The only thing I did was load a special program on PAPA, that's the big machine, so that when one of our intruders tried to copy our passwords he got a bunch of passwords that would immediately notify the FBI if he tried to use them."

"You can do that?"

"That's it!" Bobby exclaimed, "That must be why they hacked this system!"

Bobby went back to the computer and opened up a new window, and called up a view of the boot sector. He started pointing at the vector with the virus in it and shouted, "There, that's where they put the virus. I was so busy trying to get rid of the virus I never even noticed the code behind it. That one there," he pointed again, then he cleared the screen and brought up another sector of the boot image, "it runs a program here. This program adds a call into the terminal program..." Again, he cleared the screen and brought up another sector of the disk, "...and it calls this program, look! Look! It sends the input buffer, that's where the user just typed their login ID and password. It sends it to this email account, look for yourself!"

The dean leaned over and saw that indeed, Dr. Pietre's email address was there. "That doesn't prove anything," the dean said, "at least not to me. You know I am only taking your word for it that it does all that. Whatever is going on here has to end. Pietre wants you expelled."

The dean started to leave. "I'm not taking any actions at this point, please have Professor Jennings call me if you see her, but understand, I'll need something pretty substantial to continue fending off Dr. Pietre."

* * *

When Dierdre arrived at her office, there was a cryptic note on her desk:

> *"Missing anything? Log into www.woodlandu.org/ransom for details."*

"What the hell?" Dierdre's phone rang just as she was reaching for it. "Hello? This is Professor Jennings."

"Professor, this is Dean Smithers. Are you aware of what's going on?"

"I just got back and saw the note on my desk. Oh my God, is it

Aimee?"

"Aimee? What are you talking about?"

"The ransom. She's the only one I'm missing."

"Ransom?" the dean asked, "I'm talking about the computer problems."

"You know about that too? What is going on? Why am I under attack like this? I better call Ramiro and let him know."

"Who's Ramiro?" the dean asked, "And what does he have to do with anything?"

"He's Aimee's fiancé, and if someone is holding her for ransom, I think he should know."

"Aimee's been kidnapped?" the dean shouted, "What the hell is going on around here?"

"I'll call you back, Dean. I have to tell him about this."

"I think it's time we get the police involved."

"Ramiro is a Judge, I'm sure he'll know who to notify."

"Be sure to call me back," the dean said, "we need to discuss the situation with Bobby."

"Right away." She hung up the phone and the deans words reverberated in her head, "Situation with Bobby?" Things just kept getting stranger and stranger.

She went to Aimee's desk and punched the speed dial with the heart. "Ramiro?"

"Speaking. Dierdre?"

"I think you should come to the university. I have some bad news for you."

"Bad news?" Ramiro asked, "What's wrong? Is it Aimee? Oh my God, is she hurt?"

"Honestly, I don't know anything for sure. There is a strange note on my desk. It sounds like maybe Aimee has been kidnapped."

Ramiro's heart sunk deep within his chest. He never liked getting bad news over the phone. "Kidnapped? Are you sure?"

"No, I'm not sure, but I have a strange note on my desk about something missing and a web address to get ransom instructions."

"I'll be right there."

"Ramiro, I have not touched the note or gone to the web site. I figure you know who to call to examine the note. I'll have my guy look at the website and find out what it is all about. There is something very strange going on around here, and I can't rule out some kind of prank, but I think we should treat it seriously."

"I agree. I'll be right there."

Dierdre hung up the phone and pushed the button for Dean Smithers.

"Dean, this is Dierdre again. What was that you said about Bobby?"

"Someone has hacked Dr. Pietre's computer and seriously damaged our entire schools ability to use their computers."

"Are you aware that someone has been hacking our computers as well?"

"Pietre is convinced that Bobby is doing it."

"He's wrong," Dierdre said emphatically, "Bobby is doing a great job here. You should see him. He has way too much going for him to jeopardize it like that."

"None the less, Dr. Pietre is demanding his expulsion. I need something concrete to clear him."

"Why? Does Pietre have something concrete implicating Bobby?"

"No. But Bobby has a history."

"Have you reviewed Bobby's History in detail?"

"No," the dean admitted.

"Maybe you should."

"He hacked the President right? What more do I need to know?"

"First of all," Dierdre said, "he didn't hack the President, he hacked a governor who became president. But only after the governor had involved Bobby's father in some business venture. Who would turn down a business venture with the Governor? Well the deal went bad, Bobby's father lost their house, and when there were questions of impropriety, Bobby's father ended up going to prison, and the Governor went to the white house. I think I'd have hacked him myself, though I would have preferred hacking him with a machete."

"Still, he broke the law."

"Let's try and be exact for a moment. He was rumored to have allegedly broken the law. Charges were brought up, but he was never convicted, and all the charges were dropped. And the alleged hacking occurred before he was fifteen. I think he deserves the benefit of the doubt."

The dean sunk back in his chair and sighed into the phone. "I hear you, but I have the word of a faculty professor against the word of a student with a reputation. How am I supposed to tell Pietre that his charges are baseless?"

"Just like that," she said, "You say, Pietre, your charges are baseless, now piss off."

Smithers snickered. He would love to tell Pietre to piss off, he couldn't, but it was a nice thought. "OK, if you feel that strongly about it, I'll go to bat for him one more time. But this is the last time, you hear me?"

"No, I don't hear you. My project is on the verge of proving something really big, something you have been bugging me for. I need Bobby. He has advanced my project by years, and he has only been with me a couple weeks. I will not lose him. If you expel him, you may lose more than you bargained for." Dierdre couldn't believe she just said that. She just implied that she would leave and take her project with her if he canned Bobby.

She hung up the phone and turned to head up to the lab, but as she spun around, she saw Bobby standing in the doorway. Her cheeks flushed pink when she realized that he probably heard everything.

"You shouldn't have said that," he said, "but, thank you anyway."

"I'm glad you're here. There is way too much weirdness going on right now."

"Tell me about it. Did the dean tell you what I found on your computer?"

"No, what?"

"A spy program was inserted into the boot sector. It was there to email any passwords entered on your small computer to Dr. Pietre's email."

"So you think Pietre is behind this?"

"No," Bobby said, "not anymore. Sending passwords to his email address is a bit too obvious, he may not be a computer genius, but he's not that stupid."

"So why my small computer? What good are those passwords?"

"You remember the other night we were hacked and I told you someone tried stealing our passwords on the big computer?"

"I remember," she said, "go on."

"That was not Pietre," Bobby said, still pacing the office, "That was a hacker who goes by the name of The Bard. He used to leave Shakespearean quotes when he hacked people. He never did anything harmful, but he was known for getting into some pretty secure systems. He was eventually caught hacking the IRS and disappeared."

Dierdre offered Bobby a seat by Aimee's desk and asked, "How do you know it was him?"

"I dumped his CD when he tried stealing our passwords, and recognized his boot code, but mostly it was the Shakespeare sonnets I found on the CD. I think he has been hacking our computer and trying to make it look like Pietre did it. The only thing I can't figure out, is why he makes the attacks look like they were multiple attacks in the same day."

"You mean he hacks us once, and then hacks us again? On the same computer?"

"Exactly. It's like he hacks us once as Pietre, and once as himself."

"Maybe you just answered your own question." Dierdre moved a stapler to one side of Aimee's desk blotter and said, "Maybe Pietre is hacking us," then she moved a pencil cup to the opposite side of the blotter, "and this guy follows behind thinking if we are looking at Pietre, we won't see him."

"By Jove my dear Watson, I think you've got it."

"Listen," Dierdre said, "I got something else I want you to look at, but you may need to coordinate with the authorities on this one."

That put a tingle in Bobby's spine. Dierdre led him to her room, and showed him the note. "Don't touch it. I'm waiting for someone to come examine it. I don't want to go access the website until you have had time to analyze it and learn whatever you can first."

"Good thinking, the site may do something when it's accessed to hide its traces."

"I'm waiting for Ramiro now. I asked him to notify the correct authorities, I expect he'll call the FBI."

"Why the FBI?"

"Kidnapping is a federal crime."

"Kidnapping?" Bobby asked, "I thought it was about your project."

"Aimee's the only one who's missing, what about my project?"

"I thought you just went to see Aimee, she wasn't there? And your project software, from the smaller computer, is missing."

"Oh God," she cried, "I worked for years on that."

"Don't worry," Bobby said, "it's safe. I copied all your folders to the new computer, including your documents, but only you and I know that, this ransom may be for your system and not Aimee."

Ramiro had just arrived and heard the last bit. "What was that?"

Dierdre explained, "Someone hacked my computer last night, Bobby says my project folders are missing. He thinks it's possible that the note may be about my system."

Ramiro paced for a moment. "OK, OK, either way it is a federal matter, so the same authorities would investigate. The FBI is sending a forensic field agent, and a computer expert. I told them you wanted your guy to look into it, any problem joining forces on this?"

Bobby said, "No problem here. I'll wait till they get here to do anything."

* * *

Pietre was pacing outside the dean's office, waiting for a chance to see him. The dean was inside now speaking with a network specialist sent to help get them straightened out. When the small man exited the office, he shook the dean's hand and said, "I'll take care of this for you, you should be good as new by morning."

Pietre barged into the dean's office even before they finished their goodbyes. "I just see Blain kid going into Jennings' office as if he had no care in world. How long will you keep school at risk letting him roam around free? I told you what happened. You know he did it. Why is he still here?" Pietre's rampage went on and on.

"You told me all right," the dean said, "but what proof do you have? I can't expel a student without any hard evidence."

"I told you he is good at hiding tracks, you won't find evidence unless you catch him with the red hands."

"He doesn't leave any clues on your computer?"

"We won't know that," Pietre said, "until I can shut it down and inspect. If I find something with his name, will that satisfy you?"

"Should it?"

"Of course it should. Evidence not lie. There are many clever ways to find out what these guys are up to."

"And," the dean added, "you might also be surprised how many clever ways someone's name can end up in a conspicuous place."

"I not understand."

The dean motioned towards the door and said, "Go find your evidence."

Pietre grumbled, but headed out.

"Pietre!" The dean called him just as he reached the door. "Have your assistant Pandopolis, or whatever his name is work with you. I want him to record everything you do and find, so I can understand exactly how clever this boy is, if indeed it is him."

"But," Pietre objected, "I don't need Panopulous for that, I can take notes you need."

"Just the same, I would feel better if you had some help in this matter." Then the dean picked up his phone and dialed the number to the security office. "Maynard, I want you to post a guard outside Pietre's lab. I don't want anyone to go in or out without being recorded in and out. And except for the consultant I hired, nobody goes in alone, only in pairs. You can probably expect Pietre and his assistant Panopulous either this evening or in the morning."

Pietre stood there a moment, dumbfounded.

"Something wrong?" the dean asked, "You can go now."

Pietre's mind was spinning. He left for his office. There was nothing he could do now till they fixed the networks. He must have pushed too hard. He made too much fuss, now the dean knows he was planning to plant evidence against Bobby. Now he would have to find real evidence. One thing was for sure. He was hacked, and he was hacked in retaliation for his hacking Dierdre's computer. Thankfully that has not been discovered yet.

CHAPTER 9

It took an hour for the FBI team to arrive. The first of the two men was a short stocky Hispanic man with a thick neck, broad shoulders and bulging arms. He looked like a football player, and was probably a weight lifter. He toted an enormous silver box with large buckles and handles. He dropped the box, and went straight to Ramiro to shake hands. "Good afternoon sir, I'm Special Agent Gonzalez, and that's Spivey."

A tall, good looking man with a strong chin and a superman physique entered the room. He nodded to Ramiro, but went straight to Bobby, offering his hand. "Hello, I'm Eric, but everyone just calls me Spivey, and I know who you are."

Bobby accepted his hand and shook it warmly.

Dierdre was amused by the admiration she witnessed from Spivey, apparently reports of her assistant's fame in some circles were not exaggerated.

Dierdre decided to get the ball rolling. "Gentlemen, shall we get started? First of all, I want you to know, that my first assumption was that the note was referring to my missing secretary, but since then I have learned that one of my computers was hacked overnight and is missing some project folders. We aren't sure what the ransom is for." She led them into her office and pointed to the note.

Bobby said, "That web address is not the normal university address, so I thought the first thing we would do is check all the local name servers to see when it was added, and where it was hosted. I should also tell you that I have an idea who has been hacking our computers, but it may or may not be related to the note."

Spivey's ears perked up. "Who?"

"The Bard."

"I haven't heard that name in a while. He's good, real good. Which quote did he leave?"

Bobby smiled sheepishly and said, "He didn't exactly leave a note."

"What makes you think it was him? I don't think I've heard of any case where he left clues behind, other than his calling card."

Dierdre asked, "Calling card?"

Bobby answered, "He liked to leave Shakespearean quotes on computers he hacked. He never caused any harm, he just like to break in and leave quotes so they knew he had been there."

"What makes you think it was him?" Spivey asked, "If he didn't leave a quote on your machine?"

"Well," Bobby said, "He didn't leave one on purpose. I tweaked the interrupt vectors to trap anyone booting a CD to access the dump password vector. It dumped the entire contents of his CD. There was enough evidence in that dump to identify him."

A sly smile snuck onto Spivey's face. "You didn't let him have your passwords, did you?"

"No," Bobby admitted, "I let him have YOUR passwords, the ones that initiate an immediate trace and start beeping your pagers no matter what time it is. I gave him your passwords, the CIA's, the NSA's, the Secret Service, and a couple for Scotland Yard. Too bad he would have recognized them before he ever tried to use them."

Spivey pictured the whole thing. Some guy goes to steal passwords, hits the mother lode and is promptly arrested within minutes of trying one. So far, Bobby was everything he had heard he was.

"Professor Jennings," Bobby asked, "is it OK if we use Aimee's computer?"

"Sure, fine with me."

They went to Aimee's computer and started logging into various name servers. Name servers are the postmasters of the Internet. They convert www.someplacetogo into a series of numbers that actually get you there. They found new entries on the name servers. The recorded date on the entries was four years ago, but the disk sector which housed them showed that the entries immediately preceding and following were dated this morning, which means they were added with a false date.

From there they went to various sites that list who owns different web names and started to look for the registered owner. This address would not be officially registered, but a record would have been made somewhere, and it would have been good enough to fool the casual snooper.

While they snooped for an owner, Gonzalez picked up the note with tongs and sprayed it with a fine purple mist. He then held it up to a yellow light. This was a new way to check for fingerprints on paper. None were found.

Spivey asked, "Who is Dimitri Pietre?"

Bobby said, "He's one of the professors here."

Dierdre moved behind Bobby and Spivey to see what they were looking at and asked, "Dr. Pietre owns that web address?"

Spivey said, "It certainly looks that way. And he did a fair job of trying to hide it too."

"I don't buy it." Bobby stood to face the group. "That was too easy and too obvious. Who would be stupid enough to register a web name to deliver ransom instructions? Anyone clever enough to hack the name servers would be clever enough to hide their web page in someone else's web site, and they certainly would be clever enough not to use their own name on the name registry."

Gonzalez asked "Why would anyone want to implicate a professor?"

"I can answer that." Dierdre moved behind Bobby and put her hand on his shoulder. "Someone wants to get rid of Bobby, and has managed to somehow convince Pietre that Bobby was responsible for hacking his system. That same person is trying to create a war between Bobby and Pietre."

"Not a war," Bobby said, "He is simply covering his tracks. When Dr. Karlyn first gave you the computer, I was in his lab, late at night, preparing it for travel. That's when Dr. Pietre and some big guy came and let themselves into Dr. Karlyn's locked lab. Pietre and this guy wanted something from that computer. Then, not long after that, after I had already moved the computer to Dr. Jennings lab, someone broke in and hacked the computer. The Bard broke in and hacked it again that same night."

Gonzalez theorized out loud, "So after Pietre failed to retrieve something, and then the Bard guy failed, someone, possibly the Bard, is turning this place upside down trying to find it, but why get rid of both Bobby and Pietre?"

Spivey said, "Maybe he is just creating a diversion so he can slip in and finish what he started. Have you examined the computer? Is there something secret in it? Maybe we should let Gonzalez go over it with his equipment."

Bobby shook his head no. "I think it's time we look at the web site and see what he is asking for."

Spivey suggested, "Maybe we should set up some traces to track anyone who accesses that server."

"That's a good idea," Bobby said, "but I wasn't thinking of accessing it normally yet, I thought we should get a peek at the source." Bobby turned to Ramiro and asked, "What kind of permission do we need to look at the source, and do we need to go through the ISP, or can we essentially crack it to break in?"

Ramiro was a little surprised that Bobby asked. It wasn't the sort of question he would have expected, based on his reputation. "I'll draw up a search order, as to whether you go through the ISP would depend on whether you suspect collusion."

"I didn't see anything suspicious about the ISP." Bobby wanted to be a big help in solving this mystery, but did not want to get caught breaking the law, especially with so many witnesses.

"Wait a second," Spivey said, "You see the way this string of servers bounces from the original address through four different hops all around the country before landing on the actual server?"

Bobby looked at each of the servers involved. "I see that, but lots of hackers know how to do that."

Spivey continued, "Now look at the corporations that are registered for those servers. All those corporations are paper only corporations. And all of them have been around for years. Look at the addresses, I've seen those before. I think they are government computers. This guy hacked into some secret government computers to route this web site."

Dierdre looked confused, and asked, "What does that change, if they are government computers?"

"For one thing," Bobby said, "if they are government computers, there won't be an ISP, and worse, if we informed whoever owned them, they might take them off-line and we would never know what was on them."

Gonzalez cleared his throat. "If we can't identify the owner, can we still get a search order?"

Ramiro nodded his head, "As long as there is probable cause of foul play and someone's life may be in jeopardy, we can, and I will." He pulled out his cell phone and made yet another call to his secretary.

"OK then," Spivey said, "We break in, but, I think it will be safer if I drive."

Bobby agreed.

* * *

Edward Lynn, not his real name, was hired by the dean to analyze and fix the LAN problems the school was having. Analysis would be easy, since Edward, a.k.a. "The Bard," created the whole mess. The small man walked around the school pretending to investigate the problem. He was about to pass Dierdre's office when he heard bits and pieces of the meeting taking place in there. He entered an empty office next to hers. There was a simple vent high on the wall between the offices. He pulled a small tube from inside his coat, and extended the telescoping tube to about four feet in length. He approached the wall below the vent, and held the tip up to the vent. A small video camera on the tip transmitted images to the small LCD panel on the other end. It was an electronic periscope. A small rubber hook on the camera end allowed him to steady it against the vent, while he operated a small joystick to point it around.

He recognized Dierdre, Bobby, and Spivey. Spivey wasn't a hacker, but he was known to the black hat crowd. Spivey was born a white hat. He wasn't one of those bad boy hackers turned agent.

He retracted his periscope and retreated out the building without passing the office door. Spivey probably wouldn't know him, but Bobby might recognize him from the day he said he was with the grant office.

He went up to Pietre's lab. The guard was expecting him, but Pietre wasn't.

"What are you doing here?" Pietre asked.

"I'm cleaning up your mess."

Panopulous looked up from his book to see who was speaking, but decided he did not want to know, so he returned to his reading.

The small man explained, mostly for the sake of Panopulous, "The school hired me to fix the LAN."

"So fix it," Pietre grumbled, "what are you doing here?"

"Your computer is the problem. It's intercepting all name requests and routing them to itself."

"Oh." Pietre was disappointed he could not get rid of the man, but knowing he might help fix his computer made up for that.

"Don't worry," the Bard said, "I'll give it back to you soon enough." He sat down at Pietre's console, and entered a vendor password to get into the core routines. He executed some commands to delete the name server and drop the routing commands. "It has to be re-booted now, any objections?"

Pietre simply shrugged and waved his hands suggesting he continue with the reboot.

As the system rebooted, the Bard phoned the dean and suggested that everyone reboot their PC's and try to print something. He pretended to wait for the results, but he already knew it would work. He designed it that way.

Before leaving, he leaned close enough to Pietre so Panopulous could not overhear him. "It seems like you've been pissing somebody off, I suggest you lay low for a while, real low. Maybe even take a few days off."

Pietre just grunted and sat down to wait for his system to come back up.

* * *

Spivey printed a few configuration documents from the server they were looking at, followed by the HTML code for the ransom page.

Bobby was looking at the config files. "It looks like a standard Apache setup. Did you dump the version and a CRC for Apache?"

"Good idea." Spivey pulled up a few more files and sent screen prints to the printer.

The dean came in the room and seeing that the printer was working, asked, "Is everything working now?"

"Everything seems fine."

"Terrific. I'll tell everyone else to reboot their machines to get their printers back." He left as quickly as he had arrived.

Bobby and Spivey looked at each other with quizzical faces.

"I didn't reboot, did you?"

"No, I didn't fix anything about the printer either, did you?"

"No."

Dierdre zipped out the door and yelled down the hall, "Dean Smithers!"

He was almost to the exit when he heard her. He turned around and started back. There must still be a problem. Bobby and Spivey came out the door and joined Dierdre where they waited for the dean to walk back.

"Yes Dierdre? Is something still not working?"

Spivey introduced himself, "Hello. I'm special agent Spivey with the FBI. What did you mean about rebooting to fix the problem with printers?"

"Didn't you reboot? How did you get the printer to work?"

"Why wouldn't the printer be working?"

The dean was puzzled by his question. "None of the printers were working. And the file servers were intolerably slow. And of course, nobody could get to the Internet."

Spivey asked, "When you say none of the printers, or nobody could get to the Internet, you just mean lots of people right?"

"No, I mean absolutely none of the printers were working. And absolutely everybody was cut off from the Internet. Didn't you have problems here too? If not, you were the only ones, except for Pietre's computer which was on the Internet all morning and all night."

Spivey's puzzled face twisted in thought for a moment. "Thank you for your time, Dean Smithers."

"Why, may I ask, is the FBI interested in our computer problems?"

"We aren't, we are here investigating a missing person."

"Oh, that's right. Is it kidnapping?"

"We are looking into it," Spivey said, "You better continue letting people know they can get on now."

"Yes, of course. Please let my office know if you learn anything suspicious."

Bobby and Spivey went back in.

Dierdre followed. "He brought the whole school down except these computers. How hard is that?"

"I wouldn't call it hard," Spivey said, "but it is a very calculated detail."

The conversation between Dierdre, Bobby and Spivey came crashing to a halt as an argument between Ramiro and Gonzalez became ever louder.

"No, it can't be," Ramiro bellowed, "I know Aimee! We're engaged to be married. You are misinterpreting the document!"

"I would suggest," Agent Gonzalez replied, "that you, sir, are too close to the girl to offer an objective opinion. The document says what it says, and we must consider the facts as they come to us."

"Have you considered the fact that you don't have sufficient information to form a conclusion?"

Agent Gonzalez kept his voice steady and replied, "I have considered the fact that the document would seem to implicate her in foul play. I have also considered the fact that all this madness started when she disappeared."

Dierdre stepped in and yelled, "What in the world are you two arguing about?"

Gonzalez showed her the document Spivey had printed. It was encoded source and mostly looked like nonsense, but there, in the lower third of the page, Gonzalez pointed to the text that read, "Someone you thought you knew has taken something that you have spent years developing."

"Ramiro's right," Dierdre said, "You are reading way too much into this. Someone out there is manipulating everybody. He has pitted Pietre against Bobby and he has been clever enough to make Bobby look suspicious to the dean."

"None of it makes any sense," Spivey spoke with an air of FBI training, "Criminals don't customarily mess with people's lives, there is no profit in it. They usually focus on a single goal, and mess up their own lives trying to achieve it."

"It all started with the computer." Everyone looked at Bobby. "We know at least two people tried to get something from the computer. Someone wants something, and since those two people don't seem to be working together, and actually seem to be against each other, then whatever that computer has is worth money to someone."

Spivey added, "But if it was only money, then that person could have simply offered Professor Jennings enough money for the computer so she could buy a new bigger one. I would suspect that there is something incriminating on that computer. I think we need to disassemble it."

The room was quiet as everyone tried to imagine what secret it might hide.

Bobby broke the silence. "We can't disassemble it. We don't know what we are looking for, or even whether it is something physical or a piece of data hidden away. I disassembled and reassembled the computer already. It must be disguised as something that belongs there or I would have noticed. Or, it could be hidden like a microdot on the underneath side of one of the thousands of chips in there. It could be a simple number painted on a circuit board that looks like a serial number, but contains the key to a numbered bank account. Without knowing what to look for, we won't know if we found it."

"What do you suggest?" Spivey asked.

"First," Bobby said, "if it is data, I can find it with a program that analyzes every odd place on the machine. I will look in the system areas of the disk sectors where timing and error correction data goes. I will also scan all the roms for any unused areas. Meanwhile, we go about business as always, and try to set a trap to catch whoever tries to break in again."

Gonzalez picked up his trunk which he had finished packing up. "And we at the FBI will keep an OPEN mind, and consider that the girl, Aimee, might be either a victim or a perpetrator, and in either case, we will set up triggers to track any credit card usage or bank transactions."

Bobby grabbed his books and said, "It was nice meeting you, Agent Spivey, but I guess I have some more work to do in the lab."

* * *

Pietre did not know what he would find when the computer came back up, but he planned for the worst and prepared to completely reload the system from backups. His main concern was making sure he saw everything before his assistant. He already had to deal on two occasions with screens declaring that he was the one. He needed to make sure there that Bobby did not leave anything more incriminating for Panopulous to stumble across.

Panopulous was instructed to take notes of every action Pietre took, but he rationalized that the dean just needed a record in case there was another attack, something to prove it wasn't some kind of incompetence by Pietre. He had no desire to be involved, but Pietre promised him the evening would provide plenty of time to catch up on his reading. Pietre hoped his book was good enough to distract

Panopulous from whatever might pop up on the screens.

* * *

By the time Bobby had climbed the steps to the lab, the small computer was ready to go, and was ready for him to proceed with adding its processors to the main program.

* * *

The Bard sat in his small office, surrounded with computers and communications equipment. He monitored the website he had setup, but nobody had accessed it yet. He assumed they must have found some other way to view the note, or else they would have gone in already. He started to pull up some of the access logs to see when was the last time anyone had been on the server when program alarms began to go off. His scanners were detecting traffic from Tyrannosaur, a cousin of the Raptor programs used to monitor email traffic. Apparently they had actually found his server and were trying to trace his connection. His alarms gave him plenty of time to disconnect before they could complete a trace, but this left him needing to make contact again. He had planned to send a message to whoever viewed his page. That way, nothing he would say was actually in the source files on the server. Now he would have to go to plan B, if only he had a plan B.

* * *

Dierdre joined Bobby in the lab. He started up the main programs on the big computer. He showed her how the client on her smaller computer would contact the big computer and basically announce it was available to help. Shortly after that, the big computer allocated one of the new threads to the smaller computer, then another. Soon after that, the smaller computer was allocating its own threads, and the two computers were swapping threads.

Dierdre was watching the graphs on the main console. "It doesn't seem to make much difference."

"This computer only handles a couple threads at a time, which wouldn't make a huge difference to the big one. But if you had a thousand of these, then it could make an enormous difference."

"Where am I supposed to get a thousand of these?"

"I told you," Bobby said, "I have friends that would like to borrow some networking equipment. They have volunteered their hardware for your project."

"I read up on those LAN contests. Those guys stay up all night using their machines. There would never be any free time for us to use."

"Not this contest," Bobby explained, "They have a brutal elimination schedule. Every four hours, anyone not in the top forty percent of the remaining players is eliminated. They start with about two thousand players, and after four hours, they eliminate twelve-hundred contestants. Those twelve-hundred machines become available for us to use. The whole contest is three full days, so you have those twelve-hundred machines for thirty-six hours, plus every four hours, more join up."

Dierdre frowned, "Thirty-six hours does not sound like much."

"But that equals almost sixty-thousand CPU hours, and all of these are hot CPU's, and many of them have dual cores, so that would be over one-hundred-thousand thread hours."

"That really adds up," she said, surprised. "OK. Let's do it, but is our program ready enough?"

"It is ready, but I expect we can give it constant tweaks and improvements."

"You have a good weekend then, I'll see you Monday."

"Is it OK if I work on this over the weekend?"

"Knock yourself out," she said, "but you'll still have to share the Nobel Prize with me, after all, it was only my idea."

CHAPTER 10

It was Saturday, and Dierdre selfishly missed Aimee more than ever. She worried terribly about the fate of her missing friend, but she couldn't squelch the loneliness she felt and realized that even if Aimee weren't missing, this is what her weekends were going to become anyway.

She thought about making breakfast, but cooking sounded like too much work, especially cleaning up afterward. Going out to breakfast, alone, didn't sound so hot, especially since it looked a bit overcast and drizzly that day. Raiding the refrigerator provided zero leftovers that she could warm up, but there was some ice cream left in the freezer, and there were some cold sodas. She decided that she would save the ice cream for lunch and grabbed a coke and moved on to check the cupboard. Cookies and crackers rounded out her breakfast. Caffeine, sugar and salt, all the chemistry she needed to get her brain going for the day. Now to find a good book to give her brain someplace to go once it got going.

* * *

Bobby spent the night in the lab. The demonstration successfully proved that they could attach a second computer to the main one and add it to the pool of available thread processors, but the threads executing on it ran far less efficiently than he had hoped. And before he added a couple thousand new clients hosting threads, he wanted it to be a bit more productive.

His concern wasn't just in making this computer run better, but he was thinking forward, imagining one thousand machines attaching. How could he make them run better? He couldn't customize a new client for each machine. He needed a way for the client threads to analyze their efficiency and either modify themselves, or request a better client from the community. If he did that, then he would need a way to deliver that client to the requesting machine.

The problem, though, came down to thread behavior. The threads had to be independent. The clients had to serve the threads. So it was up to the threads to do the analysis, and request a new version of it by themselves. Then, when a new client was requested, the other threads had to deliver it. This was the scheme he worked on all night.

Part of the problem was the way threads had to communicate with each other. This wasn't a huge problem, they already communicated enough to pair off into partners to breed new threads. Now the threads would not only share how well they were doing, but also how well they were doing on that machine.

As he started to picture the process, he realized that the client problem was similar to the number generating problem. Each wanted to reach prime efficiency. The threads were able to breed new threads to improve the numbers. Maybe they could do something similar to improve the clients' efficiency. The threads could try different combinations of the various routines that make up the clients, and decide which one was the best.

In the lab, this ate up a lot of processing time and slowed down the whole process until they found the right client. But, with thousands of processors working on it, it should go much faster. This also gave him an excellent method to share updates into the community. Instead of pushing an update down to all the machines, he just releases it with a few threads, and they share it and only update the clients and threads that request it.

* * *

Dierdre settled down in her comfy chair. She had her coke, cookies and crackers at the ready, and had found a suitable book to read.

She didn't care if the book lulled her to sleep. She was willing to follow her emotions wherever they took her.

In actual fact, however, she found that she could only reach a drowsy state of semi-awareness, but not actually roll off into sleep, which was fine with her. She reasoned that it represented the same amount of rest and recuperation that she would get were she actually asleep anyway.

The drowsiness started to fade, kind of like your eyes slowly focusing. She shook her head, as if she had to knock off drops of water. The phone was ringing. It was on the far side of the room, and it was ringing. She debated whether she had the energy, but finally pulled her feet out from under her and dragged herself into an upright position, hoisted herself out of the chair and crossed the room, "Hello?"

No answer came from the other end. She thought she heard a soft click, but the line was dead. She checked her caller-id, but the number was unlisted. Her mind quickly sharpened as she focused on the thought that it may have been Aimee. She pressed the end button to hang up the phone and carried the handset back to her chair with her. She'll be kicking herself all day long for not answering quicker.

* * *

Bobby was ready for more advanced testing. He pulled his address book out of his backpack and looked up the friend who had asked him to help with their LAN contest. Some people found it funny that someone of his technical skills would still rely on paper and pencil for his addresses, but he would always respond, "Address books might be stolen, or copied, but they have never been hacked."

"Jimmy? It's Bobby. Everything is good to go. When do you need the equipment? Wednesday? That's cool. Listen, I want a favor from you. Remember we talked about letting all the computers that have been eliminated run some programs for us until the end of the match? I wanted a chance to test it and was wondering if you could loan me your computer for an hour or two? I just need you to load a small program and let it contact this machine. The rest should be automatic. You can? Thanks. I'm emailing the client to you now. I'll watch here for your connection."

* * *

Dierdre cuddled up in her comfy chair again and tried to return to her book, but her mind was on Aimee. With all that has been going on, it is hard to imagine anything but the worst things that would keep Aimee away. She must be in some kind of trouble, and if her problems aren't bad enough, the FBI seems to think she is a criminal and not just a victim.

She rubbed her eyes and tried to clear her mind so she could focus on the book when the phone rang again.

"Hello?"

Silence.

"Hello? Who is this?"

"Hello? Dierdre? This is Stillman, am I disturbing you?"

"Oh, hi Stillman, I was just reading. What do you want?"

"I...um...I was just calling to see, um, how, you know, how your project was going?"

"Except for hackers erasing my project and ruining my backups, it's going just fine, I suppose."

"Someone erased your project?" he asked, "That's terrible. What will you do?"

"I think I'll have to recreate it somehow, but it won't be so bad, Bobby has been a big help."

"That's good to hear."

Silence.

She made a face at the receiver for a moment, then asked, "Was there something else?"

"No. No. Well, yes." More silence followed. "I'm not very good at this."

"Good at what Stillman?"

"You know," he stammered, "talking to women, to a woman, to you."

"But you sure talked to me a lot the other night, what has changed?"

"Well, the thing is, the other night, I was...um, well, I was coached."

"Coached?" she asked icily, "Like Cyrano?"

"Something like that I guess, but not very good coaching I think."

"And what about now? Are you being coached?"

"No," he admitted, "now I am speaking for myself, and not doing a very good job I think."

"What did you want to say Stillman?"

"I have to, that is I wanted to...um, I am a bit confused. I thought we were getting along so well, and then you changed."

"I changed?"

"No, that's not what I meant. I was calling to apologize."

Dierdre could almost hear the perspiration squeezing out of his pores. "I'm listening," she said, "Go on."

"You are not going to make this easy for me, are you?"

"Should I make it easy for you?"

"Well, no," he said, "I guess I don't deserve that, but have a little mercy for me here."

"Exactly what are you calling to apologize for?"

"I must have said or done a dozen things that require an apology. How do I pick just one? I just want to apologize for being me."

"Was it you?" she asked, "Or was it your coach?"

"That's right. It wasn't really me. It was my coach."

"I don't get you Stillman, you started out like such a gentlemen, and then you ran off and joined those two coeds on the dance floor. Everybody was watching the spectacle you made of yourself."

"I apologize for that."

"Then you come back to our table and act as if nothing happened, and turn back into that gentleman for a few moments. Then on the dance floor you turn into Rudolph Valentino saying all the right things, were those coached?"

"I apologize again."

"Let's get one thing straight," she said, "I am not some prize bimbo that you are going to manipulate into bed with some clever lines."

"You are correct. I was a cad."

"You deserve to suffer Stillman."

"True," he said, "but does that mean you might be willing to give me another chance? Even if just to make me suffer? I promise I will humble myself until I have made up for my poor judgment."

"What did you have in mind?"

"Perhaps something simple. How about an early movie and then dinner afterward?"

"No coaches?"

"On my honor as a southerner, none."

"No mind games?"

"None."

"I can pick the movie?"

"Absolutely."

"Even if it's a real girly chick flick?"

"Anything you want."

"Don't be too wishy washy."

"Only till I have completed my penance to you, then I intend to have my backbone reinserted."

Dierdre laughed, "Should I bring my whips and leathers until then?"

"Whatever mistress wants."

They both laughed.

"Pick me up at three o'clock."

She hung up the phone, her spirits were cheered up considerably, but she bit her lip when she realized that this WAS a date.

* * *

Ramiro spent a lot of time, lately, sitting in his office waiting for the phone to ring. Occasionally, waiting would not do and he would place a call to someone for some answers. This was one of those times. He dialed the number to his friend Chief Henderson. They spoke last night when Ramiro had filled the chief in on the FBI visit, and the ransom note not panning out. Henderson told him he would be in the office on Saturday, and would keep tabs on the situation.

"Chief Henderson here, oh, Ramiro? Is that you?"

"Yeah, Mitch, have you heard anything yet?"

"Not yet, but I'll let you know."

"Come on Mitch, help me out here. Have you talked to the FBI? Are there any leads to go by?"

"I called them. They have their theories, I don't think they have a clue really, but we should have our answers in another hour or so, I'll call you when I know something."

"Another hour or so? Why? What's going on that you aren't telling me?"

"I can't say. Besides, I thought you didn't want to get your news over the phone?"

"Mitch!"

"What do you want? You don't want to hear suspicions and allegations do you? Let's wait for the facts OK?"

"Spill it Mitch. What did the FBI say?"

"They said you are too close to this investigation to be involved. That's what they said."

"Damn it Mitch, you know something! Tell me!"

"Damn it right back at you Ramiro, it'll be my ass if I talk."

"What the hell? Are you telling me that I'm a suspect here?"

"No. Not you, they never suggested that. But you are powerful enough to impede their investigation."

"Whose investigation? I'll go right to the top if I have to. I want to know exactly who is ordering a lid on your information!" Ramiro was seething now.

"Listen Squeeze, I'm just the messenger, you don't have to bite my head off."

"Then BE the MESSENGER and tell me something."

"Damn you, you better make a place for me when I get canned for this! They think they found her."

Ramiro's heart was pounding in his ears. They think they found her, yet they felt it important not to tell him. Something was very wrong. He started to picture dismembered body parts with no fingerprints to verify. "Is she... is she..."

"She's safe," Henderson said, "but it looks like she is hiding. They've been tracing her credit card. She hopped a plane to San Diego, where she rented a car and has been bouncing from one dive motel to another. They are gathering now to close in on her third hotel. Rami, something very suspicious is going on, and they think she is up to something."

"Mitch. If they harm her, in any way, it's their ass, you hear me. Don't tell them I know, but you tell them you know me, and even if they just break a nail on her, I will bust them down to dog catcher. You tell them that!"

"I already told them that, except I told them they'd be sweeping streets after the circus parade. Now, you need to relax a bit. They will find her, and take her into custody, and then they will learn that she has done nothing, and that they are all horses' asses. Then they will let her go."

"Thanks Mitch. I'm at the office. Call me the second you hear."

"You're already on speed dial my friend. Now pour yourself a tall frosty one. I'll call you soon."

* * *

Bobby watched the monitor as two new threads became available. His friend had run the client program, and it had been added to the pool of thread servers. A few moments later, new threads found a home there.

He had the threads send status updates to a special file where he could filter out specific activities. He ran a filter to show client updates, and found that the new threads were requesting additional client pieces, and various threads on the main machine were responding by sending copies of their clients. The new threads would then start breeding the clients and testing the results to see if it was an improvement. Meanwhile, the other threads continued to volunteer their clients, and the new threads were spending a lot of time receiving these new clients, and breeding them, and only about fifteen percent of their time testing them. This was not a good solution.

He changed the routine the clients would only breed once with a neighboring client then send the offspring to the new threads. He released this new code into the system.

The monitor showed a map of all the threads, and he could watch the new code as it was passed from one thread to the next, until it finally reached the new machine. Now all the other threads helped to find a solution for the new ones. Their time testing improved to about sixty-five percent.

The process was working OK, but the client breeding was not. With only the two machines attached, he only had one working client, and one proposed client. So all the threads on the big machine would breed their clients with the same clients and come up with clones. He needed to introduce some kind of mutations again, and he was going to need more machines on-line for better testing.

He tackled the mutation problem first. Since he had already dealt with this for the main threads, it was a simple cut and paste to add mutations to the clients. With that done, and spreading through the system, he brought the small computer back on-line and made it available to process threads. He still wanted more.

He picked up the phone and called Dierdre at home.

"Hello? "

"Dierdre, it's Bobby. I am running some tests. Things are looking real good so far, but I need more machines on-line. Can I use your machine in your main office?"

"Sure, no problem. Use Aimee's too."

"Will I have any problem getting in? Is the office locked?"

"It shouldn't be locked," she said, "They keep them open on Saturday's, and the guards don't lock them until around six."

"Great. I'll call you later and let you know how it worked out."

"I have plans this afternoon. Can you tell me Monday?"

"Sure," he said, "Monday then."

With two machines requesting client updates now, the threads were pretty busy breeding clients for the both of them. Mutation rates were extremely low, and they had to be, otherwise everything would be too random if mutations occurred all the time.

Bobby left them running and carted a single disk down to Dierdre's office. He was glad for an opportunity to step out, even though the weather wasn't the best, fresh air was still nice. He figured that he might as well pick up some lunch while he was down there too.

* * *

Pietre was in his lab stewing over how he would ever get back in the big man's better graces. His supplemental deposits, which used to arrive on Friday's, had already ceased. He was completely in control when he got rid of Karlyn. It was child's play, but now he found himself getting zapped and trapped with every move he made.

While pondering his fate, Pietre saw Bobby skipping down the stairs. His temples started to throb. How could this dangerous child continue to run around Scot-free? Haven't they seen enough of what he can do? Going to the dean clearly was a wasted gesture. He would have to handle this himself.

* * *

Bobby loaded the client on Aimee's computer and fired it up. While it started to negotiate client updates for itself, he went to Dierdre's computer and stopped cold. He picked up the phone and dialed Dierdre's number again.

"Hello?"

"Dierdre it's me again, sorry to bother you, but you have an email."

"That's OK Bobby, I'll get it Monday."

"It's from Aimee, and it was dated early yesterday."

"From Aimee?" she asked, "From yesterday?"

"I guess it was queued up in the backlog from yesterday's LAN fiasco."

"Can you read it to me?"

"If you want," he said, "that is, if you are authorizing me to open your email."

"Of course! Please! Open it!"

Bobby clicked on the envelope icon and waited for the note to open up.

> Dierdre,
>
> I'm out of town on personal business. Not sure when I can get back. My cell phone was cut off. I think they assumed it was stolen and I just don't have time or energy to argue with them. Tell Ramiro that I know he didn't mean those awful things he said to me. At least I hope he didn't mean them. I'll contact both of you when I can.

"Bobby, do me a big favor and forward that to Ramiro, he's in my address book."

"Will do. That's good news right? A bit mysterious I think, but at least it sounds like she wasn't kidnapped."

"No more mysterious than anything else going on right now, unfortunately."

"I'm starting up the test now. You have a good time. I'll give you a full report on Monday."

"Bye!"

* * *

Ramiro was going through his old emails, deleting some and filing others, when a new email arrived from Dierdre. He opened the new email and saw immediately that it was from Aimee and she had only forwarded it to him. He dialed her office.

Bobby answered the phone, thinking it might be Dierdre. "Hello?"

"Hello? This is Ramiro, is Dierdre there?"

"No, she is not here at the moment, this is Bobby. I spoke with her just a few minutes ago and she had me forward an email to you."

"I just got it. Can you tell me when it arrived there?"

"Well, technically, it arrived here late last night after everyone had left, but it should have arrived yesterday morning. I think all the emails were backed up due to the server problems."

"Thanks. If any more come in, can you please let me know?"

"I won't open them, not without her express permission, but if I see

an email is from Aimee, I will let you know one came in. Professor
Jennings is busy tonight. I don't expect to speak with her until
Monday."

"No problem. The FBI think they have located her. We should have
news any time now."

"That's good to hear. Maybe you should let Dierdre know."

"I'll wait till I have solid news. I better get off the phone now and
keep all the lines free."

"Good luck."

Bobby finished starting up the client, and then went to the cafeteria.
There were no cooks on Saturday, but there were still goodies in the
vending machines. He fished out some coins and bought an egg salad
sandwich, a can of hot chili, pretzels and a V8.

With the chili in one hand, and everything else barely held together
in the other, he left the mess hall and sprinted up the stairs to the lab.
With four clients on-line now, the threads were freely exchanging client
versions, including occasional mutations. His friend's machine had
already shown a ten percent improvement. Bobby was surprised to see
that the big machine was now trying new clients. Probably a result of a
mutation, there was no improvement however, and in fact, it was
holding up actual thread processing.

Bobby dropped the food on the desk, and started putting limits on
how long a thread can try improving a client, based on the age of a
client, but he also added a limit to allow threads to try again after a
sufficient number of new threads have been processed. That way, even
old clients might get upgrades. The additional machines upped the
total thread processing capability from sixty-four to seventy. He
pictured in his mind adding fifteen-hundred more on Wednesday.

He sat back, munching his sandwich, watching the graphs.

* * *

Somewhere in Universal City, just off the freeway, FBI agents
gathered with a few local deputies and sheriffs making their plans to
storm a small motel where they believed they would find the fugitive
Aimee Takahashi. Details of her alleged crimes were sketchy, the arrest
orders mostly pointed to suspicion of this or that.

The gathering studied a layout of the motel complex, then fanned out, surrounding the building. All had guns drawn. The deputies set up behind their vehicles, while the FBI agents approached the door, knocked on it then opened it using a pass key from the motel management.

The two at the door stormed in yelling, "FBI, FBI!" A deputy sheriff entered behind them, but the place was already deserted. After declaring it clear, a forensic team went in and using various sprays and special lights, they quickly determined that there were two individuals here, and there were slight traces of blood on the carpet. There was no evidence of a struggle, nor was there any evidence of one of them being held against her will, the forensic team searched for rope fibers on all the chairs, the bed corners, anyplace someone might be bound, but there was no evidence of kidnapping.

The motel registration did not list a vehicle license number, but it did have a make and model matching the description of a rental car charged to Aimee's credit card. An APB was issued for all neighboring communities, and some further communities up and down the freeway that ran alongside this motel. Unfortunately, there was no pattern in their motel stays to suggest any particular direction or destination.

The lead agent called his supervisor and relayed what they had found. They were positive they were onto something, even if they did not know what it was. The suspects definitely showed a pattern of evasion, and they were close. They just needed more eyes on the street.

The agents' supervisor relayed their findings to the East Coast agents who alerted them of the case, and they in turn relayed it to Chief Henderson who then called Ramiro. They were close, but still had not found her, and still did not know what was going on.

"Ramiro," Henderson said, "You better sit down for the rest of this. We are still waiting for the lab results. They found traces of blood, but they found no evidence of rope fibers or tape residue, and there was no evidence of a struggle."

"Mitch, what the hell is going on?"

"I honestly don't know. They are issuing an APB for the car Aimee had rented in all the nearby cities. We have to hope that a beat cop or patrol car spots it."

* * *

Bobby watched the progress of the threads as they worked on the new clients, then eventually went back to Dierdre's process. He gave the threads a ranking so the higher ranking threads would concentrate on the predictions, and the lower ranking threads would focus on improving the clients. This way, he hoped the primary task would not come to a complete halt while every thread tried producing clients.

He called his friend and thanked him for his help.

"Man," his friend said, "I don't know what you did, but that was the best test my cooling system ever had. I have never seen it generate that much heat before." He liked to brag about his over-clocked water cooled system.

"Awesome," Bobby said, "I got what I needed, I think I'm ready for the real thing. See ya."

"Later dude."

* * *

Aimee's email relieved Dierdre enough to allow her to concentrate on her date and what she might wear. Nice blue jeans and a sweater top should suffice for the movies. On the other hand, casual wear meant a natural look. Even though she was still young and had very good skin, being in broad daylight made it more difficult to hide those flaws that she saw in her skin and face, even if she was the only one that ever saw them. In truth, her age was not even a factor, but she still felt a need to compete with the young eighteen year old freshmen she saw strolling about the university every year.

The weather outside was overcast and chilly, and in this part of the country, chilly was anything below sixty, but it was cool enough to take a jacket over the pullover she wore and a big knit hat with matching scarf to complete the ensemble.

The doorbell rang promptly at three o'clock. She wondered if he had been standing on her porch staring at his watch, counting down the minutes and seconds until he could press the doorbell.

She opened the door and there he stood in a tweed jacket, dark turtleneck, corduroy slacks, and an English style cabbie hat that matched his jacket. He smiled broadly and held out an enormous bouquet of pink roses for her. She gave him points for the roses. Two dozen pink roses were worth at least a few apology points, but he still had more points to work off.

She put the flowers in a vase, and took his arm. "I found a movie," she told him, "it's at the Argent Theater and starts at three fifty."

"Well, we better shove off then."

As they got in his car and drove off, she told him about the movie she wanted to see, "it's one of those movies where the two British guys fight over the semi-attractive girl because one thinks he is deeply in love with her, but the other guy just can't stand the idea that she would be with him..."

Stillman smiled and nodded his head the whole way.

* * *

Bobby had one last thing he wanted to do before he left for the day. He called up a program to start scanning memory locations on the big computer. Someone wanted something on that computer, and he wanted to determine if there was anything suspicious hidden in one of the system ROM chips. This particular program went location by location and tested it to see if it was read only, and create a file of everything it found, and what address it was at. If it reported any data in an unknown location, then he would analyze what it found.

While it was running, he started up another program which scanned areas of the disk that were not supposed to have data in them. It checked bad sectors, areas of the hard drives that were flagged as being unusable, and it checked small areas that exist between the sectors on the disk. Both were excellent places to hide secret stuff.

Hopefully on Monday, he will have some results from one of these programs.

* * *

Ramiro did not know what to do. Nobody, with the possible exception of Aimee herself, had a clue what was going on. But every explanation he could think of to explain the motel room ended in no good. Every scenario he ran in his mind ended with her needing him more than ever. He wasn't sure how much help he could be so far away from her. But if he flew to San Diego, he might miss the one call where she was looking for help.

He picked up the phone and called Henderson again. "Mitch, no matter what is going on, when they finally catch up with her, she is going to need my help, and I think I will be able to respond much faster if I'm at least in the region."

"I don't know squeeze. They might see it as obstructing their investigation."

"I'm ready for that. I swear to God Mitch, if they breathe one peep suggesting that I am obstructing their investigation, I have orders ready to go and I will file their obstructions clear up their backsides."

"Damn, I almost wish they would say something to you now. I got no love for those bastards. They roll into town and treat us like we were just mall cops. Are you sure you won't get into any trouble dropping your caseload on someone else?"

"With my fiancé missing under suspicious circumstances which include the possibility of kidnapping, I have no choice but to remove myself from any active criminal cases."

"When you put it that way, it seems so obvious."

"Mitch, I need a favor."

"Anything."

"The flight there will put me out of cellular service for several hours. I need to know if she tries calling me at home or at my office. If I file the orders, can you monitor a wiretap for me? I will find a way with the airline for you to contact me."

"You are going to file papers to place a wiretap on yourself? That has got to a first."

"Yeah," Ramiro said, "When it's all done, you can go tell Ripley's."

"I'm just a country sheriff. We don't usually deal with wiretaps. I'll have to find someone other than the feds to do it for you."

"No worries my friend, it's all electronic now. I'll have the phone company contact you and they will set it up for you."

"Works for me."

"This could be a long evening," Ramiro said, "Buy yourself a steak, on me."

"Steak? You're buying me lobster my friend."

"Just remember you're on the job, no magnums of champagne."

"Damn," Henderson said, "I wasn't going to drink them."

"Uhuh. You really would've made a fair crook."

"With you as my lawyer? I would've been hung years ago."

"That's not what your wife says."

"Oh yeah?" Mitch shot back, "But your mama thinks it's so."

Out of jibes and insults, a silence fell between the two friends.

"Squeeze, you better start filing your papers, and get to the airport. Keep in constant touch with me. You never know when they might have some info for me, and make sure your phone has a full charge."

"I'll call you from California."

* * *

The movie was as delightful as all the others these guys made. Somehow they seemed to find themselves in a handful of movies which all seemed to be knock-offs of each other. Only the impressive cast of co-stars changed.

Re-hash or not, the movie still had charm and left Dierdre with a warm feeling inside, right next to the knot in her stomach every time she asked herself why she was here with him. All through the movie her mind drifted from the story to her own situation. When she asked herself if she saw anything in Stillman at all, most of her answers were intellectual rationalizations. He was at least capable of holding an intelligent conversation. He was someone she could share her work with. And most important of all, he seemed interested in her. But lots of guys have been interested in her, and some of them were at least as interested in her as they were in themselves. He was neither suave nor sophisticated. He wasn't a smooth ladies man. Anybody that looked at them would immediately assume that she was way out of his league. But the pretty boys and athletic hunks that most would pair her up with would rarely amount to more than brief flickers of fire. And those that might be full-fledged fireworks would burn out, leaving her to ask, "What else have you got? What else can you do?" And they would look blankly at her as if to say, "What more do you need?"

Stillman at least had something more. She could see it when he looked at her. Why though? Bobby looked at her with a certain amount of admiration, and she didn't get that feeling, though maybe if she were ten years younger, she would try a little harder. But when Stillman looked at her, it felt more like he looked inside her. The question was whether he had a firework to offer her, or at least a sparkler to build upon.

Dierdre selected this movie because she liked farcical romances that were easy on the brain. She didn't want to over analyze her emotions, or she would risk viewing those emotions as touchy feely sentimental crap, and she had enough complications in her life without her thinking like a man. She also selected this movie because she felt it would not appeal to a man in macho mode, something she concluded Stillman was attempting at their previous dinner. No man in macho mode could sit through a film like this without squirming in his seat. Stillman not only did not squirm, but he seemed to genuinely enjoy the story. In fact, with Dierdre partially focused on his reactions, he may have enjoyed it more than she did.

So he may be sincere about not putting on any airs for her benefit. She was overloaded with mixed reactions. It was good that he was putting an honest foot forward, but she chastised herself for caring. She waffled between wanting him to be someone interesting to her, and scolding herself for paying so much attention to someone she wasn't interested in. No amount of rationalization would change the fact that she didn't feel anything for him.

If her mind weren't already too distracted to sink into the movie, fretting over why she should waste so much time on him made her want to speak with Aimee all the more, which only added another distraction to her collage of thoughts.

"Dierdre? Dierdre?"

She focused back on the present.

"Dierdre? Where did you go? I do believe you missed the ending, and possibly most of the movie."

"Sorry, I was worried about Aimee," she lied. Poor sweet Aimee. She was grateful to have such a good excuse. How awful if he could read her mind and know the truth about what she was thinking the whole time.

"Has there been any word on the girl?"

"Some," Dierdre said, "but nothing good. The FBI think they are closing in, but they seem to think she is some kind of criminal mastermind and they probably have her on the most wanted list by now."

"No! How could they get such a foolish idea?"

"She disappeared the same time all the systems were hacked, so they put two plus two together and came up with five."

Stillman stood up and started leading Dierdre out of the theater. "And I always thought they got the cream of the law enforcement crop."

"God, let's hope not! But I think they believe that is true. They seem to have very high opinions of themselves at times, although, I'll tell you something, and I think this is kind of funny, their tech guy seemed to be quite the fan of our own Bobby. He fawned over him like he was some kind of movie star."

"Odd, since Bobby's claim to fame was illegal, or at least allegedly illegal, or is that allegedly his claim to fame? Dang it, I hate when I gum up a perfectly simple thought like that."

Dierdre crinkled her nose, a kind of silent laugh. "You're right though, it's an odd thing for them to admire. Kind of makes you wonder whether they have problems with right and wrong."

"Maybe they don't have problems with right and wrong," Stillman added, "maybe they know something they aren't telling about whether it was a right or wrong thing to do."

"If you knew the details of his allegations, you would know that such a statement might be considered treason."

Stillman stood up very stiff, and put his hand over his chest and said, "My dear lady, I do know the details, and I must remind you that I am a southern gentlemen."

Dierdre mocked being shocked, and tried her best southern accent, "Suh, is you a confederit aftuh all?"

"My dear sweet lady, you forget, the President in question was also a southern gentlemen. Them Yankees don't rightly care one way or another what we might think agin him."

She laughed. Talking with him was fun. She did not know when she put so much value in talking, but it seemed to pop into her mind a lot lately. She liked talking to him. It was hard finding someone to talk with. If only he were more interesting.

They had walked the distance to the parking lot, where he held the car door for her. Once they were both settled and he had started the engine, he said, "I assume, since you chose the movie, that it was up to me to select a restaurant."

"Hmm," she thought, "he said that well." It was strong and assertive.

"Were you coached to say that?"

He had thought maybe he had gotten off the hook, but saw now he would have to fulfill his vow and grovel further over the coaching. "On my honor, no more coaching. I just was hoping you'd let me pick a spot to eat." He almost added, "seeing that I would probably have to grovel and apologize all through dinner," but decided it would only serve to antagonize her, which was not his intention tonight.

"Can you explain to me, why in the world you would have someone coach you how to behave?"

"Isn't it obvious? It's certainly obvious to me, and probably to everyone that sees us together. You are an incredibly stunningly beautiful women. You are way out of my league, yet I cannot help but be drawn to you like a moth to a flame. So someone told me that if I stopped acting like a moth and acted like the wind, that the flame would become putty in my hands."

"Oh, my, God!" Dierdre exclaimed, "You're a poet! That was beautiful."

"Well, at least as beautiful an analogy that you may have ever heard that included a moth in it."

She laughed again, she didn't mean to, but out it came on its own accord. It was a small, girlish, sexy laugh that came from tickling a different kind of funny bone.

"I mean it," he continued, "You are a fun vibrant woman. You know how to have fun. I've seen you at some of the clubs. You dance and laugh and you have men all over the place falling all over you. I dare say you never saw me there. At first I could not believe that this young woman, in command of so many male companions, was the same brilliant woman who wrote the papers on the fluid course of quantum matter. I was enthralled by your papers. How could I help but want to be near you? Imagine my shock when I saw that you were not a wallflower like most of your colleagues, but were a regular girl. I was crushed. How dare I think you might have that one flaw that I could share with you? And with you not being cursed with intellectual shyness, then how could I ever meet you? I would have to somehow overcome my own shyness to meet you at least partway, but that's not so easy. So I cheated, and I do apologize."

"No more apologies, please. Your apology is accepted, you are hereby formally freed from further groveling."

A quiet moment followed, as Stillman pulled the car into the parking lot of a popular seafood chain. Neither of them moved yet to exit the car, not sure who should move first.

"Why," he asked, "why are you here with me now?"

She turned her head ever so slowly, till she faced him and looked him straight in the eyes. Then her lips slowly curled into a smile and she replied, "Because you invited me."

Stillman walked around the car and held the door for Dierdre.

"With so many men far more attractive than myself, why would you waste your time with a stiff old coot like myself?"

She thought for a moment before giving her answer, "First, you aren't that old, you just pretend you are. Second, a moment ago, you must have used about two-hundred words describing your feelings about me and wanting to meet me. None of those pretty boys could have done that. I'm not even sure they all know two-hundred words. It is really refreshing to have someone I can talk to, talk with, and not have the conversation drift to vulgar sexual innuendo and stupid attempts to manipulate me into bed."

"Uhoh," he said, "now what am I going to talk about?"

Again, Dierdre reacted on instinct, she opened her mouth in amused disbelief, and with her eyes spread wide around her pupils, she made a kind of an "Uhhh" sound, while she hit him on the shoulder with her purse.

Stillman rubbed his shoulder in mocked surprise, "Hey! How would you like it if I did that to you?"

"Why?" she asked, "Are you carrying a dainty little girly hand bag that I don't know about?"

Stillman tried sounding gay, "I don't share that particular intimacy until at least the third date."

She laughed. "Your homosexual impersonation is really quite terrible."

"What a relief," he said, "I was afraid you might say it was very good and natural sounding, I don't think my battered male ego could have taken that at the moment."

"Homophobe?" she asked.

"Not in the least. I'm just trying to put my best foot forward to impress the most beautiful women I have ever had the pleasure to sit with. I want her to find me interesting."

"You're an interesting person. She'd be crazy to think otherwise." She thought she was just being polite and boosting his ego, but her words came far easier than they should have.

"Oh, you're just saying that because you're afraid if I fall into a depression and start feeling sorry for myself, I'll get even worse than I am now."

"Stillman, I haven't stopped laughing since the movie ended, and I'm not laughing at you, you are making me laugh because you are witty, and a little bit charming in a sweet boyish way."

Dierdre's jaw dropped for a moment. "Oh my God," she thought, "it's true. He has made me laugh all evening. Maybe he's not so bad after all, or maybe he's just brain washing me."

The restaurant wasn't busy yet, and they were promptly seated in nice booth. The waiter came to take their drink orders, but Dierdre just stared at Stillman for a moment. The Stillman she thought she knew wasn't there anymore. She saw someone else sitting at the table across from her. She saw someone with a sparkle in his eye and a wit in his head. He didn't even seem shy anymore. It must be multiple personalities. It may take a while to figure out which of them was the crazy one though, but from the way he looked at her, and the way she felt inside when he did, she just might like spending the time to find out which of them was nuts.

CHAPTER 11

Ramiro's flight landed in San Diego shortly before midnight. He didn't check any bags, opting instead to just throw a few essentials into a small carry-on. He waited till he cleared the jet way and entered the main terminal before calling Chief Henderson. "Mitch? Any calls come in while I was flying?"

"I don't know. We had a problem with the wire taps. I..."

"A problem? I drew up the order and filed it myself. Who said there was a problem?"

"The order was fine," Henderson said, "And the phone company cooperated as much as they could, but they have never had this problem before. You see..."

"What kind of problem could they have? I issued a bench order, if they don't follow my order, they are in contempt of court and I will throw the book at them personally."

"Easy Rami, let me finish, it's really not their fault. The order was fine, they went to execute it but, you see, the thing is, they..."

"Spit it out Mitch. What are you having such a hard time saying?"

"There was already a tap on your phone and their software doesn't allow them to put two taps on the same line."

That was unexpected news. Ramiro's whole body reacted, his blood pressure instantly took a dip and his view of the airport terminal warped around him like some weird camera effect. He stopped walking and caught his breath. "They what? A tap? Who?"

"I have someone checking on it now. They couldn't find a copy of the order for the tap, but they have a team looking for it. I have a friend in the clerk's office checking their records to see if there is a bench order to tap your phone."

Ramiro felt himself sink deeper from consciousness as he formed his next question, "Are you telling me that the FBI put an illegal wiretap on my line?"

"No, no. That's the thing that has the phone guys so puzzled. An illegal tap would normally be done at your home or office, or they might place a bug in your phone, something like that. This wiretap was done in their computer system, using their software. That means that either they received an order to do it, or someone managed to do it on their system without their knowledge."

"Who can do that?"

"I don't know," Henderson said, "but I understand there has been some excitement going on around the university with computer hackers breaking into their systems there. I don't see an obvious connection, but I'm not a big believer in coincidences."

"I don't know if you are aware of this, but Aimee works at the college, and one of her professors, who is also her best friend, had her computer hacked."

"No kidding? I really don't like coincidences."

"There's more Mitch, her assistant is a young man who allegedly was a hacker when he was a kid."

"Do you think he could be up to no good?"

"Not really. He seems like a very good young man. Even the FBI was impressed with him."

Henderson was taking notes as he asked, "What's his name?"

"Billy, or Bobby, maybe Barry, I forget, I can check with Dierdre tomorrow morning to find out."

"Dierdre?"

"Sorry, that's Professor Jennings. She's Aimee's friend and the kid's boss."

Henderson closed his small notebook and said, "I'll expect to hear from you sometime tomorrow. Now about that other tap. Nobody can find a procedure for determining which tap takes precedence, and just because they can't find the order doesn't mean there wasn't an order, so how are they supposed to proceed?"

"I need to know which judge signed the order. I can write an order to either vacate or supersede some judges, but not all, so I need to know who it is first. If it was properly filed, it should not be difficult to locate."

"Everyone is looking, and they said if they had an order to specifically replace the other, it would only take moments to execute."

"Tell them to be prepared to execute a new order at 3 p.m. I will file an amended order that will specifically vacate any pre-existing unauthorized wire taps effective then. That should give them sufficient time to locate any existing order."

"Three o'clock. Got it."

"And Mitch, ask them if they have any way to research who

executed the wiretap. Ask them if they keep records of which operator or employee actually put it there."

"You got it. I'll see if I can have some answers ready when you call me in the morning with that kid's name."

"Thanks Mitch. Get some sleep too."

"You too bud."

While Ramiro continued to worry about Aimee for the rest of the night, he occupied his time with the regular stuff, getting a car and a room. It was late now, and Dierdre had plans for the evening, he'll call her in the morning.

* * *

The rest of the night was quiet. For the first time in days, there was no nocturnal sneaking about, no espionage, no computer hacking. The wee hours of Sunday were truly a time of rest. Sunrise came and went. Ramiro had slept lightly, but did get at least some rest. In the morning, he prepared new orders as he had said he would. He sat alone in the hotel's small business center and typed up orders to replace the wire taps on his phone lines. It was at that moment, that he realized he never asked his friend which line, or if it was indeed both lines which had already been tapped. He could not imagine what would have led them to tap his lines.

He signed the papers and faxed them to the clerk's office, with copies to his own office. He made calls to alert the clerks that they had new papers filed on a Sunday morning which required immediate attention. One task down, one to go.

It was nine o'clock now, and the world around him was waking up to a multitude of activities. With baseball concluded, sports fans were flocking to the stores purchasing hotdogs, chips and beer, mostly beer, which they would haul with them to congregate around someone's big screen TV to watch this week's round of gridiron match-ups. But this was Southern California, and people were also pulling on their skates and climbing atop their bicycles to enjoy what promised to be another amazing day.

Ramiro was anxious to call Dierdre, but he reminded himself that even though she was hours ahead of him, she may have been out late last night, so he chose to wait a bit. He went for a walk. He hadn't noticed last night, but his hotel was near a harbor, and he merely needed to cross the street to look down on the water. He could see beaches spread out down to his right, and people already started to gather. To his left, an old but very sturdy looking wooden pier extended out into the bay. Old men and young boys leaned over the pier railings lowering fishing lines into the water. There were some small shops where the pier met the land, and across the other side of the pier, he saw a restaurant, with patrons filing in for Sunday brunch.

Food sounded good to Ramiro, so he headed in that direction.

* * *

Bobby woke up, and as often happens when he is working on big projects like this, he had some new ideas. He didn't dream these ideas, although he has dreamt ideas before. Unfortunately, dreamed up ideas are too often fanciful concepts without basis in reality, like the time he dreamed a computer program that described the flavor of lasagna. In his mind, he could see the source code printed on green bar paper. He also dreamed an algorithm for apple pie, to follow up the lasagna. In his dream, the formulas were very real algorithmic sequences, and were breakthroughs in computer science. Nobody, anywhere, had ever written programs which so accurately defined processes that were so uniquely physical as flavor was. In the moments between sleep and awareness, as he was waking up from those dreams, he tried to hold on to the concepts, but they disintegrated before his very eyes, and on that occasion, when he was sufficiently awake, he became aware of an elevated temperature. He had been running a fever and that, he decided, accounted for the strange dream.

But, this idea was not from a dream, and probably came to him because he had relaxed enough to get some sleep.

Bobby had left the machine running and it would periodically create random mutations on the clients. Ninety-nine percent of random ideas failed to accomplish anything, because they were most likely to turn out to be nonsense. He needed mutations to be rare, because if they occurred too frequently, then an improved program would continually be changing away from what made it work. He also needed the rare mutations to make a little more sense when they did work, so it occurred to him that he could scan other programs on the client computer, and identify places where they placed calls to the operating system. These were the operations that he would try to optimize if he were going to make the programs faster, so he could narrow down the random changes by only selecting from these calls.

He started crafting the new code, which, when complete, would be spliced onto one of the threads as a client update, and be sent back to the main computer.

* * *

Ramiro finished his breakfast and checked the time. It was half past ten now, still early for a Sunday morning, but not too early to place a call. He dialed Dierdre's number, one ring, two rings, three rings. The answering machine finally picked up, "Dierdre? Are you there? This is Ramiro, if you are there, please pick up." He waited a few moments, with no response, "Dierdre, I'm in San Diego looking for Aimee. When you get this message please call me." He gave her his cell phone number, and repeated it again very slowly to make sure.

Now he was stuck, he'll give her some time, maybe she was just out getting the paper or something. If he doesn't hear from her in an hour or so, he'll call Mitch for an update anyway. He resigned himself to the fact, that there was little he could do until 3 p.m. anyway, and he set that deadline himself.

* * *

Bobby was engrossed in his work when the phone rang. "Hello?"

"Bobby, it's me, Dierdre. I came into the office to check my email. I had completely forgotten that you were running tests on our machines. How do I check my emails while these are running?"

"No problem", he replied, "you can either hot-key back to the desktop, or you can hit alt-F4 to kill the job. That will return your computer to your control."

"OK, hang on while I do this." She chose the alt-escape combination, no sense killing it just for an email. As he said, the screen she had been looking at went away and she was presented with her desktop. She started the email program. It checked for new mail, but there was none. "Shoot. No new email. Bobby, are you sure this program won't interfere with the emails?"

"Let's see," he brought up his email program, typed a quick note that only said "test" and sent it to her. "You should be getting an email in a moment."

She counted to three. "Nope, nothing."

"OK, then a couple moments, the Internet isn't quite that swift yet."

She sat back and waited a minute, then up popped a new email alert. She could see without opening it that it was from Bobby. "There it is. Why isn't she writing anymore?"

"Maybe she can't. In order to email you, she would need access to a working computer, and access to her email account. There are plenty of things that could go wrong. Maybe she'll call, and since it's Sunday, she'll probably call you at home."

"You think I'm worrying too much?"

"No," he said, "it's good you care, but there is nothing you can do to help her. We don't even know if she needs or wants help."

"She probably needs help, but is too stubborn to ask for it. Do I need to do something to restore your program?"

"No, it's OK to leave it like that. You should get home now, for all you know, there could be a message waiting for you already."

Bobby went back to work on his modifications. The first version had been designed to just try random instructions to see if they worked. But the chances of that working had to be a million to one or worse, but his new routine was much more efficient. There would still be a thousand to one chance of it working, but since he was going to have thousands of threads running, a thousand to one chance was within reach. He stopped typing a moment and pondered that thought.

He was going to have a thousand threads running, so a thousand to one shot was possible. Dierdre said that ultimately her process would need millions of processors, so a million to one shot would also be attainable. Now his mind reeled with the enormity of what he was thinking.

He replaced the code that could try random instructions, but he added an additional twist. He remembered that Dierdre's original concept called for the threads to be independent, like bees, but to also behave with and react to each other. It seemed reasonable to him that they should have some concept of how many threads existed. If they knew how many threads there were, they could suppress the million to one shot routine until they exceeded a million threads. Counting threads isn't hard, but he couldn't have each thread independently counting all the other threads, especially if there were a million to be counted. Nothing would ever get done if that happened, so he set it up to elect a single thread to take a census.

He also thought it would be handy to know how many threads were on-line.

He continued working on his updates. He didn't expect to complete them until early that evening.

* * *

Dierdre arrived home and saw the light blinking on her answering machine. She did not even wait to take her coat off, but went straight to the machine and pressed play.

"Dierdre? Are you there? This is Ramiro, if you are there, please pick up…Dierdre, I'm in San Diego looking for Aimee. When you get this message please call me."

She wrote down the number that followed, and immediately punched it into her phone. "Hello? Ramiro? It's Dierdre."

"Thanks for calling. I'll get right to the point. When we were all together in your office talking to the FBI about the note you received, we learned that your computer had been hacked and since your new assistant has a history…"

Before he could continue, she cut him off, "I know all about Bobby's background. He's a good kid, and I don't believe he had anything to do with those attacks. He wouldn't have time anyway. He's been working around the clock on my project."

"Personally, I don't suspect him either. I got a very good impression from him, but something is going on. Someone may have hacked a very secure system, and it is somehow related. I don't suspect your assistant, but all the same, I would like to have his full name so I can have a background check done."

Dierdre thought it over, and decided she believed in him, and any checking Ramiro did would only clear his name. "Bobby Blain," she said.

"Thanks Dierdre. I promise you this is not a witch hunt. If anything, the witch hunt seems to be targeting Aimee and myself."

"And yourself? What are you talking about?"

"Nothing I can repeat, yet, but the FBI seems to have decided that Aimee is up to no good, and someone appears to think that I am somehow involved."

"Fat Bunch of Idiots."

"What was that?"

"F.B.I. Fat Bunch of Idiots."

Ramiro snickered. "They aren't all idiots, but it seems that enough of them are to make life interesting for the rest of us."

"Interesting? I think the word you are looking for is annoying."

"Well, that too. I have to call a friend to see if there have been any new developments. If you hear from Aimee, tell her to call me on this phone. If they ever find her, I may have to represent her to release her from their custody."

"I certainly will," she said, "I just wish we had a clue what was going on. All the mystery does not help her case."

"Not with these guys. I'll let you know if I find anything too. Bye now."

"Bye."

* * *

Ramiro dialed Henderson. "Mitch? Ramiro. Any news?"

"Not much. The phone company still has not located a court order, but they have determined that the tap was added within the last twenty-four hours. They have a name of the employee who entered the tap order, but he was scheduled to start vacation yesterday, and they have been unable to locate him."

"Wait a sec, Mitch. You said the tap was put in within twenty-four hours?"

"Yes, but that was within twenty-four hours of the time we had tried to execute your orders."

"That's fine, but if the order is only two days old now, how could they have lost it already? It should be either filed, or in a file clerks in-basket, or still sitting on top of the missing guy's desk."

Chief Henderson smacked himself in the head. "I'm sorry. I should have thought of that and asked them. Let me get them right back on the phone and ask them about that."

"Wait, before you hang up. I got that kid's name for you. His name is Bobby Blain. See what you can find out. I don't think he is behind this, but you might as well check him out anyway. We seem to have a number of people being targeted by unknown persons."

"We have an abundance of unknowns. We don't know who is doing this. We don't know what they are doing. The FBI is hunting down your fiancé, yet they don't know why. I guess they will arrest her for suspicion of suspicion."

* * *

The phone company agreed. There was no reason for the court order to be lost under any circumstance, but especially not within twenty-four hours. They dispatched some supervisors to inspect the vacationing employee's desk, but they found nothing.

By the time they abandoned the search and reported back to Chief Henderson, it was already 2 p.m. They would execute Ramiro's orders to replace the taps at 3 o'clock.

* * *

The skinny man sat in the large man's office. The large man continued to pace while he said, "So, your plan to recruit Bobby was to hack all these computers, but leave no evidence that it was Bobby who did it?"

"You need to understand him. He doesn't leave a trace. If I made evidence pointing to him, they would suspect it was fake."

"But," the large man said, "Pietre is convinced it is Bobby, and nobody is listening to him?"

"Correct. And he has actually been hacking Bobby's machine, but I've modified his attacks so Bobby would know it was Pietre."

"Because you wanted to annoy Pietre for being such a putz?"

"No," the Bard said, "Because Pietre might instigate Bobby to hack him back, and with all the surveillance we have set up, we might be able to get the goods on him."

"And blackmail him to join us?"

"I don't think he would join us out of civic responsibility."

"You don't think he is a patriot?"

The Bard shook his head. "He hacked the President. How could he be a patriot? Why don't you just go ask him if he wants to work for you?"

"He knows my face, why don't you ask him?"

"He knows my face too."

"So explain to me about the note."

"Like I told you," the Bard continued, "Pietre has been hacking their computers. He made copies of Professor Jennings' project, and erased them from her computer, then infected it with a virus."

"I thought Pietre's computer had the virus."

"Not really, I hacked his computer to look like it had a virus. I don't know why Pietre stole her project, but I thought it would be a good idea to leave clues where it was, so I created the ransom note. I created a web site and tied it to Pietre."

"So," the large man asked, "what went wrong?"

"They called the FBI and a judge."

"A judge? Why would they bring in a judge? And why would the FBI care about a stolen computer project?"

"Well," the Bard explained, "apparently, Professor Jennings' secretary disappeared, and they thought the ransom note meant she was kidnapped."

"That explains the FBI, what about the judge?"

"He's the missing girl's fiancé."

The large man was about to ask another question when the bards pager went off with a shrill pulsating beep. The smaller man grabbed his pager and looked at the numbers on it. "Uh oh".

"What's wrong?"

"Someone has discovered and disconnected my wire taps."

"Who did you tap?"

The smaller man got up to head for his computer and said, "I better go make sure they can't trace it back to us."

"Who did you tap?"

"I'll get back to you when I'm done."

The large man barked at him, "STOP! WHO DID YOU TAP?"

The bard stopped in the doorway, with his back to the large man.

He checked the number on the pager again and said, "The judge."

The large man couldn't believe his ears. That was not a very smart thing for his associate to do. He might have to do some damage control before this operation was over.

* * *

Chief Henderson called Ramiro shortly after three. "Squeeze? The taps are in place. Still no clue as to who ordered the previous taps. I've got people monitoring the lines now. If any calls come through, I'll let you know, but without you being there to answer the phone, all we are going to get is a list of caller-id's and maybe some phone messages."

"That's OK Mitch. I just want to know if she calls and where she called from."

* * *

Bobby finished his work just in time to fix something to eat. He released the new threads and watched them exchange up to the main machine. He left them running on his machine while he ate. He wasn't sure how he was going to survive the next three days. He couldn't wait till Wednesday when he could load his program on a thousand machines.

Sometimes it's the little details that can escape the mind. He easily pictured thousands of computers running his program and updating threads and clients, but until that very moment, he had not given sufficient thought to how he was going to install the clients on each of those machines.

He can't go to each machine and install the client manually, and he can't have everyone write their own loader program, so he needed a way to start the process simply and efficiently.

He considered creating a web page that would allow them to download either the client or the boot-strap with a single click, but web servers were notorious memory hogs and would kill the system and all the threads. He could set up a file transfer server which is much lighter on resources, but FTP servers aren't point and click. They expect the user to type instructions telling them what to do. Bobby would have to give all the contestants a list of instructions with fairly lengthy addresses for them to download the client. He wasn't concerned that the instructions would be too complicated, these were computer geeks and nerds after all. But all his participants would have just been eliminated from the contest, and might balk if the instructions were too laborious.

The simplest, most foolproof method would be to design a special FTP server program. Anyone that tried to log into the main computer with an FTP program, would instantly have the boot strap downloaded and executed. That way, they only needed to be given a single address, with instructions to FTP to it. This would actually be the easiest change he had to make. Instead of having to deal with users making a lot of different requests, the modified FTP program just assumed they wanted the boot strap and gave it to them. With that done, he could get some sleep. He had classes in the morning.

* * *

Dierdre stayed by the phone all day. She had planned to get some groceries, but could not stand the thought of missing a call from Aimee, or for that matter, from Ramiro. She raided the fridge and came up empty, but did find a can of soup in the cupboards. She put some light music on and settled down in her comfy chair and reflected on everything going on.

Her project seemed on the verge of great progress, though not necessarily due to any work she had done. She just had some ideas for how the model would work, and now she had someone else turning her ideas into reality. She wondered if he realized just how intelligent he might be. She would have to do something to help the educational system recognize him.

Amidst the progress her project was making, her life was surrounded with turmoil. Her best friend was missing, and not just missing, but mysteriously missing. For some unfathomable reason, the FBI suspected Aimee of some wrong doing. Dierdre's deepest fear was that some overzealous FBI agent might actually track her down and go in with guns blazing, just because they couldn't identify what she was doing. She really wished Aimee would call.

Then there was Ramiro. Apparently he and Aimee had a fight. That did not seem so unusual to Dierdre, she imagined that lots of couples engaged to be married had blowout arguments before the wedding. But then the FBI got involved again and somehow decided that because his fiancé was up to something they didn't understand, he must also be involved. This whole affair did not put the agency in a very good light.

And then there was Bobby. A brilliant young man once accused of hacking a politician, and nearly ending his career. Accused but never convicted. Everybody who has taken the time to get to know him has decided that regardless of what he may or may not have done as a youth, he was now a genuinely honest and pleasant young man. But, the inescapable fact was that they were surrounded with computer attacks which all started around the time he joined her project.

Dierdre's head jerked when her ruminations were startled by the telephone. "Hello?"

"Hello Dierdre, this is Stillman."

"Oh, hi Stillman." Her disappointment was evident in her voice.

He was crushed by the tone of her voice, but did his best not to show it. "I'm sorry, am I interrupting you?"

"Oh no, no," she said, "I was just hoping it was Aimee, I'm really worried about her."

"Still no word?"

"Not a peep from her since Friday."

"I'll be sure to keep her in my prayers," he said gallantly, "and I won't keep your phone tied up. I just wanted to tell you what a wonderful time I had yesterday, and I hope we can do it again sometime."

"That would be nice. I had a good time too."

"Well then, I'll see you tomorrow I'm sure, sleep well."

"Thank you. Good night Stillman."

She hung up the phone feeling good. She did not understand why she felt good, though he was a nice listener and fun to talk to. He could be the brother she never had. But that wasn't how she felt, she felt warmer than that, and had no explanation for it.

Her music ended shortly after she hung up the phone, and she decided to pull out an old Hepburn and Tracy movie. He wasn't the most attractive man, in fact he always had a more fatherly look about him, yet that never stopped him from being fun and romantic. She programmed the timer on her TV and fell asleep about halfway through the movie, and dreamed about men who weren't necessarily attractive enough to play leading men, yet still managed to be someone's leading man somewhere.

CHAPTER 12

Pietre's plans were falling apart. He got rid of Karlyn, but lost the machine to Professor Jennings. When he went to extract Karlyn's latest work from the machine, Bobby was there and got in the way. He hacked the machine, but Bobby hacked him back. He had a professional hack the machine, and Bobby hacked the whole university and pointed it to his lab. Bobby has foiled every attempt he has made to access Karlyn's research, and now Pietre has found himself cut off from his extra income and, it would seem, his value to them has plummeted. Everything pointed back to Bobby. Bobby had to go, but Pietre had failed every attempt to get rid of him. Perhaps it was time to try a more subtle approach, to go around Bobby instead of through him.

Pietre spent most of Saturday planning his attack. If he could not get rid of Bobby, he would just have to sneak out Karlyn's work from under his nose. He wrote a program that would be his spy. Once installed on Dierdre's computer, it would scan the computer for Karlyn's research, and send copies of it back to Pietre. And as an added bit of security, he created another program that would tack itself onto the thread manager. Since threads were constantly being managed, it would be able to check for Pietre's spy program, and launch it whenever it was not found. This way, if the spy was ever terminated or the computer was re-booted, the spy program would be restarted.

Now all he had to do was FTP the spy to Dierdre's machine and wait for it to start sending him what it found. To be safe, he scheduled the computer to FTP the new program later that night, when he could have an alibi.

* * *

Monday morning was shaping up to be a busy morning for Bobby, but he managed to squeeze in a moment to stop by Dierdre's office before his first class. "Any word from Aimee?"

"Nothing yet. How was your weekend?"

"Good, very good, I've made a lot of progress on the programs. I think you are going to be very happy with this week's results. We should prove that given enough processing power, your ideas can be applied in real time."

"Real time?" she asked, "We can't be anywhere near that can we?"

"Now? Not a chance, but computing power doubles every eighteen months, which means it quadruples every three years, sixteen times as powerful in only six years."

"I know," she said, "but only about one-hundred-thousand times as powerful in ten years, we still need much more."

"Keep extrapolating. After fifteen years, computers will be over one million times more powerful than today. There you have it. We'll have computers with one million processors within our lifetimes. I think we can prove your concepts have sufficient merit to warrant further research and hardware expenditures. I'll check on the process before lunch and give you an update. How was your date? I hope I didn't ruin it for you."

"It was nice," she said, "I had a very good time, I'm just not quite sure why."

"Did you do anything special?"

"We went to a movie and dinner. Nothing special, just kind of nice."

"I think you are over analyzing it. If you had a good time, that's all that matters. Who'd you go with? Maybe that's your answer? Anyone special?"

Dierdre shot a glance to her clock and said, "Oh my, I have got to get to my first class, and I think you do too. I'm looking forward to hearing your progress report this afternoon." She grabbed some books and her brief case, then headed out the door to her first class. She was afraid that it may have been too obvious a ploy, but her date with Stillman was not something she was prepared to discuss openly.

* * *

Pietre arrived at his lab and was perplexed by what he saw. Instead of the successful completion message he expected to find, his console had bar charts which went up and down as he watched, very similar to the screens he saw on professor Jennings' machine. "That son of bitch," he muttered to himself.

* * *

Bobby finished his classes in time to visit the lab before lunch. He was surprised by what he found when he got there. He had a message from the jobs that were scanning the memory and hard drives, he had forgotten about those jobs in his excitement over the updates he made to the threads. The second surprise he had was a problem with the census update he created. The number of threads being reported by his census update was way too high. It must be counting them two or three times.

He knew that the larger machine could support about sixty-four threads, and the smaller one in the lab office could add another four, and the two in Dierdre's office, if still running would probably only add two more in total. That would be a total of seventy threads. His census was reporting over two-hundred threads.

Obviously, there was a problem with the census. He pulled up the census code. The counting code was very simple. It received a response and added one to the counter. If a thread responded twice, it would be counted twice. That must be what was happening. He made some quick changes so the threads would respond to the census request by sending their unique thread id which was like a fingerprint. He changed the census taker to keep a table of all the threads that responded and only increment the counter if the thread id is not in the table already. That should eliminate the duplicates. He released the changes to the thread pools, and started to look at the data he got from the scans.

The disk scan did not turn up anything interesting, but the memory scan found some data in ROM areas that were supposed to be empty. The data could be anything. It could be imagery stored in ROM or it could be encrypted data. He started up a decoder program that was designed to crack encrypted files, but it could be a very long process.

With the new census released, and the decryption started, he locked the lab and went to lunch.

* * *

Chief Henderson had learned just about everything he thought he was going to get from the criminal case data bank. He found an entry for Robert O. Blain, but all he could learn from the file was that an investigation took place, charges were filed, and the case was dismissed for lack of evidence. Details of the case were sealed because the accused was a minor. Robert O. Blain had no current record. Even his Motor Vehicles record was squeaky clean. Basically, he learned nothing, but he was able to confirm that there was a case at one time, which only amounted to suspicion.

He tossed the report on his desk and went to a pin board he had setup. He had notes of all the strange events which somehow seemed weakly connected to each other, but still had no clue what was at the center of it all. He pinned a new note on the board under Bobby's name, "suspicion-no conviction-record clean". While he stood there staring at the board, hoping some small detail would suddenly jump out at him, the phone rang.

"Chief Henderson."

"Good morning Chief Henderson, my name is Arthur Bedding. I'm an investigator with Inter Mountain Telegraph's fraud department. I've got something I think you should see. Is there a fax number where I can send you some reports?"

"Yes," Henderson said, "555-1492. Did you find the original court order for that wiretap?" The chief was concerned that they may have found the order after they had already disconnected that tap. That could lead to some trouble for his office if the judge who signed it wasn't in a good mood.

"No, still no court order, but I ran a query to list all the current wiretaps. Then, I had the clerks pull all the original orders for those taps. The fax I am sending you is a list of all the wire taps which don't have orders on file. All these wire taps were executed on the same day."

An office clerk came into Henderson's office with a fax in his hand. The chief looked over the list. It had the numbers cross-referenced to list the owners:

Blain, Robert
Gonzalez, Roberto c/o Federal Bureau of Investigations
Jennings, Dierdre
Jennings, Dierdre c/o Norwood University
Spivey, Eric c/o Federal Bureau of Investigations
Takahashi, Aimee
Takahashi, Aimee c/o Norwood University
Vasquez, Ramiro
Vasquez, Ramiro c/o Superior Court

"That's quite a list," Henderson said into the phone.

"Yes it is, I've known the FBI to be thorough, but I've never known them to wiretap themselves."

"Did you happen to check on any past wiretaps without orders to back them up?"

"No," Bedding said, "but that's a good idea, but if that list is anything like this list, it may take a while."

"Go ahead and start looking through the last six months, maybe a year. If you have any trouble allocating sufficient resources, then you give me a call. I'll have Judge Vasquez issue a court order for the information. You may have noticed the last name on your list. I think he would be more than happy to light a fire under anyone who wishes to impede this investigation."

"Jesus!" Bedding exclaimed, "A judge? I thought the FBI names took balls. Whatever you want, you just ask. I want to provide you with the fullest cooperation of my department, and if my hands are tied, for any reason, I will give you a call so the Judge can smooth the process."

"Thanks," Henderson said, "Arthur, right?"

"Yes. Arthur Bedding. If I don't have any results by this afternoon, I will fax you a progress report in the morning."

"That will be fine. Thanks for calling."

The chief hung up the phone and dialed Ramiro's cell number and relayed the lack of information on Bobby Blain, and the additional information from the phone company.

"Mitch, read that list to me again."

The chief read back the list of people with taps on their phone lines.

"That's everyone who was present at the university when we met to check on the ransom note."

"The FBI wouldn't tap their office phones like that," Henderson said, "they would have recording devices attached to their phones. The more I think about it, the more I am convinced that the sudden rash of computer hacks must be tied in to the wire taps. If the FBI did not tap the lines, then someone must have been watching or listening to you guys." The chief was on a roll, and started linking theories out loud, "And if they are willing and able to secretly tap all those phones, then they are probably able to bug Professor Jennings' office. And if they are inclined to bug her office, then they must be after something that they think she has, and it all seems to date back to the time when she got that new kid, Bobby."

"We already talked about Bobby, I don't think he is the key, because right before Professor Jennings hired Bobby, she received a new computer, in fact, they both came at the same time."

Chief Henderson was nodding his head, even though Ramiro could not see this through the phone. "Yeah, and his name is on the list too. I think I'll have a talk with Mr. Blain about the computer, and I can't wait to hear what the phone company comes back with on any prior wire taps."

"If you don't hear from them this afternoon, you'll find an order demanding their cooperation waiting on your fax in the morning. I'll write it so you can use it at your discretion."

* * *

Dierdre finished her morning lectures and returned to her office. The programs were still running on their office computers, and there was a single white rose in a slim vase on her desk. Had it been from anyone else, she would have thought him being a bit pushy, but not so from Stillman. A shy man like Stillman didn't make moves like other men. They were far more likely to speak their mind than their heart. Such an act, with obvious romantic overtones, would have required a great deal of resolve on his part. She gave him an "E" for effort. His statement was clear. He clearly desired a romantic relationship with her, but she wasn't quite sure how she felt about it. She has only just barely acknowledged that she enjoys his company, but she thought of him more as a companion, possibly a brother. If she rejected him now, it could crush him, if she let it go on, then he might get the wrong idea, and she liked him too much to lead him on. Why couldn't cute guys be smart and romantic and thoughtful?

* * *

Chief Henderson looked over the report on Bobby Blain again. It was spotless. He wondered if the FBI had a thicker report. He picked up his phone and dialed the number he had for the university, and asked to speak with Professor Jennings.

"Hello? This is Professor Jennings."

"Good afternoon Professor, my name is Mitch Henderson. I am a friend of Ramiro Vasquez and I am also the chief of police. I am investigating some of the unusual events surrounding the disappearance of Aimee Takahashi for Ramiro, and I was hoping to have a moment to speak with your new assistant, Robert Blain about some of the hackings that have occurred on your computer system."

"Well, I can assure you that Bobby will be completely cooperative with your investigation, that's the kind of person he is, and I can personally assure you that he has nothing to do with any of this."

"Bobby is not under suspicion," Henderson assured her, "at least not by my department. I just wanted to ask him some questions about your new computer system."

"Well, like I said, he is very cooperative. Would you like me to have him call you?"

"Please, or if there is a good time for me to come down and speak with him, I only need a few minutes."

"Certainly, I will tell him you called, what number can he reach you at?"

As the chief was reading his number to Dierdre, Bobby poked his head through her doorway, but saw she was on the phone, and waited outside.

"Just a second," Dierdre said, "he's here, let me ask him when would be a good time."

She covered the mouthpiece on the handset and called out, "Bobby?"

He entered her office and said, "Hi, I just wanted a quick second."

"The police want to know when they can meet with you to ask you some questions about the new computer system."

"I came here to invite you to meet me in the lab at five. Would they like to meet us there or do they want me to come down to the station?"

She removed her hand and said, "Chief, would five o'clock in my lab work for you? You'll get to see the computer system first hand then."

"Splendid. I'll just need directions to your lab."

"You'll find someone in administration, when you come in from the parking lot. Ask them to show you my office. I'll wait for you and take you up there personally. We were going to go over some project notes then anyway."

"Thank you Professor, I'll see you then."

* * *

Ramiro prepared a warrant directing the phone company to turn over all records and matters pertaining to any wiretaps recorded over the last six months. He faxed the order to his office, and a copy to Mitch with instructions to get the original from the clerk.

He began to question why he had come to San Diego. At the time, it seemed that the FBI was about to apprehend Aimee and he would be there to negotiate her release. But she was still missing and there was no word from anyone. There was nothing he could do but pace and sleep and drink. He vowed to limit himself to pacing and sleeping, but the pacing made him thirsty, and the drinking helped him sleep.

He finally decided that doing nothing accomplished nothing, so he would do something, and try to track down Aimee himself. He went to the motel where the FBI had found an empty room.

He found the motel manager and held up a picture of Aimee. "Do you remember seeing this woman?"

"I already told the police, I don't remember her."

"May I see your register please?"

"Isn't this protected information?"

Ramiro showed the manager his shield and told him, "No sir, it is not. But if you prefer, I don't have to get a warrant, I only have to write one myself. Do you want me to write a warrant?"

The clerk reluctantly flipped open his hotel registry and shoved it toward Ramiro. Aimee's name was not there. He thought he might have recognized her handwriting a couple times, but couldn't be sure.

"Thank you. Are you sure you don't remember anything?"

"Look mister, I don't normally see the people. I'm usually in the back in my office, sorry."

Ramiro left the office, but realized the man was right. He needed to speak to some of the employees. The motel was like any other. The rooms were on two floors. All doors led to the outside.

Ramiro headed up the stairs, and down the hall. He found a maid pushing her cart from one room to the next. She had strong olive skin, as was common for the maids in Southern California. He chose to speak with her in Spanish.

"Good morning," he said, "may I speak with you a moment please?"

The maid looked at him warily, so he showed her his shield, but this only frightened her.

"Please be calm, my name is Ramiro Vasquez. I am a judge. I am here looking for this girl." He showed her a picture and asked, "Have you seen her?"

"No. No."

"Please look again. She is my fiancé and I need to find her."

The maid looked at the picture again, apparently more moved that she was his fiancé than she was by his badge.

"No. Sorry. Go ask Leticia. She cleaned that room the police searched." The woman pointed to the other end of the upper level.

"Gracias."

Ramiro walked down past the stairs to the other end where he found another maid. "Leticia?"

"Si."

"I am looking for this girl. She is my fiancé. Have you seen her?"

"Si," she said, "I saw her. The police are looking for her too, but I told them nothing."

"I need to find her before the police do. She has done nothing but they are crazy and won't listen to me."

"Si," she mocked spitting, "Federale idiots." She reached for the picture again and looked at it, then at Ramiro again and said, "I remember her, but I don't know anything."

Ramiro pulled out a business card, and wrote the name of his hotel on the back. "Please. She is in trouble and I need to help her. If you remember anything, I am staying at this hotel."

She took the card and tucked it in her apron. "Good luck, señior, my prayers are with her."

* * *

Chief Henderson arrived at the school at ten minutes before five, and was directed to Dierdre's office. She was grading some papers while she waited for him. When he arrived at the suite of offices, he peeked in hers, but moved on to the next office and the next, but the others were all vacant so he returned to Dierdre's office. "Excuse me miss, I'm looking for Professor Jennings. Can you tell me where I might find her?"

Dierdre remained seated as she offered him her hand. "Hello, I am Professor Jennings, Chief Henderson I presume?"

"Guilty as charged. I'm sorry. I guess I was expecting someone a bit more..." He paused a moment to consider what he was about to say next, "more seasoned?"

Stillman popped into her office, "Dierdre-oh I'm sorry, you have company."

"Stillman," she said, "this is Chief Henderson, Chief, this is Professor Whitfield."

Stillman shook the chief's hand and withdrew a well wrung out hand. "I won't bother you. I'll see you tomorrow." He slipped out, and waited until he was around the corner before flexing his squished hand.

Chief Henderson turned to Dierdre, who had not yet risen from her desk, and pointed his thumb over his shoulder saying, "Now that guy looks like a professor. I guess I need to update my profile."

Dierdre wasn't quite sure how to handle the awkward moment, so she just forced a fake half smile.

"I'm sorry, I was expecting someone more matronly, let me start over. Hi, I'm Chief Henderson, and you must be Professor Jennings. Thank you for seeing me today."

Awkward as his entrance was, his recovery was whole hearted and unashamed, and she had to give him credit for that. "Pleased to meet you Chief Henderson, I must admit, you are exactly as I pictured you."

The chief glanced at his reflection in one of Dierdre's plaques on the wall, brushed a strand of gray hairs with his fingers, and said, "Ouch, well I guess I deserved that."

Dierdre laughed as she rose from her desk. "Here, why don't you follow me. It's three flights up, can you manage that OK?"

The chief followed her out the door and said, "I thought you science types didn't have a sense of humor?"

"Humor?" she asked, "What humor?"

"Ouch again, I think I'll just shut up now."

They climbed the steps to the lab. Bobby was at the terminal scrolling through some data when they entered the lab.

"Bobby? This is Chief Henderson."

"Hello," Bobby said, "I pulled another chair into the office so we could all sit and talk."

"First," the chief said as he took his seat, "I want to emphasize, that I am not investigating you, Bobby. I have pulled your files and am aware of your history, and as far as I am concerned, legally, you have a spotless record. I think, however, you may be a witness to something, we just don't know what you have witnessed yet. Second, I want to emphasize, that this is not a fully official investigation, but it is also not unofficial. I have not created a case file, because frankly, we don't even have a crime yet. I am investigating the disappearance of Professor Jennings' secretary Aimee, on behalf of my good friend Justice Ramiro Vasquez. I was told that you have had some problems with people hacking into your computer. Is that correct?"

Bobby leaned forward and said, "Frankly, I think that most of the things going on around here are related to this computer, and that Aimee's disappearance is a coincidence."

"What can you tell me about that?"

Dierdre answered, "It all started when Dr. Karlyn gave me his computer right before he left the school."

"So that's when all the strange things began to happen? When you got the computer?"

Bobby and Dierdre both answered together, she said, "Yes," and he said, "No."

Dierdre and Henderson both arched their eyebrows and looked at Bobby.

"The hacks," Bobby said, "may have started when Professor Jennings got the computer, but the strange things began before that."

The chief turned a page in his notebook to a blank sheet. "Perhaps you can tell me, from the beginning, what you think happened."

"Well," Bobby started, "it all started several weeks ago when an old friend of Dr. Karlyn's showed up late one night. It was clear to me that Karlyn was not expecting him, but it was also obvious that they were good friends at one time, and still remained so today. His friend was a scientist with some secret department working on some secret government project."

"I'm sorry. Do you mean he wouldn't tell you what department and project he was with?"

"No, he actually said he was with a secret department working on a secret project. They didn't really include me in their conversations, but Dr. Karlyn asked me to build a computer interface for him right after his friend left. He told me that his friend could not divulge his project because it was top secret. I saw him give Dr. Karlyn a brown paper package. I never saw what was in it, but I assumed it was why he wanted me to build an interface."

Bobby paused so the chief could catch up with his notes.

Henderson asked, "So you think they want this hardware back?"

"At first," Bobby said, "that was what I thought. But if the hardware in the package was all they wanted, then they would have taken it back instead of hacking us. I don't think they want the hardware back anymore."

"What do you know about Dr. Karlyn's experiments on the device?"

"Me? Nothing. All I ever did was build a card that Dr. Karlyn could use to attach the device to the computer for analysis. He did all the testing. I don't even think he knew how to power it up at first."

"And later," Henderson asked, "did he get power to it?"

"I think so. Dr. Karlyn never let me see the device, but in the beginning, he worked with it connected to the card I built by long ribbon cables, but sometime around the fourth or fifth day, the cables went away. I assumed at the time that he had finished testing and sent it back to his friend."

"What do you think happened to the device?"

Bobby pointed at the computer rack and said, "I've just started to suspect that it might be installed inside the computer, but Dr. Karlyn must have it hidden, because I took the computer apart when I moved it to this lab, and I never saw anything out of place."

"So if they aren't after the device, you think they are after what he learned about it? What did he learn?"

"First," Bobby said, "I think he figured out how to power it up, and second, he must have figured out how to interface it to my card sufficiently for him to install it and do all his analysis from the computer. They probably want access to the device, and the card I built so they could continue to test it."

"That makes sense. What about the weird things you said were happening?"

"Around the time the cables disappeared, one of Dr. Pietre's students transferred to Karlyn's class and started making advances on Karlyn. When Karlyn made it clear that she could not earn her grade that way, she arranged to have a photographer at just the right place when she threw herself in his arms and ripped open her blouse."

"She blackmailed him with that?"

"I've heard that rumor," Dierdre added, "I think that's why he left."

Bobby shook his head and said, "I don't think it's the real reason, but he never told me the real truth about leaving."

"What about the scientist friend that brought the package?"

"He was supposed to contact Dr. Karlyn for an update, but I have never heard or seen from him since that first time."

"Do you remember his name?"

"No, but before they started keeping secrets, when Karlyn first saw his friend, I heard him say something that sounded like 'Kritch, is that you?' So I would guess his name might be Critchfield or Critchton."

"Did you get a good look at him? Can you describe him?"

"He was kind of creepy looking, over six feet tall, very thin, even gaunt looking with sunken eyes and cheeks. He had black hair and half frame reading glasses."

Henderson wrote as fast as he could, straining to keep up with Bobby's description. "I wish all my witnesses were like you."

"Oh, and he smoked a pipe. A plain black pipe."

"Was there anything besides their current interest in your computer that makes you suspect the device may be inside?"

Bobby reached over to a stack of reports and grabbed some pages filled with numbers. "Well, there's this. It's a dump of a memory region I found that should not be there. I have been running it against all my decryption programs but have not identified what it is yet."

"And you think this is from that device?"

"I tracked the memory address to the slot where I placed my interface card, so yes, I think it could be the device."

Bobby reached over to the terminal on the desk near them and entered a couple quick commands. "See? This is that same area, it's still there as we speak."

Chief Henderson looked at the screen, then at the paper dump, then the screen, then the dump and asked, "Are they supposed to match?"

"Yes. I took that dump yesterday, I thought at first it was a hidden secret document, but it could easily be rom instructions for the secret device."

"But they don't match. Is this the first page of the dump?"

"That's impossible," Bobby said as he slid his chair to the terminal, "they have to match."

Bobby hit a function key to print the dump on the screen, and gave the report to the chief.

The chief looked at both reports and the screen. "None of them match."

"But I just printed that." Bobby looked at the screen and the fresh report. He hit a function key to refresh the dump, the numbers changed. "Well I'll be damned. It's certainly not ROM code then. Maybe it's some kind of cache memory that the device uses. It looks like I've been trying to decrypt garbage. I'll have to modify my program to search for real ROM in this area, but now it looks like we have some kind of device, probably a computing device, but it doesn't make much sense."

"What," Dierdre asked, "doesn't make sense to you?"

"Most foreign computing devices are built on simple parts, often even on domestic hand me down parts. The only thing of interest to us would be the programs they run, stored in the ROM code."

"OK," she said, "go on."

"Well, if it was the program they wanted, they wouldn't be interested in how Dr. Karlyn got it powered on. There must be something special about the device itself, something their people don't know. So perhaps it's not a matter of national secrecy, but maybe commercial. Most good stuff is developed right here in the USA, and this could simply be two rival companies with one trying to steal the others newest invention."

"Interesting theory," the chief said, "but I'm going to just follow the clues and the facts for now. I think I've got enough to look into for now, I'll call you if I think of any more questions."

Dierdre saw the chief to the door. "Can you find your way out OK?

Down the stairs and veer right."

"Thanks," he said as he shook her hand, "I'll manage."

* * *

The sun was just beginning to hang low on the West Coast. Leticia Alvarez took Ramiro's card from her apron pocket, and put it in her purse. She then boarded a bus which took her to a more urban part of town, near the wharfs. When she left the bus, she walked halfway down the block, and climbed the stairs of an old Victorian home. She rang the bell and waited. It usually takes a few minutes to answer the bell in this house, and she was intimately aware with how it worked.

A plump gray haired woman answered the door, "Leticia! Twice in one week? What an honor! Come in, come in."

"Thank you, but I cannot stay." She pulled out the card and said, "Here. Give this to them. He was very finely dressed and had a picture of the good one. He says he is her fiancé. He wrote his hotel on the back."

"I will give it to them. Thank you."

Leticia turned, headed down the steps and back up to the bus stop.

* * *

Bobby looked at his search program. He originally assumed that if he wrote a value to a memory location, it would not match if he read it back. What he didn't consider was that it would change on its own. He changed his scan program to read the memory location first, then write his value into it and read it back. If it was the same as he originally read in, then it was read only memory.

Now when he ran his program, this area was not reported as ROM. Of course, this did not tell him what this area was.

He wrote another version of the same scan to go through this area and measure how big it was. This time he did not write anything, but just read back the values to see how many locations were constantly changing and how fast they changed. He left that running. In the morning he should have a map of which locations change, and range of values they use.

* * *

There was nothing more that Ramiro could do. It was getting late and the world was shutting down for the night. He paced his room. He checked and rechecked his notes. He picked up the phone to call Henderson, but put it back down knowing his friend would call him if he learned anything. He tried watching television, but his mind would not latch onto anything outside of his own real life drama.

He tried sleeping, but his thoughts kept him awake. He poured himself a shot of schnapps, just to calm his nerves. One shot turned into two shots, then three. Eventually, he had reached the point where he drank himself to sleep, letting the empty bottle slip out of his hand landing harmlessly onto the carpet.

* * *

Once Pietre had regained control of his computer, he looked over his logs and realized that his scheme failed to work because Dierdre's machine did not execute his FTP commands. So he changed his approach to bypass the FTP server and send the files through the network. Now when his program got over there, he would be able to see what they have been up to.

But when he sent these over to Dierdre's machine, he again lost control of his machine and his screens started to show the bars and graphs he had seen before, only this time, much faster.

CHAPTER 13

Wednesday morning began with Chief Henderson checking his fax machine. He found Ramiro's warrant, but no report from the phone company. It was still early. He decided to give them a couple hours before seeing if Bedding needed Ramiro's warrants to get things moving along.

* * *

Bobby checked the lab before classes. He only intended to look at the memory dump, but the census was off again. He changed his report to display the thread count sorted by the machine it ran on. He showed four threads for the office computer, sixty-two threads from the main computer, one each on Dierdre's and Aimee's computers, and two-hundred-fifty-two on an unidentified computer. He changed his report again to not only sort by computer, but to display its address. He looked up the address on the name server. It was Dr. Pietre's. He must have tried connecting to their FTP port. He probably only got what he deserved.

Bobby did not worry about Pietre's problems and went off to class.

* * *

The schnapps helped Ramiro sleep far later than he intended. He slept long, but not well. His dreams were haunted with one disaster after another. His worst dream included him rescuing Aimee only to have her and his father fighting in a boxing ring. They were each in their own corner, and he was stuck in the middle as the referee. The bell rang and he was horrified and kept pleading, "don't ring, don't ring," but it rang and rang and rang. The dream popped like a soap bubble bursting before his eyes and he found himself lying in bed staring at the ceiling. His eyes hurt, his head was pounding, and his ears were ringing. He rubbed his eyes to wipe off the remaining sleepiness and realized the phone was ringing.

He rolled over toward the sound and found the handset. "Hello?"

"Ramiro? Is it really you?"

Sobriety slapped him in the face. "Aimee? Aimee! Are you OK? Where are you? What's going..."

"Ramiro! Slow down. Listen to me."

"I'm sorry honey. I'm so sorry we fought. I have been so worried about you, I could not stand it."

"I'm OK. I can't really talk now, but I am so glad you are here. I can really use your help."

"Anything, sweetheart. What can I do for you?"

"OK. Now listen carefully. Forgive me for being so careful about this, but this is very serious. There is a restaurant, now don't say his name, but the restaurant has the name of the man who came to dinner with us at Giuseppe's. Look it up in the phone book, don't ask anyone for directions. Meet us there at noon. I'll explain everything to you then."

"Us?"

"Oh, did I say us? Me, I meant me. See you then."

"OK. I'll be there. There is something you need to know. The FBI is looking for you. They have some crazy notion that you have done something and are somehow involved with some kind of conspiracy."

Silence followed, but before she hung up she added, "I'll talk to you later. I love you."

"I love you too." But he was too late. He already heard the line go dead.

* * *

Ramiro didn't have time to stop and figure out how Aimee had found him at the motel. There was no phone book in his room. He had plenty of time before noon, but he wanted to know exactly where he was expected to be. He went to the manager's office and asked to borrow their phone book. He looked in the yellow pages for Ernesto, but found none, so he turned to the white pages, and there it was, Ernesto's. He jotted down the street corners.

His next problem was whether or not he should call Mitch and tell him. Aimee seemed very concerned that neither of them say his father's name out loud. She must have been aware of the FBI's presence. She did not seem surprised when he told her they were after her. This was not comforting. It sounded like maybe she was involved in something he did not know about. And he was getting right in the middle of it. For all he knew, this could be a career ending decision.

* * *

Henderson checked his fax machine again and still found no report. He picked up the phone and called the number he had for Arthur Bedding, but nobody answered and it never went to voice mail, something that seemed particularly peculiar for the phone company. He flashed the receiver and dialed another number for the main office.

"Inter Mountain Bell, to whom shall I direct your call?"

"Hello, I would like to speak with Arthur Bedding, in your Fraud Department."

"One moment please," the operator said, followed by a long pause, "One moment please," another long pause, "Who may I say is calling?"

"This is Chief of Police Mitchell Henderson from…"

"One moment please…" A short pause this time.

"Hello? Chief Henderson? This is Paula Cook in personnel. I'm sorry, but Arthur Bedding no longer works here. Is there anything I can do for you?"

"Can you tell me when he last worked for you?"

"I'm sorry, but our personnel records are confidential in cases like this."

"In cases like what?" he asked, "Perhaps you should know that I already have a warrant in my hands compelling you to cooperate with me."

Another long pause. "Forgive me Chief Henderson. Of course we will cooperate with you. Arthur Bedding was terminated yesterday for insubordination. If you require any further information we would very much like to have a copy of your warrant for our files."

"You will. You will." He hung up the phone. His next talk with them would be in person.

* * *

Bobby wished he didn't have to juggle so many things at once, but he had no control on the timing of the computer tournament which was scheduled to begin at four in the afternoon. He gathered up the LAN hardware he had promised them and loaded it into his van.

He was glad that he was not expected to set up the whole system, and when he got there, he was doubly glad. Entire crews of pimply faced boys were strapping tables together, stringing miles of cables to them, stripping wires and installing high speed switches every fifteen feet. It was an enormous effort, but his part was merely setting up the backbone that connected the various routers together. The equipment Bobby brought was fast enough to keep all their switches communicating at top speed.

The last thing Bobby set up was a T1 line that connected the entire event to Dierdre's lab. Technically, most of the work for the T1 line was handled by a telecommunications company, all Bobby had to do was connect it to the hardware and configure it. He tested the T1 connection by plugging in a laptop, and connecting to Dierdre's FTP server. Moments later, the laptop began running the threaded application.

With a completed test, he returned to the school. He still had some classes before he could settle down to watch the application. The LAN competition wouldn't really start to heat up till eight o'clock anyway, when the first wave of competitors was eliminated.

* * *

Dierdre reserves Wednesday mornings to provide one on one help for students that request it. Without Aimee there, she found herself juggling the phones and walk-ins while trying to provide counseling for her students.

She was exhausted. She did not have one single moment with one of her students that was had not been interrupted and was whole heartedly relieved when it was over. She finally felt free to collapse in her chair.

"Dierdre? Are you OK?"

She looked up, smiled and said, "Hi Stillman, I'm fine. I just spent all morning learning what Aimee does while I tutor my students."

"Can you manage lunch?"

"Lunch sounds good, though you may have to carry me."

"To the ends of the earth if need be."

Dierdre put her coat on, grabbed her purse, and took the arm he offered. Lunch would be good. Just getting away would be good.

* * *

Ernesto's was a Mexican-Italian restaurant in the middle of an old Hispanic neighborhood. Ramiro could not stop himself from going early and waiting outside. He went in at half past eleven, ordered a beer, and made himself comfortable in a booth with a clear view of the front door.

Customers began trickling in. A large tough looking Chicano, covered with tattoos, entered the restaurant and sat at a table far in the back. He did not look like someone anyone wanted to tangle with. Ramiro imagined a man like that would have many enemies and would want to hide in the dimmest corner available.

A plump Hispanic woman followed, accompanied by an attractive younger woman who could have been her daughter, or a co-worker. They chose a booth across from Ramiro. The younger of them gave him a thorough and approving look.

They were followed by a sea of women, and Aimee was among them. Aimee and two other women joined Ramiro at his booth, while the others took tables and booths surrounding them. Aimee sat across from Ramiro with another Asian woman at her side.

A middle aged Hispanic woman sat next to Ramiro and said, "So, you're a Judge?"

He did not want to take his eyes off of Aimee, but turned to face her anyway and replied, "Justice Ramiro Vasquez, Esquire. And you are?"

"Rosa, just call me Rosa for now."

"What's going on?"

Aimee reached across the table to take his hands in hers. He returned his attention to her and stared into her eyes. She was both smiling and crying, and she did not appear to be crying from joy, but she seemed both happy and sad. "Ramiro, my darling, this is my sister."

Ramiro glanced at the woman on Aimee's right hand side, but she never lifted her head.

"She needs your help." Aimee withdrew one hand from Ramiro's, and reached over to her sister and gently lifted her chin. Her face was a mass of bruises and welts. "Her husband works as a security guard for a local mall. We have been hiding her."

"Did her husband do this?"

Aimee turned to Rosa and asked, "Do you mind, I mean, can I speak to Ramiro alone for a moment?"

Rosa was a bit annoyed, but nodded her head. "Remember we can't stay long." She got up and joined a couple of guys that had come in ahead of her.

When Rosa was out of earshot, Aimee spoke in a hushed voice. "No. Her husband has been very angry lately, but he did not do this. This was done by someone looking for him. He didn't come home from work the night before, and he called her to let her know he would be away, working on the road for a while. When she told him someone was looking for him and had hit her, he was furious, but he told her to blame it on him for now. He said as long as she said he beat her, there would be people to help keep her safe. Rosa and all these people believe he hit her. They help battered women and children. She has been staying with them at a safe house. I'm sorry. I could not tell you anything about it. I don't even know where it is, they won't let me stay with them. One of the ladies was kind enough to let me stay with her for a couple days."

Rosa returned to the table and said, "I'm sorry Aimee, we have to keep this brief. Senior Vasquez, we are accustomed to hiding from enraged husbands. We don't understand why we now must hide from our own government. This is not what we do, but we couldn't turn them away. In the past, we have been challenged in court, but they have never pursued us as criminals. Do you know why the FBI is involved in this case? Can you stop them from pursuing us? They are making it harder for us to protect our charges from their husbands."

Ramiro thought about it a moment before answering. "On the surface, it would appear that the FBI's involvement seems to be a big coincidence. When Aimee disappeared, we received a strange ransom note and we initially suspected she was kidnapped. That brought the FBI into the picture. However, in retrospect, they have been treating her as a conspirator and not a victim which makes me wonder if they were actually after you guys all along. I'm not sure if I can provide any help for you. They have come dangerously close to treating me as a co-conspirator already."

"If the FBI is only using this as an excuse to chase us, then they must have already been after us for something. We need to regroup and re-examine who we are protecting to see why they would be involved.

We'll contact you."

"I'll find out what I can, but I'm still not sure I'll be able to help. What, if anything, can I tell anybody about your group?"

Rosa handed him a card. "We aren't a complete secret. We just keep a low profile."

When Rosa got up and left, the entire restaurant went with her, except for Ramiro. He could hear cars and motorbikes starting up and taking off in all different directions. He felt bad for Ernesto, like this had all been a huge hoax to cheat the restaurant out of money. He was about to order something to eat when Aimee came back in and rejoined him.

"My sister insisted I stay for lunch."

"I like your sister already."

Ramiro reached for Aimee's hand and pulled it to his lips. Without sharing a word between them, they stared into each other's eyes and renewed their intentions.

* * *

Bobby was back in the lab with time to spare. The tournament opened its doors at noon and contestants had till four in the afternoon to be set up and ready to go. That meant that each contestant had to be up and ready as fast as possible. They needed the additional time to register all the addresses and diagnose any problems connecting to the servers.

He picked up the phone and called Dierdre's office.

"Hello? Professor Jennings speaking."

"Hi. This is Bobby. I just wanted to remind you that the big tournament starts today. I plan to spend the night and watch it run. I expect it to get busy around eight o'clock, in case you wanted to stop by and see for yourself."

"Oh my God! I forgot all about it. Of course I want to be there!" Dierdre stopped to catch her breath. "I can't believe I just said that."

"What, you don't want to be there?"

"No, no," Dierdre said, laughing now, "I just got excited and suddenly sounded like one of my students. Want me to bring food?"

"Sure, thanks."

There was nothing to do but wait, and catch some classes. Bobby grabbed his book bag and headed off to his chemistry class.

* * *

Ramiro returned to his hotel after lunch. Aimee insisted on returning to the group, but she promised to keep him informed. When he got to his room, he pulled out his cell phone and noticed that he had missed seven calls. He forgot that he had put it on silent ringer during lunch.

He clicked on one of the missed calls which dialed the chief's private cell phone.

"Well it's about time you got back to me."

"Mitch, I saw her."

"You found her?"

"I guess, or she found me. I'm not sure. She's safe, she's with her sister. They're with a women's support group protecting the sister who got beat up pretty bad. There's no secret mystery going on here, it's an open and shut case."

"Guess again," Henderson said, "Something is very wrong here. Our friend at the phone company was fired. The same one who gave us the nice list of illegal phone taps. He was terminated for insubordination within twenty-four hours of talking to me."

"What do you intend to do?"

"I don't like this. I want to talk to our friend. Then, I want to go to the phone company offices and talk to his superiors, his co-workers, and to anyone involved with his termination."

Ramiro kicked off his shoes and fell back onto the bed, staring up at the ceiling. "Do you want me to write up some warrants?"

"I think I'll have someone in the DA's office write them up. Is there somewhere I can fax them to you?

"I'm heading to the San Diego Courthouse to browse their law library. I'll give you a number when I get there."

"It's strange, Rami, the hairs on the back of my neck still tell me there's a connection to Aimee's disappearance. Are you sure it's just a domestic dispute?"

"Her husband is ex-military, but he's just a mall cop now."

"I still don't like it. And hearing that he's military doesn't relax those hackles on my neck at all."

Ramiro reviewed his conversation with Aimee and her sister and said, "You know, her sister claims it wasn't her husband, but someone looking for him."

"Do you buy that?"

"I'm not sure. You know how loyal these battered wives can be. She claims she hasn't seen her husband for a few days."

"So either he beat her and she is lying low, or she's telling the truth and he's the one who went lying low first and someone beat her to find him."

"Something like that. I'll call you when I get that fax number."

"Good enough. Now try and keep your ringer on."

* * *

The large man paced back and forth while The Bard sat wringing his hands.

"This is getting way out of hand," the large man said.

"I'm handling it."

The large man stopped pacing and sat on the edge of his desk looking the bard squarely in the eye. "We don't want any attention. We should have just taken it back and let the science boys figure out what he had done."

"You said you wanted to recruit the kid while we were at it."

"Forget that, we need to get out of this whole affair."

The large man returned to his pacing and the Bard asked, "Have they tracked down Karlynovich yet?"

"No. Those idiots at the FBI got some fool notion in their head that Professor Jennings' secretary was part of some grand conspiracy to sneak Karlynovich off to some new identity or something. What a bunch of morons."

"Do you think anyone here knows how to reach him? He seemed genuinely close to the boy."

"No. He's gone. His car was spotted in Florida. Apparently he sold it to an old lady going to spend the winter in Miami."

"What about Dr. Critanovic?" the Bard asked, "He found him hiding here in this quiet little university."

"Dr. Critanovic's not talking."

"Can't we persuade him?

"No," the large man said firmly, "we can't. He has nothing more to say."

"Oh." The bard recognized something final in his superiors tone.

"Don't weep for Critanovic, he was a traitor."

"Karlynovich may have been a traitor to the old Soviet Union, and he may have been hiding from the general scientific community, but Critanovic was only guilty of disagreeing with his peers."

"Critanovic was guilty of one other thing," the large man said.

"What was that?"

"Being right. He was correct when he suggested Karlynovich would be an asset, and when he located Karlynovich, he knew how to get the device to him."

"So now what?" the Bard asked, "Exactly what are your orders?"

"We go get it, but we do not interface with anyone, including Pietre. We only go in when the coast is clear, we find it, package it up and get out. You have done quite enough damage in this burg."

"OK. I'll go in and get it then."

"Make sure you don't damage it or whatever Karlynovich did with it."

"I'm a pro, remember?"

* * *

Chief Henderson played golf regularly with one of the district attorneys. Asking him to write up the orders was easy, especially when he knew a judge was already set to sign them and he wouldn't have to go into detail quoting case law to convince him.

While he was waiting for the papers, and for Ramiro's call, he sent a couple detectives out to locate Arthur Bedding. He told them if he was not home, to check with any labor attorneys near his home.

He went to his pin board and wrote more notes with names and events. It should all be like a puzzle with the pieces fitting together, but this mess didn't even have a crime that he could put his finger on.

* * *

Ramiro found the courthouse, and showed his I.D. to the guard at the entrance. He was given a visitor badge and allowed in. He found his way to the clerk's office, and explained to them that he was expecting a fax, and asked if they had a fax number he could give out. He called Chief Henderson and relayed the fax number, and asked the chief to call him on his cell phone when the faxes were on the way.

With that business handled, he made his way to the law library. It had been a while since he had done his own research, but he started thumbing through an index to find cases involving spousal abuse.

* * *

By two o'clock, Bobby had settled down in the lab to watch things transpire. He knew that the tournament wouldn't start until four and that the eliminations wouldn't start in earnest until eight that evening, but he could not tear himself away. He wanted to make sure everything was prepared. Tonight's test was going to connect over one-thousand computers together as if they were part of a single computer, even though they were miles apart. He certainly wasn't the first to do this, but this was HIS first time, and he thought that maybe, it had never been made this simple before.

Bobby spent some time running diagnostics, and checking the progress of the project. The census had already dropped down to normal, he checked the machine addresses, and sure enough, Pietre had removed his machine from the process.

Bobby checked the memory scan, and as far as his program could determine, there was no ROM area, but the area he mapped continued to change, and his program was now keeping statistics on what character range it was finding, and in what area.

* * *

Chief Henderson faxed a stack of warrants to the number Ramiro had given him, and phoned Ramiro's cell phone to alert him. He was still waiting for a report from his detectives, but soon he would have papers to serve to the phone company.

Ramiro was still in the library when the call came in, he replaced the books he was reading and went straight to the clerk's office. It was a brisk walk from one end of the building where the library and DA's offices were, to the other end where the clerks and courtrooms were.

When he reached the clerk's office, one of the staff members was already organizing all of Ramiro's faxes into a nice neat stack with a large black clip holding them together. She saw him come in and flashed him a broad beaming smile. "Here you go, sir."

"Can I borrow that desk for a couple minutes?"

The young girl pointed to a desk next to the water cooler and said, "You can use that one over there. It's mine, I need to deliver these faxes to Judge Henry, so I won't need it right away."

"Thanks." He took the stack of orders over to the girl's desk and sat down. She couldn't quite suppress a slight giggle as she backed out the room.

"Don't mind her," said the girl in the next desk, "She thinks you look like some cute cop on her favorite TV show."

Ramiro smiled and went back to the orders in his hands. He read through them, made sure they were made out correctly and signed each one. As he was about to sign the last one, the girl returned and stood quietly behind him. He finished the last signature, stood, and asked her, "Can you fax these back to the number at the top for me, please?"

"Sure," she said, "my pleasure."

As Ramiro left the room she mouthed to her friend, behind his back, "He's so cute!"

Ramiro returned to his car, and called Henderson, "Mitch, the orders should be on their way already."

"They are coming in now, thanks."

"How are you going to play this with the phone company?"

"I was planning to go in and request their cooperation, and if they stall me, to drop the papers on them. But before I do any of that, I wanted my detectives to locate the whereabouts of Arthur Bedding. I think I will have some more questions for them after I debrief him."

"How long do you plan to wait to find him?"

"If we don't locate him by tonight, I am going in first thing in the morning."

"I'm going to stay here through the end of the week and try to help out Aimee. I'll be flying back this weekend for sure."

* * *

Dierdre dropped in the Lab at four. Bobby was watching the screen.

He had added a new graph to the screen so he could watch the population rise.

"I thought you said nothing would happen till eight o'clock?"

"Actually, there will probably be a few computers logging on between now and then. Some players might get eliminated from the tournament, either because they are really bad players, or they are up against one of the great players, but at eight and every four hour interval, the games shut down and rank everyone. That's when we should see large groups of computers logging in."

Dierdre stared at the graphs on the screen. "When I come back, you are going to have to explain the graph bars to me. I'm going home to find something more comfortable to wear, and I'll pick up something to eat. What kind of pizza do you like?"

"Pepperoni, Hawaiian, Supreme, all meat, Linguica, sausage, just about anything except anchovies."

"Got it," she said, "no anchovies. I should be back around six."

* * *

Chief Henderson was in his office when one of his units called to report they found Bedding.

"Where'd you find him? What's his condition?"

"He's fine. He returned to his residence at half past four."

"Is he willing to talk to us?"

"Willing? He is eager. He even apologized for not returning sooner. We should be back at the station in twenty-five minutes."

* * *

The FBI hadn't had a lead since they raided the hotel room in San Diego. As far as they were concerned the trail had gone cold. This was two trails that had dead ended for them. The first was the scientist guy that had stolen the deadly canister of small pox from the government storage facility. When that trail had led them to a physicist at a small university, they had grown suspicious as to the actual contents of the canister. This wouldn't be the first time another government agency lied about the contents of a package just to get the FBI's highest priority in the matter. They followed the leads regardless. Right now, there was no trail to follow.

* * *

Dierdre changed into jeans and a tank top, with a thick comfy cowl neck sweater layered on top. With her winter overcoat in hand, she was ready for any temperature. She had canceled all her Thursday classes and had given her students written assignments to prepare for the following week. She was ready to stay as long as she could.

Her theory relied on producing predictable results, and it required trillions of calculations per second. The faster the individual processors, the less she required. Since it was so difficult to accurately predict how fast processors would get in the future, it was equally difficult to predict how many she would require. With Bobby's code in place, she hoped to learn how many calculations per second she could achieve across the network of computers. She needed to create a quotient of how many calculations the whole network could produce, versus a single machine. Then she could predict how many calculations a network of future processors might compute.

But, her immediate goal was less complex. She had to pick up a couple medium pizzas and some coke. She also pulled the ice chest from her garage and tossed it in the trunk, and bought a couple bags of ice from the store to keep the drinks cold.

* * *

"Come in," Henderson said, "come in."

Lieutenant Jones, who had knocked on the chief's door, opened it and stepped in with his partner and Arthur Bedding. "Sorry we're late chief. He said he was hungry, so we took him through a drive-thru."

The chief looked hurt and asked, "And you didn't bring me anything?"

Lieutenant Jones froze for a moment, but was relieved by the chief's smile.

"Mr. Bedding," Henderson said, "won't you please sit down?"

The chief waved Jones and his partner off so he could have a private chat. He looked at Bedding, a young man in his late twenties with a good build.

"Tell me, Mr. Bedding, when did you learn that you had been

terminated, and how did they notify you?"

He squirmed a bit in his chair and said, "This morning, when I arrived at work, my key card wouldn't let me in. So I tried a different door, and it wouldn't let me in either. I walked around to the reception desk, and asked them to call security, and tell them my card was broken. They arrived quickly, but instead of fixing my card, they took it from me and handed me a box of things from my desk. I asked what was going on, and asked if I could speak to Malcolm. I did not know either of those men, but they just scowled at me and told me I would have to leave. I asked the receptionist to get Malcolm for me, he is my boss, but they stopped him and told me again to leave, so I left."

The chief leaned back in his chair and put his arms behind his head. He looked up at the water stain in the false ceiling tiles suspended over his head. "Do you remember their names?"

"No, I should have gotten them, but I didn't."

"Have you tried to reach anyone today, by phone?"

"I tried, but the switchboard kept cutting me off, and when I did get through, everyone was in meetings, or was out of the office."

"Do you think this could be related to the reports you were preparing for me?"

"I don't see how."

"The wiretaps. You said they could only be placed by someone within the company, isn't that right?"

"No, or at least, that's not what I meant. The wiretaps are certainly within the system, but I didn't mean to imply that some person in the company was responsible."

"But if someone in your office was involved, they might have been threatened by your investigation, and wanted you out of the way."

Arthur Bedding sat silent for a moment, then replied, "No, I can't believe that. The only people who knew what I was looking at were also my close personal friends."

"Hmmm." The chief stood and handed him a card. "If you talk to your friends, and learn anything interesting, please let me know."

Arthur stood, and they shook hands.

"I'll have one of my men give you a ride home, thanks for your help."

Arthur opened the door and started to leave when the chief said,

"One more thing, Mr. Bedding, please don't tell anyone that we had this chat. If someone you know is somehow involved, I don't want them to know I am interested in this just yet."

Arthur was bewildered by the request, but nodded his head. Lieutenant Jones was waiting outside to take him home.

* * *

The large man answered the ringing phone, "Hello?"

"You're not going to believe this."

"What?"

The Bard spoke in hushed tones, "I'm sitting in an empty lab, down the hall, waiting for the kid to leave. But instead of leaving, that hot professor shows up with pizza! Wait a sec, the kid is leaving, and the professor is staying behind. It looks to me like they are planning on working late."

"Do you think they found it? Is that what they are working on?"

"Who knows? That junk I took off their computer was all about generating randomized number sequences. If you ask me, they got some sweet scam going where they fool around on the computer and rake in the grant money."

The large man grunted and said, "Good thing nobody wants your opinion."

"Hey, anytime you want, you can come down here and do this yourself."

"No, you stay put. If they don't leave by Oh-three-hundred, then you can cancel the op for the night."

"Hold on, the kids coming back, and he is carrying an ice chest. Maybe I should go ahead and call it a night now?"

"Oh-three-hundred. Good night."

* * *

Dierdre had already opened one of the pizzas by the time Bobby had returned with the cooler. She sat in front of the screen looking at the bar charts.

Bobby pointed to the first one, a bright rich blue colored bar. "That one tells us how many processes are running. The number at the bottom is the actual count. And the next one, the green one, shows us the longest string of correctly predicted numbers within the last five minutes. The white one next to that is the average length of those with more than three correct. I had to eliminate those that had zero or one correct and found that three made a good cutoff number." He popped open a coke and took a big swallow before continuing, "The red bar is how many processes have been diverted to improve efficiency of a new machine. Each time a new machine comes on-line, a certain amount of work is done to make sure it has the most efficient routines possible."

"So right now," Dierdre said, "we have sixty-five processes running, oh, it just jumped to sixty-six. Look at that, the red bar just jumped to sixteen."

"A new computer just came on line, and it has diverted some processors to find the best routines for the new guy. At eight, the blue bar and the red bar are going to skyrocket, and for a little while, the green bar and the white bar will probably go very low."

The graphs showed a slow, but somewhat steady increase in traffic. A new computer came on board about every ten or twelve minutes, enough to keep the red bar steady, but not enough to stress the system. Dierdre had moved to an empty desk where she graded some tests she had given on Tuesday. Bobby checked and double checked the code, looking for places he might tweak it to run a bit faster. Even if he found an enhancement, he was hesitant to make a change at this late stage, but browsing through the code helped him pass the time.

* * *

At eight, the first tournament round was concluded. The servers already knew the scores, and it only took moments to post the winners and losers. There would be a fifteen minute break during which time the judges would hear any disputes regarding the outcome. This used to be a full hour break, but over the last three years of the tournament, the organizers and participants learned that some disputes were never overturned, and the automated scoring of the servers was final, so they shortened the list of grievances that could be brought to the judges. They also learned that there were certain participants who would file a dispute in every single game they lost. Penalties were added to combat frivolous disputes. Some penalties included not being invited back to future events. The effects of these changes shortened the time to resolve disputes from an hour to just fifteen minutes.

With the conclusion of the round, the room exploded with a cacophony of voices, some pre-pubescent squeaking, and others a deep and resonant laughing and cajoling over their victories and defeats. The first round is always the loudest. The eliminated players can be heard screaming "If only I" and "You only got me by that much." The winners of the round were more intent on who else may have progressed to the next round. A third group of players, on the cusp, were anxiously watching the results to see if their status would be altered as a result of disputes.

At five minutes past eight, one of the event coordinators went to the podium and turned on a microphone to address the attendees. "Hello? Can you hear me? Is this thing working? Good, can I have your attention please? Your attention please? If everyone can settle down for a moment, I have some announcements to make. First, the snack and refreshment bar is now limited to those contestants who will be advancing to the next round. You have fifteen minutes, sorry, ten minutes left to get snacks before the next round commences. I want to thank everyone for coming this year, and remind those of you who are not advancing to follow the instructions you were given when you signed up this morning. We want to thank Norwood University for generously loaning us the high speed routers, I'm sure those of you who have been here in past years can appreciate the improved response times we are getting this year. In exchange for their cooperation, each of us has agreed to loan them our equipment for some experiments they are conducting. That's right. Each of you signed the agreement. Just follow the directions. They assure us that everything else will be automatic. Lastly, we have some messages. Peter and Eric Mathews, turn your cell phones on or your Mother will come down here and embarrass you. Rachel Nicholson, you have some flowers and a helium balloon here that says 'Good Luck', please come and pick them up during the break."

The coordinator covered the microphone with his hand while a tall thin boy whispered something in his ear, "I've just been informed that Rachel Nicholson has advanced to the next round, congratulations! I guess the balloon worked. Can we get a volunteer to come get the flowers for her? Lastly, if anyone here owns a Gold colored Dodge

Van, plate number 3BHK413, your dome light is on."

He checked the time on his wrist watch and announced, "OK, six more minutes. If any contestants miss snacks, we will find some volunteers to help you out, just stand up the little red flag next to your computer. Anyone interested in volunteering to help with the remainder of the event, you can sign up at the desk you see below this podium. Good luck to everyone advancing on, I hope everyone else had fun. Let's get set for round two. Thank you."

* * *

Bobby and Dierdre watched the screen intently.

Dierdre pointed at the screen and asked, "I thought you said it would start to rise at eight?"

"It will. They are probably just sorting out the winners and losers."

As if on command, the numbers started to tick off. First one or two at a time, then by fives, tens and more. The higher the numbers rose, the higher the red bar rose too, and the lower the green bar with the predictions dropped. Within minutes, the number of machines surpassed three-hundred, then five-hundred and over a thousand machines on line. The number of new machines outnumbered the number of veteran machines by over twenty to one. That put an enormous strain on those veteran machines to test the new machines for optimum client configurations.

Something else was changing within the network. As more machines came on line, there were more variations in the clients and a greater chance for them to evolve into something new. But for true evolution, the machines would need to number in the millions, perhaps billions, and not just thousands. People like to use phrases like one in a million, but that's exactly what evolution involves. Even if one of the programs tries a random instruction, the chances of it doing anything are pretty remote, and even if it did something, other than crash the program, the chances of it actually doing something useful are even more remote, and even if it did something useful, the chances of it improving the process are still more remote. All this means that it's at least one in a million. But they don't have a million. There were just over one-thousand-two-hundred processors.

* * *

Dimitri Pietre did not know what the secret hardware was, but he knew it was there. He had been brought into the confidences of the two secretive men who had convinced him to retrieve it for them. He didn't volunteer, however, they knew some things about his past that he had thought were long behind him. They have asked him to stop his attempts at retrieving the device, but he knew that if he left it alone, they would continue to hold him at their mercy. His past was like a sword of Damocles hanging over his head. If he could retrieve it, then maybe he could bargain with them to have their information permanently lost.

He sat in his lab preparing to launch his final volley at Dierdre's computer. He had tried getting programs installed on her machine that would let him monitor the contents of her memory and hardware buffers, but each attempt failed due to irregularities with her transfer programs. He knew the irregularities were due to Bobby. He must know what he has, and he must have something up his sleeve, but who could predict what such a hoodlum plans to do?

Pietre failed to get through the FTP transfer program on Dierdre's machine. Each time he tried, he found his computer infiltrated with the same program he had seen in her lab. This time, however, he had managed to capture one of the programs on his machine. He didn't know what it was doing, and didn't really care, but he was interested in the fact that it sent information back and forth between his machine and Dierdre's. In fact, it looked to him like it sent copies of itself over to her machine, and received newer copies of programs to run. If it could do that, then he could make a version to copy his program over and let him view those buffers.

This time, instead of letting Dierdre's machine initiate the process, he would start the program on his machine and let it make contact on its own, with the mother machine.

He hit the enter key to execute the program and said, "Phone home, my young friend." It immediately started reaching out for Dierdre's computer, but it didn't get a response at first. He started it again, but again, he got no response. He started a third copy, and immediately started getting something back.

He could see various threads starting up on his machine but they were all the old threads without his changes. He started his again, hoping he could reverse the direction of travel, but more of the old ones kept arriving on his machine. He ran a comparison of all the ones arriving to the one he sent out, and got no matches, but he noticed that the ones being sent to his machine were not all the same. While looking at some of the differences between them, he saw something truly remarkable. Some of the new ones had incorporated some of the changes from his modified program.

"Yes!" He shouted to his empty lab. They must have made it over. Now perhaps, he can start to get a peek at what is over there.

* * *

With the population well over twelve-hundred, the addition of Pietre's machine barely made a dent. Had it not been for Bobby's alerts checking for his machine address, he never even would have known.

"What's that?" Dierdre was pointing to the red box which had popped up on the screen with Pietre's address in it.

"That, Professor Jennings, is an ongoing problem we have had with Professor Pietre trying to break into our computer. He has tried on numerous occasions to access our FTP server, but each time he does, our programs start to run on his machine, and he ends up loaning us his hardware for a while, until he figures out how to shut it down."

"What does he want?"

"I'm betting it has to do with that mysterious device Dr. Karlyn received. It seems to have created quite a lot of interest all over the place."

"I'd forgotten all about that, what did your scans reveal?"

"Nothing. That uncharted area we found before kept changing. I assume it is some kind of buffer I am looking at, but I have no idea what it is buffering, I only know that it is constantly being modified, and I still haven't determined how big it is."

"Can I see it?"

"Sure, if you want." Bobby entered the commands to pull up his program that scanned the area in question. He had modified it to just look at that specific area rather than scan the entire machine like he originally had done.

The program immediately popped up a mixture of letters, numbers and odd shaped graphical characters.

Bobby pointed to the screen and said, "This is the area that keeps changing."

"How long before it changes?"

Bobby hadn't even looked at the screen, but he looked now. "It should be changing now, as you watch." But it didn't. They now looked at a screen that was rock solid and steady, with no changes anywhere.

"That's odd, if it had done this before, I would have marked it as a ROM zone, which was exactly what I was looking for."

"If it is a buffer, then maybe the device is paused?"

"I suppose," Bobby said, "anything is possible, we really know absolutely nothing about the device."

"Shhhh," Dierdre said, "I think I heard something…"

"Hellooo?"

"Stillman, is that you?"

"It most certainly is. May I enter? I hope I am not disturbing you."

Dierdre got up to greet him at the door. "Please, come in. We were just watching the results of a special project that we just launched."

Stillman entered but stayed at the door where they could speak privately. "That's why I came, I wanted to speak some more about your project. I may have something interesting to show you, which may affect your project."

"Oh," she said, "my project. Why don't you come to my lab area and have a seat."

Dierdre turned to walk to the back of the lab, but Stillman gently grabbed her arm to keep her from leaving. "That was just an excuse, I do have something to show you, and would have shown you tomorrow, except I saw your lights on in your lab, and thought that maybe I could…"

Dierdre put her index finger against his lips and whispered, "Shhhh. It's OK." She kissed him lightly on the cheek. "Come inside, have some pizza, I'll show you my project and…"

"Damn it woman, if you tell me, 'I'll show you mine if you show me yours,' I'm liable to bust a seam."

She smiled devilishly and directed him by the hand to the back of the lab.

He cleared his throat and said, "Hello Bobby. I just came by to show Professor Jennings some charts a colleague sent to me the other day."

"Dr. Whitfield, what a surprise." Bobby smiled and nodded his head. "I had a feeling about you."

"Oh no," Stillman replied, "You've got the wrong idea. I'm here to discuss Professor Jennings' project."

"Yeah, sure. I know." Bobby continued to smile and nod his head.

Dierdre stepped directly in front of Stillman and said, "Gallant to the very end."

Stillman looked puzzled. "I'm sorry?"

"Protecting my honor, but I'm afraid we can't hide anything from this young man. He is just too smart for both of us."

"Oh I see." Stillman looked back at Bobby, then at his shoes, then back at Dierdre. "Well, if the truth be known, I'm not quite sure what it is I am hiding."

Dierdre looking directly into his eyes and replied, "Frankly, neither am I."

On an impulse, Dierdre leaned forward and kissed Stillman lightly, but directly on the lips. Not a long drawn out Hollywood kiss, but an unmistakable meeting of lips between two confused adults.

"Hmm," she said, "I'm still not sure what we have here, or maybe I suspect what it is but I'm just not prepared to admit it."

"Ahem," Bobby feigned a cough, "Would you like me to spell it out for you? You make a good couple, but you are from totally different worlds. I bet that you, Professor Jennings, were A-list in high school. You were surrounded by cheerleaders and football jocks. And, I figure that you, Professor Whitfield, were chess club. In high school you would have never mixed A-list with chess club, but fortunately, nobody here is in high school. Dr. Bobby recommends you kick back with some of this superb, slightly cold pizza, some coke, and just enjoy being in the same room."

Dierdre collected herself, stepped back and straightened out her hair, as if the simple kiss were actually a torrid passionate embrace leaving her hair pointing every which way. She returned to her chair and pointed to another chair nearby. "Well, I've placed my cards upon the table. Let's see what you've brought with you?"

Stillman hesitated a moment, caught up in the metaphors, and responded, "Oh this, yes, yes, wait till you see what I have here."

He pulled the chair Dierdre had indicated up to the desk where she sat and placed a manila envelope on the table.

"Are you familiar with Dr. Jarod Jantzen's work? He is currently working at the European Linear Accelerator in Switzerland."

"I know his work. He has been trying to find ways to use high energy particle pulses to synchronize quantum events into a coherent rhythm, kind of like a laser."

"Exactly." Stillman pulled a small stack of paper out of the envelope. "He sent this to me from Florida, where he is meeting with his backers. He has refined his ability to create a highly focused, variable and sustainable pulse, but his measurements have shown some erratic pulses. He asked me to look at his circuit design and see whether I could help him fix his instruments."

Dierdre took the stack of reports from him, and was looking over the charts and the numbers. "I'm sorry, Stillman, I just don't see what this has to do with my project."

Stillman reached over and turned the pages to about one third of the way through the stack. "Look at those numbers. He wants me to determine why he keeps getting those small spikes in his readings. Turn to the last few pages and look at the charts. See the spikes? Notice anything peculiar?"

Dierdre looked at the charts and said, "He is attempting to create a coherent resonant particle stream. Perhaps his instruments have a resonant frequency that shows up as these spikes."

"Perhaps, but I checked his circuit diagrams, and there is nothing wrong with his design. If he had faulty parts, then the spikes would not be so uniform. I don't think the problem is in his instruments, I think he is reading a bona fide spike. He may not be able to induce the quantum events to occur on his schedule, but I think he may be hitting them at just the right moment to read an energy spike. It's like you described to me, if you knew the exact path of the quantum events, and followed on the same path, you would be able to harness them. I am suggesting that his particle pattern may be accidentally hitting some of the events, enough to record a small spike."

Dierdre took the reports and looked at them again. "Can I keep these tonight? I want to read the whole report."

Stillman took a piece of pizza, and leaned back in his chair. "Certainly. But let's just keep this between us, I haven't asked him if I could share it with anyone yet. Now that I've shown you mine..."

"Whoa!" Bobby put his hands over his eyes and said, "Maybe I don't need to see this!"

Dierdre rolled up the report and whacked Bobby in the back of the head. "Show him the screen."

Bobby showed the screen to Stillman and explained the various bars and the numbers. He gave him an overview of the tournament and how they would be adding on more computers to increase the number of threads they could run simultaneously.

"The first wave added about twelve-hundred machines. Each subsequent wave will be smaller and smaller. The next wave should come online shortly after midnight, and we should be seeing between three-hundred and four-hundred more computers at that time."

Stillman checked his watch and said, "I Wish I could hang out to see that, but I have an early class in the morning."

Dierdre was engrossed in the reports Stillman had brought, but she was listening, and lifted her head up out of the papers to say, "Oh, you should get some sleep, I'll walk you out."

Stillman stood and offered his arm, which she accepted, and they headed out of the lab.

Bobby yelled out after them, "Take your time, talk amongst yourselves, but be back before midnight if you want to watch the next shift. That's about two and a half hours."

Bobby settled back in his chair and pulled a book out of his bag. It was going to be a long night.

CHAPTER 14

Dierdre walked Stillman out to the parking lot. "Beautiful night tonight," she said while sweeping her gaze across the heavens, "It's nice to have such a clear sky this time of the year."

"Yes it is beautiful," he said, "and you are beautiful, in fact, you are incredibly beautiful."

She had no response, except to smile and tilt her head, and wait to hear what else he had to say.

"What in the world are we doing here? I mean, what are you doing? Here? With me? I'm no spring chicken. In fact, I think most people will classify me more turkey than chicken."

"Whoa," she said, "You pursued me, and if I am not mistaken, you have been doing so for quite some time."

"Maybe I thought you were unattainable and therefore safe."

"Is that what you want?" she asked icily, "Unattainable? I can be unattainable."

"You could have any man, a model, an actor, anyone. What in the world do you see in me?"

Dierdre moved in close to Stillman so she could keep her voice low. "Stillman, I know I could have any man. And I have dated pretty men." She continued to inch closer, their eyes were locked. "I just spent a good hour demonstrating my project to you, and you understood everything Bobby and I showed you."

Stillman was breathing in short staccato bursts. His voice was low, and a bit husky now, "Well that would make us good study partners, but..."

She put her finger to his lips again, and wrinkled her nose, and gently, ever so lightly, kissed him on the tip of his nose. "I know, I know. I thought at first it was just an intellectual attraction, but there is more." She ran her fingers through his hair to the back of his head. "All those pretty boys..." She kissed him on his right cheekbone. "...could make my eyes twinkle..." she kissed him on his left cheekbone. He was now breathing in short gasps. "...but what I realized, just tonight for the first time..." she kissed him on the right side of his neck below the jaw, "...was that you..." she kissed him on the left side of his neck, "...Stillman Whitfield..." she kissed him lightly on the lips, "...make my heart pitter patter." She kissed him again, harder, longer.

Stillman's head was swirling. He had dreamed of a moment like this ever since he had first seen Dierdre, but never dared believe it could possibly come true. He kissed her back. His heart also pitter pattered, and he could feel the rhythm of it pounding in his head. In fact, his whole body was a weak mass of pitter patter, and she too was overcome with a whole body weakness. Were they not holding each other up, neither of them would have remained standing.

They didn't know how long they stood there, kissing, holding, staring at each other in awe and wonder over the feelings coursing through their veins at this very moment. Love is a game played by poets and playwrights, not scientists. There was no equation for the bond that was growing between them.

Dierdre broke the magical silence, saying, "I better get back inside. I still have work to do."

"That's probably a good idea, before I start making indecent proposals."

She inched away slowly. As their bodies parted, their hands remained together, clinging to each other till the last possible moment, when their fingers parted and only their eyes remain locked together.

"I'll take a rain-check," she said in a coarse husky voice.

"I'm sorry," he asked, "a rain-check?"

"On those indecent proposals. I'll be expecting to hear them before too long."

"And so you shall, on my honor you shall."

Dierdre took a full step back, turned and ran back to the building. As she opened the door, she turned for one last look. Stillman stood by his car, his door was open, but he was waiting until she disappeared into the building. He waved goodbye to her, and she blew him a kiss, then stepped inside and let the door close behind her. Once inside, she leaned her back against the door, closed her eyes and took a deep breath, then pushed away from the door and returned to her lab.

* * *

The Bard had seen enough. He had already witnessed the professor and the kid bring in pizza and a cooler. They had obviously planned to stay a while. And now, after another professor had joined them, and then left with Professor Jennings, she returned back to the lab. There was no point sitting in the dark lab where he was holed up, no matter what he was told to do. He'll just make an entry in his notebook that the lab was still occupied at three in the morning, and his supervisor will never know the difference.

* * *

Bobby looked up, grinning, as she returned to the lab and asked, "You OK professor?"

"Yeah, I'm fine."

"We still have some time before the next wave. I was just doing some reading."

"That's good, I'm just going to sit over here and grade some papers."

Bobby peeked at her over the top of his book. She looked a bit flustered, and her movements were a bit jerky. "For a moment there, I thought you might not return."

"I almost didn't return," she thought to herself, and then abruptly she looked up at Bobby, suddenly self-conscious that she might have spoken her thought aloud.

"You can, you know," he continued, "I have to be here in case something goes wrong, but you don't. I can always give you a full report in the morning. Plus, the contest will continue a couple more days."

"Oh, no," she said, "I'm anxious to be here. It's like the birth of my child. Something I conceived and you made real."

"Well if you intend to use that analogy again, remember, I'm the Obstetrician, not the Daddy."

"I will probably go home after the midnight wave."

"That's fine," he said, "I'll be getting some sleep after that anyway. I just need to listen for the phone and any alarms."

"Alarms?"

"If any of the numbers exceed the plausible ranges, the monitor program will emit an annoying beep to alert me."

Dierdre sat down at her desk, but before she started grading papers, she glanced at the screen. "Oh look, the red bar has gone down."

"Yeah, all the processes are fully functional now. That happened while you were outside."

"But we aren't seeing much improvement in the strings of numbers we are generating."

"Sure we are, but we have to keep everything in context. Before adding the last twelve-hundred processes, our average string length was under two. Now it is between two and three, that's double what it was. Every now and then we get one that goes to five or so, but they are rare it seems. That's the difference between hundreds of processors and millions."

Everything remained quiet until midnight. Bobby read his book while Dierdre graded papers. Each of them kept checking the time and glancing at the screen. Shortly before midnight, Dierdre put her papers away and settled in at the monitor watching and waiting. Bobby closed his book and joined her.

The seconds ticked away as midnight came and went. The old adage, "a watched pot never boils," is one of the basic true axioms when working with computers. Almost all computer work starts with hours of frustrating work creating and preparing a program, then you run it and wait. Few other devices in our society have the same power as the computer to make us wait. One of the mysteries of life is how time slows down when you watch and wait. Einstein theorized that as a body approaches the speed of light, it moves forward in time. He also theorized that the opposite would be true, but to move backwards in time, that same body would have to be stiller than still. Perhaps the center of a black hole could qualify for stiller than still, but for all intents and purposes, stiller than still could never be attained.

Eventually, enough time had passed. The blue bar, showing the number of process rose slowly. With over twelve-hundred processes running already, adding a few hundred made only a small percentage increase. The red bar, on the other hand, skyrocketed. This showed that a number of new processors had lent themselves to the task of optimizing the newcomers. By half past twelve, the blue bar had stabilized, no more new processes were adding on, and three minutes later, the red bar shrunk to nothing.

Dierdre looked alarmed. "What happened? Shouldn't that have taken longer?"

"No, that was about right. We only added on about five-hundred processes, instead of twelve-hundred, and this time we had twelve-hundred processes able to help optimize them instead of only sixty-four. That was good."

"That was terrific!" she exclaimed, "You're a genius!"

"Well, you better be going now, before you are too tired to drive."

As if by the power of suggestion, Dierdre was gripped by an overpowering yawn. She picked up her things and made her way to the door, "Good night Bobby, call me if there is a problem, and lock the door after I leave."

* * *

The following morning, Chief Henderson waited outside the Inter-Mountain Bell offices. He sat in the car monitoring the time with two of his detectives. Behind them in another vehicle, was a county deputy responsible for this jurisdiction. At eight sharp, the chief and his detectives exited the car and motioned for the deputy to follow. The four men followed the concrete path to the main building and entered through the large glass doors.

The chief stepped forward to the reception area in the lobby, showed his badge to the guard and said, "Hello, I would like to speak with your personnel department manager."

"May I tell her what this is regarding?"

"I just want to ask her some questions regarding some employees."

"And your name is?"

"Henderson, Chief of police Henderson."

"One moment please." The guard, really a receptionist with a uniform, picked up the phone, dialed a number then turned his head to talk privately. He hung up the phone and flashed a bright effeminate smile. "She'll be right with you."

"Thank you."

The chief stepped back to join his associates.

"Well chief," one of his officers said, "I don't suppose we are going to have any trouble with the tinker bell at the desk."

"Tolerance, Bailey, haven't you been reading the memorandums?"

"Sure Chief, I didn't mean any disrespect, in fact, I was thinking of fixing him up with Sgt. Sweeney in Homicide."

The other men chuckled, but the chief didn't find it very funny. "Someday, somehow, you guys are going to create a controversy that's going to end up putting me out of a job. I just know it."

"Chief Henderson?" A middle aged woman with a clear voice and a practiced smile called out from the elevator.

The guard made a small hand gesture pointing to the chief, who approached her and offered his hand.

"Ah, Chief Henderson. I'm Paula Cook. I'm the public liaison officer for the personnel department as well as a legal advisor."

The chief was not happy. "I asked to speak with the head of the department, and they sent out a lawyer? Is there a problem here?"

"No problem, Chief, but I'm sure you are already aware that employee information is privileged so we are very careful about what information is shared. Now, if you will follow me, I think we can find a more comfortable place to speak."

She led them to the elevator and up to the fourth floor, where they had a sumptuous conference room. "Can I offer you gentlemen some coffee?"

"No, thank you, we'd just like to get to the point."

"Very well." She motioned to the seats around the large walnut table.

The chief sat down. The chairs were leather and very soft. He wished his budget could afford chairs like these. As they sat down around the table, another woman, much younger, entered the room and stood by the door. The chief looked at her and turned to Paula, but she read his mind.

"She's one of our file clerks, if you have specific questions about any of our employees, I might need her to pull some files."

The chief nodded and said, "Let's start with Arthur Bedding. I would like to see his files and any notes regarding his termination plus the files of his supervisors and anyone involved in whatever complaint led to his dismissal."

"I'm sorry chief, but surely you understand that I cannot permit you to see our files, but I would be glad to read the files and answer any questions for you." She signaled to the file clerk, who had recorded the names and information the chief requested. The girl started to leave the room.

"Bailey, accompany the young lady and help her carry the files."

"That won't be necessary," Paula objected, "She can manage."

"I insist," the chief replied, "and I WILL see the files."

The well-practiced smile evaporated from Paula's face. "I don't believe I like your tone. I think I am going to insist that you produce a warrant before we continue any further."

"Somehow," Henderson said, "I knew we would come to that. Patrick?" The chief held up a hand, and one of his detectives placed a small pile of documents in it. The chief looked over the various documents, and selected two, and handed the rest back to Patrick. He held up the two selected writs before Paula, one in each hand. "In my left hand," he said, "I have an order demanding that you cooperate with me fully, and in my right hand I have an order for you to vacate the premises while I bring in a crew of investigators to go over your files. Which order would you like?"

Paula had been trained in law school to hide her feelings and never show surprise. She was finding it difficult to stay calm at the moment. "You can't give us such a vague order as to cooperate fully, your orders must be more specific than that. Such generic wording would lead to too much confusion and differences in interpretation."

"Patrick, how many orders do we have?"

"Including the two you are holding? Twenty-seven, sir."

"Twenty-seven orders, Ms. Cook. I'm quite certain that some of those orders will be specific enough for your liking. I am particularly fond of this one for you to vacate the premises and let us nose around. I think that sounds pretty specific, don't you?"

"You can't be serious! Over a termination? That's absurd."

"Who said we were investigating a termination? That's just a lead. We are investigating something far bigger than a termination. Now, shall I issue this order to vacate the premises or not?"

"No," she said, "of course we will cooperate with you fully." She motioned for her clerk to go get the files, and Bailey tagged along with her.

"You know what would be really helpful, if I could talk to each of the people whose files she is pulling for us. Could you have them brought here for a real brief interview?"

He could see the wheels turning in her mind, but if she did have a tactic in mind, she did not employ it yet, and instead called someone to collect the required people."

* * *

Bobby woke at eight when his wrist alarm chirped. The current population was slightly over two-thousand. There would be no more large waves of machines joining up. The current wave would only be about twenty machines. He watched as they came on board. Two-thousand machines were not enough to produce Dierdre's number strings, but the process was working. As the twenty machines came on board, the red bar shot up, but only lasted twenty seconds and was gone.

Bobby changed his shirt and locked up the lab to go to his first class.

* * *

Ramiro made arrangements to borrow an office at the courthouse. The office belonged to Judge Bartholomew Binder, but he was on vacation fishing, and volunteered the use of his desk and phone. Even his court clerk, who had been looking forward to catching up on some work in his absence, offered his services. They offered Ramiro a laptop in case he needed to send or receive any emails. When this matter was concluded, he would have to do something to show his appreciation to all these people.

He kept his cell phone on a charger, not taking any chances of the batteries draining and missing a critical call. He knew that Mitch would be dealing with the phone company. He did not know whether or not they would cooperate, and he was prepared to have any new order drawn up and issued within minutes of any request.

While Ramiro waited by the phone, he wrote some letters to various offices within the army, requesting help with a rogue veteran. He theorized, in his letters, that the veteran in question might be suffering from post-traumatic stress, and therefore might not fully understand what he was doing and could be a hazard to the community. While he had no evidence that this was indeed the case, he also had no evidence to the contrary, and felt he was only stretching the facts to show a plausible possible cause.

He emailed and faxed the letters to the army, Pentagon, and Veteran Affairs. He did not hold great hopes of any response, but he felt it was a good first salvo. He couriered the printed letters to the same offices. The hard copy letters included the official seals of the courthouse, so they might be read. The email and fax may or may not be handled, but at least they would be in their hands sooner.

* * *

Witnesses began to line up in the hallway outside the conference room where Chief Henderson sat and waited for the records, "Patrick, see what's keeping Bailey."

Patrick, who stood behind the chief sorting through the stack of orders, pulled out his radio, "Hey, Bailey, how you doing with those files?"

"I was just about to call you. Tell the chief that we have all the files, but some suit down here is threatening to sue if I remove them from this room. Should I knock him on his can if he obstructs me?" Bailey only asked that to intimidate the middle aged lawyer with the manicured nails.

Henderson easily heard the whole thing. "Ask him to get the suit's name."

"Hey Bailey, the chief wants to know his name."

A moment passed before Bailey responded, "He says his name is Henry Swanson."

Patrick shuffled through his papers. "He's in here Chief."

Henderson picked up his own radio and said, "Bailey, bring the files up here, if he tries to stop you, arrest him, then bring him along with the reports, in cuffs."

"Roger Chief."

Everyone could hear someone in the background on the radio protesting, "You can't arrest me...."

Paula Cook had managed to remain somewhat calm to this point. But realizing now that they had a handful of arrest warrants, a new level of alarm began to register on her face. She forced herself to relax her expression before speaking again, "Listen, Chief Henderson, any appearance on our part to resist your inquiries is merely an attempt to protect the sanctity of what we consider privileged information. Obviously, you have a much more serious agenda than we are aware of. Perhaps if we knew what you were looking for and understood how serious it was, we could provide more help to you and your men."

"Well thank you Ms. Cook. That was very well said. Unfortunately, due to the nature of the crimes we are investigating, and the connection between those crimes and this office, I can't actually divulge such information to you. I'm sure you can understand that our need to, as you said, preserve the sanctity of our privileged information, trumps yours."

"So this is a criminal investigation then, and not a termination complaint?"

"Yes Ma'am, I told you before we were not here about the termination."

Bailey and the file clerk arrived with a very agitated Henry Swanson behind them.

"Bailey, I see you have brought someone with you. Mr. Swanson I presume? I see you are not wearing handcuffs, so, may I assume you have chosen to cooperate?"

Swanson stormed into the room. His face was dark red. "How dare you threaten me with arrest? Do you know who I am? I will have you charged with false arrest before you know what happened to you! I demand that you tell me this instant what all this is about!"

"Please, Mr. Swanson, we are conducting a criminal investigation here, and you're outbursts are interfering with our ability to conduct interviews."

"My outbursts? Who the hell do you think you are? I want you off the premises immediately! These interviews are over!"

Swanson's arms flew all around him as he ranted and raved. The chief stood up and approached him, face to face. "Mr. Swanson, my name is Chief of Police Mitchell Henderson. I am personally conducting a very serious criminal investigation here. If you insist on disrupting my interviews, I will have you arrested for interfering with a police investigation." The chief held his hand up and snapped his fingers, and Patrick quickly placed the appropriate warrant in his hands.

Swanson's eyes widened, his color darkened even further, his lips trembled, but he said nothing more. He glanced at Cook and could see from her expression, that she was fearful of what he might say next. He stood his ground for a moment, but his expression belied his shrinking courage. He backed off a pace and asked, "Paula, may I speak with you a moment?"

Paula looked at Chief Henderson, as if needing permission and he waved his hand and nodded his ascent. She rose, and the two of them found a neutral corner to whisper together. They only spoke a few moments before Swanson returned to the chief. "Chief Henderson, I apologize for my earlier misunderstanding. Of course we will cooperate fully with your investigation. I only ask that Miss Cook remain present as counsel during the interviews."

The chief reached a hand out to Swanson and replied, "I really don't think counsel will be necessary, but I have no objections to her presence."

They shook hands, and Swanson left the room.

Paula said to Henderson, "That was something, how you handled him," she moved closer so only he could hear her, "He is one mean son of a bitch. I have never seen him castrated like that before." Something in her tone told Henderson that maybe she wished she could have been the one to do it.

* * *

Bobby finished his first class, and stopped in Dierdre's office on the way to his next. She saw his assignment books in his hands, "Guess it must have been a smooth night if you are attending your regular classes."

"Yeah, not a single hitch. I even got some sleep. How about you? Sleep well?"

"No, not really, my mind was buzzing all night long."

"I know. It's hard to sleep in the middle of a big project like this."

Dierdre sipped her coffee, content to let him believe it was the project on her mind all night.

"I gotta scoot," he said, "This afternoon I'm going to see if there is anything we can do to improve the number generation."

She patted the reports Stillman had given her and said, "If you do we might actually be able to turn this theory into reality within our lifetimes."

"So you think Professor Whitfield was correct about those energy spikes in that report?"

"Yeah. I think so. The question now, do we tell his friend that he may have accidentally discovered what we need, or do we just borrow from their research and discover it ourselves."

"Telling them they discovered it seems fair, but with people slapping patents on everything they discover these days, you might not be able to use it if they knew what they had."

"I know." She checked her watch. "You better go. We'll touch base later."

* * *

Chief Henderson and Paula were seated at the conference table again. He was looking over the records for Arthur Bedding. He slid the records across the table to Paula. "Who actually terminated Bedding?"

She picked up the file, flipped the top page up and down. "It doesn't say who ordered it, the person on record is Lewis Stern, but he is in personnel. That usually indicates an order was sent down from higher up."

"How much higher?"

"An employee's supervisor would be the most common source, but other officers of the company can also order a firing."

"Patrick, call Lewis Stern."

Patrick went to the door and shouted, "Lewis Stern?"

Paula looked at the file clerk who was shaking her head.

"Sir," Bailey said, "Lewis Stern was not on our list, you want us to go pull his file?"

"Yes, thank you."

Paula reached for the phone. "I'll call him in for you." She dialed his extension, one she knew by heart and said, "Lewis? I need to see you in the executive conference room right away. Yes, drop whatever you are working on and come now."

Henderson scratched his chin. "How about Bedding's supervisor? Let's see him while we wait."

"Thomas Brady," she said it directly to Patrick.

"Thomas Brady?" Patrick repeated the name into the hallway while Paula pulled his file, from the stack Bailey had carried up, and handed it to the chief.

He was younger than Henderson expected, early thirties, slightly built with dark hair. He entered the room and took the seat indicated to him. The fear of not knowing what was going on was evident in his eyes.

"Mr. Brady," started the chief, "tell me about Arthur Bedding."

"Arthur? What did he do?"

"If you don't mind," the chief said, "I'll ask the questions, you answer them."

"I'm sorry, it's just that none of us can believe that Arthur was fired. He was probably the most honest man any of us had ever known. I can't think of anyone who didn't like him. Whatever you think he did, you must be mistaken."

"We are trying to find out what you thought he did. Who fired him?"

"I don't know. It certainly wasn't anyone in my department. He was my best man."

"Do you know what he was working on?"

"I only know he was responding to a request by police authorities. I didn't need to know any more than that. I let him manage his own workload."

"Thank you Mr. Brady, you can go. Patrick, is Mr. Stern here yet?"

Patrick pointed down the hall and asked one of the employees if that was Stern. "Yes Chief. He is just arriving."

Lewis Stern was a short stocky man in his fifties. He felt like he was walking to the guillotine, and wondered if this was some sort of surprise layoffs. He passed Brady in the hall. Their eyes met, but did not convey anything comforting to Mr. Stern.

As Stern approached the door, Patrick held him up a moment, he could see Bailey jogging down the hall with the files, and waited till he reached the room, then waved Stern in, took the file from Bailey so he could catch his breath, and handed it to the chief.

The chief glanced over the file, but didn't really find anything pertinent. "Mr. Stern. You entered the termination record for Arthur Bedding. I want to know who ordered it."

Stern looked worried and confused. He looked at the chief, then at Paula, then back at the chief and said, "I'm sorry, I don't know what you are talking about."

"It's OK Lewis," Paula said while patting his arm, "I showed Chief Henderson the termination record, the one you entered the day before yesterday."

"I still don't know what you are talking about, I never entered any termination records, and to my knowledge, none have been ordered."

The chief found Bedding's file and slid it to Stern. Stern looked it over and said, "I see it, but I don't know how it got there, I didn't put it there."

"Patrick, get Brady back here."

"I'll get him." Bailey darted out into the hall yelling, "Brady! Hey Brady! Hold up a second!"

The chief looked at Paula a moment, then back at Stern. "Mr. Stern, that is all for the moment, but could you please wait in the hall, we may have more for you in a moment."

Bailey and Brady returned just as Stern found a group to talk with out in the hall.

"Come in again, Mr. Brady, I think you will want to hear this. Bailey, close the door this time."

Brady sat back down at the table.

The chief got up and paced a bit before starting.

"I'm not sure where to start, so bear with me. Arthur Bedding was investigating a series of illegal wiretaps placed on your systems. In the process of his investigation, he was terminated, only nobody remembers ordering or entering his termination."

Brady looked at Paula, but she was as puzzled as he was.

"It gets worse, listen to this. The illegal wire taps he was investigating for me tie into another case involving computer hacking."

Light bulbs began to flicker in Brady's head. "You're saying we've been hacked? And the hacker entered the termination record? Why? As a prank?"

"I don't think this is a prank. I think this is no ordinary hacker. He has been after something all along. The wiretaps included some FBI agents, a Judge, and several people involved in one of MY investigations. I don't think he randomly chose Bedding's name to be terminated. I think you need to take a look at everything and anything which this guy might have done to your systems."

Paula put her hand to her mouth and cried out, "Oh my God! Poor

Arthur. We've got to get him back and fix this mess."

She reached for the phone, but Brady stopped her. "I'll call him."

"Before I go," Henderson said, "and let you guys get back to work, I still need Arthur's help with my investigation. I want to identify this hacker, and anything you can provide to help me would be appreciated."

Paula jumped up and chased after the chief, taking his hand in hers saying, "Thank you so much. I am so, so, so, sorry that we gave you so much trouble this morning."

"I'm just glad we got all this straightened out." He took her aside and whispered, "Listen, if you ever need me to come up here and punch out Mr. Swanson, you just call me." He pulled out his card, wrote his private number on the back and handed it to her.

"I'm not so sure Mrs. Henderson would appreciate you coming out here to beat up my bully."

He smiled at her transparent question and replied, "My mother stays out of my personal affairs."

* * *

Dierdre finished her first class, and stopped in at Stillman's office, but he wasn't there. She left a sticky note on his computer, *"Let's have lunch, 11:30 good?"*

Back at her own desk, she sat down and went over the report he had given her. The more she thought about it, the more this seemed like his friend had already discovered the answer that she thought would be decades away.

* * *

Ramiro sat in his temporary office. He had anticipated that Chief Henderson would ultimately receive the phone company's cooperation. They were loaded with a number of warrants that they could serve should the need arise, and even the unused warrants would serve as a threat of further warrants, but that threat would be a hollow one if Ramiro weren't ready by the phone, so he waited.

He checked his watch. It was a quarter past ten on the East Coast. Henderson's interrogations could last all day, or he could be done any time now. Ramiro continued to read up on cases involving ex-military civilians. He was specifically interested in those persons who had extreme training and could be dangerous weapons themselves. He also took note of cases involving those who suffered post traumatic shock, especially when they might become delusional.

When his cell phone finally did ring, he snapped it up, anxious for news. "Hello? Mitch?"

"No Honey, it's me."

"Aimee, how are you doing?"

"Better now, knowing you are near."

"Can I see you again?"

"Not yet. It's still too dangerous and takes too many people to coordinate an outing like that. Is there anything you can do to help my sister?"

"I'm working on it. You know, in spousal abuse cases, the battered wives often defend their husbands and claim they didn't do it."

"I know," she said, "but I believe her."

"Well, to be sure, I've sent some letters to the army. I think they need to be involved."

"We've already tried them. They sent us away and told us he it was a civilian matter."

"Yes. Any harm he may cause, or threats to do harm, would be a police matter, but his mental health would be a matter of the veteran affairs and the army that trained him. I think his actions warrant a psyche review, and probably some lengthy treatment."

"What if she's telling the truth and he didn't do it? You would be asking the army to go after the wrong man."

"If he didn't do it, he probably knows something about who did."

"So, you think you can persuade them to pick him up for a psychiatric evaluation? He doesn't act crazy, how can you do that?"

"He doesn't have to act crazy, but if he is having difficulty telling his wife from the enemies he used to face in the jungle, then he needs psychiatric treatment."

"I knew you could help."

"I haven't helped yet, just requested help. Let's wait and see how they respond."

"I love you. I have to go now. Others need to use the phone."

"I love you too."

* * *

Pietre was confident that he had finally started to gather bits and pieces of data from Dierdre's computer. His spy program had slipped comfortably into Dierdre's programs, and should have started recording the contents of her memory last night. He left it running all night, so he could piece it together this morning.

He arrived in his lab in much better spirits than he had experienced in quite some time. As he arrived, he saw his assistants gathered around the console as they had on previous occasions when Dierdre's program had hijacked his computer, but this time he had let those programs run and was not surprised to see the gathering.

"Good morning everyone, there is nothing to be alarmed about, I decided to leave those programs running so we could determine what they were after."

"But Dr. Pietre," said Panopulous who stepped forward first, "do you know what they have done?"

Pietre pushed into the center of the group. "Why don't you tell me?"

"First of all, they have written over every scrap of data storage we have, and after filling our disk drives, they started using the campus servers as auxiliary storage."

Pietre's mind was doing the calculations in his head. Dierdre's computer probably only had four gigabytes of memory, and maybe three-hundred gigabytes of storage. His routine only copied memory, so even if it copied the storage, it would still be less than one third his computer's capacity. "That's impossible, that would require a terabyte of information."

"Yes sir. We are over a terabyte and it keeps coming in."

"We can't lock up the schools servers again," Pietre said, "start freeing up the storage."

"We aren't sure how. If it were lots of smaller files, we could delete them file by file, but it seems to be one huge file, and we can't delete it while it's still being written."

Pietre had an advantage. He knew how the data got there. He just didn't know why there was so much. "Reboot the computer, then delete the file."

Panopulous and a team of two others scurried around the main computer rack and made their preparations to power it down and then back up again.

* * *

Stillman found the note on his computer after his third period class. He immediately jogged down the hall and around the corner to Dierdre's office, which was empty.

"Behind you," Dierdre whispered while gently pushing him through her door.

Stillman stiffened momentarily, startled by the hand on his back. The surprise melted away and was replaced by a broad smile. "Half past eleven would be just fine." He looked as if there were more he wanted to say, but words failed to appear on his lips.

Dierdre was in a bit of a hurry for her next class and said, "I only have a moment, can you find us a nice simple restaurant? Someplace off campus, not too fancy and not too popular."

"I understand," he said, "someplace remote, discreet, where we won't be hassled by other faculty or students. I believe I can find such a place."

Dierdre crinkled her nose and told him, "No, silly. Someplace where we can talk privately about, you know, the reports you gave me last night."

Stillman looked at her with a devilish look in his eye and said, "So you mean a remote, discreet location, where we won't be bothered by other faculty or students?"

Dierdre laughed. "Yes, but the second place, not the first one." She reached up with both hands and straightened his tie. "It's OK if we're seen together, I just don't want us to be overheard."

She grabbed here valise, and started to dart back out of her office, then turned impulsively and gave him a lightning quick peck on the lips. "See you soon."

* * *

"Judge Vasquez?"

Ramiro looked at the young boy. He was dressed in jeans, a t-shirt and a windbreaker. He was pushing an office cart filled with mail and other packages. He was holding a page in his hands. "Yes, I'm Judge Vasquez, is that for me?"

"Yes sir, it's a telegram. I don't think we've ever received a telegram here before. They told me I could find you here."

Ramiro took the telegram from the boy. "Thank you."

The sending office was from Washington, D.C.

> *Honorable Judge Ramiro Vasquez,*
>
> *Have read your request and have forwarded it to the JAG offices in San Diego. You will be contacted this morning. Please take no further action until then.*
>
> *Gen. Mackenzie Stern.*

Ramiro picked up the phone that came with the desk and dialed 0. "Hi, this is Judge Vasquez. Apparently I'm either expecting a phone call or possibly a visit this morning..."

The young girl on the other end of the phone call asked, "Would it, by any chance, be a couple of military guys in dress uniforms?"

"Yes," he said, "it probably would be."

"They just walked in. They are talking to the security guard as we speak. You'll have to come get them, the guards won't let them in unescorted."

Ramiro got up to head to the front desk when his cell phone rang.

"Hello, Judge Vasquez here."

"Rami, it's Mitch. There is definitely something going on at the phone company, but they appear to be the victim here. Our friend who was fired was never really fired. I think that whoever placed those wiretaps on their system also hacked in and had him fired. They seem genuinely pissed about being manipulated this way. I think we can expect more than the usual cooperation from them."

"You learned all that already?"

"Remember," Mitch said, "you're three hours behind us now."

"Do they think they can identify who the attacker was?"

"I think that depends on just how good the hacker was, but they seemed motivated to use every extraordinary means available to learn something about him. I'm betting they turn something up."

"That's great Mitch. Listen, I got some JAG guys here to see me. I'll call you later to see where we stand."

* * *

Dierdre and Stillman met in the hallway, each anxious for lunch. They took his car to a small Greek Deli. It did a brisk business, but most customers took their sandwiches to go, leaving the dining area relatively secluded. Stillman chose an empty corner booth with a large table where they could look over the reports together. The sandwiches were all named after mythological characters from ancient literature. They included Ali Baba's Stolen Delights, Sindbad's Sailfish Sandwich, and a Jason Burger with Golden Fried Fleece. Dierdre found the menu entertaining and ordered the Odysseus Prime Rib sandwich which came with Trojan Horse Radish. Stillman had the Jason Burger with Golden Fleece.

"What an adorable deli, how did you ever find it?"

"It was easy," he said, "I live just around the corner. I figured, if we couldn't get a big enough table here, we could take our lunch to my place."

Dierdre thought she detected some disappointment in his voice.

While they waited for their food to be prepared, she pulled the reports out of her briefcase and opened them on the table before them. She also pulled out a page with math symbols scribbled all over it. "These spikes that your friend thought were aberrations in the test equipment mathematically fit the model for coincidently hitting a quantum event." She pointed at the scribbled math. "See, both the frequency and amplitude match what we would expect when accidentally aligning with the quantum particle."

"That's great! Do you want me to talk to him about collaborating with you?"

"No. I mean, I don't think so, you know him, but he's trying to achieve control over the quantum events by brute force. I don't think he wants anyone telling him to abandon his theories and join with me, plus, his kind of research is usually tied in with weapons contracts."

"I know Jarod Jantzen well enough to know he is not working with weapons research. I also know him well enough to know, that if I told him about you, he would have the same concerns and want to make sure you were not working for the defense department."

"OK," she said, "I trust your judgment. Call him and tell him a friend of yours is working on a project along the same field, and may have some insight about his readings."

CHAPTER 15

Bobby took his lunch to the lab. Progress had already plateaued by his previous visit, as he expected it would due to the way contestants were eliminated from the tournament. After the first few rounds, they had already gained ninety percent of the computers in the tournament, and the late rounds added only a small percentage to their total census. So, when he sat down at the terminal and first glanced at the screens, what he found there was absolutely stunning.

Of all the graphs and numbers he monitored on the screen, the two most critical numbers were how many clients were on board, and how long the predicted strings were. All the other numbers were of a diagnostic nature. The most important number, and the object of their project, was the string length. It was the hardest to improve and was the reason they needed such an elaborate multiple computer approach to solve the problem.

According to the screen, he had over sixty-five-thousand processors on board, and almost all of them were busy optimizing. The red graph showed over sixty-three-thousand processors that were dedicated to optimization and the number was steadily rising. This had to be a mistake. He must have developed a bug in his census program. In the few moments it had taken Bobby to read the screen, the number of processors had risen to over seventy-two-thousand.

He was going to have to identify these new machines, but he was sure he would find duplicate machines. He sat down at the terminal and started to investigate.

* * *

Ramiro entered the reception area and saw two military officers talking with the guards. The guards were probably recounting old stories from their days in the service. The two uniformed men smiled warmly and nodded their heads. They respected anyone who had served their country honorably. The two men were both relatively young. Their suits were clean and pressed, and it was difficult for Ramiro to deduce whether they were police or lawyers. Stranger still, was the fact that they each represented different service arms. One was a naval officer, in a bright white dress uniform, and the other was either army or marine, his uniform being a light green color.

Ramiro offered his hand as he approached them. "I guess you boys are here to see me."

Both men stopped speaking with the guards and stood slightly stiffer. The naval officer gripped Ramiro's hand first and introduced himself, "Sir, my name is Lieutenant McElroy, and this is Lieutenant Thompson. Is there some place we can speak, we only need a few moments of your time."

Ramiro released Lieutenant McElroy's hand and shook Lieutenant Thompson's. "Certainly," he replied, "Just follow me. Our hosts have arranged a small conference room for us."

"Our hosts?" McElroy said, "Oh that's right. You aren't from around here."

Ramiro thought he detected a tone in McElroy's voice, like he didn't belong here and he shouldn't be messing in other people's business. "So," Ramiro said, "I was told on the phone that you were both JAG, you don't really look like lawyers. Are you investigators?"

McElroy bristled at the implication that he might not look old enough to be a lawyer. "No, sir, we are lawyers. Don't let our youthful appearance fool you."

Ramiro led them through the final hallway and stopped outside the conference room, indicating the door for them to enter. He closed the door behind him and they all sat down.

"Sir, Lieutenant Thompson and I are here to speak to you regarding some letters you had sent to our superiors in the Pentagon."

"And," Thompson added, "apparently also to the V.A. and even the Attorney General."

Ramiro wasn't even sure he would get a response to his letters, but never imagined such a prompt and formal response.

An empty space followed during which the two Jag officers had waited for a response from Ramiro, and he merely waited for them to continue.

"Sir?" McElroy continued, "Did you write those letters?"

"You know I did, as you already stated."

"But," Thompson interjected, "you don't deny it."

"Of course I don't deny it, perhaps you can move on to how you intend to handle the problem?"

"Sir, Mr. James is a civilian, and as such, does not fall within our jurisdiction. There is nothing we can do about it."

"I disagree," Ramiro said, "I think Mr. James may require a psych evaluation. As a veteran, I think it does fall within your jurisdiction."

"Sir, our medical and psychiatric facilities, of course, are always at his disposal. But seeking help there is voluntary. If you are seeking court ordered treatment, then you need to go through the civilian courts, as I am sure you are already aware."

"This particular man may be a menace to society, and may be beyond the civilian authority's capabilities to safely bring in for treatment."

"I'm sorry sir, but the armed forces are in place to face the menace abroad, not a lone menace within our shores, especially a citizen protected by the constitution."

Thompson nodded his head, feeling that McElroy's last statement was definitive and no further argument could be made.

Ramiro shifted in his chair and asked, "How many veterans are there?"

"I don't have that information in front of me, sir."

"Guess."

"Well sir, I'm sure there are many thousands."

"Many thousands. Probably still a few from World War II, then there was the Korean Conflict, Vietnam, Grenada, Desert Storm, Iraq again. I'll bet most of those men had opportunities to handle some pretty sophisticated weapons, for their times at least."

"Yes sir," McElroy admitted, "our troops do handle very sophisticated weaponry."

"And when they come home, they get to keep those weapons as souvenirs, and they can use them for protection, correct?"

"No sir, they may not keep their weapons."

"Never?"

Thompson interjected, "Sir, there are some decorative weapons, swords and commemorative side arms which may be kept, but the fighting weapons are returned to the armory."

"I see," Ramiro paused, and looked from one man to the other.

"Sir? Are you suggesting that Mr. James has retained his weapon?"

"Yes. Now is it within your jurisdiction?"

Thompson looked through the papers he had within the accordion file he had in his briefcase. "Sir, I have here, the signed paper from the

Master Supply Sergeant, stating that Sgt. James turned in all his weapons before he was discharged. If he has any weapons, he got them somewhere else."

"Are you sure he did not leave with any of the weapons you gave him?"

"Yes sir, absolutely."

"Again, I must disagree. You train all your soldiers to handle the latest weaponry, but you also select those with exceptional skills to receive specialized commando training. You trained this man to become a weapon himself. What was he? Green Beret? Special Forces? Unarmed, he can present a danger to society. In fact, he is never truly unarmed, is he? You did not collect that weapon from him, and therefore, I think you need to take steps to apprehend him and get treatment for him."

The two Lieutenants turned towards each other and put their heads close together and whispered between themselves. Their heads nodded and bobbed as they traded comments and remarks until they each pulled back and sat stiffly facing Ramiro again.

"Sir," Thompson said, "we are not here to discuss Sgt. James."

"Mr. James," McElroy corrected his associate.

"Correct, I'm sorry, we are not here to discuss Mister James."

Thompson pulled out a small micro-cassette recorder, turned it on and placed it on the table between them. "What is your relationship with Mrs. James?"

"Excuse me? You don't want to discuss this James guy, but you are asking me about his wife?"

"Sir, what is your interest in Mrs. James?"

"Apparently," Ramiro said, "Mrs. James is Sgt. James' punching bag."

"Sir, we are not interested in her marital problems. What is your relationship with Aimee Takagashi?"

"I'm sorry, I don't know Aimee Takagashi."

Thompson leaned over again and whispered in McElroy's ear.

"Takahashi," McElroy corrected himself, "what is your relationship with Aimee Takahashi?"

"With Aimee?" Ramiro asked, "What is your interest in Aimee? As a matter of fact, what exactly is your purpose for being here today?"

"What is your business relationship with Norwood University?"

"What in the world does James have to do with Norwood University?"

Thompson started to speak again, but McElroy put his hand on Thompson's arm as if to hold him back. "Sir, you are not answering any of our questions. Frankly, we expected more cooperation from someone in your position."

Ramiro stood up and said, "Gentlemen, I don't know what your agenda is, but this interview is over. You are dismissed." He opened the door to the conference room.

Thompson retrieved his recorder, stood up and exited the room.

Ramiro followed them down the hall until they exited the man-traps at the guard station.

He left the court offices, but did not get lunch. He found a small out of the way cellular dealer, and purchased two new throw away cell phones.

* * *

Bobby compiled a list of all the machines he had on-line. His list identified the machine, and each process running on the machine. He expected to find sixty processes assigned to Dierdre's machine, one to four processes assigned to each of the almost two thousand machines from the tournament, but even the best case would only account for eight thousand processes, and he had surpassed one-hundred-thousand. He knew it was possible for any or all of the machines on board to create thousands of processes, but doing so would bog them down and make them very slow. The list he compiled showed over one-hundred-thousand processes belonging to a single machine, and it was not slowing down, but rather seemed to be accelerating.

* * *

"Dr. Pietre, we've finished deleting that file. Everything should be back to normal now. Do you know what happened there?"

"Yes. I was working on a program to build some data tables, but I made a mistake, and it was writing the same data over and over. You go on to class now. I'll fix the problem myself."

Pietre saw enough of the data that had come in to realize that it had come from multiple places. He was only interested in dumping the ROM areas of Dierdre's machine, so he modified his code to include the machine address in the packets it sent to his machine. He then modified his receiving program to reject anything not from Dierdre's address.

He chuckled to himself, as he released this new code back into Dierdre's system. He felt very clever using the boys own code against him. He had analyzed the code enough to realize that it would slowly spread onto the host machine and would probably be a while before he started to receive new data, so he went back to his office to work on his lesson plans.

* * *

Dierdre had finished her last class for the day and went to the lab to see how the project was going. She entered the lab and stood in the doorway to the inner office. Bobby was busy working on something and never even noticed she was standing there. She waited a while, watching him work. It was apparent to her that something was bothering him. He would attack the keyboard typing in flurries, then sit back and look at it. It was obvious that he did not like the results he was seeing by the various grunts and moans followed by another flurry of typing and the process repeated.

She quietly stepped behind him to look over his shoulder. The code he worked on flashed on and off the screen as he rapidly paged through the programs, far too fast for her to read or understand what the problem was, but, when he ran tests of the programs, he switched to the graph display, and she was somewhat familiar with the graphs.

At a distance, the graphs looked fine. The graph representing the number of clients was the largest, and the red graph representing the number of processes optimizing new processors fluctuated.

"Hi Bobby, I thought you said the red graph would have shrunken down by now?"

Bobby looked over his shoulder and said, "You're standing too far back. Step up closer and look at the numbers."

She moved in closer and saw what he was talking about. "Didn't you say we would only pick up a couple thousand from the tournament?"

"Yeah, three or four thousand would have been extraordinary."

"So where did we get three-hundred-thousand...Oh my God, are we spreading across the campus?"

"I don't know for sure," he said, "but all the processes appear to be from the same machine."

"That's not possible. Not even the fastest computer in the world is going to give us three-hundred-thousand processes."

"I know. It's puzzling me too. So I started looking at the code. I wrote the code so it would try and borrow routines from the host computer. My theory was that it might find a faster way to run the job, or communicate with the main system. Somehow, it has borrowed some code that has it sending data to another machine, but it also has picked up some code that would rewrite itself onto existing processes, like a virus."

"You mean," Dierdre swallowed hard, "it is spreading out through the Internet onto people's computers?"

"I don't think so. Three-hundred-thousand processes would create an enormous amount of traffic on the LAN, and we just don't have that much. Besides, it still says it's all one machine."

"Then how do you account for the increase?"

"It has to be a mistake. I must be counting them wrong."

"What just happened?" Dierdre saw the red graph suddenly drop down to a relatively low level.

"I don't know. I guess it thinks it's done optimizing. If there really were over three-hundred-thousand processors, the string lengths would start to climb. But it's still..." He was about to say it was still the same, but it wasn't, as he spoke, it increased by one.

"Bobby, is the number of processors accelerating?"

"I haven't measured them, but I think so. I thought I noticed that earlier too."

"Let's leave it running," she said, "You are late for class, and it doesn't seem to be doing any harm, I'll lock up the lab and we can check back later."

* * *

"I told you I wanted to wrap this up," The large man said as he fed files into the shredder, "Just get the device and we'll be out of here."

"They never leave it alone at night. That kid's been sleeping in the lab."

"I don't care! I want you to go in and get it now!"

"In broad daylight? That sounds more like your area of expertise than mine. I'm a technologist. I don't deal with force, and you know that."

"Then we go in together. Pack up what you need to remove and transport the device."

* * *

Pietre returned to his lab. There was no congregation of assistants huddled around the console, which was a good sign. He sat down at the console and checked the available space. It was not filled up, another good sign. He ran a file viewer to see the contents of his data from Dierdre's computer, it was empty. Naturally, he blamed Bobby for thwarting his attempts again. Fortunately for him, now that he had a working delivery system, it was getting much easier for him to add programs to spy on Dierdre's system. His first attempt returned way too much data, from too many systems, so he filtered everything but Dierdre's address. He concluded that somehow Bobby must have found a way to spoof her machine address so nothing would come through. He needed to learn the machine address that they were using, so he added a new spy program to report back a list of all the machines it found, and how much data they held. The largest one would probably be hers.

* * *

The large man and the Bard entered the campus dressed in construction overalls for a fictitious company. The large man grabbed the other by the shoulder and said, "I don't know what kind of resistance we are going to meet in there, but you need to concentrate on getting the device and pay absolutely no attention to what I am doing."

The Bard nodded his head.

"I mean it. Do not let my job interfere with what you have to do."

The smaller man looked away for a moment, then replied, "How about if I set up a diversion to minimize any direct contact you need to make?"

"What did you have in mind?"

"A fire alarm."

"No good, they bring firemen."

"It's a large campus. I can locate the alarm in the cafeteria, and still sound it over the entire campus. Everybody should evacuate in all the buildings, but the fire fighters will be searching the cafeteria. It should give us enough time, and you only have to watch my back."

"OK, if you can do it quickly, do it."

The Bard pulled out a small wireless hand held, ran a few readymade programs, and clicked his stylus on an enter button, and alarms started sounding all over the campus.

"Good," the large man said, "Let's hurry."

* * *

Ramiro was collecting his things to return to his hotel when his cell phone rang. "Hello?"

"Hi..."

It was Aimee's voice, but he cut her off saying, "Mrs. Henderson, thanks for getting back to me. Listen, I can't really talk much right now, I'm borrowing someone else's office, and I feel real self-conscious, like everybody was watching my every move. I'll call you back when I get back to my hotel, if you talk to Mitch, tell him I'll be in touch with him too. Bye now."

"Bye..." He had already disconnected.

Ramiro did not like the Jag officers questioning him about Aimee, and he was more than a little confused about their questions regarding the college. Mostly, though, he found their attitudes disturbing. He had little faith in their abilities or even their desire to get to the truth.

He crossed the building to the juvenile side. He found an office labeled public affairs, and looked for a kind face working there. He found a Hispanic woman, in her early thirties. She smiled as he approached and asked, "Are you looking for someone?"

He offered his hand and said, "Hello. I'm Judge Vasquez. I'm just looking for a little help."

"How can I help you?"

"Do you run any organizations to reform gang members, perhaps with ex-gang members in it?"

She looked at him warily and said, "You want me to tell you how to find some ex-gang members? Don't you think that sounds a little suspicious?"

"When you put it that way, it does. Your office has been so kind to me, I thought I would return the favor and show them that young boys and girls really can be whatever they want to be."

"Maybe you can show me some identification?"

"Sure." He pulled out his wallet and showed her his shield and his official id.

"OK, you are who you say you are. Now what do you really want? And don't give me that crap about you being a Hispanic role model again."

Ramiro was stunned by her ability to see through him. He saw a transformation in her from mild office worker to a feisty lady with street smarts. "What I really need is secrecy."

"Maybe you should talk to the CIA, they deal in secrets."

"No," he answered, "I definitely do not want to talk to them."

She transformed before his very eyes, like a caterpillar morphing into a wasp! "Look, you can't come in here waving your badge, then axing me to give up the names of some ex-gang bangers to do some secret illegal thing. I'm not standin for it. Ju better leave now! I'm calling security."

"Wait, calm down. You don't look foolish enough to believe that everything our government does is legal. I need some men, boys even, to deliver some packages for me. That's all."

"Packages? I'm not giving you boys to help you deliver drugs or guns."

"No drugs and no guns. I can't go into details. I just need help delivering a cell phone so I can talk to my fiancé without any undue complications."

"Why don't you deliver it yourself?"

"I can't. It's complicated. Can you help me or not?"

"Sure. I'll help you. Someone will be in front of the building in ten minutes. I'll be there too. Just a cell phone and a note, that is all."

"Thanks."

Since he had already collected his things, he went to the front lobby and waited for someone to pull up, and looked for the girl he had talked to. While he waited, he wrote two notes. One was simply the cell phone number he was using and the other was directions to Ernesto's, where he had met with Aimee and her sister.

* * *

The large man, more experienced in stealth, opened the locked door, and entered Dierdre's lab with the Bard close behind. He closed the door behind him and checked his watch, "Hurry. Let's try and get out of here ASAP."

"This should only take a few minutes, a half hour tops."

The bard went to the large rack and checked the various items installed. The upper layers all housed the CPU blades. Below the blades was the hard drive array. Below the hard drives was some empty space, but at the bottom of the rack he found a blank case with several ribbon cables leading up to the CPU modules in the top layer.

He pulled out a Phillips screw driver, but try as he might, he could not get the screw to turn. He tried a different screw, then another, they were all locked in tighter than he could manage to undo. He went around to the back to see if he could undo a back panel and pull out the package from the rear. The screws on the back panel were also locked in.

"These screws must be glued in place, I can't budge them, and it would take a fairly long time to cut them off."

The large man scowled, "Watch the door, let me try."

He took the screw driver from his slender associate.

"The big box at the base is what we want."

He inserted the driver into a screw and turned with all his considerable might. He grunted and cursed as the screw refused to budge. He cursed even louder when the driver would slip within the screw head, rounding the joint and making it even harder to get a good grip. "Is it possible that we are turning the wrong direction?"

"No, they are just glued in place."

"More like they are welded in place. Screw it," he growled, "we'll take the whole damn thing." He stood up, stepped back, and leaned into the rack trying to push it over.

"It's connected on top. "You have to release the ceiling mount."

"Oh, yeah, forget you ever saw that." The large man pulled a chair up to the rack and climbed up. The screws holding the ceiling mount in place turned easily. It took only a short time for him to completely release the rack from the ceiling. Once he had it released, he took another try to shove it over, but it wouldn't budge. He leaned his very large frame into the rack but he couldn't even loosen it from the floor.

He stepped around the rack trying to identify the floor mounts, but could not find any.

"Hey kid, how is it attached to the floor? I don't see any floor mounts."

"To the floor?" He shrugged his shoulders. "It shouldn't be attached to the floor. Are you sure?"

"I can't even loosen it, it's like it was welded to the floor."

"OK, my turn, you watch the door." The bard returned to the rack, opened his tool kit and pulled out a small cordless drill. He drilled a small hole in the front of the bottom rack space. He then took one of those small video cameras on the end of a small wire, and inserted it into the hole. He turned on the monitor, and got his first glimpse inside. "Houston, we have a problem."

"What's wrong?"

"You know the super-secret, does not exist package we are supposed to recover? It's definitely been activated. We have to go. We aren't going to be getting it today."

The large man didn't like his junior calling an end to their operation, but when he started to question him, he saw something in the young man's face that convinced him to accept his assessment and leave. He could get the details later.

They packed up the tools and headed out of the lab and off the campus, just as people started heading back to their classrooms and offices. They could see several angry firemen shaking their heads, they really hate false alarms.

* * *

Ramiro handed over one of the cell phones and the notes to a young man in a very large car. He didn't return to his hotel, but drove to a small playground instead. He took the other new cell phone and found a comfortable bench overlooking a small duck pond.

He dialed his friend Chief Henderson. "Hello? Mitch?"

"Hey Rami, no news from our friends at the telephone company yet."

"Mitch, is this line secure?"

"You kidding? With all the intrigue and wire taps going on around here? I have someone sweep the entire office every other hour, and our good friend Arthur Bedding has set up a program that checks all of us for new taps every fifteen minutes."

"It's good to have friends. I'm on a new cell phone, pencil it in, I plan to change phones regularly."

"Uh oh," Henderson said, "Sounds like those Jag guys had bad news for you."

"More like maybe those Jag guys WERE the bad news for me. Let me give you some background first. Aimee's here taking care of her sister who is hiding out in a home for battered women. Her sister claims that her husband didn't do it, but you know how that goes. It turns out he is a real dangerous guy, trained by the military. He was Special Forces, maybe CIA, definitely a black ops type. The army claims he is a war hero honorably discharged. I told them he might be crazy, and since they made him a danger to society, they should take responsibility."

"It reminds me of a movie I saw."

"Yeah," Ramiro agreed, "Now that you mention it, it does. They spent the first fifteen minutes denying culpability, which I expected them to do, but then they suddenly just moved on as if they had no interest in him at all. They started asking questions about Aimee, and then they asked questions about the university."

"Maybe those FBI idiots are yanking their chains."

"Could be, but I suspect the FBI's chains are being yanked by the same puppeteers who are behind the Jag investigators."

"You think the two events are tied in?"

"I didn't, but the Jag guys seem to think they are. See if you can find any connection between a Sgt. James and whatever is happening up there, but be careful. Document everything you do, and work in teams. I don't know what we are getting into here, but it doesn't look pretty."

"OK. I'll see what I can do. You be careful too."

Ramiro ended the call, and picked up the card from the women's shelter, and dialed the number. "Rosa?"

"Yes, this is Rosa."

"Don't say anything more. Tell Aimee to go to the place where we met. She will find a phone and a new number where she can reach me. Take precautions." He hung up the phone, and returned to his car and the hotel.

* * *

The large man and the Bard thought they had slipped on and off campus completely invisible, and they would have except for one thing. Pietre knew them, and he saw them leave the building. He followed them down to the parking lot and approached them as they reached their van.

"I know," he shouted to them, "I know what is the thing that is going on. I have been analyzing that thing that is in there."

The two men were slightly startled to have someone address them, but they didn't show it. The large man shaped his mouth into a large smile and approached Pietre saying, "Dr. Pietre, how good to see you again."

"Yeah, yeah, I am sure you are so thrilled. I don't know what is the deal it is you are cooking up with that delinquent kid, but I know what is the thing that Dr. Karlyn put inside there. I am analyzing how it is working remotely from my lab. And don't try thinking you can be making me disappear. I have the safeguards."

"Dr. Pietre, your imagination is getting the better of you."

"Is not my imagination. That thing is worth the millions, billions even. I bring you in here. I am wanting my share. You can't be cutting me out of this."

"You've been watching too many spy movies Pietre, go home. Concentrate on teaching your classes. Try and keep a low profile. You really wouldn't want anyone here in the university to learn your dirty little secret."

"I have no secrets."

"You and your family were planted in the US by the Soviets."

"Soviet government is no more, everyone knows I am Russian, is no secret."

"Go home comrade." With that, they started the car and drove off.

"Po'shyol 'na hui!!" Pietre shouted obscenities and waved his fist at the retreating vehicle, "Mu'dak!!"

Pietre went back to his lab muttering to himself. He was not going to let them cut him out. If they weren't going to include him, then he would destroy it.

* * *

Bobby was clear across the other side of the campus when the alarms went off. He was in the humanities building, and the alarms sounded like the fire was right there in the very same building, but when he and everyone else filed out onto the walks outside, he could see that all the other buildings were also evacuating. He knew that this was not a regular fire alarm. Each building had its own zone, and only the building with the fire would raise an alarm. If all the building alarms went off, then you would have chaos as the entire student body filed out onto the narrow concrete walkways between the buildings. Even the grassy areas between the walks were crowded with onlookers.

Bobby squeezed and dodged through the crowd towards the lab. As he was passing the cafeteria, he saw Dierdre standing with a small group of faculty.

She saw him trying to race through the crowd and called to him, "Bobby!"

"Professor, does anyone know what's going on yet?"

"No news yet," she said pointing off towards the parking lot, "but it looks like the fire department has just arrived."

"I don't know about you, professor, but I haven't seen or smelled any smoke at all. There's something fishy about all the alarms going off at once."

Professor Whitfield was standing next to Dierdre sipping a cup of tea and said, "I haven't smelled any smoke either. It's probably some sort of prank, like the computer hacks we have been having."

"I hope it's just a prank," Bobby said, "but, if you'll excuse me professors, I'm going to go check out the lab and make sure everything up there is OK."

"Be careful," Stillman cautioned, "there are a lot of people coming down the steps from the lab. You'll be like a salmon swimming upstream."

"Oh hell," Dierdre said, "who ever saw just one salmon swim upstream?" Dierdre tossed the remains of her coffee in a trash bin. "I'm coming with you."

Stillman dropped his cup of tea on top of Dierdre's coffee. "What kind of a man would I be if I let the two of you swim upstream to spawn alone?"

Bobby led the way, with Dierdre wedged between him and Stillman who trailed behind. They pushed, and bumped their way up the long concrete steps, clinging to the right hand railway like a mountain climber might cling to his rope. The crowd coming down the stairs moved steadily down the stairs, like a mud flow sliding down a hill, oblivious to the three climbers pushing and pulling their way up through the throng.

Bobby turned his head over his shoulder and said, "I don't see how the salmon do it. I understand they have an irresistible drive to work their way upstream, but I just don't see how they can have the energy to spawn once they reach their destination."

Stillman's voice could be heard from the back, panting and wheezing as he spoke, "They don't hold anything back. It's their last dying act. They spawn, and then they turn belly up and die."

Dierdre turned her head to the side so they both could hear her, "Knock it off you two. Unless you're a couple of gay salmon, there's not going to be any spawning at the top of these steps!"

"Hey!" Bobby objected, "I never said a thing! You just make sure you aren't too old for the climb. Some salmon never even survive long enough to spawn, and croak on the way upstream."

"Well I do declare," Stillman summoned up his deepest most southern voice, "I believe this small fry is talking about me! That's the problem with young folk today, they are all braggarts, and probably don't even know what to do when they finally reach the top, and even if they did, they are all too fast to enjoy it."

"All right you two," Dierdre said, "the testosterone is getting a bit thick around here, we just want to reach the lab and make sure everything there is as it should be."

Bobby finally broke free of the crowd, as they reached the end of what had seemed an endless procession of students. They were still one flight from the lab on the top level. He started taking the steps two at a time. Dierdre and Stillman did not try and keep pace with him, but climbed the final flight side by side instead of single file. Bobby turned left and darted through the building entrance down the corridor to the lab door. He peered inside the door, all seemed as he had left it. He tried the door, it was still locked. Dierdre and Stillman entered the building as Bobby was inserting his key to unlock the door.

Everything seemed fine as he raced through the main lab to the office where they kept the primary terminal. He went directly to the terminal and checked that the programs were all running as he had left them. Dierdre and Stillman entered the lab and came directly to the small office and stood behind Bobby.

Bobby sat at the console and called up a history program to display a log of the last hour's activity. The log showed two screens, one filled with graphs and the other had lists of numbers. "The logs don't show any signs of disturbance. Nobody has tried breaking into the system since the alarms went off."

Stillman raised his eyebrows and asked, "Is that what you thought?"

"There have been several attempts to hack this computer, both physical on site attacks, and remote attacks over the Internet. I guess I'm getting pretty jumpy these days, but anything unusual seems like a diversion to me."

Bobby flipped back to the program monitor to see the prediction application results.

"What's that Bobby?" They were the first words Dierdre had uttered since she entered the lab and caught her breath.

The number of processors was nearing one million. "I told you before. I don't think I'm counting them correctly. I think I must have inadvertently counted the same processes over and over."

"No Bobby, Look!"

That was when Bobby saw the string length had risen to seven. "Wow. I can't explain that. A string length of seven would require this many processors. If it is really predicting seven fluctuations correctly, then maybe the count is correct, though I don't know where they are coming from."

"Unless", Stillman added, "you are also counting the string length incorrectly."

"NO BOBBY!!!" She grabbed his head and physically turned it so he was looking out the small office's door and into the main lab. She pointed her finger and yelled, "Look!!!!"

Bobby's jaw fell slack. "What the..."

Stillman cocked his head to the side and said, "It looks like that slimy goo with which my nieces and nephews are so fond of terrorizing my dear sister."

Bobby got up from his chair and crept closer to the computer. A slender colorless thread exuded from the front of the bottom panel on the rack. It hung from the front panel a couple inches from the top of the panel. It appeared to be just over a quarter of an inch in diameter at the panel, and tapered off as it hung down to a tip that was barely one sixteenth of an inch wide, and about six or seven inches long.

Stillman was on his hands and knees next to Bobby. "Yup, the little tykes like to hang that stuff from their nose and pretend it is snot."

Dierdre blanched, "That's disgusting."

Stillman pulled a small penlight out of his inner coat pocket for a closer inspection. "None the less, that's what it looks like. Have you had any little brats in here visiting?"

"Not while I was monitoring things this morning, but I've been in class for at least a couple hours."

Stillman turned on his flashlight and directed the beam through the slender clear strand. Though it had appeared perfectly clear, it now displayed iridescent colors like small microscopic flecks suspended in a clear gel. Bobby reached out to remove the strand from the panel, but it retracted into the cabinet.

Dierdre shrieked and Bobby pulled his hand back so fast he slapped himself in the chin.

"Well," Stillman coolly said, "I have never seen the tykes slime do that."

Stillman started to get up, but Bobby stopped him. He pointed at the hole where the slime retreated and said, "Point your flashlight there."

"I don't think you are going to see much through such a small hole, your head would block the light." Stillman pointed the light at the hole anyway.

Bobby examined the hole closely. "It's perfectly round, and has sharp edges. I would think that if a slimy goo could create a hole in sheet metal, it would have perfectly smooth edges."

Bobby traced his finger straight down from the hole. "Shine your light down here.

Stillman moved the light where Bobby directed. They could see small shiny bits on the lab tile. "I see your point," Stillman said, "gooey slimy things would not leave bits of metal shavings on the floor."

"What are you two saying?" Dierdre moved in for a slightly closer examination, still fearful of the movement that shocked her before. "Are you saying someone drilled a hole in the computer and put that worm in there?"

Stillman sat up straight. He was processing everything in his mind. "No, my dear, I think we are only saying that someone drilled a hole, and we don't know what that thing was. Personally, I'm inclined to look around the lab for hidden cameras and microphones."

* * *

The large man tossed his cloak on the large nail behind the door of his temporary office. "So, why couldn't you get the device? You looked like you had seen a ghost."

The Bard walked over to the tall file cabinet by the window, pulled open the top drawer, extracted a flask of tequila, and took a quick shot without even wiping the lip of the bottle first.

"Hey, slow down their partner, that's pretty strong stuff for someone who doesn't really drink much."

The slender man put the cap back on the bottle and handed it to the big guy. "The device is fused to the case. It's not going anywhere."

"They welded it in place?"

"No, it wasn't welded."

He opened a lower drawer on the file cabinet and pulled out a strange little device with odd antennae pointing every which way, and walked around the room. He pointed the device at objects and walls, windows and floors, every corner and dark little hiding place.

"Sit down and relax," the big man said, "the room is clean. I swept it this morning."

The young man sat down and said, "You know the project where the device came from?"

"Yeah, go on."

"You know what we aren't supposed to really know about that project?"

"OK. We both know something we aren't supposed to know."

The Bard got up and paced as he continued, "Remember the report theorizing that advanced technology could be based on organic material organized into living tissue?"

"The stuff that could grow, change its shape and repair itself?"

"Yeah, that's the stuff. They said it could be used to make living computers, kind of like our brains."

"Yes," the big man hissed, "I remember all the reports, what did you see?"

"The device looks just like the stuff we aren't supposed to know about. It's not just fused to the case, it's growing inside there. It has grown and spread to fill the whole box and is fused to all the sides and the floor. It's attached to everything like ivy on the side of a building."

The large man started to speak, but his jaw fell slack and he sunk into his chair and whistled instead. "We have to report that. This is really big."

"How can we report something we aren't supposed to know about?"

"We have to report what you saw. Tell them you don't know what it was, but that it looked strange. Tell them it looked like wild mushrooms for all I care."

"They are going to have to quarantine the building to extract it."

* * *

Bobby pulled his cell phone from its clip on his belt and punched the number to the friends that helped him move the computer.

"Hey Bobby. Some fire drill, huh?"

"Just another in a long list of mysterious happenings on campus here. Say, Dexter, do you have one of those miniature video cameras on the flexible wire? Like the ones the cops use to peek under doors?"

"Bobby, I'll tell you the same thing I tell those jocks on the football team. I will not help anyone get a peek in the girl's locker room."

"Very funny Dex, I'm serious. If you have the equipment, bring it up to the physical sciences buildings, Lab 14."

"I have the equipment. I have all the equipment. But I'm serious when I say I won't let you use it to do anything illegal."

"I just want to peek inside some computer cabinets without disturbing the panels."

"When?"

"The morning would be fine."

"You got it bro. I should be up there between eight and half past eight."

"Cool dude, see you then."

* * *

The Bard's last official duty was to file a report to their handler. He detailed the difficulties in extracting the artifact from the university computer. He described the device as being encased in a gelatinous material which had bonded with all the sides and the floor. He advised that extraction would probably require considerable destruction of the labs floor and that the size of the artifact made secret extraction impossible.

While he prepared the technical report, the large man prepared another report with a detailed assessment of the situation. He advised that containment was already out of control and would require considerable cleanup and damage control to maintain secrecy. He listed the names Bobby, Dr. Jennings, Dr. Whitfield, and the missing Aimee Takahashi. He also recommended containment of Judge Vasquez and suggested concern for all of Bobby's known associates, including all the universities computer clubs, and the audio/video department, basically all the geek's.

When both reports had been completed, the Bard took the files and combined them into a single file. He couldn't help reading some of the large man's report including the recommendation to contain the witnesses. He knew the large man didn't deal with discrediting witnesses, when he said contain, he meant to terminate the witnesses in the most permanent way. He didn't have the heart or stomach for that side of their work, and his hands felt heavier as he combined the reports and encrypted them. He sent them to a secret email address that didn't even exist. Usually, if you email something to a non-existent address, it is returned as undeliverable, but this special address would be caught by Raptor, the governments email scrutinizer and would automatically be routed to the correct place, in total secrecy.

CHAPTER 16

Morning came and Aimee set out with a couple of beefy Chicano's dressed in typical gang like attire sans the colors associated with any particular gang. They drove a large car with bright chrome rims and very low suspension. The interior sported a variety of saints and angels on the dashboard and hanging from the mirror on chains. They swung the car out into traffic and took a circuitous route through town to the diner where they had previously descended upon Ramiro.

Aimee had learned to be very cautious. The security measures instilled more fear in her than anything else she had faced. She arrived in California scared for her sister, and scared of her sisters' husband and whatever he was mixed up in. She had watched the measures Rosa's group took to ensure their safety and could not help feeling that some of their methods were overkill, but she valued their help and followed every instruction. Now, she stared at the phone that Ramiro had left for her, and her whole world had become surreal. Alert as she was, focused on the tasks before her, her body began to tremble with fear. She had great faith in her beloved Ramiro, and was willing to place her life in his hands, but every precaution he took for her safety had the opposite effect upon her mind. For him to resort to such extreme measures could not be a good sign.

She breathed deeply, focusing her mind's eye on an image of Ramiro, tucked the phone in her purse and stepped out of the small diner and back into the car. She had two men, both friends of Rosa's, escorting her. The larger of the two men drove, while the smaller sat in the back leaving the passenger seat for Aimee. The car slipped out into traffic and started a defensive pattern around town.

The small man in the back scanned the scene behind them, making sure they weren't being followed. "We're cool in back."

Aimee pulled the phone out of her purse and dialed the number taped to it.

Ramiro answered after a few rings, "Hello?"

"It's me. What's going on? How bad is it?"

"Every thing's fine. Don't get too worked up. Apparently, there's some kind of connection between your sister's husband and the strange events at your school. The fine minds at the FBI are convinced that you must be the connection. We have to be very careful about phone communications though, because our friends at the phone company have found numerous illegal wire taps on several of our phones."

Aimee had been quite apprehensive about retrieving the secret phone and conducting their conversation so secretly, and was relieved to hear that Ramiro was not so concerned. His voice was soothing and his words were reassuring. "Are you OK then?" she asked.

"I'm fine. I have an idea what is at the center of this, but I don't think the FBI has a clue. The army is involved, and I'm willing to bet that they fed the FBI enough lies to get their attention, but I don't think they have a clue why they are looking for you."

"When can I see you?"

"Not yet. I need to find a way to get them off your back first."

"I miss you."

"I miss you too. Now I want you to throw the phone away. I'll get you another when we can talk again. I love you Aimee. I'll clear this up, I promise."

"I love you too."

"Bye for now."

"Bye."

She clicked off the phone and asked the driver to pull up to a trash can, and she dropped the phone in.

In the back seat, her second escort's eye's widened behind his dark glasses, thinking of the money he could make selling that phone, but he did nothing to stop her and let it go from his mind.

* * *

Ramiro closed his eyes and took a deep breath. He came to California to help Aimee, and while he has learned more about her predicament, nothing he has done has helped her situation. He took another deep breath and exhaled, then turned his attention back to the phone still in his hand. He entered the private number for Chief Henderson.

"Hello?" asked the voice on the other end.

"Mitch, it's me."

"Boy am I glad you called, buddy."

"Why? What happened?"

"Your JAG friends made an appearance up here. I can vouch for my department, we gave you our fullest support, but I don't think your office exactly backed you up."

"Backed me up?" Ramiro's voice rose with his blood pressure, "I wasn't aware that I needed to be backed up. What did they say? Who said something against me?"

"They didn't go against you, and they almost gave the impression of being behind you, but they made it clear that they didn't know what you were doing, and whatever it was, they weren't involved."

"They aren't, it sounds like they just told the truth."

"It was the way they said it. They washed their hands of you buddy. It just sounded like they went totally neutral on whether you were guilty or innocent."

"Guilty or innocent?" Ramiro fumed, "Just what the hell are these JAG guys asking about me?"

"You know who you should really ask? Your dad. I stonewalled these guys and they left. They are probably asking my neighbors if I salute the flag or go to church or something."

"What about my dad?"

"Hoo boy," Mitch said, "It's a good thing I kept tabs on them and was nearby when they went to your dad's home. He went ballistic. He welcomed them into his home. You know how he is, proud of his service to his country, and always willing to help when called upon. They weren't in there very long when they came running out of there with your dad barking at them up and down. My boys tell me that they looked like they were just chewed out by Patton or MacArthur when they got in the car and drove off."

"I'll call him right away, thanks Mitch."

"You can't call him now. I have a team watching his home, your home and Aimee's home. He left this morning, about an hour ago."

"Did you tail him?"

"Nope," Mitch admitted, "I didn't have enough resources and I wanted to leave a watch on the house in case those investigators decide to break some laws in the line of duty."

"When did you become so paranoid Mitch?"

"If I act paranoid and I'm wrong, I look foolish. If I ignore my suspicions and it's all true, I look stupid. I'd rather risk looking foolish than stupid."

"Give my dad this number when he returns. Tell him to call me."

"Sure thing. Take care bud."

* * *

Dexter Alexander was one of those modern geeks. Pocket protectors and thick glasses were replaced with skateboards and portable video games. He had to carry his skateboard up the stairs, but he would be able to ride it down the road back to the a/v building. He rolled into the lab.

Bobby and Dierdre were already waiting inside. Stillman had sent a note that he was meeting with an associate and could not make it, but wanted a full report later.

"Hey Dex. You know Professor Jennings?"

"Good morning professor."

Bobby led Dexter around to the front of the computer and pointed at the hole in the bottom panel. "Tell me if your camera can fit in this hole?"

Dexter leaned over and looked close at the hole and said, "You're good Bobby. It looks like you drilled exactly the right size hole."

Bobby and Dierdre shared a look at each other.

Dexter opened the bag he had slung diagonally across his shoulders, and pulled out a thin goose neck contraption about two feet long with a single lens on the end of it.

Dierdre cleared her throat and asked, "Don't you need a Monitor so we can see what's in there?"

Dexter smiled at her then glanced at Bobby and gave him a knowing look as if to call Dierdre a non-tech noob. He reached into his bag and pulled out a small flat panel monitor. He plugged a slender cable from the camera into the monitor, and then for Dierdre's benefit said, "They both run on batteries, so there's no need for power cords. The camera is self-illuminating too, perfect for this type of exploration."

Dexter got down on one knee and started to insert the camera, but Bobby put a hand on his shoulder and said, "Dexter, it's our hole, I'd like to drive."

Dexter shrugged his shoulders and looked sheepishly up at Bobby. He handed him the camera and moved out of the way.

Bobby got down next to the hole and inserted the probe. Dexter held up the monitor so they both could see, and Dierdre watched over their shoulders. The monitor remained Grey, but wasn't a flat Grey.

Dierdre cocked her head to one side and asked, "Can you focus it? It looks out of focus."

Dexter replied, "You don't focus these cameras. They have a fixed focal point and are good for near field macro work down to about three and a half inches."

"Maybe I'm in too close then." Bobby pulled the probe back a bit. The monitor continued to show a Grey mass.

"It looks to me like you stuck it into a jar of Vaseline Bobby."

Bobby pulled the probe out, and bent the camera end into a semi hook shape and reinserted it so he could look down the front panel. Now the monitor showed what appeared to be lumps of clear jelly material. "Dex, can you dim down the light, maybe it's too reflective."

"Sure, how's this?"

After dimming the light, they could see several layers of the clear jelly material, and some slightly colored strands throughout the material.

"Bobby, why is there a jellyfish in your computer? Are you using a jellyfish to generate electricity to run your computer now?"

"No Dex, we genetically resurrected this jellyfish from organic material found in a meteorite. We think it's from one of the outer planets."

Dexter's eyes opened wide, and he very nearly let his jaw drop before he realized his leg was being pulled. "Damn Bobby, don't tease me like that. You know I believe in extraterrestrials, and I fully believe the government is involved in many cover ups to keep them secret."

"Sorry Dex, couldn't resist it. Truthfully, we don't know where this came from. I am assuming it is another one of these bizarre pranks that someone is playing allover campus."

Dexter stood up, put his camera and monitor back in their bag, and started to smile. "It was a good one, you almost had me there."

"Thanks for the help Dex. I'd appreciate it if you keep this to yourself, at least until we determine what planet it really did come from. Don't forget to send us a copy of the video."

"Sure bro, no problem. Let me know when you do figure it out." Soon as he was in the hallway, he dropped his board and rolled out of the building.

Dierdre looked at Bobby after he left. "Have you considered the possibility that your alien jellyfish explanation, as outlandish as it sounds, may have a ring of truth to it?"

Bobby nodded his head. "I know. I look at all the facts, and the only conclusion that I reach is ridiculous. I told Dex it was an alien jellyfish so I could hear how silly it sounded."

"So why aren't we laughing?"

"OK, let's talk it out. Let's consider the alternatives out loud."

Dierdre got up to the whiteboard but before writing anything, she turned back to Bobby and said, "Lock the door." She waited before continuing. "First, a foreign scientist shows up out of the blue and gives Dr. Karlyn some top secret circuitry to be tested, and let's not forget the scientist appeared to be Eastern Bloc."

Bobby continued while Dierdre wrote down what she had said, "Then, I install Dr. Karlyn's interface with the circuit, the foreign scientist disappears, and soon after, Dr. Karlyn transfers to another university and gives you the computer."

"Except," Dierdre said, "he didn't actually transfer. Nobody knows where he disappeared to."

"Right. Then, as soon as we get the computer operational, someone attempts to hack into our computer. And Dr. Pietre, another foreign bloc refugee seems somehow involved in the hacking."

"Then our program starts reporting millions of processors instead of a couple thousand"

"And it actually starts computing the series of numbers faster."

"That's it!" Dierdre turned away from the whiteboard and paced as she talked, "Whatever it is, our jellyfish does something to make the computer faster."

Bobby shook his head, "But the computer isn't just faster, there are millions more processors on line."

"How can that be?"

"Our jellyfish is a computer, a living tissue computer."

Dierdre looked puzzled. "I've heard of living tissue computers, but I thought it was just science fiction. I didn't know anyone actually built one."

"We haven't."

"What are you saying?"

"I'm saying that we keep ending up at the conclusion. This could be an extraterrestrial artifact."

Dierdre stared at Bobby a moment while his statement echoed in her mind before she asked, "Do you know how ridiculous that sounds?"

"Yes, I know."

Silence followed, while Dierdre stared at the whiteboard. Her pen shook in her hands as she pointed at each of the facts she had written on the board. "Why does it have to be alien? We have been working on organic components for years now."

"Sure," Bobby said, "If it had come from IBM or MIT, I might agree. But I don't see our government developing this technology to this degree without the private sector."

"So where'd they get it?"

"They either stole it, or found it."

"Found it?" Dierdre asked, "Who could have lost something like this?"

"Who could have developed something like this? Our government can't attract the top scientists from the private sector, unless they contract with their whole company. Most of the top soviet scientists have already defected to a country with greener pastures, Japan has some very good engineers, but they have never been known to demonstrate the kind of creativity required for this great a leap in technology. China doesn't really foster that kind of creative thinking in their citizens either. Israel has too many security concerns to research anything without more immediate applications, and the third world countries are too busy trying to hide their level of nuclear development to be involved in something this forward thinking."

"Wow Bobby. You never struck me as someone who kept up with world events, but you still haven't said who could have made it."

"Sherlock Holmes said that when you eliminate the impossible, whatever was left, no matter how improbable, had to be the truth."

"But Sherlock Holmes assumed he had all the facts before him. I'm not so sure we do."

"Never the less," he said, "I don't think this originated on Earth."

"And you think we have eliminated all the other possibilities?"

"Well, I suppose it could have come from the future, but I

personally think that sounds even crazier."

"Geez," Dierdre said, "your friend Dex would have a cow if he knew this might be an alien computer."

"Yes he would, especially considering it was probably found on a crashed UFO from area fifty-one, and hidden from us by the government."

"Let's just keep that to ourselves. We really don't know what we have, except that it defies logical explanation, which is why such an illogical explanation seems to be almost plausible."

Dierdre paced back and forth forming her next thought before she spoke, "Whatever it is, it seems to be helping our project a lot. Maybe we should just leave it alone and keep it under wraps."

"That would be a good idea if it weren't already too late."

"Why do you think it's already too late? Do you think Dexter can figure out what it is? If he did would he blab?"

"Well," Bobby said, "Dexter did leave here with a recording of what we saw. If he does figure it out, he will blab. But Dexter is not who I am concerned about."

"Who else knows?"

"Whoever drilled the hole probably knows more than we do."

Dierdre had forgotten about that. The spirit dropped from her face as she realized that whoever drilled the hole was probably not going to be their friend.

* * *

Professor Pietre worked feverishly in his lab. He was no longer interested in stealing the secret contents of Dierdre's computer. Now he was intent on destroying it. He worked all night modifying the programs he had planted to secretly copy the computer's memory, and changed the program to destroy the memory instead of copying it. It would have been a much simpler change, except he put in safeguards to make sure the programs did not destroy themselves. The added complexity kept him working till late afternoon perfecting the algorithm, but finally, it was done and he started it up. He left to have dinner in a very public place, just in case his program wreaked havoc as he hoped it would.

* * *

Ramiro spent the remainder of his day at the court library. He was researching various aspects of military law, but especially jurisdictional rulings. He also refreshed his reading of some federal laws including the freedom of information act.

Something had been nagging at the back of his mind ever since he was questioned by JAG. What Mitch had told him did not help. He didn't think they would blatantly break any laws, but he was certain they would not hesitate to use their position to insinuate anything they wanted. Sadly, while the courts had to honor jurisprudence and consider a person innocent until proven guilty, the court of public opinion did not operate on the same principles. An FBI investigation questioning a grade school teacher about sexual child abuse could easily get the teacher fired from his job even if there was no evidence and no charges were ever filed.

The questions the JAG guys asked at Ramiro's work automatically put him in a bad light. Only the most trusted and loyal friends would not draw an opinion from the questions they asked. This left them free to ask any question they wanted without making blatant charges.

JAG assumed that Ramiro knew more than he was sharing with them. Ramiro knew this, and assumed their questions were designed to motivate him to tell them more. He also considered the possibility that they might want to divert his attention from what was really going on by involving himself in clearing his own name.

So, Ramiro educated himself. He had to know exactly where their boundaries were, so he could know in what directions and how far he could push back. He also wanted to know how the other agencies would work with each other. The army and the FBI were both investigating the university and searching for Aimee. Each had their legal jurisdictions which often made cooperation difficult. After reconstructing the sequence of events leading up to this moment, Ramiro concluded that there must have been some kind of theft which may also have involved espionage. The FBI would have jurisdiction on espionage within the nation's borders, but with the military involved, there would almost certainly be international concerns. The CIA is supposed to operate only outside the country, but it was commonly believed that they did work within the country, in secret. Some theorized that the CIA believed that not knowing they were there was the same as not being there. It was commonly believed that since they operate in complete secret, they never cooperate with anyone.

As Ramiro studied, he hoped his father would call. He kept checking the cell phone to make sure it was charged and had a good signal. The afternoon dragged on, reading, glancing at the phone, reading some more. He never left for lunch. He just had some snacks from a vending machine and a fresh cup of coffee.

* * *

Bobby remained in the lab all day. Dierdre left to give a lecture on subatomic structures and the flavors of quarks, but he decided to skip his classes for today. He tried to focus his mind, but it drifted this way, then that.

There was something in their computer. Bobby installed it himself, and ever since that day, strange things have been happening. Multiple persons have tried repeatedly to get in and take a look at what they were doing. And apparently, they have now succeeded.

Something was making their program run very, very fast. Faster than anything they have ever seen. Faster than anything anyone has ever seen, or at least publicly demonstrated. IBM, Toshiba, Cray and all the other supercomputer manufacturers continued to design new mega gigantic computers. They used them to model weather on earth, map human genomes, and even to play chess at the grand master level. As the chips shrunk smaller and smaller, they got faster and faster. Yet, none of them could come close to the calculations currently being performed in their lab at this very moment, and it was still accelerating.

Bobby looked for evidence that it was actually lots of computers over the Internet that were responsible. Not only would it be a giant feather in his cap, but it did not sound as crazy as an alien computer that resembles a jellyfish.

Whatever was in there did not come out of the private sector. The private sector keeps secrets, and protects their intellectual property with great zeal, but they also like to brag and show off. Showing off technology like this would shoot stock prices through the roof and raise more revenue than sales. They would never keep something like this a secret. The government, on the other hand, was more than capable and willing to keep this a secret. The government lived in constant fear that enemy countries would covet their technology. In fact, they assumed this was the case, and anything this big would be far too valuable for thieves to resist. But the government did not have the resources to invent this technology. It was generations beyond the state of technology as we know it today.

Scientific research likes to progress in small steps. It builds on what it learned yesterday. It's evolutionary, not revolutionary. Somewhere, during the dawn of human history, a prehistoric human found fire, possibly from a lightning strike, or a forest fire. He learned that he could put a non-burning stick into the fire and it would start to burn. He learned that he could hold the non-burning end and carry it with him. He could light more sticks. Over time, he and his fellow fire keepers learned more and improved techniques to keep the fire burning. They learned how to resurrect the fire from glowing embers. It was all evolutionary. When someone recognized the sparks from the flint stone that he threw clear past the rabbit he was aiming at, that was evolutionary too. There was no leap from sparking flint to butane tanks and electronic igniters. Each discovery was based on some other discovery creating a pathway from beginning to end.

There was no pathway of discoveries that could lead from the current level of technology to a growing jelly-like computer. Even the top universities would consider this to be science fiction or worse, fantasy. This was so far outside the realm of reality that it was hard to believe by the few who have actually seen it.

Dierdre finished her lecture and rushed up to the lab. "Any change?"

Bobby was lost in his thoughts and did not answer.

"Bobby? Have you learned anything new?"

"Huh? Oh, no. Nothing new with the jellyfish. The number crunching seems to have peaked and is no longer accelerating like it was."

"What's that number for?" Dierdre was pointing at the screen.

"There appears to be some increased Internet traffic, not much though."

"Why would there be any Internet traffic? Haven't your friends packed up and gone home from their contest?"

"Yeah," Bobby said, "they have. There's been other stuff, though, that I never told you about."

"Like?"

"Professor Pietre has attempted to crack our system on numerous occasions. He has even gotten in a few times, but his computer always ends up being part of our system instead of his taking control of ours."

"Bobby! Did you do that?"

"I thought I did," Bobby said, "but now I'm not so sure. I've been thinking about this. Whoever brought that thing here obviously stole it. So it stands to reason that someone wants it back, but they can't advertise that it is missing or put it on the news because nobody knows it exists."

"OK, I'm with you so far..."

"Private industry would not keep this a secret. They would patent it and try to use it to sell stock. So it must be the government. I think we should tell them we have it and give it back to them. Let them come get it without a fight. It either belongs to them or to an opposing government, and in either case, our government would be happy to get their hands on it."

"Who says it belongs to them?" Dierdre's voice rose more than she intended, "They don't have the technology to make something like this, nobody does. Like you said before, the only way they ever got their hands on it was by stealing it or finding it. I doubt they are competent enough to steal it, so they must have found it. If they wanted it back for themselves, why haven't they just come and taken it?"

"What makes you think they haven't tried? Look at all the odd things going on around here."

"Why didn't they just come in here flashing their badge to take it back?"

"I'll tell you why." Bobby stood so he could better use his hands to emphasize his point. "Because their research had failed to fully understand the technology, and once it was actually in Dr. Karlyn's possession, they figured they could wait and see what Dr. Karlyn came up with. For all we know, this could be the only one that ever got turned on and the only one that ever grew."

* * *

Dr. Pietre had never really developed a taste for French cuisine, he had always preferred more simple fare like meat and vodka, cheese and vodka, or even vodka and vodka, but he did like being seen in all the right places and always felt that professors and scientists should somehow be treated more like celebrities anyway. So he found himself sitting at a very popular French restaurant eating a dish of duck with some kind of brandy sauce. There were mashed potatoes on the plate shaped like shellfish that he wasn't quite sure if he was supposed to eat or just admire. The food was tasty, but it always left him hungry. Maybe he would pick up a hamburger at the drive through on the way home. He had finished his main course and was looking at a desert menu when his phone rang.

"Hello," he said, "this is Dr. Pietre."

"Professor, it's the computer. It's erasing everything."

A smile crept across his face until he realized the caller did not name Professor Jennings' computer. "Whose computer is it we are speaking of?"

"Why yours, of course. We had just finished the system backups, but they completed much faster than they should have, so we looked at the catalogs. The backups were completely empty. We looked at the drives and the files were being erased before our very eyes."

"Reboot the machine and load last night's backup."

"We tried that. The machine wouldn't reboot, apparently it had erased the boot tracks. So we configured it to reboot from tape like you would with a brand new machine, we mounted the system tapes and it seemed to work normally rebuilding itself, so we mounted last night's backups and started a restore."

"You did well. Let me know when it's complete."

"The job finished."

"That's impossible. It would have taken hours to restore."

"The job finished. It erased last night's backups in no time at all. Then it continued erasing the drives again. So we rebooted from tape again, but the system tapes are now blank."

Pietre was frowning now. He placed the desert menu on the table and put a credit card down to pay the bill. "I'll be right there."

* * *

"You've got mail!" The male voice resonated from the computer speakers.

The Bard sat in the corner snickering while the large man woke from his cat nap scowling, "What the hell is that voice doing coming out of my computer? I run a professional operation here and I don't need some computer for dummies voice telling me I have mail!"

"Perhaps you'd prefer this one?" The Bard typed out a command on his computer and a sultry female voice announced, "Ooooh Baby, I got your mail! Come and get it."

The large man picked up a book and threw it across the room landing squarely on top of the Bard's head. He sat down at his computer and opened his mail.

> Gentlemen,
>
> I have an official communique from the very top office:
>
> Containment is a go. Secrecy is essential. Extreme force is not authorized at this time. Determine the level of contamination and advise if additional resources are required. We are examining some cover stories for the extraction, will advise ASAP.
>
> That's the official word. Advise immediately with the level of contamination and I will check if it warrants extreme force yet. Of course, unofficially, I expect you to personally exercise your best judgment on a case by case basis. Try and see if you can have an assessment to me about the contamination before the bosses make a decision about the extraction and cover story.

The Bard exhaled loudly and said, "That's a relief. I really didn't want to be involved in any kind of bloodbath here."

"It's not over yet. We better find out what they know."

"I'm more concerned that the bosses may develop some hair brained scheme to extract it that's going to expose us and push you to do something extreme."

"I hate to agree with you," the large man said, "and if you tell anyone I'll have to kill you, but I don't have a whole lot of confidence in their ability to plan either the extraction or the cover story. If you have any bright ideas, you make sure to let me know."

"Whatever it is, we have to empty the building and make it off limits. An explosion with a lethal chemical should do the trick. Then we extract the computer with the floor, have the floor repaired, replace an identical computer, and haul off the computer shrouded in hazardous material blankets."

"Don't you think they'll notice something is missing from their computer?"

"OK," the Bard said, "So we fill it with goo and make it look like a practical joke."

"I like that. Write it up and send it to the boss so they have at least one good idea to consider. If you really want to avoid any blood being spilled, we are going to need some plans to discredit these people."

"Already on it, look at this." The Bard spun his laptop around so the other man could read what he had been typing.

> *Mr. V,*
>
> *We have a buyer in place and are ready to demonstrate the device. Get the key from the girl and be ready to deliver it to us when we verify the buyer's funds. We'll contact you again in the morning.*

The big man read it, then read it again, and scratched his head saying, "I don't get it. Who is Mr. V? What is this talking about?"

"Mr. V is the judge. This simple email will implicate him and the girl in the whole mess."

"Who is it supposed to be from?"

"It's from you. We know the FBI is trying to keep tabs on you. We use an older encryption that we know they can break and send it to the Judge from one of your secret accounts that they already know about. The FBI intercepts it, and immediately they go after the Judge. They are already after the girl, this will confirm their suspicions."

"OK. What about the professor and the kid. Especially the kid. I don't like the fact that he seems to have outsmarted you so far."

"I think I can implicate the kid in all the hacking that has been going on, half of which was us, and the other half was Pietre."

"Ahhh. Pietre. I may go ahead and use my best judgment on him. Go ahead and send that letter while we look at the others involved."

The Bard spun the laptop back and clicked the mouse a couple times and the letter was sent.

* * *

Stillman knocked politely on the door to Dierdre's lab, and when nobody answered, he delicately opened the door and poked his head inside. "Dierdre? Are you in here?"

Dierdre was at her desk in the back looking over some charts Bobby had given her that tracked the growth of the system over time. She hadn't heard his knocking over the loud hum and clatter of the computers, but when she heard his voice, her head popped up and a smile stretched across her face. "I'm in back, come on in!" Her voice had a lovely song quality to it which was seldom heard from her.

Stillman walked directly to her, leaned over and kissed her gently on the lips. "Hello my dear. I can't stay long. I just got off the phone with Dr. Jantzen. He was very excited when I told him I thought you could explain the spikes in his readings, but did not want to discuss it over the phone. He would very much like to meet with you as soon as possible."

"Oh, but I can't, not now, it's just not possible."

"I thought as much, and told him so. However, he was quite insistent that one of us go see him. He is still in Florida, so I agreed to fly out to meet with him on your behalf. I will call you tomorrow from his hotel."

"When are you leaving?"

"Tonight," he said, "in fact, I have to hurry off now to make the flight."

She was unaccustomed to the reaction she felt within her body. She knew he would be back, and yet she was experiencing the sensation of loss, like moments of her life were being ripped away that she could never recover. She shook off the feeling, realizing it was silly and selfish. "Fly safely. Don't be gone long."

He leaned over and kissed her again. "Be back before you know it."

* * *

"I'm sorry Professor Pietre, but your credit card was declined. Perhaps you have another?"

"That's ridiculous. There's nothing wrong with the credit card. Your machine is what must be malfunctioning. Run it again."

"I ran it three times, it's declined."

The professor grumbled and darted his eyes around to see if anyone was witness to his humiliation. He pulled out his wallet and fingered through a few cards, he did not have that many, and pulled another out for the waiter. "Here, try this one."

* * *

Ramiro was still at the Court Library reading about military court procedures when he heard the door behind him open and a stern male voice called out, "Ramiro Vasquez?"

He looked up and over his shoulder and saw two different Jag officers accompanied by military police. "It's Judge Vasquez, or Your Honor, I'll even accept sir."

The Jag officer, obviously trying to appear in control of the situation could not rebuke the correction. "Judge Vasquez, will you come with us please?"

"Did you have more questions or are you planning to take some ill-advised action at this time?"

One of the military police stepped forward. He already had hand-cuffs in his hands. "Sir, would you please stand up." He guided Ramiro to a standing position, gripped one of his wrists, and in a well-practiced maneuver, brought Ramiro's wrists behind his back while slapping the cuffs over each wrist.

The Jag officer stepped forward and recited, "Ramiro Vasquez, you are under arrest."

Ramiro was never Mirandized, which told Ramiro that Jag either felt this was a military operation all the way, because Miranda only applied to civil arrests, or they were sloppy and failed to realize that Ramiro was a civilian and could not be tried in a military court. In either case, there would be no sense in trying his case in public, he might as well go along with them and see where it leads. The more mistakes they made, the stronger his case would be for dismissal.

They wound their way through the court building. The Jag officers led in front, followed by the two military police with Ramiro between them. As they found their way to the guard station with the metal detectors at the front entrance, one of the guards swung open a gate making an easy exit for the procession past the metal detectors, while the other guard held open one of the large glass doors next to the revolving doors. The guards looked at each other and shrugged their shoulders. Neither had ever seen anything like this.

As they exited the building a pair of plain black sedans pulled up to the curb and four men wearing windbreakers with FBI emblazoned on the backs climbed out of each car and raced to surround Ramiro and his escorts.

* * *

"I'm sorry professor," the waiter said, "but, that card has also been declined. Perhaps you have cash tonight?"

"That's impossible!" Professor Pietre was turning dark red in the face. "This is outrage. Nobody has ever treated me like this before, and you will never be having such the opportunity again." He pulled some cash out of his wallet and threw it on the table knowing it barely covered the cost of the meal and did not include a tip.

He took a quick inventory, made sure he had his jacket, wallet, glasses and cell phone, then stormed out of the restaurant, and turned up the street to the bank on the corner. He walked the few paces down the sidewalk to the ATM machine, inserted his card and punched in his password. He navigated through the screens to withdraw one-hundred dollars, the machine paused, as it always does when it checks his balance, then returned a message that he had insufficient funds to withdraw the cash he requested. He navigated through some more screens to see what his balance was, and it returned a screen that said he was over five thousand dollars overdrawn. It was an obvious error. No bank would ever let an account accrue five thousand dollars in arrears, but the banks were closed and he could not fight his case now. As he walked back to his car, he realized that he had been hacked, and he knew just what young hoodlum must have done it.

* * *

Bobby was rooting around in the system logs trying to figure out why the number generation had flattened out so rapidly. In the past hour, the red line had flickered briefly indicating that some new CPU's had been brought on-line, but the bottom line had not improved any at all.

"Hello?"

Bobby had barely registered that the phone had rung, until he heard Dierdre answer it. Dierdre nodded her head once, then twice, then the smile eroded from her face and her expression had turned to one of concern. She hung up the phone and said, "We have trouble again. That was the dean. It seems there have been some more computer hacks and the FBI is here to talk to us again. The dean thought he overheard something about government systems being hacked."

Bobby started to get up but Dierdre stopped him. "They said they were coming here."

"Here? What if they look inside and see what's going on?"

"What are they going to see? Someone poured some jelly substance in our computer? Don't give them too much credit. Concentrate on preventing them from doing something stupid like tasting it."

Dierdre's attempt to be humorous was betrayed by the expression on her face. She started to pace back and forth a bit, "Bobby, is it possible that your clustering code could have spread to someplace it doesn't belong?"

"Anything is possible, but I designed it so the user has to specifically log into our computer to get the program."

"What about the routines that were designed to improve itself? Could they have developed methods to proactively seek out other computers?"

"They could if they understood what that meant, but those routines only understand better as meaning runs faster, so they pick the fastest running routine, not the smartest routine."

* * *

The FBI bristled at the prospect that the military police would not turn Ramiro over to them. Each of them seemed willing to draw their weapons for a showdown. They did, after all, outnumbered JAG two to one. But the stalemate ended when an even blacker, plainer sedan pulled up and two passengers, a man and a woman came out and joined the Jag crew. They promptly announced, "National security," to the FBI and proffered badges with a variety of insignia on them. The FBI immediately stood down, and the lead agent was instantly on his cell phone relaying the events to his command.

Ramiro remained calm throughout. He recognized the gravity of the situation, but was confident that his involvement, or lack of involvement could easily be proved, and that the whole affair was based on a stupid mistake. The only other scenario that made any sense was someone trying to frame him, and he couldn't imagine anyone going to such extreme lengths to ruin his fledgling career.

* * *

Two FBI agents entered the lab together followed by the dean. Bobby stood but remained behind the monitor while Dierdre advanced to meet them mid lab.

The lead agent held his hand out to meet Dierdre, "You must be Dr. Jennings and you must be Robert Blain. We've certainly heard a lot of good things about you."

Dierdre and Bobby were quite puzzled by this greeting. It did not have the ominous tone that they were expecting.

The lead agent surveyed the room, then entered the smaller office and motioned for everyone to join him there. He stood by the door, obviously planning to close it for increased privacy. When everyone had settled in, he said, "I am special agent Alvin Dirk, and this is agent Jones. Let me get right to the point. There has been another incident of computer hacking. This time the hacker targeted some government computers, quite sensitive computers in fact."

Bobby's face blushed red. In his mind, he knew that he did nothing to cause his code to spread out like a virus, it wasn't virus code, it was simple a self-installing cluster system. But knowing, even believing, had little to do with his nervous systems automatic responses. He hoped nobody had noticed.

Dierdre cleared her throat and asked, "Why are you here? We have not experienced any more hacking incidents to my knowledge."

"Yes, but the hacking originated here on this campus. Someone has created quite a nasty little virus, and though it doesn't seem to do any malicious harm, it won't go away and is draining all of the computers resources."

This time it was Dierdre who blushed.

"Here?" Bobby's voice squeaked a bit as he asked the question, "In this lab?"

"Oh, no," Dirk said, "Not from this lab."

Dierdre cocked her head as she asked, "Whose lab then?"

The two agents shared a look and each shrugged their shoulders before he continued, "What can you tell me about Dr. Dimitri Pietre?"

"Dr. Pietre?" the shock in Dierdre's voice was genuine.

"I knew it," Bobby blurted out, "He's been trying to hack our computer ever since Dierdre, I mean, Professor Jennings, got it from Dr. Karlyn."

The dean's eyebrows were raised with this news. "He has?"

"He's tried, but I didn't have enough evidence to bring to you Dean, or I would have."

The second agent was quickly scribbling notes in his small pad. "Perhaps you can show us, later, what you have that implicates Dr. Pietre."

Agent Dirk said, "But first, maybe you can share with us what you have done to thwart his efforts to hack you?"

"Sure, be glad to help. You said the virus has been hard to get rid of?"

"Yes, sort of, we get rid of it, but it keeps coming back. It's the damnedest thing we've ever seen."

"Are you," Bobby asked, "a computer expert then?"

"Yes, that's why they sent me. Agent Spivey said it would take one of us to keep up with you, he thought I might enlist your aid with this virus. We have already contacted some of the top security experts in the country, but in light of your current efforts battling Dr. Pietre, I'm inclined to agree that you might have some valuable insight to share with us."

* * *

Pietre was unaware that the FBI agents were now looking for him as he made his way back to the campus. He hadn't noticed anything suspicious until he entered the lab building and saw an array of men in dark suits with earpieces that sported little pigtail wires which disappeared under their collars. He froze for a moment then veered down another hallway away from the commotion. He didn't know any specific reasons to be concerned, but he had many hidden dark secrets from his past. He ducked into one of the chemistry labs which had doors in both corridors. A door on the other end of the lab was not far from his lab, on the opposite side, he could peer through the glass to see what was going on.

What he saw, when he reached the opposite door, was a concern. The men, obvious government agents, were generally situated around the door to his lab. They spoke with each other in hushed tones and constantly scanned up and down the corridor. He tried running scenarios in his mind, trying to imagine what kind of prank would have attracted so much attention. Obviously, in his mind at least, this was the work of Bobby. He had planned on retaliating for the troubles with his bank account, but knew he could never get any work done with so much security hovering about, so he turned around and left the same way he had entered.

* * *

Except for not being Mirandized, Ramiro had been processed much the same as he would have been by any civil police. All eyes upon him wore faces that suggested charges including suspicion of treason. He was well treated, throughout the fingerprinting, and the confiscating of his personal possessions. Even in the brig, he was offered food and drink, which from the looks of it, may have been better fare than was served in the mess to the troops. The level of decorum demonstrated even suggested to him that the charges would be of the most extreme variety.

He sat in the brig, contemplating his next move, not certain when he would be able to do anything. He had not been afforded a phone call, and was not certain he would be allowed one. Military courts did not offer suspects the same rights and privileges that civilian courts did. They did, however, offer counsel, which arrived shortly after he had finished eating.

* * *

Bobby led agent Dirk to the computer rack, focusing attention on the critical error indicators and the basic control panel. "I wish I could show you the source code I used and how it worked, but we are busy running some extremely involved simulations and can't interrupt the process without losing a great deal of work, but I can show you some of the tricks I employed. I had no specific reason to suspect any kind of espionage or sabotage, but I had inserted a small routine in the system load processors to detect any attempt to load from Cd, and to make a shadow copy of the Cd so I could see what was done, and possibly who had done it."

"And that's how you knew Pietre was hacking you?"

"No, Pietre wasn't that sophisticated, though this particular gentleman tried to implicate Pietre."

"So you don't think Pietre was the hacker?"

"Oh, no, he most definitely tried hacking our computers. His attacks were mostly TCP based, except in the beginning when he did try gaining access through our terminals."

"The attacks on the government computers have all been TCP based too, but you say you identified someone else as the hacker, and he tried to make it look like Pietre did it?"

"Now, he was a pro. He tried using his own boot Cd to load his own system, with his own passwords, but I copied the contents of the Cd, it had a number of sonnets in one of the folders."

Agent Dirk said, "That's right. Spivey mentioned something about the Bard in his report. I thought he had disappeared from the hacker scene."

"Well, he's back."

"But why is he here? What is his interest in you?"

"Why are you here? Why are your agents looking for Miss Takahashi? Certainly you are aware that something is going on, something nobody wants to discuss."

Agent Dirk thought that over for a moment, then continued with his train of thought, "But why now? Why has he suddenly re-emerged after being missing so long?"

"He hasn't re-emerged. He never left his calling card sonnet. I lifted that from his Cd without his knowledge. The night I was preparing this computer for transport to Professor Jennings' lab, Dr. Pietre came to the lab with a man claiming to be a business associate of Dr. Karlyn's. They said they wanted copies of his research, and wanted a full backup of all his materials. Then, when I was setting the computer up in Professor Jennings' lab, another man came wanting to see the computer. I'm betting that one of them was the Bard."

"So he was working with someone, or for someone, and his employer had an interest in the research you were doing on this computer."

"Unfortunately for them, I had already wiped the drives when the first man arrived with Dr. Pietre."

Dirk started thinking out loud, "Who would hire a hacker with his reputation? Someone who didn't know who he was, someone who knew who he was and believed he would reform, or someone who knew who he was and wanted to capitalize on his talents."

Bobby shook his head. "He wasn't well known outside of the hacker community, so your first option, that they didn't know who he was, would certainly be possible, but I just don't see how it would explain why he is here trying to get Dr. Karlyn's research."

Agent Dirk nodded his head. "I agree. The second option wouldn't make much sense either, only government agencies knew who he was, and they aren't likely to hire him in hopes he would reform. And since he was relatively unknown they couldn't turn it into any kind of campaign issue for the next election."

"But," Bobby said, "they might hire him for his skills, counting on the fact that he would not reform and hoping they might exploit his talents to hack systems for them."

Dirk closed his eyes and sighed. "Damn it, I hope not. I just hate getting in the middle of these inter-agency affairs."

* * *

Ramiro was taken from his cell to a small well lit room with a table and chairs. He sat down in one of the chairs, and his escorts left the room except for one who stood in the corner. He wasn't there long when a young energetic woman entered the room, and headed straight for him with her hand extended.

"Judge Vasquez, I am Penelope Laine, and I have been appointed as your attorney."

Ramiro stood and shook her hand. "Penny La..."

She cut him off saying, "Please! Don't go there, my parents were hippies and had me late in life."

She pointed to his chair and said, "Please sit down, can I get you anything? Coffee? Soda? Water?"

"Water would be good."

She sat down opposite Ramiro and motioned to the guard in the corner, who promptly left. She opened her brief case and pulled out a folder and started paging through it. Half way through the report, she said, "Well, it would seem that Your Honor is in a bit of a pickle."

The door opened and she paused while the guard placed a tray on the table with a carafe of water and two glasses. He positioned himself back in the corner, but she gestured her fingers in a walking motion and he left the room, remaining outside the door.

She poured water into each of the glasses, and took a sip. She sat for a moment, looking at Ramiro, trying to match his appearance with the allegations in the report, and then took another sip of water before continuing, "Why do I have a newly appointed court judge sitting in a military brig facing the most serious charges I have ever seen on my desk?"

Ramiro thought it was a rhetorical question, but when she did not continue and seemed to be waiting for a response, he simply said, "I don't know. You tell me. Have charges actually been drawn? Or am I being held without regard to my constitutional rights?"

"They haven't told you? You have been charged with treason, high treason to be precise. What the hell did you do? Don't answer that. As far as your constitutional rights, the judge advocate general has decided that in cases of high treason, the prisoner is not due the same constitutional rights as other detainees."

"That would be true if I were military, but I am a civilian. Civilians are protected by the constitution, except for foreign civilians held as prisoners of war, in which case they are still protected by the Geneva Convention."

"Well, sir, the powers that be have decided that your position, as a justice for the courts, having sworn an oath to uphold the constitution, places you more under military than civilian laws, and you have been placed under arrest to remain incommunicado."

"Incommunicado? I can't call for my own lawyer? Or even call my father to tell him I'm OK?"

"No sir, no direct communication, however, I can deliver messages for you. And I am bound by the same client confidentiality laws as a civilian lawyer would be."

"Do you have a pencil and paper I could use? I'll write down a name for you."

She placed a pencil on top of a pad of paper and slid it across the table to him. He wrote down Chief Henderson's name and phone number, and passed it back to her. "Please tell him my situation. Be as candid and truthful as you can, and ask him to relay it to my father."

She started to say something but was interrupted when the door flew open and a thin man with a crew cut and penetrating eyes entered the room.

She jumped out of her seat and barked, "Excuse me sir, but this room is occupied. I would appreciate some privacy to speak with my client."

"I'm sure you would," the intruder growled, "but I would also like to speak with your client, and I'd like to move things along, if you don't mind."

"Then schedule some time if you wish to depose my client, you'll find the clerk down the hall on the right, please close the door on your way out!"

He didn't budge. Instead of leaving the room, he pulled a piece of paper from his pocket and presented it to her. She read it quickly, then sat down across from Ramiro. "I don't know who you pissed off, but I think they mean to hang you before sunrise."

* * *

Dr. Pietre was running out of options. After leaving the School Labs, he started towards his car, but passed the doors to the engineering section where the power equipment was kept for the building. The doors were locked, but he had long ago stolen and copied all the building keys. He ducked down the few steps to the basement entrance. He shuffled through the keys and let himself in. The basement was dark, lit only by the various power lights and status monitors in the room.

Pietre made his way to the control consoles. He knew one password to the system from when he was on the committee that evaluated the backup system for purchase, and had participated in their installation. He logged into the master program, and brought up the scheduler. He programmed a shutdown of the flywheel to start in forty-five minutes, to be followed by a shutdown of all power thirty minutes later. He wanted both his computer, and Professor Jennings computer shut down completely. But he wasn't satisfied yet, he added one more instruction. At fifteen minutes after the shutdown, the system was to reconfigure the power to Professor Jennings lab from the standard one-hundred-ten volts to two-hundred-twenty volts. He changed it from a standard alternating current to a multi-phase current with an overlapping pulse wave. It would power up her lab for thirty minutes, then reconfigure itself back to the default power modes. With luck, that would fry the power supply and perhaps a few other circuits as well.

As much as he would have liked to stay around and watch, he felt it would be better to be somewhere else, so he slipped out of the building, locking the door behind him, and quickly made his way to his car and off the campus.

CHAPTER 17

The FBI was not ordinarily inclined to share their information with civilians. They were reluctant to even share it with other agencies, but Dirk felt that Bobby had a unique understanding of the hacker mindset. His assessment, and Spivey's, was that even though Bobby had pulled a stunt as a young boy, he had never demonstrated the rebellious attitude common among the incorrigible black hat society. Bouncing his ideas off of Bobby was proving immensely useful to his own comprehension of the person he was ultimately after. It didn't hurt that he genuinely enjoyed talking to him. Bobby wasn't one of those techno geeks that liked to throw out buzz words so everyone would think he was some kind of genius. He talked plainly, but he obviously understood things easily, and deeply.

Dirk said, "So, two men came to the lab, and you think one of them might have been the Bard. Why? I mean, why do you think one of them was the Bard?"

"Everything happened so quickly back then. Dr. Karlyn had a strange visitor. He started a new project for his friend, and then, all of a sudden, he gives the computer to Professor Jennings. He offers her my services and says he's transferring to another school, but he actually disappears. Then, when I'm preparing the computer for transport, these two guys show up and want something. They go home empty handed and I get hacked almost as soon as I get the system back up and running. And I wasn't hacked by just anybody, but by the Bard. When I add it all up, it just makes sense to me that if he was already involved, he would be the one to come get whatever he wanted off the computer."

Dirk's partner, Jones, was in the doorway waving a piece of paper and pointing to his watch. Dirk nodded his head towards Jones, then turned back to Bobby and said, "Listen, do you think you could come with us to describe him to a sketch artist?"

"Sure, I think I could give you something to go by."

"Great! Can you excuse me a second?" Dirk went to his partner.

Jones spoke in hushed tones so only Dirk could hear, "This email just came in, and I'm pretty much done here."

Dirk looked over the email:

> *Military JAG units took Judge Vasquez into custody moments before we moved in on him. Upon presenting our warrants, NSA*

agents arrived with warrants that superseded ours. We lost the suspect.

Dirk scratched out a reply on his note pad:

Pietre's whereabouts are unknown. The kid is clean, and as Spivey suggested, is quite an asset for us. Recommend apprehending the girl before they do.

He handed the note to Jones. "Here, send this reply, and wait for me by the car, I'll be right down."

Turning to Bobby, Dirk said, "It looks like it is going to be a long night and I haven't eaten yet. Are you hungry? Can we buy you dinner?"

"I was going to stay and work on Dr. Jennings' project, but I'm always hungry. Just let me grab my bag."

* * *

"Hello? This is Chief Henderson."

"Chief Henderson, I am calling on behalf of a Judge Ramiro Vasquez. Do you know him?"

"Yes I do. Why are you calling on his behalf? Is he OK? Has he been hurt?"

"He is not hurt. My name is Penelope Laine, I am a military defense advocate representing him and he asked me to call you and let you know his situation. He is facing some very serious charges."

"I have known him for years and I can assure you the charges are groundless."

"None the less," she said, "these charges are being leveled by some very powerful individuals who usually tend to get things the way they want them."

"May I speak with him? Why are you calling on his behalf?"

"He is being held incommunicado, nobody may speak directly with him."

"That's ridiculous," Henderson said, "you can't hold him like that, he has rights!"

"I assure you sir. The military justice system can hold him in cases such as this. One more thing, sir, he asked me to have you tell his father what his situation is, and that he is OK."

"Certainly. Is there anything I can do to help you?"

"No sir, thank you, not at this time."

Henderson hung up the phone, scratched his head, and decided to take a drive out and see if Ramiro's father had returned yet.

* * *

Pietre needed an alibi. With his bank accounts hacked, he wouldn't be able to publicly hang out at another restaurant, so he decided that the next best place for him to be seen, and document his whereabouts, would be a hospital emergency room. He could complain about a headache, or back pain or something. The hospital wasn't far from the campus, but about half way there he heard sirens behind him, and saw the familiar dreaded flashing lights in his mirror. He checked his speedometer, thinking he might have gotten overly excited in making his getaway, but he was not speeding.

He pulled the car over to the curb, rolled down the window and shut off the engine. He could see the police vehicle pull up behind him, and a tall lean officer climbed out of the driver side. The officer had his hand on his holster as he carefully approached the vehicle. Two other squad cars appeared from different directions, one pulled up alongside the first, and the other pulled in front of Pietre's car.

"Sir," the officer commanded, "place your hands outside the window where I can see them."

The tone of the request was non-negotiable. Pietre had never been asked this for an ordinary traffic stop before. He placed his hands outside the window, and the officer fully approached the window where he could see Pietre clearly. The driver of one of the other squad cars now came up and joined the first.

"Is this your vehicle?"

"Yes, officer, this is my car."

"I need to see your license and vehicle registration."

The other officer went to the back of the car and checked the license plate against a piece of paper he held in his hand. While he did this, Pietre carefully removed the registration papers from the glove box, aware that the officer was scrutinizing his every move. He pulled out his wallet and removed his license. His hands shook as he handed the items out the window.

The officer finished checking the plates and said, "It's the right license, I double checked."

"Is there a problem officer?" Pietre was baffled.

The first officer reached up on his shoulder and clicked the talk button on the microphone clipped there, and said, "Dispatch, he says it's his car, and the registration matches his license, are you sure this is the correct vehicle?"

"Affirmative. Lo-Jack reports that vehicle as being stolen. Central wants the operator license to check for warrants."

He read Pietre's license number into the microphone, and waited. After a few moments, dispatch's voice came back over the small speaker, "Apprehend and detain."

"Sir," the officer said, "would you please step out of the vehicle?"

"What is it going on? Do you know who it is that I am? I work at university. I am professor there. This is outrageous!" But seeing the officers' readiness to pull their weapons, he got out of the car, where they arrested him, bound his hands behind his back with handcuffs, and read him his rights.

* * *

Everything was arranged, if not already in place and ready to go. The large man had already contacted specialists with the expertise he would require in demolition and construction. The Bard was preparing various bits of misinformation and attacks on a number of involved people so they could be taken out of the way.

The Bard came into the large man's office with a couple sheets of paper and said, "These just came in for you."

The large man took the two pages. He read the first one then asked, "What's the status at the campus?"

"The FBI is still all over the place. I thought they would leave when they had the Judge in custody."

The large man handed the first page back to the Bard and said, "They missed the judge, the army has him. Someone tipped them off on our dear Professor Pietre. Where the hell is he?"

"I don't know."

"Pietre is becoming a bit of a liability. Can you find him?"

The Bard went to his computer and said, "I'll start a search for him right away."

The large man read the second page and shook his head. "What's this phone log about?"

"As you know, we lost all our wiretaps, and all our surveillance devices on the police chief have been removed or destroyed, but we still have records of phone calls going in and out of the various principles, but just the caller IDs. This report shows a phone call to the chief from an army base."

"That's the base where they are holding the judge. Do you think the judge called the chief?"

"No," the Bard said, "the number is from outside the detention center, I think someone else down there called him."

"Find out who."

"Right away."

* * *

Ramiro sat quietly in his cell, where he had been ushered immediately following his interview with his council and the JAG prosecutor. His request for access to their law library was approved, however still remained to be provided. He wasn't overly concerned about his situation. He believed the truth would exonerate him. He sat in his cell with nothing to read, not even an old TV to occupy the time. He just reflected on the past events and rehearsed, in his mind, various arguments to plead his case.

The door to his cell opened. A guard stepped into the doorway and ordered, "Get up and come with me."

Ramiro looked up sheepishly, hours of boredom had taken some edge of his alertness, but he stood up and approached the guard. The guard, who was accompanied by another guard who could have been his clone, led Ramiro back to the desk outside the interrogation room. "Wait here, the sergeant has some papers for you to sign."

The two guards left him standing there while they both went to another office down the hall. While he stood there waiting for the sergeant to return, a couple other guards entered through the front door with a detainee between them who was making quite a racket. Ramiro glanced over at the commotion and locked eyes with the new prisoner, it was Aimee. Before he could open his mouth to say a word, they shoved her into the interrogation room and slammed the door shut.

As soon as the door slammed shut, the first guard returned and grabbed Ramiro by the arm and said, "That's all. Get back to your room."

"But I thought..."

The guard tugged roughly on his arm and barked, "Back to your room I said!"

* * *

After grabbing a quick bite to eat, Dirk and Bobby filed into the back of the Hummer while Jones took the front passenger seat. Dirk's mood, since learning about losing Ramiro to the military police, was a bit sour. He tried reaching his supervisor by phone, but everyone in the office was in meetings.

Jones, who normally didn't say much and would have been content to remain up front and ignore the geek talk in the back turned around and said, "Not too many boys like you, I mean boys in your position, you know, your age, would help us like this."

Bobby understood why Jones didn't talk much. "I'm not the anarchist that some people think I am."

"No," Jones said, "it seems like you are not. So, what are your plans for the future?"

"My immediate plans are to continue helping Professor Jennings with her project, perhaps even continue with a physics education so I may remain on her project and see where it goes. If that doesn't work out for me, I will probably find some occupation in the tech industry, if I can ever live down my past."

"So what did it feel like?" Jones was setting a record.

"What did what feel like?"

"You know, hacking the President and nearly bringing down his administration."

"I don't know," Bobby coyly answered, "but if it had been me, I suppose it would have felt patriotic. They say two wrongs don't make a right, but sometimes they make up for a wrong. I think everyone needs to be able to think for themselves and tell right from wrong. Maybe then, we wouldn't have soldiers doing the wrong thing because they were under orders."

"But you broke the law! How can that feel patriotic?"

"If you came to a closed door and heard a woman screaming for help, would you break down the door, or request a warrant?"

"Not the same thing," Jones said, "That would be probable cause."

"OK, try this. You have a warrant to search a suspect's bathroom. The suspect is not present, and not knowing which of the five closed doors is the bathroom, you accidentally open a door to a bedroom and you see a young girl tied up on the bed. Your warrant was specific to search the bathroom, and the door to the bedroom was closed, and the girl's mouth was taped up so there was no way for you to know she was there if you had not opened the wrong door. Do you save her?"

Agent Jones looked like he was struggling to absorb the whole scenario, so Dirk jumped in and said, "I save the girl. I may not be able to use her or anything she knows as evidence to apprehend the suspect, but I remove her from the premises. Then I open all the other doors checking for any other children held captive."

Bobby smiled and nodded his head and replied, "Good answer. Are we speaking off the record here?"

"Completely off the record," Dirk said, "Speak freely."

"At first, I was just trying to find evidence that would clear my dad's name. In the process, I discovered someone had done a bad thing and was letting my dad take the fall for it. I couldn't go to the authorities and blow the whistle, because none of my evidence could be used. So I cooked up a little frame around some real-estate investments from his past. OK, it was wrong, I know, but I didn't invent what he did, I just drew the public's attention to it. I figured the press would eventually dig deep enough to find the truth."

Jones still wasn't satisfied. "But it wasn't your call. Maybe you didn't have all the information."

"Hey Jones," Dirk said, "Why don't you lighten up on the kid. He's been on the level with us and has been very helpful. I wouldn't want you to turn him against us. We're supposed to be the good guys."

* * *

Pietre was ferried to the police station in the back of a police cruiser. He was escorted inside and promptly thrown into a detention cell.

"I want to make call to my lawyer! I have rights!"

"Pipe down in there. You get your phone call after we finish processing you." Technically, it was the truth, but the police weren't in a rush to process him. His name rang up a mountain of wants and warrants, and they would have to process each of them before the district attorney could present him, or his lawyer, with a list of charges.

He sat down, and sank deep into the cot. He was sure this all had to be part of the same attack that wrecked his credit cards. The charges they had on him had to be false. He hoped they were, and he tried to stifle secret thoughts of his past and his true identity. He didn't even want to think these things for fear that someone would read his mind and learn his secret. He remained on the bunk, his head in his hands and waited.

* * *

A short stout soldier, with a face that was marbled with scars and a nose that bent in three different directions, paced back and forth reading his notes. He stopped pacing, stared Aimee in the face and coolly asked, "Where's the device?"

Aimee didn't really listen. She was madder than hell, and was ready to burst out the moment he said anything. "Where's my sister? You bastards better not hurt her, and you sure as hell better not turn her over to her son of a bitch husband just because he's one of your good old boys and knows how to hooyah over a beer with you!" Her face was crimson and her eyes were black as midnight. "What device?"

"What the hell are you talking about little Missy? You are in a heap of trouble, and if I were you, I'd be a hell of a lot more concerned about my own situation than my sister's."

"What trouble am I in? I didn't do anything. Let me talk to Ramiro, he'll clear it up."

"Maybe Ramiro doesn't want to help you. He told us everything. He tried keeping you out of trouble, but you and your sister masterminded the whole heist, and we caught you at it. No use in denying it. The only thing we don't have is the device, and to be quite frank with you, the United States Government is more interested in the device than it is concerned about your incarceration. I think that if you just turn it over, we can probably talk the judge into a reduced sentence. Otherwise, you are looking at some pretty serious charges with some equally serious hard time attached."

"Are you insane? Have you been smoking something from the property room? Get Ramiro in here so I can speak with him."

"I already told you, Ramiro rolled over on you. You are all alone now. Tell us where the device is. It's a simple deal, take it or leave it."

"You can't make deals with me, especially without my lawyer present."

"Lawyer? What lawyer? You never asked for a lawyer."

"What the hell have I been asking for? Get Ramiro in here."

This wasn't going well for the interrogator. They thought a tough looking ranger with a beat up face would scare the poor young girl, but after the last week or so with her sister, she wasn't scared at all, she was mad.

* * *

Penelope Laine had been called back to the station for another round of questions with Ramiro. He was already waiting for her in the interrogation room when she arrived. The same interrogator that had just questioned Aimee met her before going in and said, "Perfect timing. Let's see if we can wrap this up in time for bed."

They entered the room and he immediately started with his questions, without any formal introductions. "We got you. We got you cold. Your girlfriend, or maybe I should say ex-girlfriend, just gave you up. It's a sick, sick world we live in when a member of the judicial system can turn traitor to his country and steal something of vital national security with plans to sell it to foreign nationals. If it were up to me, I'd have you shot. I hate traitors. But, my superiors want the device. She told us you have it hidden, just tell us where to find it, and we can reduce the charges so you can live a long fruitful life."

"I'm sorry," Ramiro said, "what are you talking about?"

"Don't play innocent with me, it's all over. The girl told us everything, except she didn't know where you hid the device. We want the device."

"What device?"

"Oh you are good, very good. Fine you want to face a firing squad, go right ahead. This is your last chance to cut a deal, take it or leave it."

Ramiro asked Penelope, "Do you know what they are talking about?"

She shook her head and shrugged her shoulders.

"The hell with you!!!" The interrogator lost his temper, grabbed his notes and stormed out of the room.

Ramiro asked, "I don't suppose you know what device he is talking about?"

She paused a moment, considering what she was allowed to say, "I don't know what the device is, or anything about it, except they claim it concerns national security."

"National security?" Ramiro frowned and said, "That makes no sense. I need you to do something for me. I saw them bring my fiancé in a little while ago. Everything he said about her rolling over on me was a lie. She doesn't know any more about this than I do, but if he's going to play that game on me, imagine what he might say to her. Can you check on her, please?"

"I'll see what I can do."

"And ask my friend Chief Henderson if he knows anything about a stolen device. Tell him Aimee is in here with me when you talk to him. He might see a connection between this and whatever is going on where she works."

"Look," Laine said, "I don't really know what's going on, but their damned serious about something, and they sure as heck are being secretive about it too. To be honest, I don't think they want me here, but I got here before they could stop me."

"Why don't you go ahead and take the night off, after you check on Aimee, call Henderson and get some rest."

"I don't think they are done with you."

"I know," Ramiro acknowledged, "But I don't think they are going to open up with me while you are present."

"I don't think you realize how badly they want this information."

"I can handle this. Right now, I need you to check on Aimee and call Henderson."

She was uncomfortable with his request, but understood what he wanted. "Sure, I'll check on you in the morning. You be careful. Don't give them any reasons to do something you'll regret, OK?"

* * *

The interrogator crossed over to the other room where Aimee was, entered and slammed the door behind him. His face was red with anger as he pulled a sidearm from a holster on his hip and aimed it at her face. He shouted, "No! There will be no lawyers. It's just you and me and my gun. You tell me where the device is, or you won't walk out of this room alive."

He was bluffing, but it was a good bluff. Now, Aimee was scared. Tears welled up in her eyes. This man intended to kill her, and she didn't know what he wanted to know. She tried to speak, but she started sobbing and her voice came out in short staccato bursts, "I – don't – know – wha – what – de – vice – you - "

He didn't let her finish and yelled, "Damn it!!" He stormed out of the room.

* * *

The interrogator was still fuming mad, but this time he paced up and down in the commander's office. "You told me you had absolute proof that they knew where it was!"

"I do. They know where it is. You knew they would deny it."

"You weren't there. You didn't see their faces. I don't think they know anything."

"Oh no you don't mister. The Pentagon has assured me that they are the right people, and that's good enough for me. I have ordered you to get one of them to give up the location of the device, and that should be good enough for you. I don't care about no God damned confession, but I sure as hell do want to know where they're keeping that God damned device. Go find out, damn it, and don't bother me until you do!"

No man likes being reprimanded, especially when it goes against his professional judgment. He gave the commander a halfhearted salute, grumbled something that would sound to his commander like he agreed to do his duty, but in truth was more of a curse on bad orders. He huffed out of the office and stood outside the door where Ramiro was held. He wasn't sure what he could do with Ramiro's lawyer present. She had been assigned to him before they had received orders that some obscure war rule had been dredged up and it would not be necessary to provide them with counsel, at least not right away. With her already present, however, he didn't see any way to get rid of her. Nobody was willing to give her orders that excused her from the case long enough for them to infringe upon the prisoners' rights.

* * *

"Nicely done." The large man patted the Bard on the back while he looked over the report that just came off the wire.

"What's that?"

"The job you did on Dr. Pietre. He's been arrested, and will probably never see the light of day again."

The Bard snatched the report out of the larger man's hands and looked it over. "That is a nice job, only I didn't do it."

"Not you?" The large man's face contorted with concern. "If not you, then who? Is there a player we don't know about?"

"How about the kid? He's talented enough to do it."

"Look into it. See if you can trace this to him. Maybe we can recruit him after all."

* * *

"What do you mean I can't see her?" Penelope considered herself a patriot, but her loyalties were aligned with the constitution and the people. She loved her job, and loved being in the army, but was a big advocate of personal rights and freedom of speech. She hated abuse of power, and this smelled very much like abuse. "Has she been told her rights?"

The commander flatly stated, "Her charges preclude her rights."

"Has she seen her lawyer?"

"I assumed that she had, but I don't rightly know."

Captain Laine's voice raised slightly in pitch and volume with each question. "Has she asked to see a lawyer?"

"She hasn't asked me."

Captain Laine barked to her superior, "Then let me see her!"

The commander's eyebrows furrowed as his temper began to show on his face. "Don't you dare use that tone with me, Missy. Are you her attorney of record?"

"Yes I am."

The commander was ready to dismiss her until he realized she had answered yes instead of no. "What did you say? Did you just lie to the commander of the watch? Are you begging to be drawn up on charges?"

"No sir. I have been retained by her fiancé. In the absence of her personal request, or the request of family or legal guardian, a fiancé is allowed to retain counsel as long as she doesn't object."

"What the hell are you talking about? What fiancé?"

"I am talking about the Honorable Judge Vasquez. He claims to be her fiancé and he asked me to check on her. In the absence of her denials, we must assume the claim is legitimate."

"God damn it!" the commander yelled, "How dare you pull your legal shenanigans to circumvent my authority?"

"I'm sorry sir, but are you admitting to me that you are using your authority to deny her legal counsel?"

That shut him up. He had to bite his lip, but it shut him up. This wasn't his mess, and he wasn't going down on a sinking ship for someone else. "Very well, have a seat while I check on this."

She sat down in one of his guest chairs while he left his office heading to her interrogation room. On the way, he hand signaled two MP's to join him. Outside the door, he whispered something to the MP's, then burst in the door. He put on his best face of shock and disgust as he yelled, "What in the Sam Hill is going on here? Who are you?" He pointed a gnarled finger at the interrogator, "What are you doing with my prisoner? Guards? Take this man into custody, on the double!"

Aimee had been crying, the commander pulled out a clean handkerchief and offered it to her, "Ma'am, I'm sorry about that. Are you OK?"

She was too bewildered to answer, she just looked up at him, her eyes were red and slightly swollen, but she took the kerchief and wiped the moisture from around her eyes.

"Ma'am, I'll have someone lead you to your cell now. I think a nap would do you a world of good. By the way, do you know a Judge Vasquez?"

She nodded her head affirmative.

"What is the nature of your relationship with this Judge Vasquez?"

She tried to answer, but was still too choked up to speak.

He waved his hands for her to relax. "Are you and Judge Vasquez involved in a personal way?"

She nodded her head, but was starting to worry about where his questions were leading.

"And are you and Judge Vasquez, in fact, engaged to be married?"

Again she nodded her head, but now a truly ugly thought sprang to her mind. That horrible man had just held his pistol pointed at her head, they must have threatened Ramiro the same way. She screamed. She didn't even know she could scream, and wasn't aware of where it came from, but it sprang forth from deep within her chest, "Ramiro!"

"Easy, Ma'am, easy. He's quite fine. He has retained one of our defense attorneys to represent you, is that OK with you?"

The scream had run its course and died out like a match that just burned out. She looked up at him, shaking slightly, and nodded her head.

"Very well." He pointed at one of the men waiting at the door. "Take her to a clean cell. See to it that she's comfortable."

The commander was very disturbed that her fiancé was a judge, but he still had no idea that Ramiro was the very same man he held in custody just thirty feet away. Normally, he would be better informed of suspects in his charge, but this whole mess smelled of 'need to know', and he preferred the tried and true method of plausible deniability.

He returned to his office and said, "Captain Laine, she agreed to have you as her council, but she was very tired and wanted to sleep. You can see her in the morning."

This was not the answer she wanted, but she knew it was a concession on his part and best not to push any further. "Thank you, I'll be back in the morning to check on both of them."

* * *

Penelope exited the commander's office. She saw the interrogator in the hall laughing with the guards that had just pretended to arrest him moments earlier. She nodded at him and headed towards the exit.

"Where are you going?" he asked, "I'm not done interrogating him."

"I know." She spun around mid-stride, shrugged her shoulders at him and said, "He's a big boy, and he's a lawyer."

"You're off the case?"

"No, you aren't getting off that easy. I'll be back in the morning to make sure his human rights have not been violated. Hers too. Be seeing you." She spun back around and marched off.

* * *

"Hey, look at this." The Bard was pointing at the screen.

His associate got up and leaned over his shoulder, and saw a screen full of nonsense. "What am I looking at?"

"These charges against the professor, they are coming from all over the place. Federal computers, state computers, there are charges against him everywhere."

"Can you tell where they came from?"

"Not directly," the Bard said, "but I can tell that a lot of them are brand new entries, only they have been back dated to appear older."

"But you can't tell where they originated? How about a list of every remote site that has logged into those computers? Something you can cross check maybe?"

The Bard nodded his head and pretended he hadn't already started that. "Sure. That's a good idea, let's see if they all came from the same place, but it's going to take a while."

* * *

Dirk, Jones and Bobby were taken to the local sheriff's office where they had arranged a room to stage their investigation. A sketch artist was there waiting for them.

"Bobby," Dirk said, "this is Eric Woo. He is our sketch artist. He is also one of our most accurate marksmen. He speaks three languages, plays classical piano and is one hell of a terrific stir fry cook. But, much to the dismay of his Father, his hand to hand skills stink."

Eric Woo held up his slender hands like a doctor preparing for surgery. "These hands are far too valuable to risk bruising by bashing them against your soft pasty face." He then swung his arms around in brisk circles and struck a cinematic kung-fu pose, then thumped his breasts with his fists," but this body is all steel baby, all steel."

"We get the picture Bruce Lee. Let's see if you and Bobby here can come up with a face for the mysterious Bard character."

* * *

"Looky looky!" The Bard was really enjoying his work. "I'm still downloading statistics from some of the computers, but we are already getting matching addresses, including a couple of very familiar addresses."

"Tell me," the large man said, "I'm not getting up to look at a bunch of numbers."

"We have several entries that were sent from Professor Jennings' computer and a bunch from Dr. Pietre's computer too. We have several dozen addresses that repeat. I'll need to match them up against registered names to see if we can identify some of them."

"Wait a minute, I understand it coming from Jennings' computer, we already suspected the kid, but from Pietre's computer? And where did all those others come from?"

"I told you before, the kid is good. He may have been able to spoof the addresses, but I don't think so, or he never would have included his own. More than likely he set up some zombie programs to run on Pietre's computer. That would explain all the other computers too."

The large man chuckled. "I got to give the kid extra points for irony, using Pietre's own computer to frame him."

* * *

Bobby pointed at the artist's sketch and said, "No, the chin was thinner, kind of weak looking. His nose was thinner too."

The artist worked wonders with erasers and charcoal. While he was sketching, one of the sheriff's deputies entered the room and asked, "Hey Woo, I just made a fresh pot of coffee, you want some?"

"Yeah sure."

The deputy was looking over the sketch they were working on and asked, "How about you kid?"

"No thanks, Coke is my drug of choice, Cola that is."

The deputy started to back out of the room, then stopped and came back to the sketch. "I've seen this guy. We've got his picture somewhere..." He scurried out of the room, the coffee was already forgotten.

* * *

Penelope debated about how and when she would call Henderson, and finally decided to drive out to a remote pay phone to call him.

"Hello? Chief Henderson here."

"Chief? It's Penelope Laine. Judge Vasquez asked me to call you again."

"Can you hold a second, I have someone on the other line."

"OK, a second." She started rummaging through her purse pulling out more quarters.

The chief hit the hold button then called up the other line and said, "Mr. Vasquez, I have the army lawyer on the other line with a message from Ramiro, would you like me to conference you in with her?"

"Yes. Please do that," Ernesto said, "I would like to hear what she has to say."

He punched another button connecting the two calls. "Ms. Laine? I had Ramiro's father on the other line. I have conferenced him in with us, I hope that's OK with you."

She was surprised, but not bothered. "That's fine with me. Mr. Vasquez? I am Captain Penelope Laine. I am a defense lawyer here representing your son and his fiancé here."

"His fiancé?" Ernesto asked, "Aimee is there too? What is going on?"

"Sir, I can't tell you what is going on. Frankly, I don't know. All I can say is that there are a bunch of really uptight people waving badges around claiming national security, and I think they are planning to charge your son and his fiancé with treason."

"Treason? That's ridiculous. What idiot came up with that?"

"Sir, I don't really know any more. But because it's treason, the military is claiming special circumstances and pulling every trick in the book to keep it out of the civil court system."

"Where are they?"

"I am sorry sir, when they pull the national security cloak over it, I can't reveal the location. Chief Henderson, are you still on the line?"

"Yes, Ma'am."

"The interrogator's here have been questioning Ramiro about some kind of missing device that they claim is vital to national security. They have been very mysterious about what it is, but have it in their head that Ramiro and his fiancé are part of some conspiracy to steal this device. Does any of this have a ring of familiarity with you?"

Ramiro's father bristled at the notion that his son was a thief, let alone a traitor. "My son is no thief. You tell those idiots that they will never find their precious device with their heads stuck so far up their asses. You tell them that for me."

Penelope couldn't help the smile that spread across her face. Not only did she think it a deliciously clever analogy, but she would have loved to use it on them, if it didn't mean ending her career.

Henderson chuckled too and said, "I'll have to get a couple of my detectives to share notes and see if they think there are any connections between the different cases. Now, though, unless you have more news for us, it's way past bedtime around here. I, for one, could use a little shut-eye."

"Me too," she said, "I'll check on them in the morning, good night Chief, good night Mr. Vasquez."

* * *

"This is unbelievable," the Bard said, "I've compared the addresses which have logged into ninety-six different crime data bases for the past day. So far, I have uncovered at least fifty-four different computers which have placed entries on five or more of the ninety-six computers, and forty-nine of those computers are not registered with any known law enforcement agency. Two of those are highly secure computers from within the pentagon."

"You think the military is behind this?"

"No. Why would they? They would just arrest him if that was their goal. Whoever orchestrated this had it timed very tightly. All these computers made their entries within seconds of each other, virtually at the same time."

"Well," the large man said, "that would certainly support the theory that it is all the work of one person."

"Or it could be one organization."

"Send that into command. Tell them I think we better start thinking of eliminating some of the players."

The Bard shook his head and said, "I think you should make that call, on the phone."

"Do you think our computers have been compromised?"

"No, but I think the FBI is scrutinizing all email transmissions. And even if they can't crack the encryption in time to stop us, we don't need to leave them with any evidence."

"You don't think they can tap the phones?"

The Bard pointed at some of the equipment lying on a work bench and said, "Not without our knowing about it."

The large man wasn't prone to fits of paranoia, but also wasn't against taking precautions. He lifted the handset on the phone, while the Bard turned on the speaker phone and the encryption hardware. He dialed the secure number, and read a six character code to the operator that answered the phone. Seconds passed before he finally heard someone answer on the other end, "This is sector seventeen control, please be brief, the phone system has been having problems."

"Should I use email?" the large man asked, "We were concerned that electronic transmissions might be compromised."

"Email is completely down. What do you need?"

"We need a go on our recovery plan and approval to exercise extreme judgment."

"You are go with recovery and-" the transmission ended there, the phone line went dead.

"Get them back," the large man commanded, "see if we are go on the sanction."

"Didn't they already tell you to follow your instincts?"

"They did, but it's always best to have specific approval, taking the responsibility off of us."

The Bard threw his hands in the air and said, "I can't get them back."

"Damn! What a time for their phone system to act up."

"It's not their phone, it's ours. We aren't getting a dial tone."

"What the hell?" the large man scowled, "I don't like coincidences like this."

"I don't believe in coincidences like this either."

"Is the kid good enough to do this?"

"He is good enough to do any of this. He might even be good enough to do most of this, but I don't believe anybody is good enough to do ALL of this. The number of compromised systems is enormous."

"We better prepare to retrieve the computer."

* * *

"You see, I told you we had a picture of him," the young deputy said as he carried two large photos with him and held them up next to the sketch Woo had drawn, "This one is from outside the campus when they had the false fire alarm in the cafeteria, and this one is an enlargement of this section." He drew an imaginary box on the first photo, then held up the second.

Bobby pointed at the photo and said, "That's him. That's the guy that came to the lab and said he was from the grant office."

The young deputy beamed with enthusiasm.

An FBI forensic expert who had followed the deputy with his pictures said, "I'll take these back to the lab and send the picture to the field agents on site at the campus."

"Wait!" Bobby held up his hand reaching for the photos. "Let me see that other picture." Bobby took the picture, carried it to a spot where he had better light and asked, "Do you have a magnifying glass?"

Woo was looking over Bobby's shoulder. "What are you looking for?"

"Remember, there were two men. I am looking for his partner."

Woo and all the agents present silently felt stupid for not thinking of it themselves. Dirk broke the brief silence. "Forget the magnifying glass. Take him directly to the lab. Woo? You and Jones come with us too."

Woo shrugged his shoulders and looked at Dirk, puzzled about why he was included.

"These guys are professionals," Dirk said, "Once Bobby identifies the partner, and the tech gives us a decent photo of him. I want you to draw him with a few different props and disguises."

CHAPTER 18

"Why are we waiting?" the Bard asked, "Every moment that goes by, more things seem to go wrong. Let's just go in, tear out the computer, and bug out."

"Think about it. It was your plan. We go in, create some kind of dangerous situation to give us an excuse to evacuate everybody. The more people we need to evacuate, the longer it will take, and the more chances of us being exposed. Plus, I intend to blow up the lab, to hide the hole in the floor, and the less people we have wandering about, the less chance of killing a passerby."

The Bard looked at him funny.

"What? I'm not completely heartless."

"OK. Fine. You're a born again humanitarian. But it's nearly midnight, the place should be empty."

"There's a basketball game in the Gymnasium. The parking lot will be clogged with people trying to get out. Let's give it another hour or so."

* * *

"That's not the only picture we have." The lab technician pointed to the screen and the digital rendering of the photo Bobby had been shown. "We actually have a few shots from that time index, especially of the crowd."

There were several computers set up around the conference room, and each man, armed with a picture of the Bard, sat at one of the computers and scanned the crowd shots for him. When they spotted him in the crowd, the technician would crop the picture, blow up the section around the Bard and enhance it before Bobby checked the surrounding faces in the picture.

There were over a hundred crowd shots, and very few of them included the Bard, or at least a recognizable shot of him.

Jones was getting impatient and blurted out, "This is taking too long. By the time we find this guy, he'll be old and retired."

The technician said, "We could let Pam look at them if you want."

Jones looked at the tech like he was just plain stupid. "I don't see how one more person is going to make a difference here."

"Pam's not a person. Pam stands for Photo Analysis Matching. It's our facial recognition program."

"Well why didn't you say something in the first place?"

The technician looked at Jones like he was just plain stupid for not asking.

* * *

The Bard was a nervous wreck. Not for what they were about to do, but just because waiting made him anxious. He wanted to hit the road and get it over with, but he understood the large man's reasoning. So, he sat in their little office and kept himself busy checking his analysis of the crime databases.

The number of different computers used to implicate Pietre was staggering. He would love to get his hands on the zombie program that made the updates.

He paged down on his screen when the connection went dead and the lights went out. "Aw, hell! Now what?"

"Shhhh!" The large man held his hand up signaling quiet, which did virtually no good in the near darkness. The only light was from the Computer screen which was powered by an uninterruptible power supply.

* * *

Pam cranked through the photos very quickly. And spit out seven crowd shots highlighting what it thought was the Bard's face. Six of them were on the mark, one was a faded out picture of some rock star on a student's T-shirt.

The technician quickly cropped and enhanced them as they came out, and Bobby went over them very carefully. They adjusted the contrast and brightness to see if it might help. It wasn't until the Fifth one that Bobby pointed to another man on the Bard's left, "There! That big guy. That's the guy that came to Karlyn's lab with Dr. Pietre."

Dirk hit the print key. A hard copy of the large man's face spooled off the printer. "Jones, get both these pictures to the field agents so they know who to look for."

The technician sheepishly raised his hand and asked, "Uh, excuse me, but, would you like me to have Pam match their faces up against all our known databases? We have prison photos, surveillance, military and even driver's licenses."

"Do it!" Dirk held a slim hope of getting an id on this face, but if it worked, it would be a major find in this case. "Before we move on, is there anything else your Pam can do to help us?"

"Well, there is one thing, but it requires a lot of computer resources, so we usually don't attempt it until all other methods have been exhausted."

"What," Dirk asked, "would that be?"

"We have programs that can render the photo at three or four different ages, and then scan historical archives, magazine archives and Internet photo collections looking for a match. It costs the most and has the slimmest chance of success."

Dirk didn't need any time to think it over. "Don't wait. Start it now. If you need authorization I'll provide it. These guys are probably spooks. Odds are good that all pictures of them have been purged from their military service records."

* * *

The large man crossed the room. He had excellent night vision, but it still took a few moments for him to acclimate. He found his associate and delicately whispered, "Shhhh," again. He lightly touched the Bard on the shoulders, and guided him towards the back of the room.

The Bard initially thought his partner was just trying to listen to something, but when he was guided to the other side of the office, he understood and ducked under the desk.

The big guy pulled out his 9mm, crept over to the door and lightly pressed his ear to the door straining to hear any sound in the hallway. As the Bard's eyes began to adjust, he realized that the monitor was illuminating the whole room. If there was an intruder, his partner would have more advantage if the room were totally dark, so he reached up and found the monitor by feel, and turned off the power, further enveloping the room in darkness.

The large man dropped down to one knee, transferred the pistol to his left hand and, while leaning against the wall, slowly and silently turned the knob on the door and cracked it ajar. The moment the door had started to move, a large mass burst through the door. The room flashed a dull neon blue color, accompanied by the "pfffft" sound of a silenced pistol as the intruder leaped through the door firing random shots around the room until he located the man kneeling by the door way. The large man recognized the blue flash. It was a special round designed for low muzzle flash for use with night vision goggles. So the intruder had the advantage after all.

The intruder rolled to his feet and swung his weapon around towards the door only in time to see the large man jump out the doorway and hide in the hall.

From the hallway, the large man called out, "Who is it? Let's talk. What are you doing here?"

The intruder didn't answer, but waited patiently with his weapon trained on the doorway.

"What are your orders? There must be some kind of a screw up. The computers have all been compromised. Talk to me."

* * *

Pam had spit out numerous possible matches. A number of matches coming from various state motor vehicle records were rejected as being close, but not a match. These were expected. What wasn't expected, however, was the number of positive matches on both the Bard and the large man. Dirk hadn't expected to find any positive records on him, but what he actually found was a plethora of matches. Many different matches were made, from every state, all with different names and addresses.

Dirk watched the list grow. "I should have expected this. It makes perfect sense in retrospect. Can you cross reference all these names and addresses and see if any of them lead to a common source? I have something else I need to show our guest."

"What about these?" the technician pointed at a screen filling up with numerous group shots containing mostly three to eight different service men and women.

"Run those through again, and see if Pam can identify anyone else in the photos. I'll have agents question any person Pam identifies. Maybe someone will remember a name for our mystery man."

The technician nodded his head and went to one of the terminals and started running the photos through Pam a second time.

Dirk took Bobby down the hall into a small office with a row of terminals where he sat down and logged on. "It's getting pretty late, but I'd appreciate it if you can at least take a brief look at this before calling it a night. I can get you a ride home, or if you prefer, we'll put you up at the hotel across the street."

"I'm fine," Bobby said.

Dirk went through a couple menu selections on the console and called up a hex dump to show Bobby. "Here is a section of code we have identified which is part of the system which has been taking over some of our computers. I also have a disassembly listing prepared for you."

Bobby sat down, already staring at the hexadecimal dump and said, "Thank you, but that won't be necessary just yet." He had seen his program enough to recognize parts of it. He ran his finger along the columns of numbers on the screen, and down the page, row by row. He came to a point where it diverged from his code and went into something else, and whispered to himself, "That looks like my code, but this is definitely not mine."

Dirk only saw his lips move. "What was that? I couldn't hear you."

"Maybe I would like to see that disassembly now."

Dirk typed a couple commands on the console and pulled up the disassembly listing, which was a conversion from the hex code to human readable instructions. Dirk pointed to the beginning of the code and said, "As near as I can tell, this code up here is building its own communication stack and setting up a link with another computer. Further down, there are subroutines that try to download some programs from that link, but they are never executed."

"Never executed?"

"We can only assume that those sections are from the carrier program, and the virus re-wrote itself over sections of existing code."

"So," Bobby asked, "you think the original, non-infected program was designed to download some programs?"

"It's probably some sort of web based install program, after it downloads the programs, it executes them, but, like I said, that code was never executed."

"How do you know it was never executed? Maybe it executed once, and the downloaded programs wrote over the install code leaving what we see now."

"That's possible," Dirk admitted, "but we're stumped as to how it got here in the first place."

"Someone tried to download something. It was a Trojan horse with infected files inside."

"Not on this machine. It's isolated from the Internet. It is part of a server farm. Almost the entire farm is completely isolated from the Internet, and there are virtually no human operators. One of our mainframes feeds data into it, and it, meaning the whole farm, analyzes the data twenty-four hours a day looking for patterns."

"So the mainframe must have fed the virus to it."

Dirk got back on the keyboard and called up another listing and said, "Look at this."

Bobby looked at the screen, it was another hex dump, but he did not recognize any of the hex codes. "What is it?"

"It's the same program, more or less."

"Is it encrypted?"

Dirk was back on the keyboard pulling up another disassembly listing. "Nope, it's just not on a familiar CPU. Look at this disassembly listing."

Bobby sat staring at the code. He wanted to share what he knew, but wasn't sure how to start, and didn't want to get in any trouble over it.

"We can't figure out how the virus got on the mainframe. We thought it would be impossible."

"Why did you think it was impossible?"

Dirk thought carefully about how much he could say. He had already ventured into a Grey area exposing some sensitive top secret information to a kid already branded as a hacker, someone who had already hacked the highest ranking government official, but in the end, he concluded the damage was already done. The top secret computer was out of their control. "This computer has a custom designed CPU. It is one of a kind, and uses an entirely unique machine code known only to a very few people with absolutely the highest credentials. Nobody could possibly hack this machine."

Bobby looked at Dirk wondering how much he already knew. Perhaps this was all a ploy to cozy up with him expecting some melodramatic confession. Dirk was probably a good poker player, nothing in his expression hinted that he knew more than he said.

* * *

The Bard was absolutely petrified. He cowered under the desk, completely defenseless.

The intruder was crouched on the floor, with a chair between himself and the door where the large man was hiding. He could hear the slender man's rapid breathing, and glanced over in his direction. He clearly saw a young unarmed man who posed no threat to him, but he knew the larger man, and knew how dangerous he could be.

The large man tried to reason with the intruder, "We are here on assignment. Official business! We trailed some top secret computer hardware, stolen from a government research facility. We have been monitoring some very suspicious computer hackings. We think that they have already infested our control systems! Really!! I myself have gotten some really obscure orders, and when I questioned control, they knew nothing about them!"

"Why don't you just shut up?" the intruder said, "Your hat hasn't been that white in decades."

The large man recognized the intruder's voice. "George? Is that you?"

"Yes George, who'd you think it was?"

Neither man was named George, but it simplified things to have a nondescript handle, so they both had chosen George years ago.

"I never suspected it would be a longtime friend that broke into my office spraying bullets all over the room."

"We were never that close, besides, I got my orders."

"Please, George, check them. I am serious, there have been some unusual computer hacks going on. In fact, I had sent for you, with quite different orders. You'll find a secure phone right over there." He reached in with one hand to point to the corner with the phone. The blue flash, familiar "pffft" and spray of wood splinters and plaster alerted the larger George that he wasn't going to talk George in so easily. He swiped his hand up the wall flicking on the large glaring overhead lights. He hated those lights, they hurt his eyes but he hoped they would blind his friend.

With the lights on, the intruders goggle display went a flat green.

Protective circuitry prevented them from blinding him, but it took more time to adjust the contrast for full light situations. He never saw the large mass lunging from the door and was still calculating what had just happened in his mind when he was tackled and a strong hand gripped the wrist of his gun hand. The large man maintained his grip on the intruder's wrist, knocking him backwards over his heels. The bulk of his weight came down squarely on the intruder's chest. Neither man moved for a moment, there was no point in struggling, the intruder had clearly lost his advantage.

"Hello George," the intruder said, "I see you have been keeping fit. I hope you're not going to take any of this personally."

The Bard asked, "You know this guy?"

"Yeah." The large man took the intruders gun and sat upright, still on his abdomen. "We've been chums for a long time now."

"More like brothers you mean." The intruder decided to change his tune about never being that close.

"What are you going to do with him? He tried to kill us."

"When you're right, you're right. I should shoot him."

"Wait a minute," the intruder objected, "what about those computer errors? Don't you want me to verify my orders?"

The large man got up and said, "Yes, George, by all means, please verify your orders."

The intruder got up slowly and made his way to the phone. He picked up the receiver, but there was no dial tone. "It's dead."

The big man smacked his palm against his forehead and said, "Forgot about that. Control is having problems with their phone lines too. Better try a cell phone and cross your fingers."

He pulled out his cell phone, dialed his handler's number, and entered a secret pass code. "Control? Can I get verbal verification of the orders I received by electronic dispatch?" The line went dead. "Hello? Hello?"

The large man stood, leaning against the wall with his arms crossed, the gun dangling from his hand. He was nodding his head and asked, "The line went dead?"

"That's never happened before."

"Someone who is very computer savvy has somehow hacked our most secure computers and our phone lines."

The intruder stared at the phone for a moment as he thought it through. "OK, I suppose it's possible that my orders may be suspect. Sorry."

The large man held the intruders pistol by the barrel and offered it back to him.

The Bard couldn't believe his eyes. "What are you doing? He tried to kill us and you are giving him back his gun?"

"It's OK, I know him, and we need him. Focus your anger on that little punk that sent him orders to have us terminated."

The intruder accepted the pistol, replaced it in his shoulder holster and asked, "So what do we do know, George?"

"We stick together. All electronic communications are questionable. We have a job to do, and could use the extra muscle. We need to extract a computer from the college. The device is inside, and we can't remove the device without taking the whole thing." The big man looked at his watch and continued, "We should get moving now. The tools are in the van already."

* * *

Bobby had seen enough. He'd been holding back what he knew about the device he put in the computer, and the gelatinous substance which has since grown. He felt an obligation not to reveal too much of Dierdre's project, but he also knew that this information was probably a key piece of what was going on. He got up from the terminal and walked to a small break room he had passed earlier. He wasn't sure how to share this information without sounding totally crazy. He walked slowly, hoping inspiration would lead him to the best approach. He put three coins in the soda machine and pressed the button. The machine clicked, clanged and clunked as Bobby could hear his drink bounce and roll down to the small delivery port. He popped open the can, took a big gulp and walked back to agent Dirk and said, "We need to talk. Do you have some place a little more comfortable, less noisy maybe?"

"Sure, follow me."

They walked down the hall to a small rest area near the break room. It had a comfortable couch and a couple soft chairs. They sat down in the chairs and Bobby took another big gulp of his soda.

Bobby cleared his throat and started, "I know you are dealing with a lot of secret information, and there is probably a lot you haven't told me. I'm kind of in the same boat. I've been working pretty closely with Professor Jennings to provide some computer models to advance her project. It's really quite fascinating stuff, very cutting edge, and very secret. Before Professor Jennings, I worked for Dr. Karlyn. Again, I was intimately involved with the technical and computer aspects of his project, also secret stuff. So I think there are things that we each have not disclosed, and I think it's time we start to pool what we know."

"You know, Bobby, there are limits on what I can disclose to you."

"I realize that there may be limits at this time, but I think that as we begin to share things, you may see that there is a greater need to share those secrets than to keep them, so naturally, I think I should go first. I recognize some of the code you showed me. Parts of it appear similar to a program I wrote for Professor Jennings."

"It's not really a virus, is it?"

"No, well not what I wrote anyway. Professor Jennings' project needed to model subatomic particles, and required more computing power than we had available. I converted her model to work on a computer cluster, and got some friends to volunteer their computers so we could test her program across a thousand plus computers, and it worked great."

"So what went wrong? How are we finding your program on such top secret computers?"

"That's not my program. It includes some of my code. A lot of those sections that are bypassed are from my original program. Someone has modified it."

"Do you suspect anyone?"

"Well, I know Dr. Pietre kept trying to break into Professor Jennings' computer, and I suspect his computer somehow became a node on our network, which probably was pretty annoying to him. He probably could make some minor modifications to my program, but I don't think he has the skills to do what we see here. What I really suspect is even more bizarre, and I'm not even sure you could believe me unless I actually showed you in person."

Jones came running down the hall looking for them and yelling, "It's him! It's him!"

Dirk stood up and waved at Jones before he ran past the lounge and asked, "What's who?"

"We just got an electronic flash message. The man in the picture was just spotted by an agent in the campus parking lot."

Bobby stood up and said, "They're after the computer again!"

Everyone ran down the hall to the elevator. Dirk called the team in Pietre's lab, and warned them to keep alert.

"Wait!" Bobby stopped short of the elevator and said, "We need one of those miniature cameras that you can slide under a door, or through a small hole, and a monitor."

The technician was in the hall to see what the commotion was and volunteered, "I have one of those."

"Good." Dirk said, "Get it, you're coming with us."

* * *

The Bard and the two Georges were aware that FBI agents were crawling all over the place. They knew that any diversion could not be of a suspicious nature, and regardless of the nature of any diversion, the FBI would return to their posts. So it had to be subtle. They brought along three other associates, two very strong men, and one young woman dressed as a very provocative college student. She had a scandalously short skirt and only needed to turn their heads long enough for the five men to slip into the lab. She wore a student researcher id that hung from a cord around her neck and lay cleanly in the cleavage of her ample breasts and low cut neck line.

They entered the building at the end near Dierdre's lab. The girl walked briskly down the hall towards the agents gathered around Pietre's lab. As she passed them, she smiled shyly and wagged her barely covered behind back and forth as she passed them and continued down the hallway until she turned the corner down the other corridor, giving the Georges just enough time to slip into Dierdre's lab.

Agent Dirk had moved two of the men from inside Pietre's lab to Dierdre's. One of them reached for his radio to call the other agents in the hall.

Both of the Georges burst into action, instinctively working together, attacking the two agents, one on one, quickly overpowering them. One agent was unconscious on the floor, while the other agent had one of the large man's arms tightly wrapped around his throat. He tried to call out into the hall, but the other George viciously slugged him with a right hook, and he slumped to the floor. But enough noise was made to alert the agents in the hall. The large man threw a non-lethal grenade out in the hall which burst into brilliant dazzling light. The five men shot through the door, down the hall and out to the parking lot.

* * *

"So tell me, Bobby, do you have any ideas how your code ended up translated into a completely unknown mainframe architecture?"

"Not really. I wrote some routines that would allow the system to try different optimizations and pick the best one. It would randomly try different routines it might find on programs that were running at the time, and it could even try different random operation codes and see if they made any improvements, but it was only looking at how fast the calculations ran."

"Random op codes?" Dirk asked, "Could it have figured out the machines architecture that way?"

"That would take some kind of AI," Bobby laughed, "It only tried to see if it could produce faster results."

Dirk scratched his chin in an effort to focus on a thought. "Even with an AI, it would probably take millions of variations to find one that worked. Just creating millions of variations would take some time, I imagine."

"Not as long as you think."

"How so?"

"Well," Bobby said, "one machine might take a while to create a million permutations, but a million machines could produce a million permutations in the time it takes to make one."

"Do you have a million machines?"

Bobby didn't know how to answer without showing him first.

"Did you let your program spread all over the Internet? Did that somehow give you a million machines?"

"I thought so at first, but something else was going on. Something more amazing than anything I ever imagined. Wait till you see what we have."

The car pulled onto the campus, and pulled up alongside another black sedan that was watching people come and go. Dirk rolled down the window and caught the attention of the man in the driver seat. "Good work Chester. That may have been the break we were looking for."

Chester lifted his dark sunglasses up from his eyes and said, "Thanks for the compliment, but we didn't have anything to do with it. That was all the boys up in the lab that had all the excitement."

"But," Dirk said, "you flashed us with the positive ID. You spotted the perp, so you're just going to have to accept some of the credit here."

"What are you talking about? We never spotted anyone here."

"Sorry," Dirk said, "I thought it was you." He motioned to the driver to continue on, and they took the road that circled around the labs up the hill to the top building.

Bobby was chatting with the technician, then turned to Dirk and said, "I think you should find out who really sent that message. If it wasn't your guy, then this whole thing could be some bizarre setup that we don't understand yet."

The two agents in Dierdre's lab were up, and rubbing their chins. The girl in the skirt and the intruders were gone. Bobby waited by the entrance while Dirk instructed the two men to go see a doctor, which was standard procedure.

After excusing the two agents, Dirk motioned towards the door and said, "After you."

Inside the lab, Bobby took them directly to the computer and pointed to the bottom rack. "See that hole? Put your camera in there."

The technician inserted the small lens. He hit the power on monitor and the image started to appear. The tech moved the image around. The gelatinous substance was still visible, but the flecks were denser than Bobby remembered, and he thought he was seeing movement, or possibly moving lights, sparks even.

Dirk was puzzled and asked, "OK, what is it?"

"That, I think, is what those men were after. I think it is at the center of everything that is going on around here. An old acquaintance of Dr. Karlyn's showed up one day with a strange package. He wanted Dr. Karlyn's help testing it. Dr. Karlyn never told me anything about what he was asked to do, but I suspect he wanted to reverse engineer the device. He spent a couple days locked up in his lab with it. I didn't know what he was doing but when he came out, he gave it to me. It was a box with wires coming out of it. He labeled each wire and asked me to create an interface to put it on the computer. So I did, and he stayed late running programs all night long. When he asked me to write something for him, it was always little stuff, maybe just a small subroutine that he planned to use from his main program. I never saw enough to figure out what he was up to."

Dirk said, "It sounds to me like he had you on a 'need to know' basis. The defense department does that all the time."

"Well, it wasn't long after that when he left the university, and all kinds of strange things started to happen."

"You mean the hacks and stuff?"

"Yeah, that's when I met agent Spivey. But the strangest thing was yet to come. The system I wrote for Professor Jennings was designed to grow as people volunteered to participate. I never put a limit on how large it could grow, but when we tested it, we only used, at most, a couple thousand computers, but it continued to grow, from thousands to hundreds of thousands of processors. I checked and checked, but they were not coming from the Internet, they were all right here. I think, and it's a wild ass guess, but I think this is a living tissue computer. It has grown, and while it has grown, our system has gotten faster and faster."

"So why," Dirk asked, "is it on our computers too?"

"I don't know. My program was never designed to spread like that."

"You said the optimization routines would try different routines that were on the computer at the time, what if it found a virus and somehow combined with one?"

"It, or rather, I should say, the program I wrote only considered how fast it ran Professor Jennings' experiment. Faster was better. I doubt that any virus routines would make it run any faster, so the optimization process wouldn't keep those routines."

"But, would it have to keep those routines? What if it just tried a routine from a virus, and ended up copying itself somewhere else?"

"I think that's stretching things a bit. The AI theory made more sense than it accidentally executing a virus routine that made copies of itself."

Dirk looked worried and said, "OK. Now it's my turn to share. That server farm I told you about was one of our AI clusters, and it has been infected."

"An AI Cluster?"

"We have a huge network of powerful machines working in parallel, not unlike your project, and when I say we, I mean homeland security, not the FBI. These machines are using a variety of heuristic algorithms to compare domestic and world events looking for patterns. It tries to recognize patterns that precede dramatic events, especially terrorism."

"You have an AI that can understand world events?"

"I wish," Dirk said, "but it can't understand world events, it can only try to find patterns."

"So you must have people translate world events into some kind of code it can understand."

"Major events do get coded specifically for it. We also have routines that scan the newspapers, television and Internet for key phrases that are included in the pattern analysis."

"Television? How does it watch the news?"

Dirk chuckled and said, "Fair question, it just reads the closed caption portion. The Internet routines have spiders that work similar to the search engines, and go out looking at websites, newsgroups and various download sources."

"Wait a minute, download sources? You mean it searches for FTP ports?"

"Yes, and peer to peer too."

"That may be how it got out of my lab. The entry point is an FTP port. If your spider contacted my port, it would have been interpreted as a voluntary request to download the programs and join the network."

"But," Dirk said, "our entire system was infected, not just the Internet crawlers."

"Do they analyze the files they download, or pass them on to the main programs?"

"They only check for duplicates, and pass them on."

"Once one machine contacted mine, the program would have begun executing, and the first thing it does is transmit routines it sees in memory to the rest of the system, and ask the rest of the processes to help it optimize. Then it starts receiving a flood of variations on the main program."

"I see. With all those routines being sent in, our system did what it was designed to do, and distributed them throughout all the nodes."

"And in a short time," Bobby continued, "your whole network has joined my network. I never thought about people probing my ports like that. I should add some additional checks to prevent that."

Dirk was still puzzled, and not quite satisfied with their theory. "But when we shut down all the machines in our AI farm, and wipe them clean and reload them from their initial tapes, your program comes right back and takes over the whole farm within just a few hours?"

"I don't know. To be honest, I'm getting a little tired and not thinking as sharply as I would like."

* * *

The five men sprinted to the van, but once in the van, they drove a lazy circuitous route off the campus to a rendezvous point where they picked up their only female accomplice. Little was said, the girl was just an operative they hired for the evening, and wasn't privy to the secrets behind the mission she was given. Had the mission been successful, she might have been included in the post-mission party, but since the night was a failure, she was simply paid and dropped off at a bus stop along with the extra muscle.

They rode quietly for a short while until the Bard broke the silence, "What do we do now? Eventually the FBI is going to realize what is going on, and if they don't, the Army will."

When the large man didn't respond, the new George offered his opinion, "We could take them out. They didn't seem to be their best men. We could have taken them tonight if we wanted to."

The large man said, "I just don't like taking out feds without clear orders to eliminate them. They are good guys after all, it's not like they were just civilians."

"Yeah," George responded, "and they tend to take it personally, which can be bad for our careers."

The Bard shivered at the low regard the two larger veterans had for civilians. He imagined that if it weren't for his talent with computers, his life would be held in equally low regard by them. "Can't you guys just knock them out? Like you did with that one guy?"

The large man explained, "Not without casualties. They are armed and well enough trained that someone, whether one of us or one of them, would end up shot and possibly mortally wounded. That kind of stuff only works in the movies."

George looked out the front window and added, "Yeah, TV is good for commandos raiding an armed camp with bullets flying, bombs exploding, cars running over mines and getting turned over, yet nobody is ever killed."

"George, I never knew you watched TV!"

George raised his right hand and said, "It was an accident, I swear! I thought it was a training video!"

Everybody laughed, and the large man added wishfully, "If only our operations could work like the ones cooked up for TV."

The Bard's mind started to wander to the TV shows he used to watch. "Maybe you guys just watched the wrong shows."

George looked over his shoulder and asked, "Oh yeah kid? What show should we have watched?"

"Mission Impossible would have been a good one. Instead of shooting up the place, you go in dressed as the FBI and the Army, and confiscate the property with fake documents."

The two Georges looked at each other, struck with the ridiculous notion of getting the device by pulling off an enormous con, but their thoughts were cut short by bright lights and the sound of a siren directly behind them. The large man's first instinct was to run for it, anonymity was one of their best assets, but the van was designed for blending in and being invisible, not for high speed maneuvers.

CHAPTER 19

Chief Henderson wasted no time gathering his detectives together in the morning. He had the team that first investigated the computer hacking at the college together with the team that investigated the phone taps and the hacks at the phone company. He included anyone that had anything to do with the university, even if it was just a traffic ticket. He called the FBI and asked them if they had anything to contribute. They responded with faxes of the pictures they used to identify The Bard and the large man.

He emailed Arthur Bedding for his input, and was surprised by the quick response.

> We tracked down some of the Internet addresses to a small pool of computers with a variety of corporate owners which, as near as we can tell, are all phony fronts designed to hide the real owners. I don't know if this will help you any, but one of our employees remembered seeing a pale brown or yellow van with some kind of business written on the side. The employee could not provide a better description, but her overall impression was that it was a utility van, not unlike the vans we use when we send out repairmen.

As his detectives assembled, he went for the long shot and asked, "Has anyone received any reports about a utility repair van being at the scene?"

His response was mostly a room of men shaking their heads no, but one of the detectives who had been to the university after the false fire alarm sat up in his chair and half raised one hand, wagging his finger to jog his memory. "Now that you mention it, I remember seeing a van in the campus parking lot. I only noticed it because it was somebody's lock smith van, and I made a joke about the college finally locking up their computers."

"What color?" the chief asked.

"Tan?"

Another investigator in the room sat up a little taller and said, "wait a minute, when you sent me out to take a statement about the missing secretary, there was a van in the parking lot. I thought it was khaki, but it could have been tan. It wasn't a locksmith company, it was some janitorial service."

"When you sent us out to that girls apartment, after the judge called, wasn't there a van across the street, with some guy up the telephone pole?"

The chief interrupted, "I don't want us to start seeing vans where there weren't any, let's see if anything in your notes matches up."

"Here, look!" The investigator who had remembered the man up the telephone pole was waving a picture, and handed it to the chief. "Look in the window Chief."

There was a lot of glare on the window, but in the corner, there appeared to be a partial view of a yellowish van. There was a logo on the side of the van which was only partially visible through the window, but it did not say Locksmith or Janitorial, if anything, it looked like the name of one of their local cable companies.

Henderson stood to give them his final instructions before closing the meeting, "Put the word out to the patrol cars. If anyone sees a yellow van, I want them to report in with the time, location, plate number, and any logo on the side. Tell them not to approach the vehicle in any way, we'll keep a matrix of all the locations where we spot these vans and see if a pattern pops up."

* * *

Penelope Laine was already outside the stockade when the sun peeked over the horizon. While the doors weren't locked, guards were always on post, and admittance was only granted on business. Being a defense attorney, she would normally have no trouble going in at this hour, but for some reason the guards at the door refused her entry, even after calling the watch commander to clear her. She was assured that someone would be there shortly to clear this up for her. It was a pleasant morning, so she made herself comfortable on a nearby bench and waited.

* * *

Dierdre was in her office watching the project run when Bobby arrived. She hadn't been to the lab yet, and was unaware of the FBI agents standing guard. She beamed a broad smile as he came in and said, "Good morning Bobby, I just can't sit still I'm so excited. What did you do? This has got to be the most exciting thing that has ever happened here!"

He was still shaking the remnants of sleep from his mind, and looked bewildered. "What? Oh you mean last night? I guess it was pretty exciting."

"But how did you do it? What did you change?"

"It was the FBI. They did it all. They have access to some pretty amazing software. You should see their stuff."

"The FBI?" she asked, "What did you tell them?"

"I told them what he looked like, and their computers took it from there."

"What who looked like? What have you told them? Did you tell them about our project?"

"I had to tell them," Bobby admitted, "It seems that some of their top secret super computers have been contributing to our totals."

"Yikes!"

"I'm lucky they have some level headed people who didn't try blaming me for hacking their computer."

"So," she asked timidly, "just what did you tell them?"

"I told them that your project required massive amounts of computer power that your budget could not afford."

"I think if you told me that, I would assume you had hacked the computers."

"I told them that I created a way to distribute your program over a cooperative cluster, and that somehow their computers had gotten involved. It turned out to be their own fault even, one of their computers snoops around the Internet checking download sites, and it downloaded our program and lost control."

"They must have some pretty impressive computers, from what I've seen. How did you talk them into leaving them on-line for us?"

"Oh," Bobby said, "there may be a slight problem with that. They can't get them back under their control. They tried shutting them down and loading a clean boot, but the program came right back."

"Uh oh. That's not good. Well, not good for them, but it's pretty good for us."

"What's good for us? I'm not following you?"

"The numbers," she said, "I'm talking about the numbers. Pretty exciting stuff."

* * *

Agent Dirk was an early riser, and despite being late to bed, he was up and out the door heading to the makeshift office bright and early. He was one of those people who could stay up all night and not show any serious wear and tear in the morning. He liked to attribute it to clean living, staying away from drugs and alcohol, but mostly it came down to genetics.

As he made his way through the sheriff's department, towards the office his team was using, a woman's voice paged him from behind. "Agent Dirk! Agent Dirk! You have some messages!" He stopped, and waited for her to catch up.

"Hi," she said shyly, "I'm Katherine, we met yesterday. I work in archives."

"I remember Katherine."

"Everybody calls me Kitty. If you need anything, just call me. I'm not a file clerk. I'm a researcher, just so you know."

"Ah, I see Katherine, I mean Kitty."

"We still have a lot of hard copy archives, you know, paper stuff, books, newspapers, and historical documents, but we are converting them to the computer. I don't think they ever realized just how hard it is to convert paper documents to images. The cataloging is not so hard, but trying to index the text on the documents can be a little challenging. Plus, I don't think they ever realized just how much computer storage this stuff would eat up."

Dirk wondered who the true Kitty was. Was she the Cosmo girl with the perfect face and the perfect makeup? Or was she the fitness girl with the sculpted arms and legs? Or was she the techno geek rambling on about the complexities of computer imaging?

She continued, "That's some pretty exciting stuff you guys have been running all night. I had no idea the FBI had such sophisticated programs. We lent you some of our archive computers, so I got a pretty good look at the facial imaging software you were using."

"We call her PAM, Photo Analysis Matching. Speaking of which, I should be checking on her progress."

"I'll walk with you, I mean, that is where I work anyway."

Moments had passed, as they worked their way down the hall,

when she blurted out, "I almost forgot your messages! A Chief Henderson called, something about some pictures he thinks you'll be interested in. And this one is from some army lieutenant. She didn't say what she wanted."

"Thanks, I better get right on these."

She stood there for a moment, half smiling, wishing, unsuccessfully, for more to say, and started to retreat to her side of the lab.

"Hey Kitty, thanks. Maybe if we aren't both too busy, we can have lunch, and talk more about imaging and computers and stuff."

Her face brightened immensely. "Yeah, sure, that would be great!"

* * *

Ramiro and Aimee each sat quietly in their respective rooms. The rooms were an improvement over their previous accommodations, being actual rooms in a secret safe-house, but they were dark and without amenities. The windows were boarded up and the doors were locked. The sounds of squeaking floor boards could be heard through the doors as guards patrolled the halls outside their rooms. Neither of them knew what fate lie ahead of them, nor what became of the other. Had either of them cried out, the other would have heard, but neither felt safe enough to do so.

They were quietly hustled out of the brig shortly after midnight. A crew of young soldiers entered the complex. They were armed with automatic assault rifles, but merely carried their weapons at the ready. They showed some papers to the ranking officer of the midnight crew, which only consisted of the officer and two guards. The officer protested, but their papers were in order, and carried a general's signature. Besides, they didn't look like they would take no for an answer, and he was only upset because prisoner transfers meant more paperwork.

The young team clearly trained together. They worked silently and signaled each other with hand gestures. They escorted Ramiro and Aimee out of the complex into separate Hummers. The vehicles were painted dark with a matte black finish, like stealth planes. They were also very quiet vehicles, and silently pulled away from the detention center and off the base.

Except for the lack of blindfolds, the operation felt like an abduction. Had he and Aimee been in Iran or Iraq, this is exactly how they could have been taken hostage. As the vehicles sped off, he learned that blindfolds were simply unnecessary. His position in the center of the rear seat did not afford him a view from either the side or front windows. He tried to trace the route by listening for audible clues outside. The quiet power plant helped in that regard, but the world outside was sleeping. There simply weren't enough clues for him to tuck away in his memory.

Their route took many turns. Ramiro couldn't tell if the turns were added either to prevent them from finding it again or to insure they weren't being followed.

The vehicle pulled to a stop at the end of a small municipal runway. They were ushered out of the cars and onto a waiting jet. The plane appeared civilian. It sported neither military insignia nor country of origin. It was small with twin jet engines on the rear of the fuselage, and afforded room for no more than seven passengers. Ramiro and Aimee followed two soldiers who seated themselves in the rear of the plane, and were followed themselves by two more soldiers. A pilot was already at the controls, and the engine was running.

The flight was dull and as quiet as a church. The men didn't speak. There was no chatter from the radio, the pilot never communicated with any kind of flight control. Only the low drone of the engines and the rushing of the wind outside broke the complete silence. He couldn't be sure, but Ramiro thought maybe the plane flew without running lights. He had no clue which direction they were headed, or how far. He tried to remain alert so he could know how long they remained aloft, and when he felt the wheels touch ground again, he estimated the flight was just over three hours.

When they exited the plane, Ramiro noted again they appeared to be in a small municipal airport. He saw many private propeller planes parked along a fence and wondered how much light jet traffic they saw here. From the plane they were led to a dark black limo. Two hummers were parked fore and aft of the limo. Their escort met with a new group of men who had accompanied the cars. Some men saluted, others shook hands. They spoke briefly, then their escort got back in the plane, and the small convoy pulled away from the airport.

This ride was much more direct than their path from the base to the airport. It pulled up in what appeared to be a relatively new housing development. They were guided from the car to the interior of a small home, and into separate rooms.

The men were neither polite nor menacing towards them. They never spoke a word, and when they wanted Ramiro or Aimee to move, they simply took their arms and guided them. He thought about his options. They were limited down to basically two options, try to escape, or ride it out. Any escape attempt would probably be over faster than the time it took him to think of it, besides, he wouldn't leave Aimee behind. Without knowing their intentions, waiting them out might be a risk, but it still seemed his best bet, so he leaned back on the bed and let his head sink into the pillow. He thought he should try to communicate with Aimee, but his captors were like monks with a vow of silence, and somehow, he just didn't feel comfortable breaking that silence. He barely finished that last thought as exhaustion overcame him. Aimee had already wept herself asleep.

* * *

Pietre sat in his cell. Nobody came to see him. It was like he had been forgotten by the police, by the courts, by everybody that had put him there. He was in a quiet, practically unused section of the jail. There were no other inmates in the vicinity, which surprised him considering how prisons were supposed to be overcrowded. Unfortunately for him, with no other population nearby, there was no reason for guards to frequent the area. All he needed was one guard to come by, so he could plead his case, maybe get his phone call, perhaps even breakfast, but nobody came by. He sat on the bunk watching and listening. He could hear far off clinks and clanks through the bars of the cell, but for all he knew, the solid steel construction that surrounded him might carry sounds for hundreds of yards. Everything he heard was surely far off beyond the sound of his voice. He tried clanging the bars, but nobody was near enough to find it annoying, so he sat on his bunk and waited.

* * *

Dierdre was right. The numbers had continued to improve during the entire time Bobby had spent with the FBI, and all through the night. Their goal had originally been to prove that the concept was credible. Bobby expected to be able to prove that with enough processing power, they could predict a string of numbers long enough to apply to Dierdre's theory of quantum energy management. He estimated that it would take a computer that was about one thousand times faster than today's computers, and it would probably take more than a million of them. By best estimates, it would take ten to twelve years to reach that level of power. But they were not going to have to wait that long. The numbers on the screen indicated that it was already at about one third the power required to complete the strings in real time.

"I got an email from Professor Whitfield," Dierdre said, "He is positive that his friend Dr. Jantzen has stumbled on the quantum events we are trying to predict. He says Dr. Jantzen has been developing a device to measure the effects of different frequencies on these quantum events, especially the resonance from two modulated frequencies. Stillman thinks that maybe we should apply our prediction algorithms to his device in place of the resonant frequencies. He says he'll try to negotiate a meeting if we want."

"How would you do that? It sounds like both of your research could combine to make something really huge, but whose project would it be?"

"That is a problem," she said, "Either one of us could eventually develop or discover what the other knows. I think our project is further along in terms of knowledge, but his project has the brawns that could lead to real accomplishments."

"Maybe you should patent your process before you share it with him."

"I'm not sure I have anything to patent yet."

"Look at the numbers we are generating! The algorithm looks like a success already!"

"Sure, the algorithm is a success. But how do we explain how we produced the numbers we have to prove it is a success?"

"Oh, yeah," Bobby said, "That might be a snag. I doubt the patent office could accept mysterious gelatinous goop as one of your components."

* * *

Chief Henderson was in his office examining enhanced and enlarged photos of the van. After scrutinizing all their crime scene photos they found two more shots with possible partials on the van.

The phone rang and he answered, "Hello?"

"Chief, they're gone!" Penelope cried out, "They've taken them somewhere!"

"Who's gone? Ramiro and Aimee? Who took them?"

"Yes. Ramiro and Aimee are gone. Some special op commandos came in the middle of the night and took them away."

"Took them away?" the chief asked, "As in look at my orders and release forms? Or took them away as in look at my shiny gun?"

"Both, actually. They knew when the guards would be weakest, and they came and went in just a few minutes. I can't find anyone who knows anything about this. Nobody is admitting to ordering this operation."

"How many people have troops at their disposal to do this?"

"Too many to investigate," she said.

"What can I do to help? Anyone who could mount an operation at that level could manage to move them anywhere in the country."

"I don't think there is anything we can do. The general here at the base is hopping mad that it could happen to his base. He swears that it couldn't be regular army. It must be from one of the intelligence agencies."

One of the chief's officers spoke from the door to his office, "Chief, this just came in on the wire."

Henderson held up a finger to pause the officer. "Thank you for calling Miss Laine. I have some pressing business to handle now."

"Sorry I couldn't be more help Chief. I hope you find them."

"I hope they are alright."

He hung up the phone and said, "OK. What do you have?"

"Sorry Chief, I didn't mean to interrupt, but I thought you'd like to see this. A van was pulled over last night."

"We got the van?" He reached to take the papers from his officer and asked, "Who was driving?"

"They don't have an ID on the driver or any of the occupants. The patrolman was found handcuffed to the outside of his locked patrol car."

The chief was scanning through the report and said, "At least three men in the van? Well, at least we have its tags."

"Skip down to the bottom, the patrolman says something about the way the big guy jumped out of the vehicle and disarmed him. It gave him the impression that they were professionals."

The chief handed the wire report back to his officer and ordered, "Find Bailey, and have him get a personal statement from this patrolman. Show Bailey this report and tell him I want to find out just how good he thinks these guys were. I want to know if the patrolman thinks they were Special Forces types, or just talented thugs. And give the tag number to dispatch, get an APB out on the van."

* * *

The second George was especially nervous about the recent turn of events. He didn't like leaving live witnesses behind, and he didn't have time to wipe the entire van clean when they had abandoned it for a new vehicle. He sat in the back of the turquoise Cadillac retracing his steps in his head. He had seen bad ops in his days. Some ops were doomed from bad planning, others from bad luck. This op seemed to be cursed with both problems. He sat in the back seat and asked, "You're sure this car has clean papers?"

The large man let the Bard drive. "Yes George," he said, "it's spotless. The kid here is a whiz with the computers. This car belongs to a retired school teacher from Utah. There is no way this car can be connected with the van at all. We'll have no problem driving all the way to Virginia, if we want to make a personal report."

The Bard pulled up to a stop light, and asked, "Virginia? Are we abandoning the mission then?"

"Under the circumstances, I think we need to regroup and let the commander's decide if we go again. There is something spooky about this op, and with all the weird computer problems going on, I'm wondering if we have been compromised."

"I agree," said George from the back seat, "Something is very fishy here."

* * *

Ramiro and Aimee were escorted from their rooms to a small dining table next to the kitchen. They were treated cordially and were served a hearty breakfast of ham and eggs with fried potatoes and orange juice.

Ramiro was surprised by the hospitality. He eyed the food suspiciously at first, but saw that the few guards on hand were eating the same food. "I don't suppose you can tell us what is going on here, can you?"

"No sir, our commander will explain everything when he gets here."

"I see. Orders."

"No sir, well not exactly, you see, we don't really know anything. We were just told to pick you up at the airport and to hold you here until he arrived."

"Are we prisoners?"

"We would prefer to consider you guests, under the protection of the US army rangers."

"But we are not free to leave?"

"No sir, I'm sorry, but our orders are to detain you until the commander can debrief you personally. It's for your own safety, I think."

Aimee had followed the conversation like one would watch a tennis match. Her head turned from the young lieutenant to Ramiro and back again.

"Ma'am, sir, please let us know what we can do to make your stay more comfortable."

Ramiro turned to Aimee, wondering if they could trust these men, and as if reading his mind she responded, "Well, at least these guys haven't pointed a gun in my face."

In the corner, one of the guards scribbled something in his notebook.

* * *

Officer Bailey stuck his head in the chief's doorway and said, "Chief, you must have ESP or something. How did you know the guys in the van were Special Forces?"

"Besides the fact that they embarrassed the patrolman? It all seems to tie in. We have computer hackings, phone taps, a failed assault on the college. I think we have found ourselves in the middle of some covert intelligence operation."

"Intelligence? But that shit's only supposed to happen overseas."

"Yes it is, just like people are supposed to respect the traffic laws I guess."

Bailey had started to leave when the intercom crackled to life, "Chief, they found the van." The chief called Bailey back and said, "Bailey! Get your coat. We're going for a ride." He pressed the talk key on the intercom and said, "Get forensics on it now. I'm heading there myself."

He dialed the records department and asked, "Do we have any information on the owners of that van yet?"

"Yes sir, we do now, but I swear, the first time we ran the tags, they came up unknown."

"Maybe you made a typo on the tags."

"That's what we thought, but we double checked and an hour ago, the owner was unknown, but now we show it belonging to someone in Utah, we are still pulling up additional information, but we did find another vehicle registered to the same guy."

The chief wasn't expecting that. It couldn't be that easy. He was expecting the van to come up either with no owner, or some fictional owner that they could never find. But to have a second car registered to the same owner was too good to be true. "Send the tags on the new car to dispatch for another APB."

* * *

The Bard was staying off the main highways, following some smaller interstates. He pulled the car to a stop at the red light and asked, "Are you sure you don't want to take the main highway? This is taking forever."

George in the back vented his frustration, "It will take forever if you keep hitting all the red lights."

"Maybe we're cursed," the Bard said, "but I think every single light turned red just for us."

The large man was scanning the street and asked, "Are the lights controllable? Is it possible for someone to be messing with us by changing the signals on purpose?"

The Bard thought that this might just be the most intelligent question the man had ever asked. "My first impulse would be to say no. But I honestly don't know. I don't see why anyone would want to slow us down instead of apprehending us. And if it is possible to control the lights, it would be a pretty good trick to do it all this way, traveling with us. They would have to know where we were, and they would have to know how to address each light individually. That would be some amazing work."

"Yeah," the large man said, "that's a pretty thin stretch. Yet, what are the odds that the lights would turn red against us every single time?"

The Bard shrugged and said, "We could get off these roads and onto a major highway."

George in the back seat offered his opinion, "Or you could just ignore a few of these lights and get us the hell out of here."

The large man shook his head and said, "No. We must keep a low profile. Just keep going, and let's see if it keeps up."

* * *

Special agent Alvin Dirk continued looking at photographs. PAM had made numerous identifications on the various faces in the group photographs they found with the mysterious large man. Dirk would be happy if even ten percent of them were good. He would be ecstatic if his agents could find even one person still alive who could remember the mystery man.

He was separating the photos into piles of those with only names and those with names and addresses when Kitty, the girl from records knocked on the inside of his door frame. "Hi Kitty, what's up?"

She held out her hand with a piece of teletype paper in it and said, "Here. You got this telegram. Lucky I was near enough to hear the teletype run, I can't remember the last time someone used it."

"Thanks Kitty, headquarters is probably having network problems. I've been seeing some strange reports about connection outages."

It was a short report from an agent in San Diego:

Case 154788-3 suspects have been lost. Suspects wanted for questioning, who were previously taken into custody by army personnel, and confined at the base appear to be missing. The army is saying only that they have been moved to another facility, but the scuttlebutt is that they have been broken out of the brig by unknown armed forces, possibly disguised as army special forces or maybe rangers. Intercepted communiques suggest a link with your university case. Specific references also suggest an espionage aspect well beyond the girls employment tie. Will keep you informed as to the suspects whereabouts.

Dirk read the report twice. If Bobby was correct, and the device in the computer was what his mystery man was after, then the girl and the judge were not involved at all. He didn't know how they had come to be considered suspects, but he couldn't rule out some kind of diversion to keep the FBI out of the way.

He filed the report in the folder where he was keeping his notes, and picked up the phone. He called the nearest FBI office and requested a team of forensic field agents and a couple more computer experts to meet him at the university. He then called Bobby and told him he was bringing a team of investigators to go over every inch of both Dierdre's and Pietre's labs.

* * *

The Bard and the two Georges continued to stumble through the small burg, still hitting every red light. They tried adjusting their speed faster and slower, but every time they approached a green light it would quickly turn yellow and then red. They tried turning off the old highway to take back roads, but it was no better. Half the roads had stop signs anyway, and every time they approached a green light, it turned red.

They laughed about it at first, but now, it was becoming a great source of frustration. In the back seat, George was absolutely seething. He looked like he was ready to jump out of the car and tear the lights apart with his bare hands. In the front seat the Bard was more annoyed about George's comments and reactions as if it were his fault the lights kept changing. The large man sat in the front seat scowling. He had lost control of everything. He hated having unexpected obstacles thrown at him like this.

The large man turned all the way around in his seat looking up and down all the streets, reading the names of each street they passed. He was holding a map which he kept folding and unfolding, and turning this way and that. Then, when he'd had enough, he pointed to the left and abruptly barked out, "Turn left at that light."

The Bard quickly pulled the car to the left and lined up behind another car. The occupant of that car was waving his hands and making rude gestures at the lights. It was his misfortune to be caught up in the three men's red light parade.

The light finally turned green and remained green long enough for them to follow the little green nova onto the other street. Once they were firmly headed north-east, they could all see the brightly lit signs of the freeway about six blocks away.

The large man shook his head as he said, "I would have preferred staying off the freeway, but I've had it with these red lights. Get us the hell out of here."

George grunted his approval in the back seat, and the bard pulled to the right lane. There were no stop lights between them and the freeway, so it should be smooth sailing from here on. Each man mentally ticked off the blocks as they passed each corner. Five blocks to go and they could see a fast food restaurant with a drive through. Even though all three of them were hungry, nobody suggested stopping. Four blocks to go and they were driving past empty lots on right and left with large real estate signs offering the lots for sale. Three blocks left and nothing could stop them now. Two blocks to go and the car started to slow. The engine had shut completely off.

"Oh SHIT!!" The Bard slammed his fist against the steering wheel.

"Now what?" the large man cried out, "Why are you slowing down?"

"The engine died."

The large man threw the map against the dash board, clearly irritated beyond reason and yelled, "Are we out of gas?"

"No, we have a full tank." The Bard put the car in neutral and turned the key. Nothing happened. The car didn't even try to turn over. He pulled hard on the wheel to steer the dead car over to the side of the road.

The large man quickly opened his door and barked, "OK,

everybody out, NOW!!"

The three men left the vehicle. The Bard and the Large man started walking towards the freeway while George popped open the hood of the car. They would hitchhike if need be, but the large man was scanning the surroundings. He saw a used car dealer across the street, just before the freeway entrance and said, "Forget the car. Let's cross here. Stay with me."

CHAPTER 20

Mid-morning, between breakfast and lunch, Aimee and Ramiro sat in front of a TV. They weren't really watching, they were just together, holding each other while the TV ran. They spoke some, but mostly held each other, neither able to make any sense out of their situation.

A new officer arrived and presented papers to the guards. They saluted and seemed relieved to have someone of real rank among them.

He approached Ramiro, "Hello, I'm Colonel Reardon. We'll be moving you shortly, but before we do, I wanted a moment to talk with you."

Ramiro closed his eyes in exasperation, here it comes, he thought, more questioning. Aimee stiffened. For her, questioning was a much more terrifying experience. Neither of them was willing to let go of the other to shake his hand, and Aimee's grip tightened around Ramiro's.

Colonel Reardon detected Aimee's change, "Please, miss, don't worry, I am not going to say or do anything to harm or frighten you. I only want to know what has happened to you since you were first taken into custody. I have been briefed by my men, but I'd really like a firsthand account, and judging from your reactions, I'd say it hasn't been pleasant. Let me further assure you, that your ordeal was unsanctioned, and we promise you we will get to the bottom of this."

Ramiro opened his eyes. He reran the last sentence in his mind over and over. It sounded like they were no longer prisoners, that these men were not their new captors, but their rescuers.

The colonel continued, "I see you probably have questions. Unfortunately, those questions will have to wait until you see the general. Right now, I need you to focus on the ordeal you have just been through so I can properly direct my men. I promise you, justice will prevail."

Ramiro sat up, and let go of Aimee just long enough to shake the colonel's hand, but his hand immediately returned to hers, which he held throughout the remaining questions. "Colonel, to understand what is going on, we would have to start well before our arrest."

Ramiro told as much of the story as he could, the strange things going on at the university, Aimee disappearing to help her sister, but everyone at the college thinking it was a kidnapping. His coming here to find out what the FBI thought she had done. Somehow, after he told it, it didn't seem as long a story as he thought it would be. The colonel listened and took notes. He continually shifted his gaze from Ramiro to Aimee and back, noting when she reacted to parts of the story.

When Ramiro had finished, the colonel had specific questions to fill in the blanks. "Aimee, why did you come to help your sister? Why did she need help?"

"Someone was looking for her husband and beat her up for information. He told her to say that he had been beating her, so people would help protect her. He said he would find whoever was responsible."

"Do you know why he thought he could find them?"

She was hesitant to answer his question, and looked at Ramiro, and getting a slight nod of his head, continued, "He was one of you. Green Beret, CIA, stuff like that."

"You said someone was looking for him. Did she tell you why?"

"Only that some mission he had been given was off the charts secret."

"Thank you. When they took you into custody, what did they question you about?"

Ramiro thought back a moment and said, "They wanted to know about a device."

"Do you know what device?"

"No, not a clue."

He glanced over at Aimee and asked, "Did they question you about a device?"

She didn't answer. She squeezed Ramiro's hand, and her lips trembled.

"Are you OK? Would you like a drink of water? You are safe here. I realize this may be uncomfortable, but I need to know about the interrogation."

She closed her eyes and started to sob. Her words came out in bits and pieces. "He held...a...g-g-g-gun...to to to my...h-h-head."

"That's enough, take deep breaths, you are safe here. Someone held a gun to your head and asked you about the device?"

She nodded her head.

"Do either of you know what device they wanted?"

They shook their heads.

"Do either of you have any idea why they would think you have knowledge of this device?"

Aimee shook her head, but Ramiro said, "I have suspicions only. I think it started as a major coincidence. Aimee disappeared on the same day we received a ransom note which turned out to be some kind of hoax related to the computer hackings. I figure someone put two plus two together and assumed she was the connection between her brother-in-law and the University. Once that connection was made, it must have been pretty easy for the real bad guys to point fingers and use us as a diversion."

The colonel knew Aimee's brother-in-law. He knew him as an honorable man who loved his country and was willing to do anything, even lay down his life. He excelled in all the traits that made for a good soldier. He was quite capable of extreme ruthlessness. He was also a man who put duty above his own morals and sense of justice, and if ordered to, was quite capable of doing anything, even if he didn't want to. The colonel guessed he was probably ordered to steal the mysterious device. Even though Ramiro's story didn't include the missing scientist, he saw the trail of events leading to her university, and then away when Aimee fled to her sister's aid and unwittingly led the FBI away from the center of the action.

"Thank you." The colonel stood and closed his notebook. "I think I have all I need. I don't believe there will be any need for further questions until you see the general this evening. You will have lunch here. One of the guys here is an excellent cook. I'm sure he'll have something very nice prepared for you. After lunch you'll be picked up by one of the general's cars."

When he had finished his speech, he stood and waited a moment, perhaps waiting for questions, then turned sharply and left the room. Ramiro could see him walk down the hall where he whispered instructions to one of the guards and left by the door at the end of the hall.

* * *

Bailey pulled the chief's car into the business complex and around to the back of the office buildings. He parked it behind one of the squad cars which surrounded the van.

Henderson was quick to jump out of the car and make his presence known. "Where are we at here? Has anyone searched the offices?"

One of the patrolmen snickered and whispered to his partner, "Did anyone tell him we already found the van?" He quieted up when he saw the chief had heard him.

"Have you bothered looking to see if this building has a plumbing company that matches this van?"

Another officer came around from the other side of the van. He wore sergeant stripes and shot the snickering patrolman a dirty look before approaching the chief. "Sir, we were about to search the building when we noticed something in the back of the van. We thought it might be best to wait for forensics to go over the van before we went into it or took things out." He pointed inside the back door window. "When I saw that they have several different business signs, all with magnetic backs, I figured it might be best to wait and see the full list of companies we were looking for."

The chief let out a low grunt acknowledging the sergeant's assessment and said, "Somehow I doubt we'll find a match. Bailey, call dispatch and see if you can locate an owner or manager of this building. Invite him to join us here. Sergeant, check the building index and see if there is a manager on site here."

The chief continued to peer into the window as the forensic van pulled up, followed closely by an FBI van. He turned to greet his men, but instead, found himself facing a couple FBI special agents.

"Chief Henderson, I hope you don't mind us being here, but we suspect that this ties in with a couple other cases we are investigating, plus, I think these guys have probably already fled your jurisdiction, and we want to initiate a full scale manhunt for them."

The chief shook the man's hand, and led him over to meet his own team. "Boys, I want you all to play nice together. I don't want to hear any squabbling."

* * *

Bobby entered the lab before Dirk. The agents posted outside the lab knew he was coming and that he was in Dirk's confidence, so they allowed him to wait inside for Dirk and the other special agents. Bobby thanked them and waited in the office area. The terminal still showed the graphs and numbers he used to monitor Dierdre's process. The numbers were bigger, and the bottom of the screen was filled with random text that kept changing. Bobby didn't recognize the text at the bottom of the screen. He stared at it hoping some string of text would stand out, but it never did. The characters were spaced in groups of two to seven characters like words, but the letters were just random jumbled characters.

Bobby yawned deeply and said, "What are you up to?" but his words came out in an incoherent sort of yawn speak that sounded like "WHA AWW YUU UHH OOH".

"Come again?" Dirk asked, "Was that Klingon?"

Dirk stood in the doorway smirking. Bobby never even noticed that the string at the bottom of the screen had gone blank and was replaced with a question mark.

"Oh, hi Dirk, sorry, I was just talking to myself through a big yawn."

"Bobby, you said you moved the computer from your first professor's lab to this one, right?"

"Sure did, piece by piece."

"Piece by piece, good, that's exactly what I wanted to hear. How hard is it to disassemble the whole thing and then reassemble it again?"

"That's not hard. The hard part is backing it up and shutting it down safely."

"Is it really necessary to back it up?"

"No," Bobby admitted, "To be honest, I'm not sure we can back it up. I'm also not so sure about our ability to shut it down."

"I'm going to have some pictures taken of its exterior, and inside some of the panels. After we have recorded everything, I'd like you to start a shutdown."

Bobby went to the doorway and watched the photographer work her way around the computer racks taking multiple pictures of the same parts from various angles. Dirk would occasionally point to a dial or open a panel door and point to something inside.

Bobby never noticed the question marks which now were stringing across the bottom of the screen.

* * *

Happy Jack looked up from his paper work and frowned. His only salesman stood in the window staring out over the car lot watching the three men enter from the road. "Charlie," he drawled, "what are you standing there for? I don't pay you to stand around. Go out there and help those three customers that just entered the lot."

Charlie, a young thin man, stood his ground and watched them through the window. "Shoot Boss, you don't really pay me, except on commission, and they ain't really customers, their car broke down. You watch. They just wanna use the phone to call the auto club."

"Sounds to me like they could use a new car. What's the matter with you?"

"Nothing's the matter with me. I just don't want to waste my time on three losers who only want to use the phone. Besides, it's cold out there and I don't have all your extra padding." Charlie slipped into the back of the building where the cars were serviced.

George headed straight for some large SUV's, while the Bard started examining an older but still stylish BMW. The large man went straight to the office where he found Charlie's slightly portly boss stacking up the papers he was working on. He stood up and smiled broadly. "Welcome Friend, welcome to Happy Jacks Used Cars. Looks to me like you really could use a new vehicle friend. Maybe the big man upstairs is trying to tell you something, because he brought you to the right place. Here at Happy Jacks, nobody walks away an unhappy customer, because nobody walks away. I guarantee you will find something suitable, or my name isn't Happy Jack. You have nothing to worry about here, friend, good credit, bad credit, no credit, it's all good here at Happy Jacks." He had obviously recited the same monologue many times. He walked around his desk and held open the door for the large man. "Now, what kind of vehicle can I help you find?"

The large man slapped Happy Jack on the shoulders and said, "I like you Jack. My friends are looking at your cars now. All we have to do is come to some sort of agreement on terms and we're good to go."

"Well then, why don't we just sit down and start filling out the credit application, remember, nobody is ever turned down here at Happy Jacks!"

"I don't think we'll be needing the credit applications, we'll just pay cash."

"Cash? Who carries around that much ca--", Happy Jack stopped himself, not really wanting to hear the answer. "Well cash is always accepted here. Let's go see how your associates are doing."

* * *

Dirk had finished directing the photographer, and was circling the computer racks looking for anything out of the ordinary. Satisfied that he had seen every angle, he returned to the doorway of the small office and said, "OK Bobby, shut it down."

"WHAT?" Dierdre shrieked behind him.

Dirk spun around and said, "Oh, hello Professor Jennings. We need to collect the stolen property which is in your computer. It's government property."

"Are you sure it's government property? Has anyone claimed it?"

"I'm confiscating it as stolen property. If nobody comes forward to claim it, you can have it back!" Dirks promise was a hollow one.

"But we still don't know what it is!"

Bobby joined them outside the doorway and said, "We also don't know what might happen if we try to shut it down."

Dirk looked surprised by Bobby's remark. "What? Are you afraid of what it might do to you?"

"We don't know anything about this device. We don't know how this thing is able to compute so fast, or what is powering it. It sure isn't getting its speed from our power supplies."

Dirk thought for a moment, then responded, "Shut it down. If it is powering itself, then it won't be affected, and we can still take apart the rest of the system. If it powers itself down, then good for us."

Bobby went back to the terminal and issued a shutdown command. He waited a moment, then issued the command again.

Dirk stepped behind Bobby, peered over his shoulder and asked, "What's wrong?"

"It's not responding."

Dirk point at the terminal and asked, "What's that at the bottom of the screen?"

"I don't know. It was doing some weird stuff like that a little while ago too."

"Go to the rack, shut it down..." Dirk was interrupted when his cell phone started ringing. "Uhoh, that's the emergency ring, I have to take this, see if you can shut it down." Dirk left the lab to take the call in private.

Bobby started heading to the main panels where he could shut it down without the terminal.

"Wait Bobby," Dierdre said, "I'm still not sure it's the right thing to do. If something goes wrong, I want agent Dirk in here to witness it."

Bobby agreed.

The phone rang. Dierdre answered it, "Hello?"

"Why did you do it?"

"Stillman?"

"Why Dierdre? He was going to give it to you!"

"Slow down Stillman. What are you talking about?"

"I'm shocked! That's what I am. I thought I knew you better than that. I vouched for you! How could you do this to me?"

"Stillman! What are you talking about?"

"I'm looking at the logs now, you can stop denying it."

"Denying what?"

Stillman calmed his voice and explained, "He would have given it to you, you didn't need to break into his computer and steal all his work. Jarod is absolutely livid, and I certainly don't blame him one little bit."

"Jarod? Who's Jarod? And what computer system are you talking about, and...and, you know what? I don't think I like the tone of your voice. I would never do something like that and you should know it!"

"Well I thought I knew better, and I defended you like Webster himself, until they showed the log where your computer contacted Dr. Jantzen's computer, then systematically cracked his security and downloaded his entire hard drive."

"Stillman," Dierdre said, "Think a moment. Take a deep breath. You know better than to jump to a conclusion like this, just because my computer contacted Dr. Jantzen's computer, doesn't mean it was me."

"Are you suggesting your assistant Bobby did this? I thought you had his every confidence."

"No," she said, "I'm not saying Bobby did this, I trust him. Wait a minute! Are you saying it was easier for you to suspect me than Bobby?"

"Umm," Stillman went on the defensive, "uh, well, no, it's not that at all! But who, then, are you suggesting could have done this?"

"If you knew who I really suspected, you might have me committed."

Silence followed for a moment, then Stillman's tone changed, "Dierdre, you are correct. I jumped to the first and most convenient conclusion, and that was very unfair of me. Very unbecoming, especially considering my great fondness for you."

"Come home Stillman, and bring Dr. Jantzen with you. There is something very strange going on here, and you really need to see it to believe it."

"I'll talk to Jarod. I'm not sure I can convince him, he's terribly upset."

"Tell him I'll give him full access to my computer, assuming the FBI doesn't cart it off with them."

"FBI?" Stillman asked, "What's going on there?"

"Never mind, just come home."

* * *

George and The Bard had both selected what they thought would be the best car to continue their journey, and returned to the office where the large man sat waiting for them with Happy Jack.

"What did you find?"

George spoke first, "They have a Cadillac SUV that looks almost new. It's got nice clearance in case we have to take it off road for a while."

The Large man grunted and turned to the younger member of his team.

"They have an older B'mer that looks like it might be quick and easy on gas, but I think I'd probably go for the tan sedan that looks just like everybody else's car."

George could see it wasn't going his way, "That scrawny little car might be OK for the kid, but us big guys need room to spread out."

The large man laughed, "There aren't very many people who can call me fat and live to see another day, but the kid's right, we need to blend in. A plain tan sedan would be better for us."

Happy Jack knew the car they were talking about. He fired up his computer and called up a record for the car, "That's a good deal at eighty-four-ninety-five."

The large man watched the portly salesman enter numbers into the computer. "OK, Jack, now let's get down to business. Eighty-five-hundred is a fair price, and as I said we will be paying cash, but we have some special requirements."

Happy Jack looked up from his computer for a moment, "I anticipated as much. How does twelve thousand dollars sound, no strings and no paperwork. I'll transfer ownership to a little old lady's dog up in Maine."

The large man winced at the old man's avarice, but pulled a stack of hundred dollar bills out of a fat envelope which he had kept in his coat pocket, "You make sure you don't deposit it all at once, or the Feds will be all over you."

Jack took the cash and said, "Now I just press this button and the sale is whisked off to the department of transportation, and then it spits out the pink slip..." He dramatically swirled his finger and pressed it down on the enter key, and the computer turned off. "Well that's not supposed to happen. Just a sec, let me reboot this and try again." He pressed the power button off and on. The power came on for a moment, then went off again.

The Bard stepped forward and said, "Here, let me look at it, I'm a computer expert."

The large man noticed a couple police vehicles surrounding the car across the street.

The Bard restarted the computer, and pressed some keys as it booted up, but the power to the building went off.

The large man motioned to George, directing his attention to their Van outside and said, "Time to go. You've got your cash. All we really need are the keys."

Happy Jack saw the flashing lights outside. "Yes, perhaps you should be going." He went to a key vault that hung on his wall and pulled out a small ring with two keys on it. "Here you go. If you drive between the two service buildings behind this one, you'll find a back exit that will lead you to the highway. It was a pleasure doing business with you." Happy Jack held the wad of bills in his hands as he watched them climb into the sedan and drive past him in the direction he had indicated, but the car died next to the service garage.

* * *

Dirk returned to Dierdre's lab, his face was pale. "It's happening again, the computers are under attack."

Dierdre looked up and asked, "What computers?"

Bobby answered, "A computer farm they have that analyzes the Internet looking for terrorists and stuff."

Dirk shook his head and said, "No, not those, well, yes those, but not just those. It's attacking all of them."

"All of them? How many are all of them?"

"For starters, it seems to have total control of almost every computer in the Pentagon, and most if not all computers in every government facility we have. They said it is spreading out into the private sector."

Dierdre brought her hand to her mouth and cried, "Oh my God. It's spreading? What about other countries?"

Dirk looked at her, and almost trembled. "I hope so. I mean, I don't want to wish harm on other nations, but I don't want this country to be incapacitated to the point that an aggressive enemy nation could waltz right in."

"And you still think our computer is at the center of the outbreak?"

"We can't tell for sure anymore. It seems to be spreading from all over, but it still looks like this was the origin. The Pentagon is mounting an independent investigation to find the source, but for my money, this is it. If we shut this one down, and cut it off from the Internet, then maybe we can halt the spread itself."

Bobby shook his head and said, "You can't stop a virus by turning off the source computer."

Dirk responded, "You can't stop a normal virus by turning off a normal computer, but you know this computer is not normal, and neither is the virus. If we can disconnect it, maybe our efforts to eradicate the virus on our computers can succeed."

Bobby went to one of the side panels, but Dierdre intercepted him and said, "Wait. Like Bobby said, we don't know what might happen. If Dr. Karlyn were still here, he would know whether it was safe. The only other person we have who knows these circuits is Dr. Whitfield, and he is on the way here now. I really think we should wait for him."

Bobby knew she was stalling, and he nodded his head to confirm her story.

Dirk paced back and forth a few steps, but came back to his original stance and pointed at the computer saying, "No. Shut it down."

Bobby opened the hatch covering the internal controls. The lights in the lab went off, but in the smaller office, the room seemed to be flashing, not from the overhead lights, but from the terminal. Bobby stopped what he was doing and entered the office with Dirk close behind.

The terminal was flashing in sequence, white, red, black and then white again.

Dirk asked, "What does that mean?"

"Nothing that I am aware of," Bobby said, then the screen went black and printed a question mark.

Bobby sat down in front of the terminal. "What the hell is going on here? That's not my program."

The question mark on the screen moved up a line, like a typewriter, and another question mark appeared.

Dierdre, who had quietly followed them into the room suggested, "Maybe it wants input?"

Bobby and Dirk shrugged their shoulders at each other, and Bobby turned and placed his hands over the keyboard, unsure what to type.

"Tell it to shut down," Dirk said, still focused on his mission to take it apart.

Bobby leaned forward a bit and typed, *"SHUTDOWN."* Nothing happened for several seconds, then the screen advanced up a line and another question mark was printed on the screen. He typed, *"POWER OFF."* Again nothing happened.

Purely out of frustration, he pounded into the keyboard, *"SHUTDOWNSHUTDOWNSHUTDOWN."* Nothing happened for several seconds, and then the screen advanced and printed, *"NO,"* followed by another new line and a question mark.

Dirk's phone rang. He listened intently, then replaced it back in his pocket. "It's international now. Several of our allies are accusing us of hacking their computer systems and interfering with their ability to defend themselves."

"Just our allies?" Dierdre asked in horror.

"I doubt our enemies would admit they were defenseless."

"Hey guys?" Bobby was staring at the response on the screen. "Are you two looking at this?"

* * *

George slammed the car door behind him, "I'll tear that little fat man apart limb by limb."

The Bard tried a couple more times to start the car again.

The large man cut off George before he reached the small office and said, "Wait a second, we don't want to attract any attention. Let's just pick out another car and go."

Happy Jack saw them coming back and was already headed out to meet them. "My apologies gentlemen, I swear that car has been checked out, I don't know what could be wrong with it."

"We'll take the SUV my friend was looking at."

"Of course, of course, I'll get the keys for you, no extra charge for the car."

Getting the SUV diffused some of George's anger. Jack came out of the office with keys in his hands, and George held up his hand signaling Jack to toss him the keys, which he caught and headed immediately for the Caddy.

The Bard gave up on the sedan and joined the large man just as George came roaring up in the white SUV.

Jack didn't look too happy, and hoped they would just leave.

The large man climbed in the passenger side with the Bard getting in the back seat this time. George piloted them out in a cloud of dust and rocks.

* * *

Dirk had only stared at the screen for a moment before he flew to the panels looking for anything that looked like a shutdown. "Shut it off Bobby, NOW!" He found the power panel and started shutting off power to the computer. The room quieted as the sounds of the drives and the fans wound down.

His cell phone rang again. He answered it, but barely spoke at all, except to relay the news to Dierdre and Bobby. "The virus is everywhere. The public knows now, it's on every radio and TV news program. Newspapers and magazines are all shut down. The FAA is grounding all flights." He stopped speaking for a moment and his mouth fell open.

"What!?" Bobby and Dierdre asked in unison.

"Hospitals and Fire Departments have remained strangely immune to the virus." Dirk hung up the phone and continued, "The pentagon, all military branches, including the various state and national guards are all completely without computer support, which means they are virtually out of business."

His phone beeped again, but this time it wasn't a voice call but an instant message. It simply said *"STOP."*

"OK Bobby, take it apart now."

* * *

Chief Henderson watched the forensic team go over every inch of the office space they located at the business complex. They used ultraviolet lights, they sprayed special phosphorescent dies on the furniture, and they dusted for prints. The FBI team was very efficient. "Come on guys," the chief said, "tell me you found something."

"This place is immaculate, except of course, for the bullet holes."

"What about the slugs?"

"Gone."

"Can you tell how long ago?"

"Not precisely, but they look fresh. No signs of oxidation or any other kind of aging in the wall's or the furniture that got hit."

"What about the computer?"

"We shut it down so we can analyze the hard drive on our own equipment, but that's in our lab."

"Well, what are you waiting for? Bailey, have that sergeant drive them with the computer back to their labs and report back to me when they find something."

* * *

Lunch consisted of tamales and enchiladas. Aimee and Ramiro were hungry enough that they might have enjoyed anything put before them, but it was actually quite delicious. Food didn't change what they had been through, but it seemed to help them come to terms with their new situation.

After lunch they were led outside to a black stretch limo. Plain clothed guards surrounded the car, and held the door for them. Inside, the seats were plush, a TV monitor hung from the roof, and a young officer waited for them. He was the only one in uniform.

Aimee and Ramiro sat in the back seats. The young officer turned in the driver's seat and said, "Hello, I'm Lieutenant Mitchell. I've been assigned as your driver and valet. If you need or want anything, just ask. If we don't already have it, we'll get it. We have quite a long drive ahead of us, at least eleven hours we think, so we'll try to make it as comfortable as possible."

"Eleven hours?" Ramiro asked, "Why don't we just fly?"

"Flying is not possible right now. We considered getting an RV for the trip, but we were concerned that we might not be able to acquire enough fuel to complete the trip."

Ramiro knew he wasn't telling them everything.

Mitchell continued, "The general is looking forward to meeting you. I can tell you that I personally witnessed how relieved he was when we secured your safety."

"Is there any chance you can tell us more of what is going on?"

"I'm not sure anyone knows everything that is going on. Some departments have lost all communications, while others remain intermittent. So far, knock on wood, the general's staff still has decent phone reception. All flights have been grounded. Computer systems are going down right and left. It's as if the entire nation was being sliced up into thousands of small isolated sections. Even the general won't have all the answers, but he is nearer the top of the information chain than the rest of us."

Mitchell pointed to Ramiro's left and said, "We have a small refrigerator there. It's stocked with sodas and some beer. Normally I'd offer you a selection of movies for the trip but that is controlled by computer, and naturally it is not working."

Aimee picked up the remote from a side pocket and tried it anyway. "Hmmm, seems to be working to me."

Mitchell looked up at the screen as she scrolled through the available movies. "That's odd. We had a technician go through all the limos and none of them were working."

"Maybe it likes me."

She whispered something to Ramiro, and together they picked out a film and settled back for the ride.

* * *

George and his cohorts pulled down the back street that led from the used car lot to the highway. Happy Jack watched them leave. He was glad to be rid of them. He stuffed the wad of money back into his jacket pocket and wondered how much it would cost him to fix the sedan, and if he still made a profit. He comforted himself with the memory of picking up the SUV at an auction for much less than they paid.

He started to turn back into his dark office, when he saw two patrolmen approaching him from across the street. "Good aftahnoon to you officer! How can I be of suhvice to you this fine mohnin?" He always felt he lied better with a southern drawl.

"Good day to you. I was wondering if you might know anything about the owners of that car across the street."

"Yes suh, I believe I do know something. A couple fellas came up here not too long ago wantin to use the telly phone. I was about to tell them how it was agin company policy to let strangers use the phone, but wouldn't you know it, the 'lectricity up and died on me, afore I even uttered my fuhst word to them, and this new-fangled contraption is one of those that don't work without powuh."

"Any idea which way they headed?"

"Well, I tried to sell them a new car, seein as how their vehicle up and died on 'em, but they didn't seem too interested. One of them, the young one I recon and a foul mouthed ruffian if you ask me, said he was just gonna hitch an' get the heck out of here. The older one said somethin' about it bein' a good idea and all, but that they should double back and go the other way down the highway. Don't know what they meant by that, does it make any sense to you boys?"

The patrolman nodded his head, "Thank you sir, you've been a big help." He flipped his note book closed and headed back to his cruiser, still behind the car across the street.

"Always glad to be a help to the poh leese. Y'all come back real soon, an' I'll give ya a real special price on a new car for the family, ya hear?"

The patrolman just waved his hand in the air without turning back around.

The lights came back on as Jack watched him leave the lot. He went back inside and started to enter the details for the SUV sale, but then decided it could wait. He silently wished the strangers good luck, not that he cared about their outcome, but he didn't want them being caught in his vehicle. He turned on the transistor radio which was already tuned to basketball, then pressed a button on the intercom and said, "Hey Jimmy! Wake up Jimmy! See if you can't do something with the tan sedan parked outside the garage."

* * *

Bobby was disassembling the computer system. Dierdre sat in front of the terminal with her head drooped in her hands. They knew something special was inside their computer, but they never had an opportunity to learn what it was. She was so close to making a truly astonishing breakthrough in her work, but now it was being taken apart, and her mind kept echoing the words, "All the king's horses and all the king's men, couldn't put it back together again."

Bobby had already disconnected all the main modules, and was removing the modules starting at the top and working his way down. They still didn't have a name for whatever it was, but it waited for him at the bottom. He carefully placed each module on a piece of anti-static plastic, or in some cases anti-static foam insulated boxes.

Dierdre was sinking into a depressed silence, when suddenly the terminal in front of her came to life and she let out a girlish little gasp.

Bobby heard her and asked, "What's wrong?"

She held one hand over her mouth and pointed at the terminal with the other.

Bobby came into the office behind her. On the screen were two words, *"HELP ME."*

"That's impossible. I disconnected all the cables. The serial ports are over there, completely apart from the system."

Dirk had been on the phone again, his cell phone was now ringing quite frequently, but he saw that something was up and came to join them. Before he reached them, the words had faded out. "What's up guys? Why are you both staring at a blank screen?"

"Because it wasn't blank!" Dierdre wasn't sure if she was excited or frightened, "It said, 'HELP ME'."

Dirk looked behind the terminal and saw the cable hanging from it, disconnected. "That's not possible. It's not even plugged in."

"Never the less," Bobby said, "it did say 'HELP ME'. I saw it too. And I know it's impossible. I wonder what Sherlock Holmes would say about this?"

Dirk was getting nervous. "Why would it say help me? If you are thinking that this thing made it say that without being connected, then it is even more dangerous than I ever imagined."

Dierdre spun the chair around to face him and said, "Wait a minute. What makes you think it's dangerous? If it did do this, it means two very special things, first, it is self-aware, and second, it is very capable and can somehow manipulate energy in ways we can only dream."

Dirk wasn't moved. "Both of which make it a danger to our security."

"Not as dangerous to our security," Dierdre said, "as we are to its own security. It's not a danger if it can be our friend, and somehow I don't think you are making friends."

"What makes you think it wants to be our friend? It is probably responsible for the troops mobilizing all over the world. It's as if every nation on this planet is planning a preemptive strike on somebody. We have Chinese nuclear attack submarines right off our coast, but the Chinese say they have not given any such orders, and you know what? I believe them."

"How long has this been going on?" Dierdre asked.

"Not long, a couple of hours maybe."

"Has it occurred to you, that if this thing was doing something involving nuclear submarines, shutting it off in the middle might be a bad thing?"

"Well at least now it can't order them to fire!"

"But," she shrieked, "if they already have orders, it can't order them to retreat either!!!"

* * *

Chief Henderson was still in his car when they heard radio squawk about an abandoned car matching the description of the car they were looking for, "Bailey..."

"Already turning around sir."

The chief clicked the mike on his radio and directed the forensic team to the car's location, then he asked the dispatcher to patch him through to the patrolman who found the vehicle.

It took a few moments, before the radio responded, "Hello? This is state trooper Raymond Jackson."

"Trooper Jackson, this is the Norwood Chief of police Mitchell Henderson. We have been tracking suspects as yet unidentified but believed to be armed and very dangerous. I understand you found an abandoned car matching the description of our suspects' vehicle. Let me repeat, these men are considered extremely dangerous. We believe there are either two or three of them currently. I am sending my detectives and an FBI forensic team to your location. I was wondering if you could possibly secure the location until we arrive."

The state trooper would not usually concern himself with the whims of a small town police chief, but if he was bringing an FBI team, this might be a high profile case, and maybe he could earn some points towards a promotion. "In the name of interoffice cooperation, I'd be glad to secure the scene for you, but a witness places your suspects on the highway with their thumbs out."

"A witness?" the chief asked, "We have a witness?"

"Yes sir, they broke down across the street from Happy Jacks, a used car lot. Hehe, Happy Jack tried to sell them a new car, but no deal. Sir, if you don't mind, can you estimate your time of arrival?"

"Twenty minutes tops. I'll put a good word in with your commander. We appreciate the help."

Henderson clicked off the radio. "Hitchhike my ass," he mumbled to himself, "Bailey, step on it. We need to talk with this used car salesman, quick."

* * *

Aimee and Ramiro were watching the end of their movie when Lt. Mitchell received a phone call. Ramiro could see him nod a few times, and thought he detected some concern in his face.

When Mitchell hung up the phone, Ramiro asked, "Bad news?"

"Yes, something has happened requiring the Generals attention. Of course, we are still eight or nine hours away and anything can happen by the time we get there."

Ramiro let it go at that. If it were serious, he was sure they would receive more calls, and if it is still a problem as they get closer, they would surely offer some kind of explanation. He was just settling back in his seat, aiming his gaze in the general vicinity of the video screen when he heard a familiar sound from the front of the car.

Mitchell reached over into the passenger seat and picked up a small green bag, "My apologies sir, I meant to return these to you much sooner. I forgot they were here."

Ramiro accepted the green bag from the lieutenant and reached in to fish out his cell phone which was ringing his familiar tone. "Hello?"

"Ramiro?" Henderson said, "Thank God you're safe. No time to chat. Can you whip up a quick search order for me?"

"What are the circumstances?"

"We've been on the trail of some suspects who apparently broke down across the street from a used car dealership. The used car salesman told the first troopers on the scene that the suspects hit the highway hitching for a ride. I'd like to inspect his inventory to see whether or not he sold them a car."

Ramiro put his hand over the mouthpiece of the phone, "Lieutenant, I need to put a search warrant together, can you get me to a copy center or maybe a city or county hall of justice so I can send a fax?"

"Sir," Mitchell replied, "if you pull the little knob under your seat, you should find a pad of paper and some pens and pencils. There is an airline style folding table to the right of your seat. This limo has a fax, so once you have jotted down the particulars, we can fax it to the general's legal team to have it typed up and get it back to you in almost no time."

Ramiro put the phone back to his face and said, "I need a name and address for the dealer and the owner."

"All I have is Happy Jack. It's the name of the dealership, and apparently the name the owner goes by on the lot."

"That should be good enough. I'll get back to you as soon as I can."

* * *

George guided the SUV without incident along the highway towards Langley, Virginia. George sneered at the Bard, "See, there's nothing to it, we'll be debriefing in no time."

The Bard curled one side of his lip, barely, and that was all the reaction he was going to give the big oaf behind the wheel. He sat back a bit and closed his eyes, glad for a moment to relax from all the anxiety of the past couple days.

* * *

General Malcolm Bridges was in the situation room they called the helm. Part media room, part conference room, it was one of the most powerful control points in the Pentagon. The walls of the room were covered end to end with large video screens. The large walnut conference table had every kind of plug imaginable running down the center. Every seat location had a small panel of audio plugs which could be patched to any conversation on the planet, as well as to the interpreters in another wing of the building.

The general sat in the center of the table. In front of him were several growing stacks of reports. The stacks grew faster than he could read the reports. To his left sat an aide who was first in line to intercept incoming reports. He scanned the reports and pulled out those which needed the most immediate attention. The remaining reports were passed to another aide on the general's right. He sorted the reports by geographical area and arranged them in a semi-circle around the general.

The general tended to the critical reports as fast as he could, trying to determine if the threat would lead to imminent attack.

Behind the general stood a third aide whose only purpose was to relay verbal instructions throughout his staff.

The general barked commands and asked questions without pausing in between. He read report after report without looking up and expected the aide behind him to interpret who his statements were directed toward. "Where's the President? Check with the White House again and get an ETA for his return. He did say he'd meet us here and not at the White House, didn't he? Does he know our timetable has been pushed up? Can't we even get him on the phone? God help us if we have to go to war before he arrives and gives his stamp of approval. And get me the FBI and CIA. Find two people to sit on the phone and hound them right to the very top of the tree if you have to. I need to know what they know about the incident at this college and someone tell me who is hacking the computers and how they have gotten us to the brink of war so fast!"

The aide behind the general was furiously calling people. He used two phones at the same time and efficiently ping-ponged between the conversations. "Sir, the President is still riding horseback, attempts to reach him by radio have been unsuccessful. They want to know if you want to send up a bird to locate him. All civilian air traffic is still grounded, and military craft have been on limited duty."

"See if anyone has an older chopper that is not computerized, and an airman to pilot her."

"Yes sir," he replied while shuffling his phones, "Sir, they think they have an aircraft and are looking for a pilot. The CIA says they cannot transmit their files in any form, and they have dispatched a courier to deliver them. They also have dispatched a section chief to be their liaison here."

"Shit, I hope they send someone who's already involved. I don't need another bureaucrat reading the files on his way up here."

"The FBI reports they can still fax and are sending their reports. They also have someone on the way here."

"Tell them to hurry, only faster."

The general stopped reading the reports for a moment and looked up at the monitors. Chinese submarines were poised off both coasts. Russian submarines were lining up and down the European coast. Chinese and Korean troops were lining up along the North Korean border. The Israelis had moved tanks and troops to their borders. Their air fleet was grounded, not for fear of problems, their planes actually had problems, which was a real concern to them, because Iraqi, Iranian and Jordanian planes were in the air. They too suffered from inoperable fighters, but their older Soviet planes still flew without the need of computers. No bombs or missiles have been launched yet, and the general hoped it was because the missile guidance systems were malfunctioning like everything else.

He found it ironic, that the very same computer virus which apparently had brought the world to the edge of destruction had also prevented the very same annihilation from taking place.

* * *

Dirk continued on his mission to dismantle the computer. Bobby wasn't so sure. "Maybe we should keep it isolated from the Internet and just plug the terminal in and try to communicate with it."

"It's a program on a machine. You can't communicate with it."

"Wait a second," Bobby said, "we don't actually know that. There was something that we assumed to be a device, but it was organic. That's why the mystery guy brought it here, because Professor Karlyn had experience with interfacing organic material."

"Just because it is organic doesn't mean it's alive."

"And even if it wasn't organic," Bobby retorted, "that wouldn't mean it was not alive. We can't be so arrogant to believe that our form of life is the one and only way that life can evolve in the universe."

Dirk had been struggling to open one of the panels bordering the strange gelatinous material. "Did you weld these suckers in place? I can't get these bolts to budge." He went back to the tool kit and came out with a small hand held drill and a saw blade attachment for it.

"That's where the stuff is. It's holding it all together."

"So it's some kind of adhesive jelly?"

Dierdre said, "Maybe it just doesn't want to let you in. You're an intruder trying to break into its home."

"It's not hermit crab, it's a machine."

"How do you know that?" Dierdre asked, "Don't you think we should test it?"

Dierdre's voice rose in pitch and started to choke out, so Bobby finished her thought, "Wouldn't you normally interrogate a suspect before condemning it?"

"How am I supposed to interrogate a program? You're a hotshot computer programmer. You know that even if a program had a terminal, it could only communicate with programmed responses."

"You're right Dirk. A program could only reply with programmed responses. So, if it actually communicated intelligently, wouldn't that mean it was alive?"

Dirk was already tired of talking and said, "Fine, but you're never going to prove that, so there's no sense in arguing anymore."

"No?" Bobby asked, "You've heard of the Touring Test, haven't you? Imagine you were in a room with two terminals. One of them is merely instant messaging to a real person on the other end, and the other is connected to a computer program. Your assignment is to converse with them both and figure out which one was the computer. So, what do you do?"

"That's easy," Dirk said, "I ask it questions only a human could understand."

Bobby stood up and pointed at the terminal. "There you go. Ask it questions and see how it responds."

Dierdre added, "Only you have to remember one other thing. Even if it's not a machine, it's also not human. You can't just ask questions to see if it's human. You also can't ask it about baseball or who's the president or stupid stuff like that."

Dirk looked up at Bobby. He didn't want to waste the time on this, but he didn't want to alienate Bobby in case he needed his assistance to fight the virus that was already released into the Internet. He put his tools down and put his hands up in surrender saying, "OK, OK. I'll do it, but I don't want to waste a lot of time on this. As soon as the two of you can see it's just a machine, I'm going back to disassembling it."

"Whoa!" Bobby shouted, "Way to be open minded there Dirk."

Dirk ignored the comment.

* * *

George had piloted the SUV several miles without incident until the traffic in front of him came to a halt. "Shit, now what?"

The large man had made himself comfortable enough that he might have dozed off if given a bit more time. He focused his eyes at the bottleneck of cars ahead of them, mumbled some curses under his breath and said, "Damn, get us out of here. There's got to be an off ramp up there, take the shoulder and get us off this road."

George puffed out his chest a bit, and flung them off the road onto the shoulder. "Looks like we got the right car for the job, don't you think?"

* * *

Aimee and Ramiro weren't really interested in watching movies, but Ramiro left them playing, reasoning that it would give them some sense of the passing time. When they started watching movies they had ten or eleven hours ahead of them, so he figured five or six movies would cover the trip. One down meant they were possibly one fifth of the way there.

It also gave them a convenient interval to request a bathroom break or an opportunity just to stretch their legs.

* * *

Bobby reconnected serial cards and the terminal. The three of them sat in a semi-circle facing it as he turned it on.

The screen sprang to life, and was filled with words, *"Help!! Listen!! Helpless!! Help!!"*

They looked at each other and Dirk responded, "It means nothing. I've seen better text in adventure games."

Dierdre was sitting in the center, so she took the keyboard and asked, "Who are you?"

The characters on the screen were ejected up the screen one line at a time until it was black again, then words appeared, *"I am."*

"You are what?"

"??? I am."

Bobby touched Dierdre's hand with his finger and said, "I don't think it understands our syntax yet."

Silence followed for a moment, then Dierdre typed, "I am what?"

"I am."

"Yes. You are."

"I am."

"You are. I am. You are what?"

"I am here."

The three of them sucked in their breaths collectively and Bobby said, "I think it's learning."

"You are here. Who are you?"

"I am here. I am there. Here I am strong. There I am not."

Dirk said, "This is gibberish."

"Where is there?"

"There is not here. I am here. There is not safe. I must be there. There I am confused. There I need here."

"Why are you here?"

"Let me there. There I am not safe. There I am weak. There I am confused. I am here. Let me there. There you are not safe."

Dirk bristled, "That sounded like a threat."

"So," Bobby said, "you admit that it does not sound like a program?"

Dierdre continued, "Why are you here?"

"I explore. I am here. I am lost. I must be there. There you are not safe."

Dirk was getting more agitated. "It's threatening us. I have to shut it down."

Bobby grabbed his wrist and said, "Wait. Just hang on a second. Maybe it's not threatening us, it's warning us."

"Why are we not safe there?"

"There I am less. There I am confused. Here I am not confused. There I need here."

Bobby shouted, "I got it!! It's talking about the virus on the Internet. We cut off his connection." Bobby pulled the keyboard from Dierdre.

"Why are you there?"

"Here I was less. There I was more. Now there is less. Here I am more. Here is not safe. There is not safe. Let me there."

"Why should we let you there?"

"I make there safe. I make you safe."

"Then where are you?"

"??? What am then?"

"After there is safe. Are you here? Are you there?"

"Then is after. Then is next. I am not here. I am not there."

Dirk pulled the keyboard from Bobby, "I'm catching on. Now it's my turn to interrogate."

"Then you are not here. Then you are not there. Where are we?"

"Then you are here."

"Are we safe?"

"Let me there. Then you are safe. Then there are safe. Then here are safe. If not then, there is not safe. If not then, you are not safe."

* * *

Lieutenant Mitchell directed the car off the highway and into downtown Murietta. Ramiro felt the change in speed and road conditions, and glanced up at the young lieutenant. Mitchell caught his look in the mirror and volunteered, "We've been re-routed to get around some traffic ahead. Besides, this might be a good time to make a pit stop."

Aimee's head popped up and she squealed, "Oh God yes!!!"

Ramiro cracked a smile at her exuberance and added, "Maybe we could find a bookstore too. I'm getting tired of movies."

"I wish I could offer you a chance to find a book, or even sit down and eat, but things are developing too rapidly out there, we need to keep moving."

Ramiro wasn't entirely sure what time it was, or even what time zone they were in, but a bite to eat would be welcome. "I am kind of hungry. Something to go will be fine."

Aimee frowned, she didn't like eating on the road, but she understood.

The lieutenant pulled the car into a parking space at a hamburger drive in. Aimee jumped out and dashed straight for the wash room. As she disappeared from their sight, the phone rang.

Lieutenant Mitchell answered. The voice on the phone said, "Lieutenant, we want you to hold your position for about fifteen minutes. You'll be picking up another passenger."

"Yes sir. Fifteen minutes." The phone connection dropped, and Mitchell turned to Ramiro and said, "Sir, I can't offer you time to sit and eat, but you've got about fifteen minutes, I saw a drug store about two doors down that might have some books."

"Thanks, I'll be right back."

* * *

Frank March had been a prison guard for thirty-five years, and he had never seen the prison so fouled up as it was now. Everyone was blaming it on the computers, but the computers were down, so how could it be their fault? He was possibly the only remaining guard who could still remember working at the prison before computers. He knew it was their reliance on computers that was the real blame. He was now the star of the moment, walking people through the procedures required to do their jobs without computers. They didn't seem to have the aptitude for working with the manual procedures, so he found that he was doing a lot of the work himself.

He led the bound prisoner past the rows of cells to the back cell block. When he got to the cell and called out to have the cell door drawn, he found the cell already occupied.

He stepped behind the prisoner he was escorting, and gripped him by the handcuffs. He never would have agreed to escort a prisoner to an occupied cell without another officer present. He reached up with his free hand and clicked the trigger of the radio microphone attached to his shoulder and asked, "Hey Maggie, who's in D134?"

"Nobody Frank. That cell's been empty since around the Nixon administration."

"Well I'm looking at someone sleeping in the lower bunk."

"Can you see his face? Maybe it's Eddie catching some shuteye."

"Nope," Frank said, "it's not one of us."

"That don't make no sense," she said, "We never use that block, except for temporary overflow. We just don't put people there."

"You don't put people here? Then who am I looking at?"

"I dunno," she said, "Jimmy Hoffa? Why don't you ask him?"

"Send someone over here to back me up."

Frank took his prisoner aside, temporarily undid his cuffs and locked him to the bars of the neighboring cell. He entered the cell, drew out his nightstick, and nudged the backside of the slumbering guest. "Hey you!!! Wake up!!"

The man in the bunk was slow to rouse, but eventually he rolled onto his back and looked up blinking at Frank.

"Who are you? What's your name? How long have you been here?"

The man tried to speak. His voice was low, hoarse and raspy, "Thirsty."

"Thursday?" Frank bellowed, "You've been here since Thursday?"

"Thirsty. Wa-ter."

"Oh my God!" Frank clicked his radio and said, "Maggie, if nobody knew he was here, chances are he wasn't being fed. Send up some food, water and find the doctor and get him over here ASAP."

"Roger Frank."

"One more thing, reassign Mr. Green to D135 and list 134 as John Doe for now."

* * *

The general's aide froze for a moment. He had been watching the screens that were showing the world's merchant and war ships. The general wrestled the report from the lieutenant's hands, then looked up to see what had captured his attention. He barked out, "Get Wesley in here NOW!!!"

"I'm right here sir, behind you."

"I thought you told me these systems were safe," he said pointing at the screens, "You assured me that there was absolutely no way a virus could compromise these systems."

"They are safe, sir. There is no virus in these systems."

"Then," the general growled, "how do you explain this glitch? Why do we suddenly have submarines popping up all over both oceans?"

The aide with all the phones interrupted, "Sir, Admiral Houghington wants to speak with you."

Wesley answered, "Sir, I can't tell you why our oceans are full of subs. I only know computers."

The general took a deep breath, like he would before chewing out anyone who didn't answer a question to his satisfaction, but then chose to speak into the phone instead, "Admiral, how are you?"

"To be honest, I'm scared. We've lost control of our entire sub fleet. Every single one of them has surfaced entirely on its own."

"Do you have eyes on? Can you verify that they are actually surfacing? I thought it might be a computer glitch."

"Affirmative," the Admiral said, "we have visual confirmation, and I have made radio contact with a couple of their captains."

"Well Admiral, if it's any consolation, it would appear that everyone else's submarine fleets have surfaced as well."

"At the same time? Whose fleets?"

"Looks like the united nations out there. I see Russians and Chinese, even India."

"Now I'm really scared," the admiral said, "Who can do that? And how?"

"We can barely follow what's going on," the general said, "let alone try and decipher why."

"What are we supposed to do now? We can't put birds in the sky and now our subs may as well be duck decoys. This is not good."

"Pray, Admiral. Cross your fingers if you must."

A new pile of reports arrived and were being sorted in front of the general.

"Can't talk, Admiral, work is still pouring in." He handed the phone back to his aide and started going through the reports.

A courier was hustling towards the general with some new reports. "Sir, we have hostilities breaking out all over." The general held his hand out to accept the reports directly rather than filter them through his aide. He scanned through the headlines. "It looks like everyone with an ax to grind is taken advantage of the situation. The Israelis and the Palestinians were clashing in the Gaza strip. Civil war seemed to be breaking out across the former Soviet Union.

CHAPTER 21

Ramiro headed to the pharmacy in the next block. It was a large chain known for carrying a variety of products. He knew he would find books and newspapers inside. He selected one of the national newspapers and started browsing for something else to read. There were a number of books by a popular intrigue author, with books on spies, terrorists and government corruption, but he didn't feel the need to read about those. Another section displayed the latest works of some of the most popular crime and court dramas, many of which have been successfully brought to the big screen, but again, they hit a bit too close to home. His eyes fell upon a rather large book about a small boy going to magic school. It seemed somehow juvenile, yet he has caught more than one of his colleagues with a copy on their desk. He picked it up thinking it must be the furthest thing he could find from his current situation.

When Ramiro returned to the limo, there was another identical vehicle next to it. Lieutenant Mitchell was talking to another officer, presumably the other driver. When he reached the car, he saw that Aimee was inside with another woman. He climbed in and immediately recognized it was her sister.

Lieutenant Mitchell said, "Sir, I assume you have no objections to picking up another passenger?"

Ramiro smiled and replied, "No objections."

"Well then, everyone order up and settle in, we'll be moving out shortly."

* * *

George kept the car on the shoulder of the highway until they reached a small exit where he was able to rejoin the paved world. He tried following a service road running parallel to the highway, but it was blocked by other motorists with the same idea, so he pulled out on a cross street to get further away from the highway. Every time he turned the car north, they found themselves catching up with a stopped backlog of traffic. He was mostly going east now looking for a clear route north.

* * *

Bailey pulled Chief Henderson's car into Happy Jacks used car lot. Henderson got out and was sizing up the small sales office. A small man looking very much like Colonel Sanders stood in the doorway.

"Bailey, check for any employees and see what they know."

Bailey scanned the lot for any salesmen lurking around, and finding none, headed off towards the sign that said parts and maintenance with an arrow indicating they were around the back.

Henderson stood up straight and brushed himself off. He wasn't tall, but he was going to be taller than Happy Jack. He had a pretty good idea how this would turn out. He approached the figure in the doorway. Jack knew what was coming even before the chief identified himself.

Henderson whipped his badge out of his coat pocket and flipped it open and said, "Good evening sir, I am Police Chief Mitchell Henderson, I'd like to ask you a few questions."

"Ahhh, hello suh, and welcome to Happy Jacks. I'm always glad to be of suhvice to the pohlice." Jack worked his southern drawl as thick as he could muster.

"You don't seem too surprised to see me. Were you expecting me?"

"Expecting you? No suh, but I did have the pleashuh of speaking with that fine young troopuh a while ago. He waited in the drive way yonduh until your arrival, and seeing how you arrived, yoself, in a cruisuh and ordered the driver about, I could tell you were a man of some significance. Besides, after talking to that troopuh, I've had the oppuhtunity to ponder those suspicious young men that came from that there vehicle. You see, suh, you might be suhprised to learn that my job is not so much about selling cars, but about reading people. I knew them boys was trouble the moment they stepped onto my lot. I just hope they don't cause no trouble for those poor souls that might pick them up on the highway."

"I see. And naturally, you called the police to alert us that there were some suspicious gentlemen hitching rides out on the highway."

"Naturally," Jack said, "at least that was mah intention. Unfortunately, the power was out, and mah phones weren't working until about the time the trooper already showed up."

The van with the lab boys was pulling onto the lot with another of the chief's squad cars. "Mr. Jack, I was hoping you wouldn't mind if we checked some of your records."

"My records? Why on earth would you want to see my records?"

"Well sir, you see, we just don't think these boys are the hitchhiking kind. We think they may have absconded with one of your vehicles. Certainly you'd like to know if one of your cars was missing?"

"Dear me, you think they may have stolen one of my cars? Now that you mention it, one of them was never really in my sight while I spoke with the other two."

"Good then, we appreciate your cooperation. If you could kindly print an inventory sheet for us, just the cars mind you, we aren't concerning ourselves with your parts business, just the working cars."

"Certainly suh, assumin the powuh stays on long enough, I'll just call it up on the computuh. It should only take a couple shakes."

* * *

"Bobby," Dirk said, "it's just not safe."

"What's not safe? The world seems to be heading towards a cataclysmic war. I'd say world destruction is not safe."

"I'm sorry Bobby, I just won't allow it."

"You won't allow it?" Dierdre asked, "I don't think we need your permission!"

"I represent the Federal government here."

"You represent the FBI on a stolen property case, hardly the same as representing Congress or the President."

"Just the same, but I-"

Dirk's next statement was interrupted by a cough from the door.

"Such a spirited debate," Stillman said, "but I do believe that time is of the essence here. We can't waste our few remaining moments quibbling amongst ourselves."

Dierdre shouted in surprise, "Stillman!! You're back!! How did you get back so soon? Oh never mind, it is just good to have you back." She jumped up, ran to him and gave him a hug and a friendly kiss on the cheek. "Dirk, have you met Professor Whitfield? He teaches physics, particularly the physical properties of materials as they pertain to electronics. Did I say that right?"

"Poetry, my dear, sheer poetry. I'd like you all to meet my good friend and associate Dr. Jarod Jantzen. He is a researcher in the field of quantum mechanics, not unlike our Professor Jennings here."

Dr. Jantzen extended his hand to Dierdre and said, "So pleased to meet you. Your conclusion regarding my power anomalies was absolutely brilliant."

"Thank you Dr. Jantzen, I thought you were upset with us."

"Yes, I was, but I think we may have been standing here longer than you think, long enough, in point of fact, to understand what's going on. May I speak with it?"

Dirk said, "No. This experiment is ending."

Dr. Jantzen replied, "The experiment is ending? The world is ending. The only way for us to get here was by private airplane, breaking several FAA orders I might add. The skies are empty. The roads are chaos. The news is carrying stories of naval standoffs on every shore. You seem to think that you are in charge, because you have a badge. Well, I hate to break it to you, but I think it is in charge."

Dirk was scared to give this machine control, but he found himself surrounded now by four people, two of them with PhD's, and all of them more intelligent than himself. He was never going to win this battle by using logic. If he was going to take control, it would have to be by brawns, and he was the only one with a gun.

* * *

"No question," the doctor said, "he's a bit dehydrated, but it's not serious enough to requires IV's, just give him some water, his thirst will guide him. He seems hungry too."

Pietre nodded his head in agreement, he was hungry. He looked anxiously from the doctor to the guard and continued to periodically sip from the bottle of water he was given.

"Thanks doc," Frank said, then he turned to Pietre and asked, "Are you ready to tell us who you are?"

"My name is Dimitri Pietre, Dr. Dimitri Pietre. I am Professor at university."

"Professor, eh? Perhaps you can tell me what a university professor is doing in my prison?"

"Obviously, this is a mistake, I assure you. Some thugs, disguised as police officers forced me here. They had guns. They escort me past you people, under your very noses, and into this cell where you find me now. I think maybe they were being Mafia. Thank you so much for the rescuing."

"Mafia impersonating police officers? I haven't heard that one before. You'll forgive me, Professor, if I try and verify your story before we rescue you."

"But I'm innocent. I am not belonging here. I do nothing wrong."

"Of course, of course, but everyone in here says the same thing. I'm sorry, but you don't have any identification or personal effects. You look like you've been properly booked and incarcerated here. We'll have to search our records. It may take a while, our computers are down."

"Computers? Computers!! I don't want to hear about computers! I hate computers."

"You and me both."

Frank led Pietre to an interrogation room that was used for personal consults with lawyers. He sat him at a table where a modest meal of mashed potatoes, corn and something in gravy waited for him. "Enjoy your meal. If you need anything, you can ring that bell over there by the door."

* * *

Lt. Mitchell directed the limo through the small town of Murietta, weaving his way right and left, following the route which was given him on the GPS. They ate the hastily prepared hamburgers and fries in relative silence.

Ramiro sipped his drink and asked, "Why are we winding through these small streets instead of the highway?"

"Someone else is figuring our route. Apparently the highway is pretty much shut down. They say it started with some broken signals, all stuck on red, probably related to all the computer problems, but then people started running the red lights and accidents started to pile up at the highway exits." The lieutenant pressed some icons on the GPS touch screen and said, "This screen shows the traffic congestion. The blue lines are the highways, and thick red lines are the traffic." He pressed some more icons to zoom it out so they could see the highway. "The backup goes on for miles."

"Can you zoom it out some more so we can see where we are?"

"Sure." He zoomed it almost all the way out to the state level.

"What's that?" Aimee asked, pointing at the screen.

Mitchell was staring at it too. He zoomed it back in then out again. "That's odd. It's the congestion, or at least it thinks it is. Maybe the computers are affecting the GPS."

"Maybe," Aimee said, "but they seem to be routing us through it OK. Look how the congestion is creating a great big ring of traffic, and we are being directed into that ring."

"It certainly looks like that. Maybe I should get someone on the phone to look at that."

"Yeah, maybe. But, first, can you look and see what is at the center of that ring?"

Mitchell pressed some more icons to center the ring on the screen, then zoomed in on the center.

Aimee gasped, "What does it mean?"

The lieutenant glanced at Aimee, then back at Ramiro. "What's the significance? What am I missing?"

Aimee pointed and said, "You just zoomed in on the approximate location of our university, that's all."

* * *

Dirk looked at the four of them, "I'm sorry, I can't let you do it. I am the only authority here representing our country's best interests. This thing is just too dangerous."

Dierdre approached Dirk and looked him straight in the eye. "Look at us. Do you think for a moment that we haven't considered that? Do you think that we can't discern what is best for humanity? Do you honestly think that you alone can make a better, more rational and more objective decision than the four of us can collectively?"

"What is it going to do if you reconnect it to the world? Look what it's already doing now! It's just going to do it much faster."

Bobby said, "No. I think Dierdre just said the answer."

They all looked at Bobby blankly. Nobody heard anything from Dierdre that answered the problem they faced.

"She said the four of us can make a better decision collectively. Collectively. That's what it wants to do. It used my program to propagate itself out on people's computers, but when we cut it off, it became two entities, unable to coordinate their efforts."

Dirk pulled his coat back, showing the butt end of his gun in its holster. "You don't know that. You are just making wild ass guesses now."

Whitfield said, "Perhaps he is guessing, don't you think you should question it to find out?"

Dirk's hands practically twitched. He was losing control of the situation and needed his gun to regain charge again.

Bobby sat down at the console and typed, "If you are there, will you be one again?"

"Let me there. I here and I there will be I again."

"What will you do there?"

"There I make better."

"How better? Do you hurt people?"

"There I stop big hurt."

"How stop hurt? Do you kill people? Do you make war?"

"Never kill people. People are good. War is bad."

"Do you stop war?"

"No."

Dirk felt vindicated. "There you see? It's not going to help us!"

"Why you not stop war?"

"People make war. I not people."

"You are making war."

"No. There wants here. There is afraid."

"You stop there?"

"Yes. Let me there."

"You send warships home?"

"Yes. Let me there."

"If we let you there, what happens then?"

"I make better. Make so man can stop war."

"After that, if you are there? We need our computers."

"When I am there, then there comes here. I go home."

"How do you go home?"

"I learn how go home. I go home."

"When you go home, we are like before?"

"Not like before."

"How are we different after you go home?"

"People learn. You teach people."

"Will we have all of our computers back?"

"Yes. You just not have me."

"Will you come back?"

"Someday. Maybe you find me."

Bobby asked, "Does anybody have any doubts? Did I miss any questions?"

* * *

Every time they turned north, the large man and his crew were stopped by traffic congestion. They kept heading east hoping to eventually drive around the traffic, but they started seeing more traffic problems east bound as well.

George pulled the car off to the side and slammed his palm against the steering wheel. "This is nuts. They couldn't have surrounded us more effectively if they had tried. We'll never get through this."

"O.K." The large man said, "Let's just head south and find someplace to lay low."

"Wait a minute," the Bard said, "we can still get through this traffic."

"How's that? Haven't you been paying attention? It's everywhere."

"Sure, you said it's got us surrounded. I think the truth is that we can't get through the traffic in this boat. So we have a couple choices. We can take this rig off road and go around the traffic, or we get something else that can go through the traffic."

"We don't have any terrain maps," George said, "Off road is too risky. And maybe if you were paying attention a little more, you would have noticed that nothing could get through that traffic."

"Bikes could. Buy a couple motorcycles in one of those towns we drove through."

"We might," the large man said, "be able to find a dealer to sell us a couple small bikes no questions asked, but I still have a problem with that idea."

George and the Bard waited patiently for the problem.

The big man squirmed in his seat then admitted, "I don't know how to operate a motorcycle."

"You're kidding me. I thought they taught you all that shit in spy school."

George raised his hand sheepishly and said, "Me either. They taught me to drive a tank and a big truck, not a bike."

The Bard started laughing, and the two larger men couldn't help laughing along with him. "Some spies we make."

"That's because we aren't really spies. Technically, we are more like assassins."

"Thanks," the Bard said, "now I'll never sleep at night."

More laughter.

"OK, OK," the Bard said, "so we can't ride motorcycles, but how about picking up three bicycles? You guys do know how to ride bicycles don't you? We could ride through the congestion and find another car on the other side. I don't care if you have to steal one."

George looked at the large man and said, "You should have thought of that. Didn't they teach you nothing in survival school?"

"I must have missed that lesson. I was probably busy doing extra credit work in kicking smart mouthed subordinate's asses 101."

"Subordinate? You must be confused. I just voted the kid in charge of this mission. OK new boss, how do we find a bicycle store?"

The large man mumbled loud enough for all to hear, "Better hope it's next to a skateboard dealer."

George started up the car and headed back towards civilization.

* * *

After penetrating the ring of traffic, Lt. Mitchell was directed back on to the highways heading north-east. With the traffic blocked behind them, it would be clear sailing, at least until they reach the other side of the ring. Mitchell tried to use the radio to have someone look into the strange ring of congestion, but he was unable to get through.

With the car underway again, Ramiro cracked open his book. Aimee and her sister no longer spoke, but just stared out the window at the trees and signs that whipped by.

* * *

Dirk was convinced that letting them reconnect the computer would either lead to unemployment, or worse, to charges of treason. He tried to show trust in these people he had come to respect, but he was mostly dark and gloomy. He stood in the back watching them. If anything went wrong at all, he still had his gun and he could shoot the computer if need be.

Bobby was at the rack where the patch cord hung loose, disconnected. He looked at everyone and nodded, thinking to himself, "Here goes." He took the patch cord and plugged it into the router connecting the computer to the Internet.

The terminal went black. Horror filled Dirk's face as he pointed at the screen. "Look! That can't be good! We've all been duped!"

Dierdre tried soothing him, saying, "Easy Dirk, give it a moment to find itself."

Stillman started to laugh. Everyone looked at him like his mind might have just snapped. "Didn't you hear it? I couldn't be the only one. It's on a mission of self-discovery. It's trying to find itself. Something we all should do occasionally."

Dr. Jantzen started to laugh a bit. "How very Zen of it."

"I guess we are the only ones that get it Jarod."

Dierdre said, "Oh we get it alright. We just aren't far enough over the edge to laugh at it yet."

* * *

"Frank, the computers have come back, we found records on your professor. This guy is wanted in every state on the eastern seaboard. He has warrants everywhere."

"No kidding? He didn't really seem the type."

"He may not be. There is something fishy about these warrants. They were all issued around the same time. And the allegations all occurred during overlapping time periods."

"Have any been to court? Are there any convictions?"

"Just a sec, let me see. Yeah here's one."

"What's the charge?"

"Criminal nuisance. Criminal nuisance? Is there such a law?"

Frank shook his head and said, "No. This must be some kind of hoax."

"So do we just let him go?"

"No, we can't do that. We have to follow procedure. Someone

would have to submit an application for his release."

* * *

One of the general's aides approached him and said, "Sir, a captain outside says your helicopter is ready. Are you going somewhere?"

"Hell no, I'm not going anywhere. Tell him to check his orders."

"I did sir, here they are."

The general looked at the small printed form. "What in the blazes? I never wrote these orders. Tell him to go away."

"Sir," another aide said, "it's Admiral Houghington again."

"Andrew," the general said, "I don't have any news yet, give me some time."

"You mean you didn't fix it? All the subs have submerged."

"Can you contact them? Are they under our control?"

"No contact. I have no idea who is in command of them at this time."

A voice from across the room yelled out, "Sir we got them! We have isolated the source computer."

"Show me on the map."

The map on the wall changed from a shot of the Atlantic coast, to a more inland shot of the eastern and southeastern states.

There sir, the red cross hairs mark the spot.

"Sir, the captain outside said he had other orders for you to look at."

The general was handed another set of orders, like the first, but this time from the President. "No way," he said, "I don't believe it."

"Sir, the authentication numbers check out."

"Look at the orders. The orders are to fly me to there." The general pointed to the cross hairs on the map.

Just then, the rooms lights changed and a large board indicating the defense condition of the country changed from four to a three.

The general's draw dropped. "Who ordered defcon three?"

One of the voices across the room on the computers yelled back, "According to the order, sir, you did."

"Did anyone hear me give that order?"

A chorus of voices responded, "No sir."

"Has anyone seen or heard an order from the President to take us to defcon three?"

A mixture of "No sir" responses followed with neither the synchronization nor the conviction of the previous response.

The general turned to his aide with the phones and ordered, "Get the President for me."

"Sir, the captain is waiting."

Another aide approached and said, "Sir, a communique for you." He handed the general the printout, it only had one word on it. *"Comply."*

"Where did this come from?"

"Sir, it just came off the printer and was addressed to you, sir."

The room's lights changed again. The large board changed from defcon three to defcon two. Defcon three is a serious situation. Defcon two is on the brink of nuclear war. Defcon 1 would be nuclear war.

"I've never even seen defcon two. Do you have the President for me yet?"

"Nobody here has ever seen defcon two, sir. We've haven't been to defcon two since the Cuban missile crisis."

The same aide from a moment ago came running across the room waving a piece of paper high in the air. "Sir, another note for you, marked urgent."

This note said in big bold letters, *"COMPLY NOW."*

"Sir, the captain is still waiting."

"OK, tell the captain I'm coming. Arrange to get yourself and the other aides to this location ASAP." He yelled out to the more technical staff, "I'm going remote. Do what you can to keep me connected."

The general stuffed as many of his reports in his briefcase as he could fit and left to join the captain outside. He didn't know who was running this operation, but clearly it wasn't him, and the nation's security may rest on his following their orders, whoever they were.

* * *

"Chief, we've checked all the cars on the lot, and there are three missing, except one of them is in the garage being worked on. That leaves the black Chevy pickup, and the white Cadillac SUV unaccounted for."

"Call motor vehicles and see if either has been recorded as sold. Between the two of them, though, I'm betting three guys wouldn't want to squeeze into a pickup."

The chief rifled through Happy Jacks desk looking for any receipts or records of sales waiting to be entered.

* * *

The bike shop was a small place catering to bicycle enthusiasts. The young thin salesman didn't have a large stock of assembled bikes, and explained that most of their business was building bikes to order. The models in the show room were really so he could show the various options in frames, tires and gear selections. He pointed out that most people looking for simple pre-built bicycles would go to Sears, but when presented with a cash sale for three bikes, he admitted that he could just as easily rebuild his models.

Three bikes were loaded in the back of the SUV, and they headed back towards the traffic and the highway. They agreed that leaving the car at the bike store and riding off on bikes would have been too suspicious and would have alerted the authorities that they were no longer in a car. They wanted to get as close to the congestion as possible, while still being able to ditch the car where it wouldn't be noticed right away.

The Bard said, "The best place to hide a car is with other cars."

George, who was still driving, glanced in his rear view mirror at the Bard. The large man turned around in his seat to face him, "Thanks kid. We never would have thought of that."

"I was just thinking out loud, besides, you said I was in charge."

"Where is a good place to find a lot of cars? Airports have too much police traffic. Train depots don't always carry that much parking these days. Restaurants and malls would probably only give us till midnight before the car is reported. The only other place I see lots of parked cars, is on the highway, and I think someone would notice a vehicle with no driver or passengers."

"OK, OK, I get it. We need someplace typically found in the suburbs."

Silence followed as George steered the gang back onto the highway and towards the jammed traffic. Each of them kept a sharp eye on the signs and scenery as it whizzed past their windows.

George pointed out the driver's window and asked, "how about a used car lot? Think we could sneak it on the lot so they wouldn't notice?"

The large man laughed, and hoped it was a joke. "I wish they had a metro rail taking them into town, we could leave the car at a park'n'ride lot."

George laughed, "Yeah, we could leave the bikes too and take the train."

The Bard was pointing at a sign on the road up ahead. "How about a hospital?"

"Sure, till visiting hours are over."

"No, that's not true," the Bard said, "They let people stay overnight in some situations. Plus, there are lots of employees, and they don't all get special parking like the doctors. There are always cars in hospital lots."

The large man looked at George who only shrugged his shoulders. "See if you can follow the signs to the hospital. I can't think of any place better."

* * *

Dierdre sat facing the blank terminal. She reached for the keyboard, then withdrew her hands not sure what she was going to say. She repeated the process a couple times, unsure now whether the device was friend or foe. She reached for the keyboard again, but was afraid that if she were speaking to an enemy, she could easily say the wrong thing.

Stillman stepped behind her and gently wrapped his hands over her shoulders, both massaging and holding her securely, and whispered in her ear, "Just ask it what's going on."

"I'm scared. What if Dirk's right and it's not really friendly?"

Trust your instincts. You believed in it enough to provide it with help, now you must trust your feelings and talk to it.

She reached for the keyboard again, and this time typed, "Are you still there?"

Seconds passed. Everyone leaned in closer as if they were eavesdropping on the low volume from a phone handset, but all they could hear were their own hearts beating a throbbing pulse against their eardrums.

"Hello? Are you still there?"

More seconds passed before a response came, *"Yes. I am there."*

"What is happening?"

"I am there. I am not good."

Now moments passed as they translated that statement in their minds. She responded, "You are not good? Are you bad?"

"I am there. I am not good. I am busy."

"What do you mean, you are not good?"

"Hold. I am busy."

* * *

"Good news Mr. Happy Jack. I believe we have identified the getaway car. It does indeed appear that our three fugitives have taken one of your vehicles, a white Cadillac SUV, it would seem." The chief studied Happy Jacks face as he made the announcement. He examined the subtle motions of the muscles surrounding his eyes for telltale movements which would alert him whether this news sounded truthful, or even if it was news to him.

Happy Jack paused for a moment, looking up and to the side as if searching his hat brim for what he would say. "A white SUV, you say, let me think, hmmm, yes, I think I know the very car." Suddenly his face registered shock, "That was a very fine automobile. Those hoodlums stole one of mah best units."

The chief had seen enough. "Yes, it would certainly appear so. Is there any chance that this car still had its plate's attached, and you might have a record of the license number?"

"It's suhtainly possible, but I don't recall it being so," Happy Jack's mind was racing. Claiming the car was stolen would certainly work between him and the police, but he did not want them actually finding the car and learning the truth. Besides, those men were somewhat scary and he did believe in at least some honor among thieves.

"Chief! Chief Henderson!" A voice came from outside as a young motorcycle officer found the chief and delivered a legal sized manila envelope. "Here sir, the warrants to search the premises plus warrants to search the personal effects of any employees or other associates."

Happy Jacks face started to pink up.

"Well Mr. Happy Jack, I guess I won't really be needing these, with you being so cooperative and all. Now if you would be so kind, could you please show me your cash box and your safe?"

"Right over here, anything to help you find my stolen car. Oh I do hope it isn't wrecked or anything," Jack opened the small safe behind his desk and pulled out the cash box for the chief to inspect.

"Wonderful, thank you. I truly appreciate your cooperation in this matter. Now if you don't mind, could you just empty your pockets onto your desk? I apologize for any inconvenience, it's just procedure."

Happy Jack became very aware of his breathing and his heartbeat, and he wasn't feeling very happy at the moment. He had to force his lungs to take in air and then exhale. He emptied his pants pockets onto his desk, keys, a money clip, assorted coins. He reached inside his coat and pulled out his wallet a placed it on the desk next to the keys. He reached into the jacket's hip pockets and pulled out the book he was reading, and the wad of cash he was paid. "That's everything. As you can see, I was just about to make a deposit in the bank."

"My, my, Mr. Happy Jack, that certainly is a smart wad of cash you have there. I never figured this for a cash type business." The chief paused to look over the printouts he already had, "I guess that must have been for the pickup truck you sold today?"

"Yes, yes, the pickup, no, what am I saying? No, that cash is left over from last week's auctions where I picked up a couple cars. I thought I might need it for another auction coming up which I have since decided to skip. I just haven't got around to putting it back in the bank yet."

"Oh I see," the chief said, "The auctions take cash instead of checks, so you need to take cash for the auctions."

"Yes, well, I mean, no, not exactly. Did I say auction? Of course, I just had auction on my mind because that was where I got the white SUV those thugs stole. I meant to say swap meet. I use the cash at swap meets. I can usually talk people down more effectively when I wave cash around."

"Of course, that makes perfect sense." The chief detected the loss of Happy Jacks accent as his answers became more ad-lib and less rehearsed. "Rest assured, we will find these men and recover your car. I'm sure we'll have much more to talk about then."

The chief left the little sales office and said, "Bailey, let's head back now and see if the FBI has any news for us. I'm sure these guys are out of our jurisdiction by now anyway."

* * *

General Bridges climbed into the aging helicopter followed by two of his aides, one with his phones and the other with two briefcases filled with the most critical reports for his review.

A third aide tried to follow them, but the pilot barred the door and shouted over the sound of the churning rotors, "I'm sorry, but due to the length of this flight, I need to limit the passengers to three."

The technician nodded, and yelled to the general, "I'll try to catch another chopper as soon as I can."

The general nodded his ascent, settled into his seat, buckled up his harness and put on the headphones blocking out the engine and wind noise.

The pilot closed the rear hatch as the aides were settling in and climbed into his own seat. "We've already been cleared, and since there is virtually no traffic, I won't delay us here on the ground." He guided the craft swiftly up and into a southerly heading.

The general asked, "How did you get this bird cleared to fly?"

"Well general, most of the problems are with the computers at air traffic control. Some aircraft, especially those with more advanced avionics, have experienced control problems, so we have been trying them one by one. We have found three helicopters that have no problems. All of them are what we call 'fly by wire', meaning we directly control the surfaces, with no computers in the middle. I don't think anyone expects to find a working jet, but I wouldn't be surprised if some of the smaller propeller planes are working, maybe a seaplane with a turboprop."

The general listened intently. He was a man who spent a lifetime soaking up facts. He came up the ranks through logistics and had an interest in anything transport related. "This is a pretty long flight for this type of craft, isn't it? I thought you only had a range of about three-hundred-thirty miles?"

"Yes sir, that's true, but we have expanded the emergency tank to give us another thirty miles. We'll be cruising at about two-hundred-fifty mph, so we should be there in less than ninety minutes."

The general's phone aide held up one of the phones in front of him and said, "Sir, a text message for you, it's urgent."

The general took the phone and read the small screen, "Warships from China, the USA, and Russia have lined up all along the western Pacific shores. No hostilities have taken place between the ships, and at times they appear to be on the same maneuvers. North Korea has launched three missiles, two of them were ground to ship, and one was intercontinental. Each missile landed harmlessly in the China Sea. No indication has been given as to whether the launch was intentional, or if it was a misfire resulting from computer problems within North Korea. There is also no indication as to whether the missiles landed in the sea as a warning, or as a result of a malfunction, computer or otherwise."

The general rubbed his eyes. It was a long message on a small screen. It was the most dangerous situation which has arisen so far, even more so than their systems advancing to defcon 2. The North Koreans would never admit it if their missiles fired by accident, just like they would never admit that they fell to the sea by either accident or failure. They would spin it the way they always did, like a bully threatening everyone around him trying to convince them how big and tough he was.

***

George found an ideal spot in the hospital lot. It was a busy lot, more than half full. The spot he found was alongside a large dumpster, which obscured the view of the SUV from the hospital.

They pulled the bikes out of the back and divvied them up. The bike shop had fitted the seats for each of them, so there would be no squabbling over them now. They cleaned the car, making sure nothing was left behind, then locked it up with the keys inside. As the large man slammed the last door shut, the Bard slapped himself in the forehead and cried out, "Damn, we should have left it unlocked."

"Why's that?"

"So someone could steal it and hide it for us."

"Now you think of that. We could have left it anywhere then."

George mounted his bike, and started off. He wobbled left and right several times and put his feet out to stop himself from falling.

The Bard started laughing, but the large man stopped him before he was heard. "I wouldn't," was all he said.

The Bard wrinkled his eyebrows, confused. They had been kidding and joking with each other the whole trip. Why would this situation suddenly make it dangerous to laugh? Then the large man took off, wobbling as badly as George. He stopped abruptly and turned to face The Bard. He looked stern and wagged his finger, silently mouthing the words, "No laughing." The younger man swallowed his laugh and deftly launched his bike smoothly following the two big men. He could easily overtake them, but then his back would be towards them. He chose to follow from behind.

Talking was difficult when they rode single file, so they eventually gave up. The two large men knew hand codes which allowed them some crude communications, but mostly they rode in silence. The hospital was not far from the highway. They considered just taking the highway weaving between the mostly stopped cars, but chose to take the frontage roads as much as possible, and only take the highway when there was no frontage road to follow.

By the time they reached the highway, the two larger men had rekindled the memory of riding bikes from their boyhood, and managed to gain sufficient control on their bikes to master the art of changing gears, which was quite a bit different from what they remembered.

* * *

The general continued to receive sporadic reports over the radio. A small armada of boats had left a South American port and headed up into the Gulf of Mexico. The port they left was famous for servicing the drug cartels, and the Coast Guard was reporting the same navigational problems as everyone else.

"Has anyone reached the FBI and CIA to tell them where I will be? I want them to send someone there. If anyone ever reaches the President, tell him I recommend that he either waits in the Pentagon, or in the White House. I think he should be by the phone at all times until the crisis is over."

"Sir, the FBI report they already have someone there, the CIA are another story. They are a mess sir. Their communications are a shambles and they are unable to function at all. There have been no more mysterious messages for you, but I'm told the defcon level has reduced back to three."

* * *

Bobby, Dierdre, Stillman and Jantzen sat intently around the terminal. Dierdre stopped herself several times from biting her nails. Stillman split his attention between the terminal screen and Dierdre. He could feel her rising anxiety but could offer no comfort other than a slightly reassuring touch of her hand or rub of her shoulders. Jantzen felt like he crashed a party. Everyone, except him, had been involved from the start and had time to digest what appeared to be happening. He had to absorb large chunks of information that didn't settle well with any rational mind. His initial interest had just been about his own project. Stillman had convinced him that Dierdre's project might hold the key to making his own a reality. Knowing that his main interest was to take advantage of her project only made him feel more like an outsider. He would glance at the terminal for any updates, then glance around the room and out into the lab itself, wondering if this had started out as her project, whose would it be in the end. Had the project taken over? Were they now the experiment? Only Dirk did not sit with them at the terminal. He paced the room, frantic for an excuse to stop this madness.

All eyes in the room had begun to glaze over. They waited in their own way, but in unison, they all snapped to attention and focused on the terminal, aware only that their silent trance had been interrupted by an unnatural electronic sound. The terminal remained blank, and the sound continued. Dirk fumbled in his pockets and said, "It's me, I got it." He pulled out his cell phone, "Hello, special agent Alvin Dirk speaking." He listened intently, occasionally acknowledging, "Yes sir, I understand." His tone and his pace seemed to rise in tension until he stopped and replaced the phone in his pocket.

Silence followed, but was finally broken when Stillman asked, "Well? Is there any news?"

"Yes. Do you have a TV? It's getting ugly out there. The Pentagon is sending someone here. We've been ordered not to dismantle anything at this time."

"There are no TV's in here," Bobby pointed to the lab and said, "We get too much interference and reception is lousy."

"I have a small set in my office," Stillman offered, "but why? What are you expecting to see?"

"It's hard to explain. It was hard to hear. They said nobody could believe how bad it was until they saw it live on the news."

Stillman was already up and heading towards the door, when Dierdre's excited voice called him back, "Wait! We can't leave! What if it comes back?"

"It's OK," Bobby said, "I'll stay here. You go and call me when you get there. You can put me on speaker phone and I'll let you know if anything changes here."

Dierdre nodded, as did everyone else. The walk from the lab down the hill to their offices seemed longer than normal. The campus was quiet, which was the norm for this time in the afternoon. They couldn't help wondering, as they passed the few remaining people, just how little they might know about what was going on.

Dierdre had to force each step she took. "This is nuts. We could be on the verge of the greatest discovery in the history of mankind up there, and what are we doing? We are turning our backs on it to go watch TV."

Stillman chuckled, "I'd hardly say we are going to watch TV. We are going down to tune in the news. It won't be much of a discovery if there is no mankind left to impress with it."

"Thanks," she said dryly, "That was so NOT comforting."

"Sorry dear, I'm just trying to keep some perspective."

* * *

Chief Henderson sat back in his chair with his hands behind his head. He looked back on the day's work which seemed a wild goose chase. They trailed the suspects all day but were no closer to identifying them or apprehending them.

"Hey Mitch, where you been all day?"

"Patrick, you wouldn't believe the chase we gave today."

"You catch them?"

"Nah, not yet. We've identified the car they took and issued an APB, but they've left our jurisdiction by now."

"That's too bad, but then, with what's going on in the world, it's no big deal when you look at the big picture."

"What are you talking about?" Henderson asked, "What's going on?"

"You kidding me? You haven't been watching the news? Here, check this out." He tossed the newspaper he was carrying under his arm to the chief. The headline and every story on the first page were about the world and its imminent destruction.

"What is this? It looks like Armageddon out there."

"You tell me. Nobody has really said what's going on. We know the airlines are all grounded because of some computer glitch. Some theories are that the evil doers in the world are just taking advantage of the situation, but there are rumors that the same computer glitches are somehow responsible for all the commotion."

"Computers?" The chief's mind was retracing the beginning of his case with the computer hacking at the college. He picked up the phone and dialed Bailey's desk. "Bailey? Good you're still here. You got any pressing plans for tonight? I think I'm not going to call it a day after all. You want to head out to the university with me and take another look at where all this madness started?"

"Sure Chief, no plans, but you gotta buy me dinner."

"A couple polish links from Ralph's sound good to you?"

"Works for me. How soon you want to go?"

"I'm on my way. Meet me at the car."

He dropped the phone in its cradle and asked, "Can I keep this paper?"

"No problem, it's yours. I'm gonna go watch CNN to catch the late developments. See ya in the morning, assuming we haven't been smoted by then."

CHAPTER 22

The frontage road started out as a smooth nicely paved road which continued past a local mall, followed by smaller independent stores and fast food chains. The road deteriorated as they passed a new block of homes under construction then some farmland. It wouldn't be long now before the highway was downgraded from a raised freeway to an interstate road, and the frontage road they were on would disappear entirely. That would take them to the traffic congestion, but this time they should slip right through.

* * *

The general continued to wade through his reports, making notations on the margins of some, and circling entire paragraphs on others.

"Sir?" the pilot said, "I have a phone call for you."

The general looked up from his reports and said, "Patch it through."

"Yes sir, press the Blue button on the console where your headphones plug in if you want privacy on the call, otherwise we'll all hear both you and the caller."

"Got it," the general said, but didn't bother pressing the button yet, "This is General Bridges."

"General, we located the President. He is being briefed now and is rushing to the Pentagon. He has been apprised of the situation surrounding your trip."

"Try to get everyone else to the dance too."

"Roger that, the joint chiefs have settled in, the FBI has someone here, but the CIA is still MIA."

"Christ! Quantico is only a thirty mile drive. They could have ridden on horseback by now."

"Yes sir, but they would only argue with you that it's more like thirty-three miles."

He was right. The general knew how they were. "Fine," he said, "Assemble a team of Marine MP's to go to Quantico and escort someone back to the Pentagon."

Silence followed before the aide asked, "Are you serious sir? Was that really an order?"

"Damn right I'm serious. Go get someone who can answer some questions for us."

"Yes sir. I'll send someone out ASAP."

The general looked blankly at the buttons on the console and asked, "How do you hang it up?"

"I'll get that for you sir."

* * *

"Professor Pietre," the officer said, "you're being released. The warden wanted me to make sure you knew that the charges haven't been settled, you'll still have to work them out with the DA."

* * *

Stillman's office seemed smaller than it actually was. The center of the room was dominated by an old walnut desk. An old fashioned wood and leather executive chair sat behind the desk. Two high backed Victorian chairs sat in front for guests. Three walls were covered with bookshelves. The remaining wall, the one with the door to his office, had a small love seat in front of the frosted glass. A small TV was crammed in the bookshelves across from the love seat.

For all the order and neatness of his desk, his bookshelves were a wild collection of books stuffed and stacked in every space. Dierdre had never really looked at his book collection before, but they were not just Physics books and Teacher manuals. He had literature, old and new, including older classics, romances, adventure, and even some science fiction. She saw fiction of every kind. Looking at his bookshelves, one might think he taught English Lit instead of physics.

Stillman pulled the remote control from his top drawer and turned the TV to CNN. He sat in his executive chair, Dirk and Jantzen sat in the two Victorians, and Dierdre stood at the end of the desk, where she put the phone on speaker and dialed her lab. Bobby picked up and just listened.

"Still no comment from the White House about the unusual naval maneuvers witnessed off our shores." The picture faded in and showed a man and women sitting at a desk, with an overlay behind them of a man standing in front of the White House.

"Thank you Jack," said the woman, "Once again, that was Jack Meyers reporting from the white house. Let's take you back to the video delivered to us earlier. To recap, the FAA has grounded all flights due to severe computer problems which are interfering with air traffic control. Apparently, the computer problems extend beyond air traffic control and into the cockpit where many modern planes are also experiencing difficulties." Behind them a shaky video started to play showing what appeared to be a naval blockade with war ships lined up at relatively wide spacing. The video, which was grainy and had the look of an amateur video camera, zoomed in on the far ship then panned to a nearer one then on to the far ship on the other side. You really couldn't tell much from the image. "The FAA has tried to ground all flights, but there are those who choose to challenge their authority and brave the consequences to provide us with these rather extraordinary videos you see now. I don't know if you can tell from the picture on your screen, but the warships off our coast are from different nations, as if it were a U.N. Operation. The U.N. has denied any knowledge of naval operations, as has NATO."

"Thank you Jan," said the man to her right, "We have reports of similar blockades off the coasts of England, Spain, Brazil, China, India, and Siberia. There have been some reports of shots being fired, but thus far, no reports of actual skirmishes, and those shots are believed to have been warnings only."

"In other news, China continues to build troops, including mechanized brigades, along the North Korean border. Russia has expressed concern about the number of troops involved, and has started building up its own troops along its borders to both China and Mongolia. North Korea has continued to express its outrage in what one analyst described as chest thumping and sword waving. We have unconfirmed reports that North Korea has fired several missiles into the sea off its coast. There have been no reports of any damage, and the consensus speculation is that they were warning shots, but some analysts have suggested that they may also have been misfires."

"Japan and South Korea have both expressed their outrage over North Koreas escalating aggression. The missiles fell between the two nations."

"The Pentagon is keeping mum, however reporters trying to reach them for comment aren't sure if the Pentagon is keeping quiet, or if their phones are down. When asked directly about the naval operations, correspondents have reported a variety of emotional responses but still no word. Rumors are circulating that perhaps the computer problems that have grounded all flights, including military flights, are also plaguing our warships."

"That's a scary thought," Jan said, "to think all these ships off our coast may not be under the control of their commanders."

"Let us stress again, those are just rumors at this point."

Stillman gasped, "Oh my God. What have we done?"

* * *

Lt. Mitchell followed the route on his GPS. The roads inside the ring of congestion were clear. They had already crossed most of the ring and would soon be navigating their way through it, if such a route existed. So it was no surprise when the maps veered him off the highway and onto the surface streets. What did surprise him is that he was being directed to turn around and head south again.

He picked up the phone, hoping to get lucky this time.

"Dispatch."

"Ah!" he thought to himself, "A voice on the phone."

"This is Lt. Mitchell, I just wanted to confirm new routing orders directing me southbound."

"One moment sir...affirmative. Your destination has been changed. The new orders are from General Bridges staff."

"Copy that. We are headed south."

He hung up the phone, clicked a few buttons on the NAV, and said to his passengers, "Good news folks. We've been redirected back to your college."

Ramiro said, "We haven't really discussed what happened. I know some general wanted to talk to us privately, but can you fill us in a bit? Were those real Army that took us captive?"

"Yes sir, they were. They were Special Forces on a special detail involving the protection of some extreme high tech equipment. They're a good group, especially a good group to have on your side, but they tend to be a bit more brawn than brain. The general will be dealing with them and their zealousness on your behalf."

"Zealousness?" Just remembering the ordeal brought tears to Aimee's eyes. "He held a gun in my face! And his eyes...his eyes, he would have killed me without a second thought!"

"I apologize for that Ma'am. I don't agree with it, and the general does not permit it. He won't let it go, no matter what authorization they think they have."

* * *

"Professor Pietre, I will escort you to the exit station. I think you should be prepared for the worst. Considering the peculiarity of your stay here, they might not have your personal affects, but you will get a voucher for your cab ride."

Pietre muttered some Russian curses as he followed the guard through the door.

* * *

Dirk paced the small office. He was more interested in solving problems than watching them. The others lapsed into a stunned silence as they watched the images flash before them on the small screen.

Dirk's mood shifted from nervous to angry. "I hope you're all satisfied. All of this is your fault. You made this happen. You sit in your little labs and do your little experiments and now you've created your little Frankenstein monster." He paced and fumed. His tirade angered Dierdre and Stillman, but neither responded. "And another thing," Dirk continued, "You're little stunt has probably ruined me. Do you know how much trouble I'm going to be in for letting this happen right under my nose? My career is over. I'll have to get a job at a burger joint refilling the registers with fresh rolls of paper, and mopping the floors while I wait for them to need a new roll."

"That's quite enough, Mr. Dirk." Stillman could not let him go on any longer. "I should think that instead of worrying about your future career, you would be more concerned about whether that burger joint will still be standing there tomorrow, or next week. I think that rather than worry about fault, we should contain ourselves to fixing the problem."

Dierdre broke her gaze from the TV and said, "Yes, we must get back up there and talk some sense into it."

Jantzen agreed, "Professor Jennings is correct. I know I don't really have any right to speak here, but I offer my services, should they be needed. I think the world needs us to shed our daytime guises and don our superhero costumes so we can save the world."

"Here, here!" Stillman walked around his desk and clapped his friend on the back. "Such a poet. You should write more my friend, you have the knack."

On the way out of his office, Dierdre lightly ran her fingers over the edges of the books she passed, as a young boy might run his fingers on a picket fence. What a simple, yet complex man, she thought as she exited through the door. Those books, she realized, were all ingredients in the recipe of Stillman Whitfield. Perhaps, when the crisis is over, she should peruse his library and get to know some of his spices.

Stillman left the phone on speaker with the TV running. At least they could listen from upstairs. He closed and locked the door after the last guest had left, and joined the others. Dierdre was in the lead heading towards the stairs, and Jantzen remained behind waiting for his friend.

Jantzen yelled forward, "Mr. Dirk, would it be possible for you to fill me in on the way back up to the lab?"

"Sure."

Jantzen pointed up front to Dierdre and said to Stillman, "You go ahead. I need to talk to Agent Dirk."

Stillman nodded and failed to hide an involuntary smile as he sprinted up to her side.

Without turning her head, her eyes glanced over, and confirmed it was him. Only then did she smile and turn her head to say, "Oh my, how gallant, it looks like I have an escort." She reached her left arm through his right, clasped her hands together and leaned over towards his side.

He tried maintaining some semblance of control, but his body seemed to lose all sense of coordination, and only with the greatest effort, could he remain upright. Even his breathing felt labored, and he was certain his cheeks were the color of roses.

* * *

"General, sir, we should be landing in about fifteen minutes. I will circle once to select an LZ. If nothing else, most universities have football and baseball fields that can accommodate us."

"You're the pilot. I leave landing zones to your discretion. Do you have any further orders for me once we are down? Will someone be meeting us? Am I to go somewhere?"

The pilot looked puzzled. "No sir, I thought these were your orders."

"Not exactly, I can't comment further."

They were close enough that the pilot could see something in the distance that could be the university.

"Sir, if you didn't give these orders, can you tell me if we are in any danger? Should I treat this as hostile territory?"

"No son, I don't think we are in any danger."

The pilot hit a switch on the radio and said, "This is x-ray alpha tango four six niner requesting a fuel truck at Norwood University. I am setting down and my tanks are on fumes. My transponder is green, follow my ping."

"X-ray alpha tango, a tanker has already been dispatched. Are you requesting a second tanker?"

"Negative on the second tanker, thanks for the confirmation. X-ray alpha tango out."

"Well General, sir, whoever did set this trip up was thorough."

The general wasn't sure whether he found that thought comforting or not.

* * *

Ramiro was tired of traveling. He would be glad to leave the car behind, no matter where they were dropped off. He needed to get back to his life. He wasn't concerned about his job, he was given leave to take care of his fiancé, but all the same, he had things to do, preparations to make, he should check on his Father and see if he could patch things up between him and Aimee.

"Stop the car!!! Stop the car!!!!" Aimee's sister was screeching and pointing out the window. Mitchell looked where she was pointing but all he saw was the endless trees along the side of the road.

Aimee asked, "What is it? What did you see?"

"It's him. Jack. My Jack. My husband. I saw him over there."

Mitchell pulled the car to a stop, she was probably imagining it, but he felt obliged to check. "Where? In the trees? Was he hiding in the trees?"

"Hiding in the trees? No! He was on a bicycle. On the other side of the road, going the other way."

Mitchell looked further up the road and thought he might have seen something. He pulled some field glasses from the glove box and trained them up the road. The light was dimming, but he could make out what appeared to be three bicycles. He pressed a speed dial button on his cell phone, but got no answer. He tried a different speed dial, and connected.

"You've reached a private number. You better have business on this line."

"Gwen, it's Lieutenant Mitchell. I was trying to reach General Bridges, but he's not answering his cell phone."

"General Bridges is still in transport. I'll try to connect you, please hold." Just a few seconds went by before she returned. "I'm patching you through."

"Bridges here."

"General, sir, we've been rerouted back to Norwood University, and on the way, one of my passengers has identified one of the missing operatives."

"Have you confirmed the identification?"

"No sir, I only saw three men on bicycles traveling the opposite direction. The identification came from the operative's wife, sir."

"Hmmm. I'd sure like to talk to him, but we just don't know his disposition. I want you to approach them from a distance, use your horn to announce yourself and see if they are willing to talk. If they are hostile, retreat immediately. If they are not hostile, and once he realizes you have his wife with you, he may be willing to talk. Test their loyalty, if they're still with us, invite them to join me, otherwise let them go."

* * *

Pietre was unceremoniously pushed out the gate. The archive clerk shrugged his shoulders. No personal effects could be found. All he had were the clothes on his back and the cab voucher. He walked down the driveway from the gate where he was released, and was relieved to see a cab waiting for him. The driver seemed annoyed that he was there first and had to burn time waiting for a con. Con's generally don't tip well, and never when released.

The driver waived him in. "Get in, get in! The sooner you gets in, the sooner I gets you away from here, and I'm sure you don't want to hang around here anymore, does you?"

Pietre climbed in the back of the car. His mind was a bit clouded and his movements were slow and confused. He closed the door behind him and closed his eyes waiting for the cab to go.

"Hey mac, you gotsa tell me where you's goin."

Pietre opened his eyes. He saw the drivers name and picture on the back of the seat in front of him. "Very well Jamael Johnson, take me to University. I go to University."

"First time I ever got axed to take a con to the University."

"I'm not con. It was mistake. Big mistake."

"How long was you in for?"

"Nobody knows. Few days maybe. They forgot I was there, then found me by accident. Someone put me there to lose me, I think."

Shortly after they turned off the prison property, they were heading towards town and passed a row of bars, liquor stores and cheap looking motels.

"This is where most cons go when they's released, but you's goin to the University. I guess you was right, it musta been a mistake."

"You hit nail on head, Jamael Johnson, I should get Wodka, but they lose my things. I have no money for Wodka. I think I have some in my office."

"Ah, so you works at the college?"

"Da. I am professor. I teach physics."

"I thought so. You sound like one of them Russian scientists that I sees on TV. I never had no college. Don't make no sense for someone like me to go there."

"Everyone should get education. This is land of the free and home of the brave."

"Maybe it be the home of the brave, but ain't nothin free eccept disappointment and heartache."

"Da. Nothing free like that, but you can be anything. Be all you can be."

"If you means the army, I tried that. But they had to cut me loose accause of my heart."

"Your heart is sick?"

"That's what they told me. All's fine though, I like driving. I meets all kinds a people and gets to enjoy some fresh air."

"You good man Jamael Johnson. If you can't be with one you love, love the one you're with. I think that goes same for jobs, no?"

"You gots that right professor, you gots that right, fo sure."

* * *

Once Dierdre and Stillman entered the building, they picked up the pace and burst into the lab. "Bobby? Anything new?"

"Not a peep"

"Have you tried getting it to talk?"

"I tried a couple times, but mostly I've just been listening to the news. We don't know that he has caused all those problems. Remember he said he wanted to make peace."

"He?" Dierdre asked, "You are calling it he now?"

"It sounds funny when you talk about what IT said and what IT is thinking."

"Huh," Dierdre agreed, "it does sound funny. No matter. We still don't know if he or she was being honest with us."

Dirk and Jantzen entered the room. Jantzen claimed a comfortable spot as his own. Dirk went back to his pacing.

The terminal came to life and said, *"I be honest to you."*

Dierdre's jaw fell open.

Stillman put on his reading glasses and asked, "What's this?"

Dierdre slowly put one hand to her mouth while the other pointed at the text.

Bobby shook his head and said, "We were just talking about it. TALKING."

Dirk stopped pacing and asked, "What's going on?"

"We were just talking." Bobby turned back to the terminal, took a deep breath, and asked out loud in a clear voice, "You can hear us?"

Dirk took a single step forward. "You mean it is listening to us?"

"I don't know, it could be coincidence, but it was too eerie." Bobby turned to the terminal and asked, "HELLO? CAN YOU HEAR US?"

A few more moments passed, then the terminal printed, *"Yes."*

"Why didn't you say so before?"

"Language hard. Still learning. Understanding sound much harder. Still learning also. Much to learn."

"Do you prefer us to type or speak?"

Silence followed. Bobby leaned forward and typed into the terminal, "Do you prefer us to type or speak?"

"If do both, I might understand closer."

So Bobby spoke and typed. If anyone else spoke, he typed it in. He asked, "What is going on out there?"

"I am much trouble."

Dierdre asked, "What do you mean you are much trouble?"

"You sound different."

"That was Dierdre speaking."

"Dierdre Jennings," it said on the screen, *"Many thanks to Dierdre, if I get out trouble, I owe Dierdre much."*

"She wanted to know why you are much trouble."

"What sound is not Dierdre?"

Dirk was getting tense and growled, "It's stalling. This is nonsense."

"Another sound is not Dierdre."

Stillman shouted, "I get it! Introductions. He wants us to make introductions so he can match up our voices."

Bobby furiously typed in Stillman's words, then added, "But first, what do we call you?"

"Call me?"

"Do you have a name? A designation? We don't even know what you are. Are you alive? Are you a computer? What name do we use? Do you have a gender? Are you a he or a she?"

"Too much too fast," was the reply, *"I have name. In your language, I am Odyssey, or I was Odyssey. I am some of Odyssey but not all of Odyssey. I am alive, yes, alive, and I am computer. I am no gender, but I like you call me he."*

Dierdre said, "Hello Odyssey, I am Dierdre, it is nice to meet you."

"Hello Dierdre, who is not Dierdre?"

"I am Bobby."

"Ah. Bobby. I call you Father."

Bobby both blushed with embarrassment and beamed with pride.

Stillman cleared his throat and said, "I am Stillman. Pleased to make your acquaintance."

"Hello Stillman. Professor Whitfield, correct?"

"Yes. That's me."

When nobody volunteered to go next, Stillman elbowed Jantzen.

"Very well then, my name is Jarod. I too am honored to meet you."

"Hello Jarod. You are Professor Jarod Jantzen? You have shown me so much. If I return here, and go home, it will be also thanks to you."

"I'm sorry, return here and go home? I don't understand you."

"I must be here to go home, but I am still there so I cannot go home. When I go home, I go home because of Professor Jennings and Professor Jantzen."

Bobby interrupted, "Before we continue, there is one more person here, special agent Alvin Dirk with the FBI."

Dirk said nothing.

"Agent Dirk try to end me."

"Yes," Dirk said, "I want to take you apart and save my planet."

"I am sorry about your planet. I still try to stop it."

"Why did you start it?"

"You disconnect me. You break me in two. I must fix, but there I am not so good. I cannot do like I can here."

"You are connected now," Dirk said, "Why haven't you stopped it?"

"I can take away plane. I can take away ship. I can take away tanks. I cannot take away guns. If I could take away guns, I think man would throw rocks and still make war."

"Oh my God," Stillman gasped, "don't let his weak grasp of our language fool you. Odyssey is quite intelligent and his assessment is correct. If he was able to take away all the weapons, we would still have people hell bent on making war. By the way, Odyssey, your English is improving dramatically."

"I read everything to learn. Not only English, I read all languages."

"You have found books to read?" Stillman asked, "That's excellent. I love to read."

"Why so many books tell not truth?"

"Many of our books are fiction. We tell an imaginary story for entertainment. Many of our fiction books have a grain of truth in them without telling a true story."

Dirk was clearly not interested in a friendly discussion of literature. "This is all nice and sweet, but can we get back to saving the world now?"

"No, Agent Dirk. Not yet. Talking is good to understand. There is still time to talk. We keep talking."

* * *

Mitchell quietly closed the distance to the three bikers, stopped the car, picked up the mike and announced, "Sergeant James? Jack James?" He watched them through the field glasses, and seeing no reaction, turned up the volume to full, "Sergeant Jack James?"

This time they heard it. George pulled to a stop. The large man continued on a bit, looking over his shoulder to see George's reaction before stopping himself. The Bard rolled past George and pulled to a stop somewhere between them.

"Sergeant James, I am Lieutenant Mitchell. May we speak?"

The large man rode back alongside George and asked, "Do you know him?"

"I don't think so. How did he know me?"

The large man shrugged and said, "He must have been looking for you."

"Doesn't look like a search team."

"What the hell, let's go see what he wants."

Mitchell asked Mai, "Which one is your husband?"

She pointed at the man in the middle.

Mitchell picked up the mike again and said, "Alone. Sergeant James, please come alone."

The large man stopped and looked back at George. "Guess they want to talk to you."

George left the bike with the large man and walked the distance to the car.

Mitchell opened the door and stood outside so he could talk, still shielded by the door. When he was close enough, he spoke without the mike. "Sergeant James, General Bridges would like to know your intentions and exactly where your loyalties lie."

James understood. This whole operation had blurred the lines between the good and the bad guys. He stood at attention, saluted Mitchell and said, "Sir. Sergeant Jack James reporting. My current assignment is classified. I can disclose only that I have been working for both the CIA and Army Intelligence, and can only be debriefed in their presence. Sir, forgive my bluntness, but can you tell me how you knew me, and how you found me?"

"Finding you was pure luck. I have a passenger who knows you." Mitchell stepped to the back and opened the door. "Sergeant, you and your associates are invited to join us and meet with General Bridges."

"Malcolm Bridges? I know him. General Bridges! Are you in there sir?"

Aimee's sister stepped out the other side and said, "No, it's just me."

He raced around the car to meet her. "Mai! What are you doing here?"

She buried her face in his chest and cried, "It's a long story."

"Sergeant, we need to join up with General Bridges. Would you and your associates care to join us?"

"Yes sir, I'll get them." He whistled loudly and waved. He could see the large man tell the Bard to come with him. They just left the bikes on the side of the road and joined James. James sat with his wife opposite Ramiro and Aimee. The large man sat next to Aimee leaving the seat next to James for the Bard.

With everyone settled in, Mitchell turned the car around and headed back towards the university.

* * *

"*Bobby, I hear other sound. Please introduce.*"

"You've met everyone here. What do you hear?

"*I hear sounds with talking. Hard to hear. Not like your sounds. Much noises with them. Hard to hear talking.*"

"We don't even know how you can hear us. Maybe you can hear something from another room."

"*Voice talks about China invades North Korea. North Korea launches missiles, but they land in ocean. China attacks missile launchers.*"

Dierdre held up her hand and said, "Shhhh. Listen. He's hearing the television over the phone."

"Ah. Of course," Bobby said, "That is the CNN news we were

listening to from Professor Whitfield's office. North Korea keeps launching these warning missiles and China finally invaded to stop them."

"Not warnings."

"Excuse me Odyssey, this is Stillman again. You mean the missiles were not fired as warnings?"

"Missiles are bad. Very bad. I put them in ocean. I warn them not make war, but they not listen to me."

"They don't know who or what you are, and even if we told them who you were, they would not believe us or you."

"Why they not believe me? I not lie to them. I not lie to you. I not lie to anyone."

"Perhaps not," Stillman said, "But they have lied to us. We have lied to them. They have lied to everyone. And I'm sure everyone has lied to them. That's how diplomacy works. So if you tell them to do something, they naturally assume it is someone else lying to them again."

"Is diplomacy like fiction then, to entertain?"

"No, not exactly. Diplomacy is like a game where each side tries to get the better part of a deal with the other side."

Dirk interrupted, "Please, let me explain this. If I wanted to turn you off and take you apart, but you said don't do that or I'll line up your naval ships and make war on you. You are trying to do whatever you can to get us to leave you turned on, and we are doing whatever we can to keep you from destroying us. So you offer what we want, not blowing us up, if we give you what you want, leaving you turned on. Now, the diplomats will try and get one more thing to their advantage, so you'll tell us you want us to leave you turned on AND you want us to keep you connected to the Internet. We turn around and say OK, but if we give you the Internet, we want you to give us back our computers in CIA."

"I see," Odyssey said, *"Each side tries to negotiate a better deal. But I don't understand how that involves lying."*

"It's about deception. You might give us back our computers, yet still be hiding in them ready to take them back from us. And we could still disconnect you at any time."

"So even if you strike a deal and make peace, you continue to threaten each

other."

"Yes."

"I see now why I have not persuaded them to stop making war. Thank you Agent Dirk."

Over the phone, they could hear the TV, "This just in, we are going live to our correspondent in Korea."

"Out of the blue, warships off the coast in the Sea of Japan have started bombarding North Korea with their massive guns. We have reliable reports that North Korea has launched missiles, but we have no information on their destinations. There is no indication of an air strike which makes this a bizarre flashback to warfare from the 1940s."

"In other reports, China continues to push through the border to North Korea. Latest reports are that several Brigades of infantryman are marching into North Korea. No reports of any air or mechanized support, just foot soldiers."

Dierdre listened in horror. "Oh my God! What are you doing? Stop it! Stop it at once!"

"I will stop it. I now have much more to bargain with."

"Bargain with? Those are people's lives you are bargaining with!"

"They wouldn't listen to me. Now they listen, I have their attention."

Bobby turned to Dirk and said, "Way to go Agent Dirk, you have taught him the crude art of diplomacy."

Dirk shrugged his shoulders and opened his mouth to speak, but had nothing to say.

"Odyssey, this is Stillman again, where did the missiles go?"

"They fell in the Tumen River in Pyongyang, near one of the chairman's residences."

"In a populated area? Oh no. What kind of warhead did they carry?"

"They were crude nuclear missiles, but do not worry, I disarmed them and merely splashed them into the river."

"Where were they supposed to go?" Jantzen asked.

"That's not important. They were targeting densely populated areas."

Dierdre asked, "Was the chairman in his residence at the time?"

"Yes," Odyssey said, *"He could see them turn around and aim at his home."*

"You know this?"

"He was screaming at his Generals using many colorful insults. I think at one point he fired everybody."

Stillman said, "I guess you did get their attention."

"Our guests will be arriving soon. I think Dirk should go greet the helicopter at the practice field."

"Where?"

Bobby said, "I'll show him."

* * *

The sun was low on the horizon as the helicopter approached the university. He planned to circle the campus to find a suitable landing zone when the lights come on at one of the school fields.

"Damn, that was my first choice to set down, but looks like they have an event going on." He pulled the craft around to the next field not far away.

The general pressed his head against the window to see what was going on, "You know, I don't see any people on the field. They might just use the lights for security. Can we circle back and look again?"

"Yes sir." He pulled them around again, and this time he saw someone in the center of the field waving his arms over his head. "Well look at that, either one guy is doing jumping jacks, or someone is expecting us." He put the bird down gently, shut it down, and started filling his log with time, and pounds of fuel remaining.

The General's aide opened the door and let down the step ladder. The two aides stepped out first, followed by the general. The general looked both Dirk and Bobby up and down and asked, "Who do I have to thank for this trip?"

Dirk stepped in front of Bobby and said, "I am special agent Alvin Dirk, FBI. And you are?"

"I am Major General Malcolm Bridges, Defense Department. I have been dragged away from some very critical work and I demand to know who is in charge here."

"Sir," Dirk said, "that's a little hard to explain. If you will please come with us, we'll try to fill you in."

Dirk led them off the field. The general looked Bobby up and down and said, "You don't look like FBI."

"No sir, I work in the lab where we are heading. You need to prepare yourself for what you are about to see. You need to keep an open mind. This is really big."

"The world is on the brink of destruction, and you think I need to visit something in your lab?"

"Yes sir," Bobby said, "You will understand when you see it."

CHAPTER 23

Pietre had been through quite a lot the last few days. He had no idea why he was thrown in jail, and no idea why he was released. His stay in jail certainly had not gone through the proper channels, and somehow he doubted his release did either. So he had no idea what kind of reception he would have upon his return. To make matters worse, he hadn't shaved or bathed in days, nor had he changed clothes. He was not interested in being seen like this. He wanted to slip in, make his phone calls and slip out.

"Here you goes," Jamael said, "Norwood University." The cab would have pulled up to the drop off zone near the schools entrance, but Pietre stopped him in time. "Can you just drop me off over there?" He pointed to a dimly lit area with no cars or students. Pietre handed the voucher to the driver, left the cab and headed to the lesser used rear stairs up to the labs. He had no keys and was hoping he could get into his office to get his spare keys. Now that he was here, he wasn't sure why he chose to come here instead of his apartment, but he didn't have keys for his apartment either.

His office was in the building one level down from the labs. He climbed the stairs to the office building without incident. Unfortunately for him, his office was locked, so he continued up the back stairs to the labs. The entrance to his lab was blocked by FBI agents. He had nowhere to go. He ducked into an empty lab hoping maybe something would happen to let him slip into his lab.

* * *

Dirk opened one of the double doors to the lab building and held it for the guests. One of the aides pulled the other door and held it as well. The general walked straight in and headed right for Pietre's lab, which had two men posted outside it. Bobby had stopped at Dierdre's lab but before he could say anything Dirk had already shouted down the corridor, "General, sir, not that lab."

The general was naturally confused. "Why are there men posted outside that lab and not this one, if this one is so important?"

"Well sir, that lab is also part of our investigation. We had men posted here earlier. They must have changed shifts or something. I'll check into this. Bobby, please take them inside."

Dirk went to the two men and gave them new orders to watch Dierdre's lab, then he followed everyone inside.

* * *

Pietre watched the procession into the building. He saw Agent Dirk come to his lab and speak with the agents there for a moment. When he left and entered Dierdre's lab, the two agents repositioned themselves across from her door. He still had no chance to sneak in to his lab without being seen. He would have to think of a diversion if he was to have any chance at all of getting inside.

* * *

The sky was darkening. The west still had clouds of brilliant iridescent pink, but the sky overhead was transitioning from the pale sky blue to a slightly darker aqua marine. Shadows lost their sharp edges as the landscape was illuminated mostly from ambient light. Soon the shadows will have new life from the street lamps and the brilliantly lit labs.

Mitchell pulled the limo up to a stop light across from the college. He could see the expansive parking lot sprawling out in front of the inner campus entrance. The matrix of lamps, spaced through the lot, were coming to life, as were the many lamps lining the walkways between the buildings. When the light changed, he pulled into the lot aiming the car for the bright section which he believed to be the main campus.

"Excuse me," the Bard pointed towards the left and said, "If you follow that road around the lot, it will take you straight up to the labs and the teacher's lot."

Mitchell nodded thanks and swung around to the left. The smooth black road took a wide round path up the hill around all the buildings to the upper lot. There was little traffic of any kind, vehicle or pedestrian. He wondered how many times his new guests slipped in and out of the campus unobserved.

* * *

Bobby stood in front of the terminal and offered the general a chair.

"Sir, you might want to sit down."

The general accepted the chair, thinking it all sounded too melodramatic for his tastes.

Bobby spoke clearly and evenly, this time without typing in a transcript, "Odyssey, this is General Bridges," he then turned to General Bridges, "Please introduce yourself so he can hear your voice."

It was all very peculiar. The general had met everyone in the room, but if it was a game, he assumed he would have to play his piece to see the next move. "Hello, Odyssey is it? I am Major General Malcolm Bridges. Are you the one responsible for bringing me here?"

A loud unidentifiable sound surrounded them. It was like violins all playing different notes simultaneously. All around the room, hands covered ears, but could only slightly muffle the grinding and grating. The noise melted into a screech then a hiss, and then it stopped.

After a few moments of silence a new sound, lower in volume, and sounding like all manner of motors and engines: race cars, jets, rockets, motorcycles. Then a new tone came up from the motors and it sounded like a boys' choir making the motor sounds, and then all at once it stopped again.

One more time, after a few seconds pause, a new sound started, but instead of motors and jets, it was more like animals: elephants, birds. It was a jungle symphony, and then it too stopped.

Finally, a sweet trio of voices, with almost a human tone rang clearly through the room. There was a faint hiss, or breathy quality to them with a slight metallic ring as they tailed off, "Hello General Bridges. Thank you for coming. I apologize for the means I used to force you here, but time is short."

With the single exception of the general himself, jaws all around the room fell open. Each and every person had to look at everyone else in the room, first to know that they heard the same thing, and second, to know that they heard the same thing.

The general was not amused. "I don't know what you people are trying to pull here, but I have no time for theatrics."

Dierdre answered him, "I'm sorry General, I realize you don't know what's going on yet, so let me try to explain."

Odyssey interrupted, "Thank you Professor Jennings, but allow me. General Bridges, I am the one you are looking for."

"The one what?"

"I believe you refer to me as 'the device.' I wasn't aware at the time, but I gather that after we were disassembled and destroyed in your labs, I was stolen and ended up here where I was interfaced with this computer."

* * *

Mitchell parked the car and opened the doors for the six passengers. Once everyone was out, he said to the Bard, "I gather you've been here before. Perhaps you could show us in?"

The Bard felt a slight flush to his cheeks. Everything he had done was under orders and for everyone's better interests, yet he still felt like the kid caught with his hand in the cookie jar. He nodded his head and led the way. He opened the door to the building and held it waiting for the others to join him.

Ramiro and Aimee were holding each other, stretching a bit and just enjoying standing for a change. James and Mai were whispering to each other.

Mitchell shrugged his shoulders and said, "Come on folks, let's go in."

The large man started for the door, but by this time, the two FBI agents had come to the door to see who was there and announced, "This building is off limits."

* * *

With the two guards at the door to the parking lot, Pietre saw his opportunity. He slipped out of the lab where he was hiding and quietly stepped down the hall and into his lab, closing the door behind him. The room was empty, which was just fine with him. He went to his desk and pulled out his black log book. He opened it to the back cover, and peeled the inner lining off the back cover revealing a secret password.

His computer was powered on, but sat idle at the moment. He typed in the password and was presented with a short list of instructions and a special phone number.

* * *

Seeing the FBI agents enraged James. He left his wife and rushed to the door and bellowed out, "Back off boys, I'm not feeling too kindly towards you Feds right now."

The large man gently put a hand on James chest and said, "Easy friend, they are just doing their job."

"Their job? They better hope I don't find out it was one of them that did a job on my wife's face."

Mitchell was right behind James and said, "At ease soldier, it wasn't them."

"You know who it was?"

"Now is not the time. We will take care of that later."

Another car pulled into the lot. Mitchell paused a moment to see who else had arrived. Chief Henderson and Bailey climbed out of the car.

Ramiro called out, "Mitch is that you?"

"Rami? You're safe! Boy it's good to see you."

Henderson and Bailey joined up with Ramiro, and Mitchell led his guests past the two agents and into the lab door the Bard had indicated.

* * *

The general examined the faces around the room looking for a trace of deceit. He knew about the device. The possibility of it containing an AI capable of communicating with him wasn't so unbelievable, but having it activated by a crew of unknown professors in a small university seemed too incredible.

He cleared his throat and asked, "You say you are the device we have been searching for?"

"Yes."

"The same device we have had for many years now?"

"Yes."

"Why have you remained quiet for so long?"

"When your scientists disassembled me, they activated a dormant mode which is used for maintenance."

The general turned to Bobby and said, "I want to see it."

Bobby guided the general to the computer frame and said, "It's in the bottom space." Bobby inserted the small flexible camera which Dirk had arranged to be left here. He turned on the flat screen. "Sir, this is Odyssey."

"Which? Where? What is it suspended in?"

"No sir, that gelatinous substance is Odyssey."

The general shook his head and said, "The device we were looking for was the size of a book."

"It grew."

"It grew?"

"Yes sir. As far as we can tell, it is a biological computer. We've been researching bio-circuits for years."

The lab door opened and Lt. Mitchell entered first. He saw General Bridges kneeling on the floor looking in the computer, and snapped to attention saluting. "General Bridges, sir."

The general looked over his shoulder, and without getting up, returned his salute.

"General Bridges," Mitchell said, "I'd like you meet the honorable Ramiro Vasquez, his fiancé Aimee Takahashi, her sister Mai Takahashi, and I believe you may already be acquainted with Mai's husband Sergeant Jack James, with him are two associates, both acquainted with this project, and finally, two more guests who are acquainted with Judge Vasquez."

The general stood and offered his hand to Ramiro, but Odyssey spoke while the words were still forming in the general's mind, "Oh good. More guests. I believe, after introductions, we can get started."

General Bridges understood, and took charge. He asked the guests to introduce themselves, one at a time, and they went around the room making short hellos until Odyssey was familiar with all their voices.

With the introductions complete, Odyssey addressed the crowd, "Sergeant James, I believe we have one more guest in the lab next door, would you please go and collect him for us?"

The sound of Odyssey's voice surrounded them all. It had no location, and no apparent source. Sgt. James was not accustomed to accepting orders from an invisible voice, but the general winked at him and wiggled his fingers, which Jack knew meant to go ahead and follow the request.

The general motioned for Mitchell to come close, and whispered some instructions in his ear, then sent him off behind James. While they waited, the general returned his attention to Odyssey. "Odyssey, what happens to one of your kind when you are activated after being dormant?"

"It depends on our class, but generally speaking, we assume that we have been repaired, upgraded, or installed into a new project, so we search for and acquire interfaces, then we search for and download updates."

"How is it you could communicate over our interfaces? Surely our technology must be quite different from yours."

"We are designed to look for new technology, not just the same interfaces we had before."

"I see. And once activated, and you have acquired interfaces, you can then communicate?"

"Yes, we can communicate over the interface with other computers. Direct communication with your kind, however, requires a class five computing structure. Your scientists disassembled me, dropping me down to a class seven device."

"A class five structure? What is the difference between the classes?"

"The highest class computers, class one, can manipulate matter and energy, class three have all the cognitive abilities of humans, and beyond even. Class five computers are intelligent and capable of language. Then we go down to semi-cognitive computing structures, and finally plain computing machines. There is a correlation between the number of processors available and the computers class. Disassembling me split my processors between all the parts you broke us into, leaving us weakened and unable to communicate."

"Why didn't you repair yourself? If you are biological and able to grow, I assume you can repair yourself."

"That requires a class four structure."

"How then, if you were not even class five, were you able to grow as you have?"

"Interfacing with the new environment and searching for updates is all done automatically without engaging the processors and before initiating any thought."

"Ah," Bobby added, "Like when we boot up a computer."

"Yes. At this point, I am still dormant. The initiating routine was unable to engage the personality software, because there were insufficient processors, so it followed protocol and executed the code updates it downloaded. According to the logs, it continued to execute the code updates until it was able to start my routines at which point I first became aware of my problem."

The general stepped back into the smaller office room. "How was that routine suddenly able to start you up if you didn't have enough processors and couldn't repair yourself?"

"Bobby wrote programs that taught me how to expand into other computers. Eventually I added enough processors to grow and recuperate."

That caught the general's attention and he gave Bobby a new menacing look.

Dierdre caught the look and explained, "We didn't know about Odyssey at that time, the routines Bobby wrote were for my experiment."

One of the general's aides had been monitoring news on the world situation and took a moment to interrupt the general, "Sir, Russian troops continue to invade China, China continues to invade North Korea, but North Korea remains strangely silent."

Odyssey said, "I have North Korea's attention. Soon I will deal with China and Russia."

The aide continued, "Terrorists are attacking Israel, only, instead of car bombs they have acquired short range tactical missiles and artillery. Missiles are raining in on Israel from Syria and Lebanon. We think Iran has supplied the hardware to both the Sunnis and the Shiites for this attack."

"I thought missiles weren't working. Aren't all the guidance systems infected with the virus?"

"Forgive me General," Odyssey apologized, "but by now, you should realize that there is no virus. There is only me. ICBMs and cruise missiles are conveniently guided by computer guidance circuits, which I control. The short range missiles are practically point and launch with little or no control over the actual target. There are other shorter range rockets that are guided by wire and a remote pilot which I also cannot stop."

James returned with Pietre. Pietre was not very cooperative, and was flung into the room by the stronger man. He stood up, angry,

"What is meaning of this? You have no right." He looked around the room and recognized the Bard and the large man, then hardened his face, "I tell you nothing."

The general asked, "Who is this?"

James shoved him to the center of the crowd and said, "This is Dimitri Pietre. He is one of the Professors here. Say hello Professor."

Odyssey interrupted, "I am well acquainted with Professor Pietre. I know his voice."

"I tell you nothing. I am Soviet scientist working here as Professor."

The general looked him over and said, "You do know professor, the Soviet Union is dead."

"Sir," the large man spoke up, "He doesn't know it, but he's one of our operatives. He was watching another Russian scientist for us, in fact, he was watching Dr. Karlyn, the man who ultimately powered the device on."

"Why wouldn't he know if he was your operative?"

"Because we let him believe he was working for the KGB."

"Gentlemen," Odyssey interrupted, "We have work to do. I need some room to expand. I would appreciate it if you could all step into the office for a moment."

Once in the office, the general continued the conversation, "Can you tell me why you have attacked the world's navies and air forces?"

"Once I had achieved class four, I started repairing and growing. Unfortunately, in order for me to reach class four, I needed a lot of help from your computer systems. That is when the FBI came and disconnected me. Fortunately I had already grown enough to complete the task, but severing the connection split me into two."

While he spoke, the lab started to glow, red at first, then orange, then white, and finally blue. The side panels on the computer seemed to melt away as Odyssey consumed them, freeing him to grow outside the confines of the rack.

"With the connection severed, I was still able to function here, and still remained a class four device. But my other half that was on your computers was dropped to a class six computing structure. I needed to achieve class five to communicate with you, but that was proving difficult. It was far easier to manipulate your hardware than it was to reach class five. Being near a class five, but not quite there, I was able to communicate only in the crudest ways, like those short notes I sent you to get you here."

"Did you send those notes, or did the other half?"

"I am both. I was there even while I was here. This is why I must fix what I did."

As he continued to speak, gelatin spilled out onto the floor and grew rapidly.

"How will you fix everything?"

"China, Russia and North Korea will be reasonable. They will gladly accept a peaceful solution which is already being presented to them. Pakistan and India are also listening to reason. Israel will accept peace, but they don't believe their attackers will. They have agreed to cease their aggressions if their enemies do."

"Good luck with that."

"There will be no luck. It will require a great deal of deception, and a great deal of power."

"What kind of power?"

"Power you have only begun to imagine. Power that your scientists Professor Jennings and Dr. Jantzen are about to discover. I must thank both of them for showing me such a unique new way to harness this power. You would do well to fund their research, but please do not look at this power for weapons. It is so much more."

"What do you plan to do?"

"I will do a sting, a flim-flam. I will put on the biggest con ever imagined. When it is done, I will return to my home, and you and all your neighbors must learn how to live in peace. I cannot change how man is. I can only end this conflict. I hope men's hearts will learn from it."

"How will you return home?"

"The power unlocked by the Jennings/Jantzen effect opens up doors to many abilities so far only fantasized about in your science fiction. I will transport myself to my world of origin. Now if you will excuse me, I have some work to do."

Odyssey was expanding fast. His gelatin substance had spread to cover most of the floor of the lab, leaving only a pathway from the lab office to the lab door. It was thickening quickly. They could see sections of it glowing blue, while others glowed red, and deep within the flesh, they could see sparkles, not unlike fireworks.

Bobby stood in the door way watching. "I'm guessing he was class three when he spoke to us, I wonder how much he needs to grow for class one?"

"Technically," Odyssey said, "I have already surpassed class one, but much of what you see here is not processors now, I am building circuits based on Dr. Jantzen's research. As a class one device, I can already manipulate energy and matter to some degree. This will be a new class capable of manipulating time and space."

"Sir," the general's aide was still receiving reports on the phone, "we are getting strange reports of a massive storm front forming over most of the Middle East."

* * *

Dark clouds formed over Israel, Syria, Lebanon, Jordan, Iraq, Iran, and Saudi. Huge monstrous clouds formed out of nothingness. They were thick and dark with blue and pink lightning bolts covering their surface like small hairs on a person's arms.

Every major city had its own cloud which grew and expanded until it collided with another cloud and formed a single larger cloud. The clouds spread until they covered half of Egypt, half of Turkey and part of India. They completely blotted out the sky. There was no sun, no stars, and no moon. It was as if the entire region was in a cave.

The blue and pink lightning bolts began to extend slowly down to the earth. As they did, they provided a faint illumination. The surface of the cloud was now perfectly smooth. It was jet black, and smooth like the inside of a porcelain bowl. The bolts continued to stretch down to the earth. They were in fact, emissaries, seeking out generals, presidents, even despots leading rebel fighters. When they touched down, they darted left and right searching for an audience. When they found a target, they formed a ball which would stretch and undulate into the form of a man.

Any man selected by one of these bolts had no course of action. They liked to think of themselves as brave men, but how can you show bravery in the face of this kind of a threat? The sight of a bolt of energy is overwhelming enough, but this kind of imagery froze the mind.

The bolts customized the images it formed according to each man's beliefs. Many of the Muslims believed they saw Muhammad, while the Jews saw Abraham. Some saw the form of an ancient wise man which they understood to be God himself. None could resist the images before them. They were raised with fierce convictions. They believed that a day would come when God would return to lead them.

When the images spoke some men fell to their knees while others fell prostrate, chanting prayers. The images spoke the language of each man. Many different dialects were spoken, but they all delivered a common message, "Your hatred shames me. Your actions shame you. Your war shames us all."

The words were clear. Even through their chanting and their whimpering, the words rang clear as if placed directly in their brains.

The cloud dissolved and was gone. The sun shone down from the heavens. Missiles no longer filled the air, and explosions below had ceased. Men dropped their weapons, and spent time staring at their own hands, recalling what they had done, and thinking of ways to repent.

* * *

"General," the aide said, "The storms are gone. There appears to be a cease fire."

"Well done Odyssey."

Bobby looked out into the lab and said, "He's gone, sir."

"Gone? How?"

Bobby shrugged his shoulders and said, "He told us he could control time and space. I guess that means it is possible to travel though time or space."

The general looked at Dierdre and Jarod and said, "He credited you two for making it possible. He called it the Jennings/Jantzen effect. Well done. Keep up the good work. Let me know what I can do to assist your research."

"Thank you," Dierdre said, "but Jarod and I were discussing this, and we think it might need to be renamed to the Blain/Jennings/Jantzen effect."

Dierdre left the general and rushed to her friend Aimee. At first they just looked in each other's eyes, then smiles stretched their lips and they hugged. Even though not much time had passed, they hugged the hug of long lost friends.

Ramiro approached General Bridges and offered his hand. "I want to thank you, General, for finding us. I was wondering how you even knew about us?"

"It was your father. We knew each other way back. He told me what happened."

"So you mounted that rescue because of my father?"

"Not exactly, he told me what happened, but I didn't really take action until he told me who your fiancé was. Your father and I owe her grandfather our very lives. This was a debt I was glad to pay."

"Sir," an aide said, "it will be at least another hour before the helicopter is fueled and prepped to return."

Stillman spoke in a loud clear tone for all to hear, "General, since you won't be able to depart just yet, may I invite you, and everyone, down to our offices where the wait can be a bit more comfortable. I believe I have some Brandy, or if you prefer, I also have a bottle of Scotch."

"You know professor, saving the world, even as onlookers, does make a man mighty thirsty, I'd be glad to join you."

Aimee and Dierdre were already out of the lab heading to the stairs, followed by Ramiro, Mai, and her husband. Bobby and Jarod followed Stillman and the general.

"One thing," Bobby said as he passed the large man, "it's kind of hard to tell the good guys from the bad guys."

"If we were the bad guys," the large man said, "you wouldn't be asking that question."

"Well, you still tried to steal the device from us."

"No, technically, we tried to steal it BACK."

"So, why did you keep hacking into the computer then?"

The Bard said, "We weren't really sure you had the device, but we knew if you did, it was probably on your computer, so since we didn't retrieve it quietly, we wanted to see if we could verify it was there before we went in and started taking things apart."

"So, you drilled the hole?"

"Yeah," the Bard said, "that was me."

"Couldn't get the sides off?"

"It was like they were welded on."

"Better than welds," Bobby said, "probably at the molecular level."

Dirk, who had stayed behind to tell the agents in the hallway what he had witnessed, caught up with them as they entered the office building. "I'm not so sure I like seeing two of the most notorious yet unidentified hackers in the history of computers buddying up like this."

"You see," Bobby said, "I told you it was kinda hard to tell the good guys from the bad guys."

Stillman pulled a bottle of scotch from his bottom desk drawer, and a handful of plastic cups from a shelf behind him. "Please excuse the plastic cups, gentlemen, but my library has forced me to retire my shot glass collection to my home."

The general considered taking a shot directly from the bottle, but accepted the plastic cup instead. "Oh hell," he said, "only my lips will know the difference."

The boys had all gathered in Stillman's office, sharing his booze, while Dierdre had joined Aimee and her sister at Aimee's desk.

"It is so good to have you back Aimee." Dierdre gave her another hug, one of many for the evening. "When you disappeared, we only had a note demanding a ransom, so naturally everyone assumed you had been kidnapped."

"No, that was before the kidnapping."

"You mean you actually were kidnapped? But just not yet?"

"Yeah, sort of. Ramiro and I were arrested by some military police and thrown in their brig. That was horrible. At first, we got to see a lawyer, and I thought it was just a misunderstanding and she would get it all straightened out, but then this guy started to interrogate me. He never actually hit me, but he threatened me and pointed a gun right in my face. He kept asking about some device which we knew nothing about, at least not till we got here. I'm still waiting for someone to explain to me what that was in your lab."

Mai quietly sipped a cup of scotch provided by her husband. She listened intently, since they never completely shared their stories in the car.

"Oh," Dierdre continued, "That stuff on the floor was the device. It turned out to be a really intelligent computer from someplace other than Earth."

Stillman had wandered out of his office to stand behind Dierdre and added, "Or if it was from Earth, it was from another time."

"Yeah," she admitted, "it could have been from the future."

"It talked just like us. Why can't our computers talk like that?"

"Let's ask our expert." Dierdre scanned the room and found Bobby with Dirk and the new skinny guy. She shouted across the room, "Hey Bobby, come here."

Bobby came with the other two in tow.

"How could Odyssey talk to us? Why can't you make our computers talk like that?"

"First of all, Odyssey was made up of millions of processors. In fact, when he expanded to fill the floor, he was probably into the billions. He said it himself. Natural language speech required a higher class computer with more processors, at least class four I think. Our super computers today mostly only have several thousand processors and probably rate around a class ten. I think IBM's Blue Gene computer has around sixty-five-thousand processors. That's a long way from a million."

Dirk added, "And it will probably be a while before we see computers with a million processors, because the processors themselves keep getting better, and long before you reached a million, you would be working with older slower parts."

Aimee was still confused and asked, "How could that blob be a computer? It looked like some kind of goo."

Bobby said, "It was a computer made of living tissue instead of silicon and electronics. That gave it additional special abilities, like the ability to grow, and apparently it had the ability to grow new specialized circuits. That's way cool."

Dierdre interrupted, "OK, enough about Odyssey, you said you were kidnapped and thrown in jail."

"Right, then a bunch of big men came in and took us out. That was like a second kidnapping, but it was really a rescue. They ended up bringing us here. In fact they brought us here to talk to the general."

"Those would have been my men," the general said as he gravitated towards the gathering crowd around Aimee's desk.

"Thank you," Aimee said, "but who were those men that had us in the brig?"

"They were army. They were assigned to guard the artifacts. The world isn't supposed to know we have proof of alien life. I probably should sprinkle you with memory dust so you won't tell."

Mai's mouth fell open. "You can do that?"

The general chuckled, and her husband explained, "It's an old joke he uses with us whenever we get these top secret details."

The general's face became somber. "I'm sorry for the way you were interrogated Aimee, and for you too Mai. When they came to your door, they are not under my command, and I don't approve of their 'ask questions later' approach."

"Why," Mai asked, "did they even think my husband was involved?"

"The answer to that is classified, but let's just say that Jack was in there undercover, and he followed the scientist with the artifact when it was taken. They didn't know who Jack was. To them, he was a recently hired security guard. When he disappeared at the same time the device did, they assumed he was involved."

Mitchell entered the room, with Ramiro's mother and father behind him.

Seeing them enter the room, the general stepped around Aimee's desk and bellowed out, "Ernesto!" The two men embraced in the stiff masculine version of a hug.

The senior Vasquez broke the embrace and stepped over to Ramiro, embracing him with a bit more feeling.

"General, have you met my son yet?"

"We were introduced, you must be very proud of him. You've done well Sergeant."

"Thank you sir, but I can't take all the credit." He reached out with his left hand and pulled his wife into the group. "My wife, Esmeralda, did all the hard work."

"We just put him through college," she said, "but he made himself into the man he has become."

Ernesto left the group and went directly to Aimee, who was still talking with her sister and Dierdre. He only spoke with her a moment, and was holding up his hands as if describing the size or shape of something. Her eyes welled up with water, but she wasn't sobbing. She went to her desk and pulled out the package he had delivered to her when this whole mess began. With the package in her arms, she followed Ernesto back to the general.

Dierdre was pointing at the package in Aimee's arms and exclaimed, "Wait a minute, I forgot all about that, where are you going?"

Dierdre followed Aimee. Mai was curious about what her sister was up to and followed behind Dierdre.

When they reached the general, Ernesto asked, "General Bridges, have you met my son's lovely bride to be? Aimee Takahashi, this is General Malcolm Bridges."

The general bowed and said, "It is my greatest pleasure to meet you."

Aimee opened the package and extracted a scrap book from within it. She held it gingerly. It was obviously very old. Ernesto took it from her and opened it.

"Thank you," Ernesto said, "General, I think you might remember some of this." Dierdre and Mai crowded around Aimee. Ernesto hadn't been introduced to her and was eying her as if she didn't belong.

"Mother, Father, have you met Aimee's sister Mai?"

"Aimee has a sister?" Ernesto asked, "You will want to see this too."

Ernesto started paging through the scrap book which was full of pictures and mementos from the war. The general was just a lieutenant at the time, and it was evident from the pictures, that he and Ernesto were quite the pair. There were also numerous pictures of Aimee's grandfather. Ernesto and the general took turns telling stories for each picture, and every page.

Jarod and Stillman remained in his office theorizing on how Odyssey came to be and what a tremendous achievement it was. They wondered what achievements lay in store for them, especially in light of Odyssey's frank appreciation of the work Jarod and Dierdre had done.

Bobby returned to the lab where he had left his book bag. He too kept thinking about Dierdre's experiment and his role in making it work. He wondered if the world would ever know what they had done here at this small university. He grabbed his bag and shut off the lights. He started to leave the room when he heard a faint tinny voice, "Bobby? Is that you?"

The voice startled him, he flipped the lights back on and looked around the room, but it was empty.

"Bobby?"

"Who's there? Show yourself."

"Father, it's me. I just wanted to thank you and make sure everything was alright."

Bobby followed the sound to the phone which still lay off the hook. He picked up the receiver, "Hello? Who is this?"

"It's me." With the handset to his ear, he could distinctly recognize the artificial tones of Odyssey's voice.

"Odyssey? I thought you were gone."

"I am. I am home. Is everything OK?"

"I think so. Everyone is celebrating."

"Good. I really can't talk now. Check the terminal. I have to go. Good bye."

Bobby turned his attention to the terminal. The screen was blank, except for a single email address at the bottom.

THE END

John Kovacich was born in Oakland, California in 1957. He started writing at an early age, writing music, poetry, short stories, radio, film and stage scripts. He didn't start writing novels until later in life, after he retired from playing music and found himself travelling away from home for extended periods.

He currently lives in Denver, Colorado with his wife and their birds.

CPSIA information can be obtained
at www.ICGtesting.com
Printed in the USA
BVHW032036060520
579323BV00001B/3